RUNNING WILD NOVELLA ANTHOLOGY, VOLUME 6, BOOK 2

EDITED BY LISA DIANE KASTNER

RUNNING
Wild
PRESS

CONTENTS

Running Wild Novella Anthology, Volume 6, Book 2

Published in North America and Europe by Running Wild Press. Visit Running Wild Press at www.runningwildpress.com Educators, librarians, book clubs (as well as the eternally curious), go to ww.runningwildpress.com for teaching tools.

ISBN (pbk) 978-1-955062-47-3

ISBN (ebook) 978-1-955062-38-1

SINGLE FEMALE, 21, AT THE END OF THE WORLD

BY ANNA K. YOUNG

PART ONE: NUMBNESS

JULY 2032

I went to my favorite park after things really started going to shit.

Came back with six ducks, all shot neatly through some part of the head or neck, and six bloody arrows jammed in my canvas quiver. Proudly I marched those ducks through the empty streets, each bird dangling by the feet from my hands. They left a messy trail down my khakis to the asphalt.

Each of those little ducks had waddled right up to me. Didn't have to shoot any further than ten feet. I thought myself pretty dang clever—while everyone rushed the stores and tore each other to shreds, threw bricks through windows like wannabe anarchists, I had fresh dinner for the next few weeks.

Except I got back home, and my shoes were sticky with blood. And my khakis were ruined. My dying yard was cluttered with giant slabs of drywall, loose nails, wood planks, and broken glass. And the sky was dim with ash, dismal as it had been every day for weeks. And I realized I didn't know what to

3

do with six dead ducks, now that I had them. And the guilt of luring friendly ducks who liked bread crumbs only a little more than they liked me started to weigh in.

You're scum, you're scum, you're scuuuuum, crooned my brain, and I threw the bow and arrows back into the trunk of my car and shoved the ducks messily in my barren freezer and laid face-down on my bed for a few hours.

But eventually I got hungry—O Gluttony, my Folly, my greatest detractor of Morality—and so I took out a duck. It had a shiny green head and cute little bead eyes that I ignored. I couldn't think what to do, so I pulled feathers out in ragged clumps, randomly, until that sorry duck looked like a doll who got an untimely haircut from a three-year-old. The stupid thing was stiff and matted and cold from its brief foray in the freezer.

I wished I had a grinder in the basement—could have just thrown the whole ugly bastard in and enjoyed the tantalizing anonymity of mystery meat—but I settled on hacking off a naked wing with my hooked Pakistani skinning knife and throwing it in the Crockpot.

* * *

MARCH 2032

"You need to get your own charging cord," my boyfriend Emery said, months before the ducks, late in the winter. He threw a balled-up napkin at the back of my head as I gleefully escaped with the prize in question.

Safely beyond napkin reach, I turned and leaned on the chipped doorway of our bedroom. "Yes, what shall I ever do once I'm on my own?" Then, dramatically, I sunk down and covered my eyes. "Stop! I shan't speak of such things."

"You're insane," Emery grumbled, already back to scrolling

through some dire news article. Our new dog Misha laid across his feet and shot me a misty, doleful look.

"You're a copout," I said back. "If you really wanted to prove a point, you'd break up with me right now and take your charger with you." I couldn't stop the teasing, even though Emery had long checked out; the vibrant light of the setting sun broke through the blinds right over the strip of freckles over his nose. It splashed his irises with honey-gold and left me a little weak in the knees. "Look, if you're going to take the charger with you, can I at least come see it on the weekends?"

He kept ignoring me. Once I had ways to get his attention away from the disaster feed, the pipeline of all things grim and world-ending. Some of those things involved few words and fewer articles of clothing. But, suddenly very tired, I plugged my phone into the low bedroom outlet. I sat in the growing dark and stared at the startup screen, only to turn it off when the notifications came rolling in.

AUGUST 2032

I shouldn't have tempted fate.

Not only did Emery break up with me, but he took his charging cord and everything else of his in the apartment. We even shared his laptop after mine perished in a mysterious coffee-related incident, so that went out the door with him. Then my phone died, the world ended for real, and suddenly the stores ran out of charging cords. And then the weeks went by and they ran out of everything else.

The power is still on, miraculously. I'd guess not for much longer, what with all the flickering. The phone lines may still work, and I'd bet the internet is still flashing red-and-black government warnings. But people are dead, even more probably than I think, and things just keep getting worse.

Or so I assume. Disconnected, I have no one left to talk to. No Emery, God knows if he made it across the country. Never heard a syllable from my family even when my phone wasn't dead. God knows I tried to reach out. I called every emergency outline, pounded my fist at every busy signal that droned on for hours, reached out to relatives who barely knew my name.

I think they must have died early on. My parents and brother and all our tight-knit relatives lived right near Yellowstone, not that it mattered. All that's left of the entire state, and some of the others around it, is a big smoking hole and a nasty series of reactivated fault lines. If I wanted to know what happened, I'd have to go scraping through the mountains of ash and wreckage to identify their charred bones myself. That much became clear.

And I'm here, chowing down on a soggy, tasteless, weeks-old duck wing. At least I don't have to pay bills anymore.

I should be upset. Fear should paralyze me. The grief of losing everyone should have struck me the minute I felt the caldera collapse.

But something in me is as dead as my phone. Maybe the emotions just haven't caught up yet. I think that's the best I can hope for.

"What is wrong with me," I say out of obligation between greasy bites of duck. The words ping off my cracked alabaster walls, maybe chipping the yellow paint in the kitchen a little but not doing much to stir tragedy in my heart.

Once true darkness falls (late, too—who would have thought everything would go to shit right at the peak of a hot, sexy American summer?), I haul my parents' ancient tube TV out of the creepy concrete basement. Emery had a slick, 72-inch TV hookup complete with internet streaming and video games. I think I hate him most of all for taking it with him.

I haul up the DVD player next. I shake a dead spider out of the slot, blow the dust off a disc, and laugh my ass off at *Better Off Dead* for the next hour and a half. The electricity is even so kind as to stay on for the whole movie.

* * *

I sort of hoped for a "girl and her dog at the end of the world" kind of story, full of tropes and tribulations and, obviously, triumph against the odds. Maybe telepathy, but hopefully not cannibalism. Emery and I got a dog once university classes got cancelled halfway through March, a somber Corgi named Misha, who seemed to follow me out of duty to her ancestors. I'd never seen such a serious dog, but the humane society assured me Misha was full of love.

Her previous owner died horribly. Nosey me, I couldn't understand why someone would give up a perfectly good, depressed dog. The answer was suicide, and Misha probably saw the whole thing. Bloody mess, figuratively and literally. I read it in the weekly online obituaries: "Samantha was survived by her parents, three sisters, and her loyal fur baby Misha." And, lo and behold, a picture of 24-year-old, blond Samantha holding a very happy, ears-perked-and-tongue-lolling Misha.

Loyal and loving. I'd have wondered why no one took the dog in if the world hadn't already started sliding toward disaster at that point. A big caldera starts rumbling and, what do you know, people want to move in a hurry, or they start spending their money on bomb shelters. The humane society burst with animals people either couldn't feed or didn't think they'd be able to soon. So I scoffed at the doomsday morons and adopted the saddest dog ever.

Me and my dog at the end of the world. I'd learn soon enough what an adorably naive notion *that* was. It didn't occur to me until a bit later, when my own store-bought food supplies were nearly gone, that walking around with a chubby sausage of an animal might look like flaunting to certain people. People who weren't hungry enough to eat human, yet.

Good taste.

It was karma, I suppose. Misha watched her owner shoot herself in the head, and I watched Misha earn the same fate. Right in the front yard, too. Obviously I was too late when I rushed outside after I heard the gunshot. Couldn't even get to her body in time to keep the pack of half-starved wackos from taking off with it.

Rattled, I wasted more gas than I should have racing over the crumbling city streets to the humane society. I stumbled on trembling legs through the busted front door, tripped my way through the different wings. The stark, concrete building had held up better than most, but my voice echoed hollowly in each empty room.

Someone set them free, someone set them free, I kept trying to convince myself, *someone set them free,* but too much blood smeared the walls for that to be true.

I shot the ducks the next week.

* * *

Someone tries to break in that night. They probably saw the hazy glow of the post-credits TV static sparkling through my open blinds. I hear them try the doorknob and fall off the futon before the first crash, run into my bedroom and back out before the second, throw the lock and wrench the door open before the third.

"Get away!" I scream, and flail my gun at the shadow I've

just knocked backwards off the concrete steps. In the ashy lavender tint of the summer night, I can see terror chiseled into the young man's face. He scrambles to his feet, trips over his own weapon—an aluminum baseball bat, by the sound of it— then scoops it up and crunches across the debris in my yard to the trees across the street.

I'd thought my parents were total screwballs when they took me to get that Ruger nine millimeter two years ago, when I moved out of the dorms. *It's not like I'm going to need it for anything*, I'd said. I'd kept the eleven bullets needed to load the thing and left all the others at their house in a box in my old bedroom, under my frilly baptism dress and a stack of old elementary school artwork.

It's not even loaded now. I scoff at the cowardice of the would-be intruder to cover up the sound of my hysteric wheezing. It's part of this hobby I've taken up—talking to myself to fill the ongoing silence.

"What was—" I start, choking on the words and taking a second to catch my breath. "What was he going to do, give me brain damage and steal a bunch of freezer-burned duck parts?"

I don't sleep after that, just stare at the darkened ceiling, the unloaded gun clutched over my chest like funeral flowers. First light hits like a slap to the face when I see my front door is cracked now; the flimsy piece of shit. I venture to open it and notice a little rectangle of red plastic lying on my sidewalk where the intruder fell.

It's a student ID card, like the one still clipped to my backpack. Connor Michelis. I think we had an etymology class together. He always asked overly-complicated questions to assert his superior intelligence in class, and read Old English Bible passages in a horrible cross between Shakespeare and Bob Dylan.

Now I remember for sure. A literature major, in the

English genus with me but a completely different species. He was on the club baseball team.

I rummage under my stained kitchen sink for a toolkit, also a moving-out gift from my parents. I stand out on the front step and nail Conner's ID to the door, driving the point right between his half-lowered, smug-looking eyes.

* * *

MAY 2032

I got my first taste of real fear—not anxiety, not worry, *fear*—when Emery said he was leaving.

"But why?" I begged. I sounded so whiny and juvenile that even I recoiled, but still I pressed him. My bare feet dug into the gray carpet of our bedroom. "I can't be alone out here."

"My family is still alive," he replied, not quite looking at me as he zipped his hard-shelled blue suitcase. "I have to go be with them."

"But what about me?"

"You should come with me. I promise my parents will let us stay, whether you think so or not."

Misha circled around Emery's feet as he collected things around the room, tripping him up. I tried to entice her over by kneeling down and calling her, but she stayed glued to him. My face and ears burned, half from shame, and I rose to stand awkwardly in the center of the room. Emery bustled around me to scoop up his pile of neckties and box of earrings.

He paused. "Is this yours or mine?" he asked and held up a black eyeliner pencil.

Then the room lurched, and we both scrabbled for holds. I reached for him, but he stayed latched onto the closet door frame, and I stumbled to my knees. Misha whined.

Emery seemed not to notice. Once the wobbling subsided, he checked his phone, spelunked its ugly glaring depths and came up with pinched eyebrows. "Another aftershock," he mumbled, not really to me. "They can still feel them all the way in Pennsylvania."

I pretended to check my phone, too. The animated cherry blossoms on my background floated into wavering grass, and I counted twenty fallen blooms before jamming it back in my pocket. "I'm sure they're fine over there," I muttered and felt something thorny snake up my throat. "We're way closer to the Rockies here, and we're fine."

"New faults opened up across the country, Caz." Emery's voice, usually a sweet, raspy baritone, fell flat. "I'm not going to explain it again."

"We can't all be geology majors," I said lightly, and at last he looked up at me. A mixture of confusion and contempt crossed his dark, angular features, but whatever he thought he kept to himself.

I followed him outside as he loaded the last bag into his decrepit old Jeep Cherokee. As he slammed the creaky back door shut, I broke the stony silence. "You can't leave this late," I said. "Just stay until the morning. Please."

I couldn't see his expression in the dark, couldn't interpret his sigh as wistful or irritated. "I still can't believe you won't come with me. Or at least go to some family. Cousins or something," he said.

"Yeah, right," I said, and eyed the flatscreen's silhouette which poked up through the piles of luggage in the back. "If I could think of someone who would actually care, they'd probably just tell me to stay put until these aftershocks die down."

"You don't know what else might happen."

Finally, the thorns in my throat whipped out. "What else?" I laughed. It turned into a smoker's cough. "You're turning into one of those idiots who's building a bunker because they think this is the reckoning and not just some stupid, coincidental shit."

"Cassidy," he growled.

"You gonna start hoarding canned yams? Corn? Spam?"

Emery stalked around the Jeep and opened the door, got in, started the engine. I followed him.

"God forbid it rains while you're out there." I ploughed on, terrified now that I could see his hand on the gear lever, illuminated in orange by the check engine light. "Am I at least invited on the ark?"

He shut the door and stared at me for a long moment before he backed out of the gravel driveway. The apartment door left open, Misha wandered outside and tried to trot after the Jeep, but I scooped her up before she could slip past me. The Cherokee paused once in the road, and for a second I thought he might come back.

The headlights flicked on. Emery drove away. He kept to a cautious, in-town speed limit for as far as I could still see him. The last thing I saw was his blinker flash red as he turned onto the highway out of town.

"I guess it's just you and me now, Mish," I said. "Time for a girls' night?"

Misha just whined.

The earthquakes kept coming every day. I wished Emery was around to explain what that meant for us, but my phone died before I could build up the courage to call him. My only source of communication, cut off. I guess I was too distressed by the loss of my boyfriend to remember the custody battle for his charging cord.

* * *

AUGUST 2032

The power shuts off in the middle of *Better Off Dead* a few days after the attempted break-in.

It's at my favorite part, too, where the little jerk on the bike chases down John Cusack to get his two dollars. Except he never gets it, and eventually he falls off a snowy cliff. Cinema at its finest.

I guess I'll never get to see how the movie was going to end this time around, I muse to myself as I lay in the sudden darkness for a few minutes. Who knows, it could have been different. Schrödinger's film.

I stub my big toe on my desk chair while stumbling through the living room and swear. In the kitchen, I flick the light switch, then immediately remember the power is out. The hacked-up chunk of duck in the Crockpot is mostly cooked, at least.

I trip over the pile of clothes on the floor in my bedroom and try to flick on the lights again. In the bathroom, I brush my teeth in the dark and turn on the water, which only runs at about half-pressure.

I lurch back into the kitchen and grab all the pots and pans I have left. (Cooking was more of Emery's thing, so that's a grand total of two scuzzy black pots and a frying pan.) Then I haul armfuls of cups—mostly mugs with sassy quotes and novelty pint glasses—in and out of the bathroom, filling them up with water while the pots fill up in the kitchen sink. Then I fill up my coffee pot, cans in my now-defunct recycling bin, empty candle jars with a sheen of cider-scented wax around the interior. It takes probably an hour. The pressure keeps going down.

My eyes adjust to the dark. I fill every container I can find and put them in rows on the living room floor. It looks like a cityscape built by Dr. Seuss. The glass containers especially catch the waning, hazy moonlight through the window on shiny rims.

Which reminds me to shut the blinds. And, tip-toeing through the skyline below, I lift my desk chair and set it squarely in front of the door.

"May anyone who passes this way stub their toe," I say and make the sign of the cross before I grope my way to the bedroom and wish it had a door and a lock too.

* * *

OCTOBER 2031

I never followed politics. That was more of Emery's thing too. He tracked debates and debacles as if his life depended on it. Which, I guess eventually, it did.

"Can you believe this?" he said one morning as I shuffled into the kitchen. Autumn was settling in for the second time since Emery and I had moved in together. It was 8:30 a.m., and Emery had already been up for at least an hour.

"No," I mumbled and caught a blurry glimpse of the red-and-blue banners around the daunting block of text on Emery's phone. I had to look away at the pretty fall leaves outside. "I can't believe you're already reading that shit. It's like you can't wait to start every day in abject misery."

"I don't know how you ignore 'this shit,'" he said.

"You got me."

"They're talking rations." He waved the coffee in his left hand. It sloshed over the front, leaving a stain on the floral pattern which read *I Might be High*. "Stockpiling in case the caldera does go off. Nobody's going to take that well."

I yawned and reached past the coffee for Earl Grey. "Isn't

the government always coming up with ideas they'll never actually do? It's like their trademark."

"No," Emery replied gravely. "This is different."

I ruffled his dyed-black hair, admired the iridescent edge of deep blue made visible by the light streaking through the orange and yellow trees outside. He scrolled, agitated.

"I think it's gonna be super nice today," I said. "We should go up to the park. Those ducks are probably starving without our weekly breadcrumb donation."

He didn't hear me. I stared at him for a few long minutes before he looked up. His hand extended.

"Can you refill my coffee?" he said, eyes already trailing back to the news bombardment.

"You don't need any more, you psycho," I muttered, but refilled his mug anyway.

* * *

AUGUST 2032

A huge earthquake thunders through the apartment that night. I pull the black comforter over my head in the dark and curl into a ball. I hear a lot of things crash and a *crack* that's extra deafening amongst the racket.

I was sixteen the first time I felt an earthquake, and it would be almost four years before I ever felt another. That first one woke me from a dream where I stood on a boat in a storm and clung to the railing. When I realized all that rocking was real, I fell out of bed and crawled into the doorway to my bedroom. By then it had already ended.

This one goes on for a long time, but I don't hunker under doorways anymore.

In the morning I see even more parts of the ceiling have

collapsed and knocked over half of my containers of water. It's basically down to the wood framework overhead now. There's also plunging cracks widening in the walls. The windows barely hold their own against the warping old duplex. Of all things, the door looks most intact, maintaining the baseball bat damage but not getting worse.

"The rental company is never giving me back my deposit now," I mutter, and gather up the tipped-over containers to take them to the kitchen sink.

The water's off. I head to the bathroom and flick the switch, remember the power's off, check the faucet there.

Nothing.

That makes all of the utilities, at least for me. The internet could still be up and running somewhere, but I was only using the water and lights, and now they're both gone. And of course the gas heating shut off long ago, after a bunch of the pipelines ruptured.

I wonder if my next door neighbor is alive. I've been too scared to check, haven't heard a thing in weeks. I have to hope the lack of a smell means he got out before things went downhill.

* * *

APRIL 2032

"There's a nationwide lockdown going into effect," Emery told me when I got home one evening. I'd just been called into work, along with everyone else, to find out we were all laid off and the restaurant was closed until further notice. I'd kept myself from rolling my eyes throughout my boss' spiel, but couldn't resist nudging my coworker Jasmine halfway through.

"I don't know, man, I think we should stay open," I'd said.

"We might really benefit from rebranding our products. 'Chocolate Quake Shakes' could really sell right now."

Jasmine had just stared at me.

"A lockdown?" I repeated and tossed my tacky work hat on the futon next to Emery. "Are we really going full Cold War right now? How is this about Yellowstone blowing still? Don't the experts keep saying it's probably all a false alarm?"

"We're supposed to stay sheltered at all times, and there's a curfew from 6 p.m. to 10 a.m. to minimize people leaving their houses," Emery said. "It's on every website I've searched. Not just the news sites, all of them."

He turned his laptop toward me. I searched *where to buy heroin* on Google and opened the top result. A banner appeared over it: red background, bold black letters. Everything Emery had said, with an all-caps note at the bottom: VIOLATIONS OF SAFETY REGULATIONS ARE SERIOUS. APPROPRIATE POLICING WILL FOLLOW AS NECESSARY.

I turned the laptop back. "What Nigerian prince did you try to contact?"

"For fuck's sake, Cassidy, this is serious."

I squeezed my eyes shut against his biting tone and took a deep breath. When I opened my eyes again, Emery didn't look any less pissed. "They can't do this," I argued. "It's idiotic. They're not doing anything useful. Do we even know what the fuck is happening?"

Emery's lips pinched tighter. "No," he said at last, "but there's no precedent for this. Even if Yellowstone doesn't blow, this is serious. *Insanely* serious."

"But how do we know we're any safer inside? Or is this just like those old nuclear bomb drills where kids would hide under their desks? What kind of threat—"

"I don't know!" Emery slammed his laptop shut and

pressed his hands against the top. The muscles in his arms twitched. "Nobody knows. But can you just promise me you'll stay inside, and stay safe? Please?"

I watched the sleeves of his T-shirt quiver, saw how hard he tried to control himself. I knew the feeling, anger seething from the heart of fear. He was terrified.

"Fine," I said, and walked to the kitchen. He got up to follow me. "But when everyone starts running each other over to get to the grocery store between 10 and 6 tomorrow, we'll know what the real threat is."

* * *

AUGUST 2032

I can't stay here anymore.

It's like that last earthquake set off something crazy in the town. Everyone who's left, anyway. In these past few days, it's been nonstop gunshots, yelling, screeching cars, people running by themselves or in pairs across streets and through the overgrown grass around the crumbling houses. The occasional gunfire, I could handle, but after two days of hearing at least one round every hour, I load the Ruger. I don't want to. But I have to.

Two more people try to break in, one through the cracked door, another through the window.

I can't take risks. I fire a shot at each of them—well, not at them, but into the dark next to them. It works, but I see after the second time that the intruder has a gun too and wonder why he didn't fire. It makes me look like the crazy one.

It's not just that, anyhow. I'm running out of water faster than I thought. Pieces of the ceiling keep crashing to the floor, the counter, my bed. The insulation in this place is shit, so I'm just as freezing cold at night as I would be outside. And I can't watch *Better Off Dead* anymore, so really, what's the point of staying? It was hardly safe inside to begin with.

My car has almost a full tank of gas. I have a nice bike. My bow and arrows, the gun. And, if worse comes to worse, I have a couple pairs of running shoes and a few years of high school cross-country under my belt.

Now I just have to figure out where I'm going.

* * *

APRIL 2032

"Who could have guessed," I said to the top of Emery's head as he hunched over his phone one evening, scrolling furiously through the latest article about a Walmart trampling death. We both sat in the living room, him at the desk chair, myself on the wood floor. His roots were growing in blond. "I guess 10 a.m. to 6 p.m. isn't nearly enough time to buy all the bulk Skittles one might need for an apocalypse."

No response.

"But, hey," I continued, "at least we get to enjoy Black Friday early. Except it's every day. And instead of killing each other over discount TVs, we can beat business majors to death over a ten-dollar can of tuna."

To my surprise, that got Emery's attention. He lifted his head just enough to give me an unblinking Kubrick stare under his too-long bangs. More and more, I found his expressions unreadable. I couldn't tell if the dark circles around his eyes shadowed concern or pure rage. The phone glowed in his lap: red screen, black letters.

"Why?" he said. "Why do you have to make a joke out of this?"

Stunned, I almost couldn't answer. Almost. "I'm not making the jokes," I said at last. "I'm just laughing at them."

"Why can't you just be afraid, even a little bit?" he shot back. "If not for me, at least for yourself?"

I ran both hands through my tangled hair. Dark brown knots came away with my fingers. "Oh, you worry enough for the both of us."

"I'm worried because you aren't." His phone screen grew dim, then dark. He didn't notice, though his hand still cradled the case. "I'm worried you're going to do something to get your-self hurt."

"I'm not five, Emery," I said and shook the loose clumps of hair twisted around my fingers to the floor. "And you should realize by now, the real danger isn't any of the shit you think it is. How many have died because Doomsday McGee just *had* to get the last thirty-eight cans of alphabet soup?"

Emery stood up fast. He didn't stop looking at me until his phone buzzed a few moments later and the screen lit up. It took that tiny bit of extra light to see the thick gloss over his pupils, pooling along his eyeliner. I stopped pulling out my hair and tried to say something, but he turned just as fast as he stood and strode to our room, letting the curtain over the doorway fall behind himself.

"God damn it, Cassidy," I said, and stood up as well. "God *damn* it."

I didn't follow Emery to the bedroom. Instead, I found my girly-girl whipped cream vodka in the freezer and went back to the living room. I sat in my nest of fallen hair and added to it until it got dark.

* * *

AUGUST 2032

I clear the freezer of its alcoholic contents the night before I leave the duplex for good, and when I wake up in the morning, I'm only the third-most hungover I've ever been. The second-most was the night I spent in jail.

The first was the night I met Emery.

* * *

SEPTEMBER 2030

"Oh my gosh, yes, I *love* that show," I said. "Hey, I think they're starting a game of flip cup in the kitchen. You should go play!"

"Yessss." The girl—Lauren? Laura?—stood on wobbly legs and steadied herself against the coffee table before she looked back at me. "You have to come too!"

"I will," I said, not budging from the patchy brown recliner. My legs were asleep from her sitting in my lap. "I just have to use the bathroom first."

"Okay!" She wandered into the hall, and joined the drunken stream of college students eager to find more excuses to drink. I thought I'd finally be alone with my Dasani, but then this blond kid with terrible eyeliner held back from the group and flopped down on the couch across from me.

"That was rude," he said, and took his phone out of his pocket and scrolled through it. He wore a plain blue sweater, cable knit, brown buttons. "Did you just ditch that girl?"

"Um. Yes." A tidal wave of cheers erupted from the kitchen. "Something tells me she won't miss me. She's been telling me all about her boyfriend who's hiding somewhere around here."

He stared at me for a long moment, then nodded toward my water. "You don't drink?"

"No, I do, just not when I have to drive."

"Ahh." He shut his phone off and slipped it back in his pocket, finally meeting my eyes. I got a good look at the freckles across his nose. "Got stuck DD-ing."

"It wasn't even that." I leaned forward. The recliner croaked as it tilted with me. "Fuck, I wish. I asked my shitty roommate for a ride to the store since she was already going, and she said she was gonna stop by and talk to her friends here 'just for a second!'" I did an impression of her voice that sounded like a cartoon mafioso's dumb sidekick. "'Don't worry Cassie, it will just take a minute!' God. I should have just taken my own car."

"That's the worst."

"I waited in her electric spaceship of a vehicle for twenty minutes before I realized that, as per usual, she wasn't going to be right back."

"Electric cars are so weird."

"I can't even find her now, and she's got the keys. Or the astronaut I.D., or whatever you start those things with. So now I'm stuck at a random party with people I don't know in some shitty campus apartment."

The blond guy looked like he held back a smile. It didn't work. He started laughing just a second later.

I couldn't help it. He was adorable, even more than Laura/Lauren. I laughed a little too. "What?"

"I don't know. Roommates suck." He spread his hands upward. "Especially when you share a shitty campus apartment with four of them."

I almost laughed again, then realized what he said. "Oh shit," I said. "I'm sorry. It's not that bad—"

"No, it is." He pointed at my right leg, which I'd been jostling since he sat down. "Do you always do that?"

I didn't bother trying to stop. "No," I said. "Sometimes I pull all my hair out instead."

He glanced up at my top knot, then back down. Usually I couldn't look someone in the eyes so long, but for some reason it didn't make me nervous when he did it. "You shouldn't pull it out. You have nice hair. I wish mine was dark like that."

"Thanks, I'm cured." He just laughed, and once again I couldn't keep from joining in. "But really, thanks. You could just dye your hair, you know."

"Yeah, but that would just give my roommates another reason to call me the F-slur."

"Ugh." I glanced down, feeling a brief spike of discomfort. "How old-fashioned of them. I'm sorry."

"Don't be. They're a bunch of morons. I don't take them seriously." He reached for an unopened Smirnoff Ice on the low coffee table between us and cracked the lid with a cheap-looking bottle opener. "With all that's going wrong in the world, you think I have time to be stressed about *their* bullshit?"

I watched him take a long drink and felt bold. "Since I've already called your apartment shitty, can I insult you again?"

He raised his eyebrows behind the bottle and nodded.

"Your eyeliner is terrible."

He turned away and swallowed hard to keep from spitting all over the coffee table. "I know," he said with a snort. "I just tried it out tonight because I figured they'd all be too drunk to remember tomorrow."

"Well, hey." I waited for the sudden surge of noise from the kitchen to die down a bit. "You still have the pencil?"

He nodded. "One of my exes left it here. She had a whole bag of them."

Something warm rose in my chest, but I hid it by turning

up my nose like a disgusted socialite. "If you wash that atrocity off your eyes, I can help you redo it."

"Oh boy." He tapped the bottom of his Smirnoff on the table. "I might need another one of these before I can do that. I think there's some in the fridge, if I can get through the kitchen." He stood. "I know you're not drinking, but do you want something else? I think we have Mountain Dew."

I wrinkled my nose. "I'd rather drink toothpaste." He smiled, and I stopped bouncing my leg. I pointed at his near-empty bottle. "I'll have one of those. If I'm gonna be here for a while, I might as well enjoy it."

* * *

That one drink turned into a makeup session, which turned into more drinks, which turned into a makeout session, which turned into my roommate finding me stumbling to the bathroom at 4 a.m. and asking if I was ready to go, which turned into me saying no and her leaving with my groceries.

Emery and I didn't hook up that night, or the next day—we were both too hungover, so we just cuddled and watched dumb game shows and drifted in and out of sleep together. By the end of the weekend, though, we did, after which he told me he was bi and had just recently come out to his family. Apparently, it hadn't gone over too well.

It's okay, I told him, *I think I'm...something too, my family wouldn't be cool with it if they knew either, it's okay to be upset, just let it out.* He couldn't even cry properly without sprinkling in a bunch of jokes, and he'd always laugh when I joked back.

That's when I knew I loved him. I couldn't deny what I felt. Maybe it was naive and silly, but inexplicably I knew there was something between us. He understood me in a way few people ever had. Better than that, he accepted me, and I admired his openness, his ability to tell the truth even when it sucked.

Neither of us had been in a real, lasting relationship, though his history was far more expansive and varied than my own. We were both sophomores without any close friends outside of classes. Both had terrible roommates. Both craved closeness, honesty.

Three weeks of constant contact later, we found a miraculous apartment opening, a cute little off-campus duplex, and moved in together.

AUGUST 2032

Even being only the third-most hungover I've ever been, I spend half the morning unable to do much but collect containers with lids and dry-retch over the sink. It doesn't help that I'm trying to save water, so I didn't drink any last night and try not to drink a ton this morning. It won't be any use to me if I just throw it up right away.

Fortunately, I have Tums, and ibuprofen, and a tub of precooked, plain quinoa I find trapped behind the fridge. Those three things get me almost to a functional level, and I manage to consolidate the rest of the water into the right containers and put the remaining duck bits into a cooler. My bow and arrows are still in the trunk, and I've been keeping the gun on me since the most recent break-in. There's nine bullets left, which simultaneously feels like too many and not nearly enough.

The world has only been getting colder with the constant ash cloud darkening the sky. It occasionally parts to give a bittersweet reminder that hey, any other year, it would be sweltering right about now. I have a beat-up canvas bag, army surplus, that I stuff full of winter clothes. Gloves. Leggings. A high school soccer sweatshirt that isn't mine, the scent of jasmine perfume still lingering on it. It's not too cold during the day, but I'd bet a handful of shitty insulation it's frigid at night.

I don't waste too much time with my on-the-road outfit. The trip shouldn't take more than a few days, and at this point, no one is going to fault me for wearing the same clothes three days in a row. So a plain burgundy crew neck sweatshirt and distressed mom jeans it is. Ones with big pockets. A belt, too, since I seem to need one these days, pulled to the second-to-last hole. And, of course, I refuse to leave without my signature eyeliner. I'm not an animal.

I toss my bike, the army pack, a gray sleeping bag into the backseat. Think about tossing my wallet into the overgrown grass along my driveway, but keep it in the glovebox just in case. Stuff my phone in my pocket, where it thumps against my leg whenever I take a step. Check the air pressure in my car tires. Crouch behind a rosebush when a disheveled young woman trudges down the street. She takes a long glance at my car, and I worry I'll have to shoot at her, but then she keeps walking. She might have a limp. I wonder how many people still have fuel in their cars, or electricity to charge them.

Before I drive off, I stand out front and look at the house. My neighbor's car is still there, but I haven't heard him walking around or seen him outside. He might have left with someone else. I'm not morbid enough to peer through the windows even though the blinds are up.

The half of the duplex Emery and I lived in is by far more decrepit, and now it's got a hard lean from the collapsing infrastructure. I remember when we moved in, we were so excited to live in some semblance of a real house, away from shitty campus apartments and shittier roommates. I had a south-facing window to put my plants in, and Emery wasn't forced to pay for the wonky campus internet. Between my restaurant job and his geology lab work, we could afford to live better than either of us had before. We only noticed the quirks as time went on—the outages, the lack of insulation, the sulfur smell if you didn't run the hot water often enough.

And the cracks in the ceiling. Can't forget that one when it keeps crashing down next to my head.

At any rate, one thing is now certain: the landlord was definitely overcharging us.

* * *

LATE APRIL 2032

Possibly the only reason Emery and I survived the caldera was because I was belligerently drunk and ached for everyone to be as pissed as I was.

It didn't take long for Emery to find me even though it was pitch-black outside—there was a new moon, I remember. I don't know how he did it. Other than the fact that I found the tallest hill in the park and stood at the top, waving my vodka and screaming into the dark, I hid myself pretty well.

Maybe all the cops showing up tipped him off.

They got to me at the same time, Emery and the police. They had my stiff, frozen wrists in handcuffs by the time Emery stopped yelling, fog puffing from his mouth like a steam engine, probably because they told him he'd be in trouble too if he kept it up. He said he'd meet me at the station, but the cops told him to go home until curfew ended in the morning. I didn't get to watch his silhouette stalk away into the dark, because it took three police officers to stuff me into the backseat, and they kept blocking my line of sight.

I was the second-most hungover I'd ever been when I woke

up in holding the next morning. I cried when I thought Emery wouldn't show up right at 10 a.m. and stopped crying when he did. I watched the attending officer grimace as she scraped a handful of my hair off the floor of the cell and threw it away. Then she led us both to another room so they could return the belongings they confiscated overnight.

Then, suddenly, I heard a phone ring down the hall. Then another. Then all the phones rang in a cacophonic mess, and people raced around past the doorway.

I tugged Emery's arm. He stared stone-faced straight ahead at a blank wall. "What's going on?"

He didn't move.

"Emery, come on. Did something happen when you came in?"

"What do you care?" he said. "You don't care what happens to other people."

"That's not true. Emery. Please. Just ask someone."

He pulled out his phone instead. Strangely, the screen was already on and flashing when he took it out of his pocket. He unlocked it and read the notice that popped up.

I'd never seen someone go pale before, but he did. Sirens wailed outside in a growing cacophony. I spun my head to look for a window, but we were in a central room.

"Emery?" I asked as he spat a single curse under his breath. "What's happening?"

"Come on." He stood and headed to the door.

"What?"

"Cassidy!" He leaped back and yanked me up by my arm. He started jogging, pulling me along behind him.

"Emery, stop!" I pulled away and lurched backward into a police officer, slamming us both into the cinderblock hallway wall before hitting the ground together.

Emery reached down, but instead of helping me up, he

grabbed the officer's arm and pulled him close. "Where's the nearest exit?" he shouted over the noise, people running past in every direction.

The officer shoved him off. Emery stumbled back and fell, and I tried to crawl to him. Someone stepped on my hand, hard. The officer got up and tried to leave. Emery grabbed the guy's pant leg, but he kicked him off. His scuffed black shoe thumped into Emery's cheek.

"Stay out of the way, kid!" the guy barked as he raced down the hall.

Emery curled and cradled the side of his face. I finally got across the hallway and huddled next to him, trying to move his hands. The hard blue carpet scraped my knees. "Emery," I begged. "Let me see."

He grabbed my arm again and stood fast. "Come on."

This time I stayed with him, swerved through officers and secretaries and other bedraggled, hungover suspects. No one tried to stop us, but they would shove us ahead or backward if we were in the way.

We burst outside as the shockwave hit.

It felt unreal. Everything passed in a violent blur, and suddenly I was on the ground, slammed into the concrete on my back so hard it ripped one sleeve of my sweatshirt almost completely off. Noise crashed down like a tidal wave—screaming, sirens, a pounding in my ears, and a deep, guttural rumbling, roaring over everything else. The searing morning sunlight pounded behind my eyes, and my stomach churned as the ground lurched hard once, twice, then settled into a sharp rattle before fading altogether.

I wanted to cry but couldn't. I gasped for air and coughed, the wind knocked out of me. The cacophony continued, the rumbling still audible but growing more distant. Above me, the clear blue sky and cheery sun made a mockery of the chaos I saw when I finally managed to roll over. All around the station, buildings had started to crumble, shards of brick and drywall piled along the newly cracked streets. With a groan, I sat up. Bruises stabbed along my ribs and the vertebrae of my spine. Emery lay nearby, trying to push himself up from where he had landed facedown in the patch of tulips surrounding the station's flagpole. A tender red splotch marred the side of his face under his eye.

"Emery!" Though I could feel the power behind my voice, it sounded gritty and quiet. My ears rang as I wobbled to my feet and walked over to him. A horde of ambulances peeled past us as I knelt next to him and tried to help him up, and I heard echoing, muddled screaming. It seemed to be coming from all around.

"Emery?" I asked again, my voice pockmarked and raspy. "Are you okay? What just happened?"

He sank to the ground, and his back cracked against the flagpole. He looked half-dead, his mouth partly open and his eyes unblinking. I dropped to my knees next to him, crushing a red tulip.

"Emery? Emery!"

"It wasn't supposed to happen," he whispered hoarsely. "They said it was just going to be a few small eruptions."

"What?" I searched Emery's face as if that might explain. His eyes were bright red, the color of the sun, lined with darker red veins. My stomach lurched. "Was that another earthquake?"

He stared back, and finally, I could read him clearly. There was no contempt, no rage, no concern. It was just pure fear.

"Yellowstone just erupted," he said slowly. "Millions of people just died."

* * *

Had I been in a normal mood, I would have thought him dramatic. To be fair, not as many people died in the initial explosion as you might think. It was everything that came after that killed people off for real, but I got the point. For a while we just sat there in front of the precinct. Chaos exploded around us in what seemed like a dream.

All I could think was, *I was right all along.* The lockdown didn't save us from the eruption any more than it saved the people who trampled each other trying to horde food.

We went back to the apartment. Emery's Jeep bumped over potholes and debris, both of us dead silent. The first miracle was that the duplex still stood, though parts of the roof had sloughed off into the front yard and some of the windows had cracked. Opening the door, I couldn't do anything but stare at the carnage inside for a full minute, Emery breathing heavily next to me. Enormous chunks of the ceiling had shattered on the floor, and the heavy ceramic lighting fixture in the living room punched a hole in the wood floor. Shuffling through the wreckage, I saw that our bedroom had fared the worst—the ceiling hardly existed anymore. Giant slabs of drywall and wood planks laid squarely on our bed.

So, in reality, I probably saved both of our lives by disturbing the peace and breaking curfew. Emery could have died, been crushed to death by the very roof over our heads. But, thanks to him feeling responsible for my humiliating outburst, he spent the whole night awake in his Jeep, hands clutching the steering wheel, gritting his teeth and waiting for 10 a.m.

PART TWO: DISORGANIZATION

AUGUST 2032

The drive is almost kind of fun. I feel like a Mars rover, powering through all the dust storms and ashy orange sky. I reach for my phone for the first time in weeks when I get sick of the static on the radio and want some music. However, despite my best attempt at optimism, the thing is still dead, and I still don't have a charger. It goes right back into my pocket.

I find myself regretting replacing the old tape deck with a Bluetooth hookup. I could be listening to the same eighteen Beach Boys tracks on repeat for seven hours if I hadn't. My mom's old tape still lives in my glovebox, gathering dust with my insurance card and a bunch of greasy fast-food bags.

Getting out of town was weird. The few people I saw outside all stopped and stared as I drove past. Luckily, the highway near town was almost entirely abandoned. I only ever saw one other car, and it was right on the exit heading back toward the college. I can't imagine why someone would be heading that way.

But then again, they were probably thinking the same thing of me heading south. Away from the Canadian border, which is right there? Closer to the caldera? Possibly through some of the major cities that suffered big time damage? Man, that bitch must be crazy.

Well, maybe I am. But odds are Yellowstone won't blow up like that again for another seven bajillion years, and the utilities are all out of commission, and the days are getting shorter. Darker. Colder. The ash, even though it's settled a bit, isn't helping. And I heard someone say on the street that they closed the borders up north, no exception, *weeks* ago.

So I'm heading to Mexico like some kind of spring breaker. Will they let me in? Who knows. The irony of desperately seeking refuge there is not lost on me. I already spent a good ten minutes laughing about it. That's why I tried to turn on the music—the car seemed so quiet afterward, even with the static buzz.

I fancied the idea of traveling east only for a second. But here's the thing—I'm 21, single, and something like half the nation's population is dead. I think I'll have a better chance of getting over Emery if I don't spend every day wondering if maybe I'll get a glimpse of him on the street.

Now to work on my Spanish.

* * *

NOVEMBER 2030

"Scientists just detected some unusual seismic rumblings under Yellowstone."

"Oh yeah?" I worked the goo over Emery's head and let my gloved hands savor each strand of hair. It had already been twenty minutes, but I couldn't stop messing with it. "Are they sure it's not just a stampede of incoming tourists?"

"They said it's stronger activity than normal." Emery flicked his thumb over his phone screen one last time before shutting it off and tossing it on the shelf over the sink. He looked up at me, with his big amber eyes and clean face and an old, grubby towel over his neck and shoulders. "It seems like it could be serious."

"Nah, they detect that shit all the time. It's happened a few times before." I slicked my hands together, giving Emery a spiky mohawk. "You should style it like this."

Emery stood to look in the mirror. "Awful. No."

"Are you sure?" I came up behind him in the mirror and draped my arms around him. A spine of his hair brushed my chin and left a dark spot. "You look very punkish."

"Emphasis on *ish*," he said. "I look like a ninja star."

"A very handsome ninja star," I said and squished my cheek into his to smatter kisses on his face.

He snickered and tried to pull away. "Caz, stop! You're gonna get dye everywhere!"

"'To dye is not the opposite of life, but a part of it.'" Finally pinning him in the corner opposite the mirror, I lowered my eyelids and brought my face so close our noses touched. "Then let me dye with you, my Emery."

He remained tense until the end of our kiss, and when I opened my eyes, his were already open. His face looked a little red, but it could have been from our play fighting. The corners of his lips curved up slowly.

"You literature types are weird." And just like that, he spun me around and gave me a little shove. "Out. I'm going to wash this stuff out."

"I'm not a literature student," I called through the closed bathroom door just as the water started running.

He emerged from the shower a different man, and not just because of the hair. Or maybe I was just looking for it. I always loved the symbolism of baptism, the changes it brings, new beginnings. We'd been together for two months, and every day felt like something new, yet something timeless. It was fall, sophomore year, and the trees were dying, but we were just coming to life. It felt like we'd been together forever. But not in a bad way. It was a perfect forever.

Reclined on our too-small bed, I felt an unshakeable tension grip my body. "You look..."

Emery waited, I know, for some snarky comment, a silly joke, a battle of wit that would only end if he preoccupied my lips. But he must have realized I wasn't going to come up with something. For once I couldn't be anything but serious. Maybe that's when *he* knew I loved him.

"I know," he said and climbed in next to me.

* * *

AUGUST 2032

I find a gas station just short of 400 miles into my trip. Miraculously, the pumps still work, and even more miraculously, they still demand my credit card. Good thing I hung onto my wallet. Since it seems trivial anyway, I let it eat up most of the money I have left in my account and fill up my near-empty tank.

The gas station must have a backup generator, which would excite me more if I had any use for it. My car is an old thing, reliable but not electric or even hybrid like most people have. I guess that was another thing to unite me and Emery—our shitty cars. His Jeep was three years older than my car and half the seatbelts were frayed into clumps of fuzz around the edges.

I wonder if he made it to Pennsylvania okay.

Another car pulls in while I'm standing there under the smoggy sun, too fast for me to crouch behind my car. It zips to a charging station and screeches to a stop, its weight lurching over the front wheels before settling back. A couple of girls hop out, one on each side. The one on the passenger side hooks up the charging cable. The driver, short but with arms that could kill me in an instant straining the sleeves of her green T-shirt, leans against the driver's side door and stares me down.

I wiggle my fingers in a weak wave. She stiffens, then barks something over her shoulder at the second girl.

The passenger rounds the front of the car to meet up with her companion. The gas pump clacks, my tank full, and I fumble to remove the head as the girls head toward me. They look about my age, both very pretty. That doesn't soothe me even the slightest.

The gas cap keeps screwing on lopsided, but I finally give up once the girls are within thirty feet of me. "Hey!" the driver yells as I duck into my car and lock the doors. "Hey!"

I ignore her. Fortunately, this isn't a horror movie—the ignition rattles to life on the first try, and I swerve around the pumps and thump back onto the highway even as the muscular girl tries to run after me.

Heading south, still.

* * *

SEPTEMBER 2031

The ducks started getting friendly enough that if I ran out of bread crumbs, they'd nibble my fingers instead.

"Look, Emery," I said, prompting him to glance up from his phone. "Dr. Quack is getting his green feathers back."

36

The mallard sensed our interest and ruffled his wings as he waddled over. He rooted through the dry yellow grass beside Emery's purple high tops and, finding nothing, looked up and tilted his head sideways to peer at us. He quacked once.

"Sorry, Doctor," Emery said, showing his empty palms. "I'm all out."

A few other ducks wandered close, and Dr. Quack took a moment to chase off another male. Heads lowered, the two barreled through a patch of dead clover until the smaller male plunged into the algae-slicked pond. Satisfied, Dr. Quack swaggered back, victorious, unperturbed that Emery and I were laughing at him. He stopped again at Emery's feet and let out an insistent quack.

"We're still out of crumbs, sir," I said to him.

Quack.

"Maybe we better leave," Emery said, and zipped up his striped hoodie. "I think we're about to get jumped."

I stood too and wrapped a protective arm around Emery. "Fine," I said, "but the AMA will be hearing about this, Doctor."

The ducks scattered lethargically as we passed between them to get back on the gravel path through the park. As we twisted through the clusters of parched spruces and aspens, the latter showered golden leaves on our heads. I leaned on Emery's shoulder. "We may have to start closing our windows at night," I said. "I don't think Doc will accept defeat so easily."

"We might have to start closing our windows at night anyway," Emery said. "Have you seen what's happening lately?"

"Autumn?" I asked hopefully.

"If only it were just that. They got more readings from Yellowstone yesterday."

"Blah." I rubbed my face on Emery's hoodie, which muffled

my voice. "Readings-shmeadings. I've got a paper due tomorrow that I haven't even started yet."

"Activity is picking up again."

I groaned, released Emery from my grasp so I could push my bangs back from my face. "When isn't it? That place is a bubbling cauldron. It'll settle."

Emery glanced at me, then up at the misty September sky. "You're probably right," he said with a sigh.

"I'm always right," I said. I bent over to scoop up a handful of leaves and held them in the crook of my left arm while I pulled out my phone with my right. "Now smile."

He looked at me, and after a moment a genuine, contented smile crept over his features. We'd been dating for just over a year. It made my heart flutter to know that, even after that long, even with everything going on, I could still get Emery to smile.

I threw the leaves in the air, pulled Emery close, and snapped a photo as they showered down around us.

* * *

AUGUST 2032

That picture is still the background on my phone. Or, at least, I assume it is. I even gave up my beloved lock screen—a picture of a goblin shark, the ocean's ugliest living fossil—in favor of that portrait of me and Emery. Despite his worries, in the photo he really does look happy. I remember our heads clunked together a little as I pulled him in, and it made us laugh, our eyes matching dark crinkles of black eyeliner and crow's feet. There's a blur of a leaf covering half of my mouth, the photo itself a little motion-fuzzy. If I could have, I would have printed out a giant poster of it to frame on the wall as our family photo.

If I ever end up living in a house again, I'll probably have to make do with a poster of a goblin shark instead. Keeping a giant poster of your ex is a little weird.

The crazy thing now is, despite the circumstances, I've been having decent luck. I got nervous when I ran out of water around the *Welcome to Nevada* sign. The highway went past a big body of water, Walker Lake, and the town next to it, but the few people I saw walking around freaked me out. They looked rangy and not too nice. Stared down my car as I went past. I wasn't sure I trusted lake water, anyway.

But then it happened—I found a dusty RV park about 45 minutes later. Looted, and the dry ground around it cracked and upturned. I stopped to root around for cans of food but wasn't finding anything. I almost left, but something drew me to a camper with its door falling off the hinges. Maybe it was all the "Hike Nevada" pamphlets I saw on the cheap linoleum just inside. I stepped over those into the tiny kitchen, and lo and behold, someone left behind one of those water purifier pumps for camping, a gem in all the wreckage.

I might have seen a face peering out from a flipped-over RV, but I think I've just been a little jumpy. I really did expect to see more people along the way. Walker Lake had probably half the people I'd seen the entire time. There's definitely been a few cars, but it looks like most people ditched the rural towns around the highway long ago. That, or they died.

Both are very possible.

At any rate, I needed to find something drinkable, ASAP, or else all the moisture would leach from my body and I'd become a bleached skeleton behind the steering wheel. So I turned around and drove the 45 minutes back to Walker Lake.

I didn't go all the way back to the town, though. Once I saw a break in the railing alongside the highway—they're pretty frequent, what with the earthquakes and all—I drove slowly off the road and through the sagebrush to the water's edge.

There's the broken remains of a wooden fence around it, and unlike the lush foliage that sprouts around the lakes where I grew up in Montana, it's surrounded by hard dirt and rocks. It's not anything special—just sort of a massive puddle. Then again, most bodies of water are. It's covered with a mucky, thin layer of ash, but below the surface it seems okay. At any rate, I'm glad to have the pump, because there's no way I'm going to contract giardia after coming this far.

The hazy lilac twilight settles in over the desert, and after sleeping cramped up in my stuffy car last night, I'm tired and more than willing to camp out under the stars. Even if it means wearing a wet cloth over my mouth and waking up with stoner eyes. So after refilling all my jars and water bottles and lidded bowls, I shut the top of a blanket in the driver's side door and prop the other end over some big rocks. The key stays in the ignition in case I have to make a quick escape, and the window stays down in case the car locks itself for some godforsaken reason. My phone stays in my pocket, because I guess I haven't gotten over that habit yet. It's heavy enough to make my pants sag below my hips, and I have to tighten my belt to the last hole.

I drag my puffy gray sleeping bag out of the backseat and flop it on the ground underneath the blanket fort, the canvas backpack full of winter clothes doubling as my pillow. The cooler full of melted ice and duck parts might not pass an FDA examination, but it's all I have, so with the help of some emergency lighter fluid and my handy-dandy box of matches, I start a campfire and grill up the least suspicious cut of meat.

It sucks, of course. I should have known to bring hot sauce as one of my essential items.

But I stomach it, and then I lay down, draping a damp white T-shirt over my nose and mouth. The sky stays light for a long time despite the faint haze, but soon the stars creep out.

Most nights since Yellowstone they've been hidden by smoke, so it's nice they're visible.

Emery and I used to stargaze at the park, before everything, so I know a lot of the summer constellations. The Big Dipper is obvious, pouring over the lake. I can see Lyra, and Cassiopeia, and I know where Andromeda is supposed to be even if I've never connected the dots, literally. The North Star is allegedly obvious, but I never seem to know which one it is.

What I need is a southern star. Or maybe an encyclopedia. Or a Spanish-English dictionary. Based on a crinkled map I found in that trailer, I think I'm heading toward Tijuana. I don't know anything about it other than that it's a huge city. It's also on the ocean, which is nice. I've always wanted to live on the beach.

That's what I focus on as I drift off, converting the watery brush of Walker Lake on the rocky shore to the crash of waves on a Tijuana beach. My campfire still burns, trailing pale smoke into the night sky.

* * *

MAY 2032

When Emery finally told me he was leaving, about an hour before he actually did, I managed to get ahold of him long enough to sit him down on the futon and look at me.

I choked. "You can't," I said, all I could come up with after a moment of tripping over my words. I started unraveling the loose yarn from the red afghan we kept draped over the armrest.

"Caz." He put both hands on my shoulders, anchoring me to him despite my shaking. "You have to think ahead. Be serious."

41

"I *am* serious!"

"You're not thinking this through."

"The worst of it is over," I insisted. My voice sounded thick in my head, but I hoped I sounded calmer on the outside. "And where is there to go? You can't escape what's happened. Might as well accept it."

His bottom lip curled in, his dark eyes framed by sympathetic eyebrows. "I'm sorry, Caz. I know you were close to them."

I couldn't speak. I clenched my teeth to keep from making any sound.

"I know I haven't been here for you like I should have been," he admitted. "But you didn't seem to even care. I was worried, but I didn't want to say something and—"

"My parents didn't know anything about me," I said, and unraveled my hair from its top knot. "They probably wouldn't have liked me if they did."

"I'm sure they still would have loved you, Caz. Even though you never got to tell them—"

"Why do you even want to go back to *your* parents? Until now you hadn't talked to them in, what, a year and a half? Who's to say they even want you to come back?"

That stopped us both, all the other sentences between us fading as that statement crushed them to death. Emery's face froze in open, vulnerable shock. I think my expression looked the same, but I guess I'll never know.

Misha whined.

"That's low, Caz," Emery said, his voice quiet but close to boiling over. "They may not understand me, but they'd never—"

"I didn't mean it," I said, feeling as though I was backtracking uphill—blind, stumbling, able to see the steep drop just ahead of me. "I know you care about them and...and I'm sure they care too. But I..."

He didn't give me the respite of filling the silence. He just waited.

"I care about you," I said at last. My eyes felt like sandpaper. "Every part of you, everything. I want you here. Things have to get better. It'll get better."

Emery stood from the futon and headed to our bedroom. I dropped the afghan and followed unsteadily after him as if tied to him by a kite string.

"If you stay, we can find a better place to live," I said as he crossed the carpet. "Safer. Electric heating. Earthquake-proof. They have to start up classes again eventually. We were almost done."

Nothing. He rummaged through clothes on the floor, pulled things up and threw them back.

I couldn't think. Couldn't convince him. My mind threw a Hail Mary. "The ducks at the park won't know where you went," I said. "Someone has to keep feeding them!"

Emery's back turned to me as he dug for suitcases at the back of our closet and started throwing clothes in. "I have to go home, Caz," he said.

I just stood there in the empty center of the room, closer to Emery than anything else, the words *But why?* ready to springboard off my tongue and into the air; unaware of the aftershock that would hit moments later, unaware that it would send me sprawling while Emery clung to something sturdier.

Fully aware, then, that nothing I could say would change his mind.

* * *

MARCH 2031

"Well, that's wonderful, honey." My mom's words sounded tinny through my cheap earbuds. "Does this mystery man have a name?"

"Uh, yeah," I said, and held the tiny microphone bar up to my mouth. Emery widened his eyes and tilted his head forward insistently, sitting on the bed across from me. I hesitated anyway. "Emery."

My mom *hmm*ed with interest. "That's an unusual name."

"He's really smart. Geology major. He's working with one of his professors."

"Geology, huh?" I heard my dad say in the background. "Can't tell us anything about those crazy little tremors we had in the fall, can he?"

I shrugged even though they couldn't see it. "Dunno. You'll have to ask him sometime, I guess."

Emery nodded encouragingly. His artificially black hair shifted to fall over his eyelashes.

"We, uh," I continued. "We're...thinking about moving into the same apartment next fall."

There was a staticky pause. "Oh," my mom said at last. "Are you sure, Cassidy?"

"He could be a serial killer with a collection of hands, for all you know," my dad piped up again. "Or maybe he has a thing for eyelids. Ones with lots of eyeliner."

I do, Emery mouthed, and it soothed my nerves enough for me to stifle a giggle. "He's not."

"He could secretly be a psychotic paper boy who just wants your two dollars."

"Not everything is *Better Off Dead*, Dad."

"Do you trust him?" my mom said, cutting us off. "That's all we really want to know."

"Uh, yeah, you know. I think I trust him."

"Then if you think it's a good plan, you should go for it," my mom said. "It doesn't sound like he needs your hands or your eyelids anyway. He already has your heart."

"Ugh. Mom."

She blew out air, making the speaker crackle on my end. "Your father started it."

"Yeah, but he wasn't corny about it."

"Well, maybe not." She sighed. "I'm happy for you, Cassidy. He sounds like a nice young man."

"He is."

"Sometimes we worried about you in high school, you know, and even last year. You never brought anyone home."

"Oh," I said, the word feeling sticky. Emery cocked his head. "Yeah?"

"Not that you have to date someone all the time, of course. We just didn't want you to be...lonely."

While she talked, I paced out of the bedroom and into the living room, doing laps in and out of the kitchen. Emery followed me as far as the bedroom doorway. "Well, I'm not lonely," I said. "I told you about Hal in high school. And, you know. I have like, classes and stuff. I keep busy."

"Oh, I know," my mom said. "We're just happy for you, Caz."

We said goodbye and I hung up a few minutes later, yanking out my earbuds.

Emery gave me a slow clap. "Well, that was almost the truth," he said.

"They'd be horrified if I said I moved in with you three weeks after we met," I said, watching snow fall outside the kitchen window. It glowed an eerie orange from the streetlights forced through the gray dusk. "And they'd crucify me upside down if they knew we've been living together since September.

They asked how Jeanine was doing, for fuck's sake. I haven't talked to her since the day I moved out and her wack-ass boyfriend took over the lease."

I marched into the living room one last time and flopped down on the futon. Emery came and sat next to me, an arm over my shoulders. "What's wrong?"

"Oh, nothing," I said. "Just a lethal dose of infused subtext."

Emery shook me lightly back and forth. I let my head roll limply against the back of the futon. "Use your civilian words."

"*We didn't want you to be lonely*," I repeated. "That's just code for 'We're over the moon that you're actually into men, or anyone at all, because we were wondering.' At least you and your parents are up front with each other."

Emery leaned his head against mine. "And we all know how well that went."

I sighed, picked at the sleeves of my red sweater. Emery reached over and grabbed my hands to keep me from pulling a loose thread from one of the cuffs.

"One step at a time," he murmured by my ear. "You told them we're together. That's more than you were going to do."

"Only because you bullied me into it," I muttered back and stared at the dark kitchen floor. The square of faint light from the window over the sink wavered with shadows of the bare trees shifting in the wind. "I swear you could convince me to do anything. I'd follow you straight into Tartarus if you said it was a good idea."

He squeezed my hands tighter. "Good thing I would never do that to you."

* * *

AUGUST 2032

I awake crying, or having just done so. Disoriented. Salt encrusts my face. Maybe my eyes are just watering from the ash and campfire smoke. Heat already rises around me even though the sun is just cresting the dusty horizon. I think I'm suffocating.

Something is dragging me over the rocks.

The fabric of the shirt over my mouth, not quite dry, suctions hard as I gasp. I screech, thrash, trapped in my sleeping bag, the mouth of it tight over my shoulders. Dark, fuzzy silhouettes loom above me, shouting now. My gun, that unyielding lump of metal I've slept next to since the first break-in attempt, sinks down by my feet.

The shirt catches on something and slides off my face. "Help me!" I scream over and over, then stop when the back of my head thumps into a rock. My vision goes blurry, but when it clears, I get a better look at the two people dragging me. A guy and a girl. Both have red hair, the girl's in a high ponytail, so maybe siblings. Same ski-slope nose too. Freckles over the bridge, just like Emery. Matching blue bandanas tied just over the mouth, matching gray shirts. The shirts might have been different colors at some point. As with the girls at the gas station two days ago—was it really only two days?—they look around my age.

Guess I'm not the only one crazy enough to be wandering around like this.

Raw anger rips through me. Fear. It's back. Now I'm screaming without words, guttural growls that rise to glass-shattering shrieks.

"Shut up!" The guy hops on one leg to plant a boot in my side, and I gasp again. Now the tears are streaming for real. He snorts, jerking his head to flip his chin-length, shaggy hair out of his face.

The end of my sleeping bag flops around, the weight of the gun giving it a life of its own as the maybe-siblings toss me down. Immediately I try to get up, but the girl straddles my chest and keeps me down as the guy watches over. He seems satisfied, though I'm still hollering and fighting, and he walks back toward the car.

"Let me go!" I scream, trying to sit up. Damn, this girl is heavy. Her freckled hands pin my shoulders.

"Shut up," she repeats, with the same inflection and half-curled mouth as the guy. Definitely siblings.

I finally fall back. Her knee crushes my chest. I'm exhausted, and light-headed. Nausea settles into my throat and head. Dizzy. The murky sepia sunlight pierces behind my eyes. "Please," I croak, meeting the girl's copper eyes. "Don't—don't take my stuff. Or let me come with you."

She doesn't say anything, but her pale eyebrows dip for a second.

In a piercing moment of clarity, I suddenly think of Misha. Then the Donner Party springs to mind, unbidden. My thumping heart stutters. Oh my God. "Nevermind," I slur. My ears ring. "Take it." I'm not nearly as cute as a Corgi. Oh God. This girl looks thin. I thought she just had nice cheekbones, but her face is like a skull. "Just leave me here. Don't kill me."

"We don't need your blessing to take your shit," she snarls. "And you're not worth killing. Just shut up and I won't break your face."

The girl eyes me as I blubber, having barely heard her response. I can't tell if I'm crying now or if my eyes are just watering from hitting my head on a rock and getting booted in the ribs. Her face wavers like I'm looking up at her from underwater.

Survival. Survival. Walker Lake. I think I was closer to the water just a second ago. Why can't I remember moving? "I'm Cassidy," I say, one thing I know for sure. I think this might help with survival. "I'm...21 years old. A senior in college. Or, I was."

The girl's eyebrows pinch again, and this time they stay there. Without shifting her weight she looks sharply over her shoulder. "Cameron!" she shouts. "Hurry up!"

"I'm...single now, too," I say. That's funny, but I can't laugh. Red hair. Ponytail. I feel like one of those lame dating app dudes. *Girl, you're too beautiful to be stealing my car. You come here often?*

"Key's already in the ignition," the boy shouts back, his voice gruff. "Think it's a trap?"

The girl looks back at me. Her face is pulsing in and out of focus. She calls something else to her brother, and it takes a second for the words to catch up to me. "I doubt it."

I hear the engine rumble to life through the back of my head, feel it vibrate in the earth. I start to shake, and the intense nausea makes me gag, every breath hitched. I can't think. "You're beautiful," I say, the only words I remember.

The girl reels back a fist, I think to hit me in the head, but stops short. "Shut up," she says one last time, the words warbled. Something drips onto my neck as she lifts her knee from my chest and starts to stand.

Another clear moment strikes like a slap to the face. I somehow kick the gun up toward my hand and force open my sleeping bag. The zipper buzzes as it splits. "Stop!" I yell.

My thumb clicks off the safety through pure muscle memory, but it's too late. My vision slips again, and I'm back on the ground, my head bouncing off the rocks, the girl on top of me, the gun knocked from my hand and skittering across the beach.

"You're beautiful," I repeat, my world a blur of dirty colors and wheeling motion. I don't remember who I'm talking to. Or where I am.

Red hair. Siblings. *I had a brother too. I'm hungry and scared too. We should stick together. We should go on a date. A real one.* I try to say all this, and other things, out loud, and maybe I do.

It doesn't stop her from breaking my wrist and leaving me there in the sagebrush.

* * *

THE PAST

My dad took me and Frankie out shooting a couple times when we were both in high school. It was just for fun. Dad paid for a membership every year so he could sight in his rifle before hunting season, but he also had a decent stash of handguns for recreational target shooting. We'd go to this range halfway up the mountain pass leading out of town. Dad would pull up to the heavy iron gates, and Frankie would hop out with the key and swing them open so we could get to the rutted dirt parking lot.

The first time we went, I was a sophomore and Frankie was a junior. I was excited but terrified at the same time. I'd been around guns my whole life but never shot one. I wasn't a hunter like the others; when we went up to the grandparents' for hunting weekends, I'd stay in with Grandma and play cards all day, waiting for the others to come back in their snow-caked wool pants and Army surplus boots. They'd have either a good catch or a good story. I'd have brownies ready to warm them up.

But I wanted to shoot a gun, at least once. My parents also

wanted me to shoot a gun. Or, really, they wanted me to know how.

It was raining when we got to the range. I jumped out of the backseat of the truck into the mud and stood a few feet away, watching as Dad dug around in the stacks of black gun cases and crisp, shiny boxes of bullets.

Frankie squelched over to stand in front of me. "Why are you wearing ballet flats, you doofus? It's raining."

My feet were already soaked and freezing, but I wasn't going to tell him that. He had the hood of his green raincoat over his long crew cut. Slim-cut khakis. Sturdy black boots. "They're just what I was wearing yesterday when it was nice out," I said. "I was at Sadie's house overnight."

He fluttered his eyelashes and clasped his hands together, spoke in a mimicking falsetto. "Ooh, Sadie, your ginger hair gives me butterflies."

"Quit!" I looked around him to see my dad still searching the back of the truck. He didn't seem to have heard. "I didn't have time to change my shoes after she dropped me off."

"It would have taken you five seconds to change them."

"Oh my God, you guys were already in the garage when I got home, and I didn't want to hold you up," I said, exasperated.

Frankie smiled. "Whatever." He stomped his boot in a deep rut, splashing water toward me.

"Stop!"

"What are you two doing?" my dad asked. "Help me move this stuff inside." He handed us both a couple of gun cases, and we ducked inside one of the awnings set up over the shooting area. It was just as cold in there as it was out in the rain. I rubbed my hands together to warm them up. Frankie took off his bulky raincoat and tossed it on the single plastic chair on the concrete floor. While Dad was still busy setting up new paper targets on the pulley, I squeezed water out of my low ponytail onto Frankie's arm.

"Cassidy!"

"You two better settle down," Dad said, frowning. People said Frankie and I looked nothing alike, but somehow we both looked like our dad. Same dark hair and sharp jawline, for me. Same round eyes and square forehead for Frankie.

That forehead looked pretty serious right then, so me and Frankie stopped screwing around. "Which one are we starting with?" Frankie asked.

My dad opened one of the cases. The handgun inside was mostly silver, with a narrow barrel and black grip. "Probably the .22 for Caz," he said.

"Can I start with the nine millimeter?" Frankie asked.

"In a second. We're going to let Cassidy focus."

Dad held up the gun. He showed me how to load, how to use the safety, where to put my hands, how to aim, how to stand. He fitted some giant, clunky earmuffs over my head. I started to feel more and more overwhelmed the longer he explained things. There was more to screw up than I originally thought.

But at last, he handed it to me. "Load it when you're ready, the way I showed you," he said. Frankie stood off to the side, fake-aiming a couple lanes over. "Squeeze the trigger, don't pull. And remember to hold steady the entire time."

I held the gun facing forward in my lap so Dad couldn't see my hands tremble. The air was damp and cold, the gun's grip sticky like sweat on skin. "Okay," I said. "I'm going to load it now."

"Remind me again about the three rules with guns?"

I looked at Frankie. He stopped pretending to shoot and gave me a thumbs-up. Then I looked back at my dad, those same round eyes serious and encouraging, the jawline we shared not hardened like it was when he got angry. The earmuffs around my neck pressed against my collarbones through the soccer sweatshirt I borrowed from Sadie. It still smelled like her jasmine perfume.

"Don't load until you're ready to shoot, and treat every gun as if it's loaded," I said. The gun felt clammy in my hands. "Don't touch the trigger until you're about to fire.

"And don't aim at anything you're not willing to shoot."

* * *

AUGUST 2032

I wake up with a pebble pressed into my right temple, sweat drenching the side of my head up to my eyebrow.

No, not sweat. Water. The lake. My right arm is stretched into Walker Lake, fingers splayed into the faint waves lapping the shore. My eyes sting. My throat stings. The dim sunlight fondles the left side of my face with a burning hand. I try to push myself up with my left arm and immediately puke liquid into the rocks at the edge of the water.

This is now the most hungover I've ever been. And I didn't even drink. For a few minutes I only have one thought: *I can't believe I left the* fucking *keys in the ignition.*

I kind of remember ending up by the water after that asshole broke my wrist, but I don't remember crawling over. I do remember screaming a lot. It hurt like a motherfucker. I've never broken anything before.

I've also never gotten a concussion before, so I can check that off my bucket list.

I keep laying with the top of my head in the water, trying to remember what to do if you have a fucked up wrist and a fucked up head. The thin slick of ash floats on the water and

53

sticks to my hair. Finally I sit up and fight the ensuing burst of nausea. There's nothing left in my stomach anyway. It's late afternoon and dry, hot. The smoke in the sky keeps the sun from beating down too hard, but this is still the desert, and it's still...maybe August? August, I think. My head swims like it does when I have a fever. Treading molasses.

The car is gone, of course. And almost everything with it, even my stupid bike and the arrows in the trunk and the water pump, all those jars and Tupperwares I filled. They must have pulled the canvas bag of clothes out from under my head right before I woke up. I can see my sleeping bag unzipped and flung into a lumpy mess maybe twenty feet away. The T-shirt I draped over my mouth is still there near it, a flag of white against the gray. A symbol. Surrender.

There's a spot of black a few feet from both.

With an involuntary groan, I try to stand again. It takes a minute for me to reconnect with my legs and get them under me. My knees scrape against the hard dirt between the pebbles. I plant my left hand and narrowly avoid my former stomach contents, push myself slowly up. My ribs complain where the guy kicked me, but it's nothing serious.

I know better than to put weight on my right hand. It hurts even before I see it emerge from the water like some horrible deep-sea abomination. Swollen and bruised, ugly purples and yellows. I thank God it's not sticking in some weird direction or else I might have thrown up again. The ache is awful, but it's nothing like the sharp pain from before. I don't know why I thought plunging it in lukewarm lake water would help, but that's just the concussed brain for you.

I'm lucky I'm not dead. Or, I should feel that way. Even though those psycho gingers didn't kill me, passing out with a concussion should have.

Maybe. Or maybe not. I'm just trying to remember what I

learned in health class when I was a sophomore. I think Sadie got a concussion playing soccer once in middle school.

Maybe I don't have a concussion at all. Maybe I'm just crazy. I think I told the redhead girl I loved her.

The thought makes me dizzy, and I have to sit down again.

* * *

They left the gun.

I don't know why. The redhead girl could have picked it up and shot me while I writhed and wailed on the ground, half-conscious. Delusional. I wouldn't have blamed her. In fact, I probably wouldn't have even known it was her. Things got sketchy there for...well, a while. I don't know how long.

But instead she left it lying there, almost where I could have grabbed it. Once I feel stable enough to stand again, I zombie-walk over to it. A spot of black next to the gray sleeping back, next to the white T-shirt, which is dirtier and stained up close. There's still nine bullets in the clip.

That's probably good. That means I didn't get a chance to shoot.

I don't know if I would have, given the chance. And that's the worst part. I was aiming right for her ponytailed head, or at least trying. Trying to line up the little knob with the notch on the end of the barrel. If I hadn't been seeing extra knobs and notches, I might have gotten there.

My finger was on the trigger. I remember that specifically. It seems like it should have felt cold, but it wasn't. Because it was already mid-morning. The metal was the same tempera-ture as my fingertip.

My puffed-up hand can't wrap around it now. I paw at it for a while, suck through my teeth at the pain as it jolts through my wrist. I switch to my left hand and pick it up. I try to aim at the stub of a crossbeam jabbing out from one of the old decaying fence posts. The sights bob up and down like waves, never quite lining up. I brace the inside of my left wrist with my deep-sea-abomination hand. My left pointer finger creeps to the trigger. It's warm.

The safety is still off.

Squeeze, not pull.

The recoil knocks my left hand backward, and I cry out as it rattles my broken wrist. Then, cursing, I set the gun down hard and kneel on the rocks, cradling my arm and gritting my teeth.

"Shit. Shit. Shit." It feels like it's throbbing again. A sharp sob erupts from my throat. "Jesus. Fuck."

Still sucking in air, I reach over and clumsily click the safety back into place. I spend a few minutes curled over my knees on the ground. It creates a dark cave, a false sense of security. The angled sunlight speckles the tops of my thighs with pockets of red, crisscrossed by denim stitches.

Finally, I blink the last of the wetness away. The pain retreats to a dull ache again, and I stand up. I walk the dozen yards or so to the fencepost.

"Great," I mutter. It's perfectly intact.

I spend a while searching the area around the post and beyond. My feet scuff the ground, but I never hear the *clunk* of discarded metal. The dirt, rocks, and sagebrush are as pristine as they ever were.

The only thing I find is a dead raven. It's sprawled across the hard-packed dust, one wing splayed out, the oily feathers flattened to the bone. There's not much left other than that, feathers and bone. Crusted eye sockets. One of the feet is missing, and the other is a pallid black, dust lining the ridges up to the claws. It makes me realize I haven't seen a live bird in a long time, and also that I'm hungry.

In fact, I've been hungry. I've been hungry since I murdered those stupid ducks at the park and ripped all their feathers off. And now that's all gone too. I haven't wanted to look, but I'm probably just as skinny as that redhead with her gaunt face and angry eyes. Maybe looking down at me struggling on the ground was like looking into a mirror for her. Maybe that fleeting look of pity she gave me wasn't sympathy for me, but for herself.

There's nothing left of the crow to eat anyway.

The sun is going down. I'm going to have to camp out here again.

I wish the internet was still around so I could go online and leave a bad review for Walker Lake.

* * *

NOVEMBER 2031

"People think I'm an impostor." I scrolled through the comments on the side of my essay, all the way to the bottom and back up to one in particular. I clicked it over and over, the highlight over the text blinking on and off. The room felt too bright, mid-afternoon light reflecting pure white light off the November snow outside each window. "They hate me."

Emery stood hunched over the desk behind me, his hands on the top of our black faux-leather office chair. I looked back at him. He squinted at the screen. "'This is an interesting issue,'" he read, and reached forward to stop me from clicking on the comment again. I let go of the mouse and ran my hand through my long bangs. A couple loose hairs fall onto the keyboard.

"Don't do that," Emery said. "Let's just look at it for a second. 'This is an interesting issue. The experiences of queer women are underrepresented. However—'"

"However," I repeated. My head fell back, and I looked up to where Emery's faintly stubbled chin met the top of his black cashmere turtleneck.

I maintained a low groan as Emery kept reading. "'However, perhaps this is an issue better told by a member of the queer community. There are plenty of straight writers whose opinions have already been heard.' Hmm..."

I knocked my head against the back of the chair in a slow pattern. *Thump. Thump.* "I knew this was gonna happen," I said. "I knew I should have just written about something else. Literally anything else."

"They just don't know, Caz," Emery said. He pressed his other hand to my forehead, stilling the *thump*ing. He scrolled through a couple more comments. "I don't think you'd even disagree with most of these."

I gripped the arms of the chair. "Why don't you just clamp my eyes open so I'm forced to keep looking at all these people calling me a straight-splainer, *droog*."

I blew a stream of air up onto his hand, and the ends of my bangs flew outward. Emery let go and spun the chair around, kneeling so we were face-to-face. "Okay," he said, smiling gently. "Better?"

"I'm gonna throw myself off a rooftop."

"Absolutely not." I looked down, and Emery crouched even further to meet my eyes. "Hey, don't be upset. You know you were the right person to write this, and that's important."

"Is it?" I swiveled the chair from one side to the other. My fuzzy blue socks trailed across the hardwood, picking up lint. "Because my classmates think I'm a hack."

"You're not, and it's none of their business." As I spun by, Emery reached out to grab my hands and held them between us.

"I guess."

"What if you mentioned that you have a strong, sexy, proud bisexual boyfriend to back you up?"

I scowled at him. "Great. Then they can tell me I'm flaunting you for diversity points." I looked down again, muttering. "Using you. They wouldn't be wrong."

"What? Caz, come here."

He stood and pulled me up, though I sagged against him. He half-dragged me to the futon, tripping over my reluctant footsteps. I couldn't fully protest, finding it hard to speak, as he sat us both down and arranged it so the hard bar pressing up through the cushions rested in the space between us. I pulled the fraying red afghan piled on the armrest up to my chest and put my head on Emery's leg, facing the kitchen so I wouldn't have to look at him.

"Okay," he said once we were settled. "What did you mean? You're not using me."

"I don't know." I sniffled, then cursed myself inwardly. *Fuck you! How dare you make this about yourself!* I draped one arm to the floor and traced over the shallow wood grain. "It's like, since you're a guy, everyone thinks we're straight. And that..." *Oh God, you're actually going to say it!* "...it just, it makes it easy to date you. Because I don't have to hide you. I can just pretend and no one ever has to know."

Emery's arm tightened around me. I couldn't see his face, but when he spoke next, it sounded like he was about to cry. "So that's the only reason you're dating me."

"No!" I sat up fast, an apology hanging on the edge of my tongue.

But I stopped. He was smiling. Almost laughing, not crying. "You just want me for my Y chromosome," he said. "And all this time I thought you loved me."

"I can't believe you think this is funny," I said, a little hurt. The futon creaked as I brought my knees to my chest and buried my face in the afghan again. The darkness felt nice. "I hate feeling like this. I *am* a fake."

"But Caz, you really do love me, don't you? We've been together over a year."

"Yeah?" I peered up a little. The fuzz from the blanket created a frame at the bottom of my vision. "What is this, a test?"

Emery pulled the edge of the afghan, and I relented, letting it slide from my grip. He draped it over both of our legs. "No, it's the opposite. That's the point I'm trying to make. If you love me, what does it matter? There's not some kind of identity test you have to pass."

I didn't know what to say. I leaned my head against his shoulder after a moment. He mumbled something reassuring, and I breathed in deep. He smelled like the apple cider candle he liked to burn in the kitchen while he made dinner.

Across the room, the laptop screen went dim, then dark. It caught my attention. "But what about that?" I asked, pointing.

Emery shrugged. My head bobbed with the motion. "That assignment is done anyway, isn't it? And the semester is almost over. So who cares." He brushed his fingers through my bangs, but in a soft way, not how I always ripped through the roots. "You can tell them or not. Don't let them force you into it through a couple of comments they probably wrote five minutes before the deadline."

"I guess." I let my hand drop. My fingers rolled a loose yarn in the afghan while we sat together. "Who knows. Maybe I'll—"

Suddenly the room shook violently. I gripped Emery around the waist as one of my potted plants toppled from the windowsill and shattered on the floor. Shards of terracotta scattered into the corners of the room. Our ceramic dishes clanked together in the drying rack. A subwoofer-like noise rumbled beneath the rest of the chaos as the room tossed us back and forth. Something continued a high-pitched ringing for several seconds after it stopped.

Emery's chest slowly deflated between my arms as he exhaled. I couldn't slow my breathing so soon. His hazel eyes, wide and stunned, looked strangely piercing in that pale snowy light from the windows.

I clutched him tighter, handfuls of black cashmere. He never pulled away and never let go of me, either.

"What was that?" I asked

PART THREE: REORGANIZATION

AUGUST 2032

The Israelites allegedly wandered in the desert for 40 years, waiting and hoping for something better. It's been one day and I'm already thinking about offing myself.

To be fair, I don't have somebody dropping me glorified chicken and waffles every step of the way. But I guess I have to be fair to God too. Twilight hasn't hit yet, so there's still time for quail in the evening, and maybe I didn't get up early enough for the manna.

I *did* wake up right before sunrise. I just didn't ooze into an upright position until noon, and I only accomplished that because I got too stiff laying in the sleeping bag.

My mouth was dry as sawdust and tasted about as good. I tried striking a rock with a stick, but alas, no water sprang forth. I thought about shooting the damn thing. But instead I sucked it up and drank the ashy, algae-ridden water from Walker Lake, saving those last eight bullets for emergencies.

If it comes down to it, I'm gonna be real pissed if I find out I have nine lives.

I stumbled along the highway all afternoon. Not right on it, of course, but in the dust and scrubby plants alongside, far enough from the road that I can hope I look small and insignificant. I go through a shabby cluster of shacks and trailers marked by a "Lobster Crossing" sign and head south on Highway 360 when I see it.

Sometimes cars go by, more than I think I ever saw while I was driving. The majority are electric ones that are too quiet for my liking. Maybe I just didn't notice as much. It's easier to ignore potential threats when you're hurtling along at eighty miles an hour and yelling Beach Boys hits to yourself, all nice and protected by fiberglass and aluminum or whatever the fuck cars are made of.

They're much more obvious when I have to dive into a sagebrush to avoid being seen.

Half those drivers probably saw me anyway. It's so flat out here, I might forgive someone who lived here for thinking the Earth isn't round. The lush mix of ash and dust might be enough to reduce me to a grainy silhouette, but I'm not taking chances. I'd dive right into a nest of rattlesnakes if I thought it would hide me better.

I can't tell quite how long I've been walking. When I started, the sun was its usual red smear pretty much right overhead, and now it's dripping down the sky off to my right. So a few hours. If I'd run instead of shambling like a reanimated corpse, I might actually have a better idea. They called me the Human GPS Watch in high school cross country—we could run around town for some unspecified amount of time, and when we stopped, I could nail down the distance we'd gone to the tenth of a mile.

But I've avoided even glancing at mile markers and those

shiny green signs for upcoming towns. The highway is practically barren anyway—I haven't seen any semblance of a town since leaving the lobster place. It's just sagebrush, and distant low mountains, and sometimes a rift or hillock in the parched earth beside the road.

My white T-shirt, which I dipped in the lake and tied around my mouth before leaving, is stiff and not even slightly damp. Hardly white anymore, caked with dust. I keep it around my face anyway, because there's a breeze blowing and it's got the smell of sulfur on it. The sky is darker than it's been in maybe a week. My eyes wouldn't stop watering earlier today, but now they feel gritty and impossibly dry. Every time I blink, it feels like I'm gently caressing them with a pumice stone.

Even though the water at Walker Lake tasted like the inside of the fishtank, I'm craving it hard. I chugged it until my stomach bloated before leaving, thinking that had to at least get me through the day.

It got me to pee about a hundred times between there and here, but now I swear I'm even more dehydrated than I was before.

Emery always told me I was the hangriest person he knew. If I had to wait more than four hours between a meal, the claws came out. He swore I almost ripped the handle off the front door after I came home from a work meeting that ran twenty minutes past my scheduled dinner time. I tried to explain the feeling: *there's a barracuda circling in my head, see, and if I don't drop fish flakes in the tank on a regular basis, he starts chomping on the part of my brain that makes me nice.*

Well, Emery should see me now. There's no cute word for the feeling when every drop of water has been sucked from your body. I simultaneously want to cry and logically realize I shouldn't waste the water. My throat sticks to itself. Coughing fits erupt without warning. Every time the wind rustles up a swirl of dust, it's all I can do not to scream. Terror, rage, both. My brain feels like it's too big for my skull. It throbs with my sluggish heartbeat, which throbs with my wrist, which hurts enough to almost distract me from the tender egg on the back of my head. The only thing keeping the sweat from evaporating off my back is my sleeping bag, strapped across my chest by the buckles meant to keep it rolled up.

I look like a tortoise with twice the vulnerability and half the speed. And none of the survival skills. I don't know why I thought heading into the desert was the best course of action. I lived by a university, for God's sake—there had to have been some boring old professor who knew how to dredge up drinking water, or divert it from the river thirty miles out of town. Someone who could have pulled the feral college kids together and formed a new civilization from the rubble. I don't know why I thought I was better off on my own.

The gun doesn't leave my hand during the day. As it gets later, I entertain the idea of shooting at the tires of the few cars that go by. I'd probably miss, but it'd be fun. Like Russian Roulette. *Who knows if I'll hit, comrades? If I have to walk, so do you!*

But every time I think that, my busted wrist gets a shock of pain, and the doldrums in my thoughts get a little current. If I hit, they'll get out of the car and come find me. They'll pin me to the dust, scratch my skin with sagebrush spines, and break my other wrist. They'll either steal my sleeping bag and clothes and whatever else I have left, material and otherwise, or they'll kill me and leave my body to rot like a dead crow alongside the dented Highway 360 marker. Or worse.

Since none of the options sound all that good, not yet anyway, I keep my finger off the trigger. And eventually, it drops out of my hand, and I don't even think about picking it up.

* * *

THE PAST

Sadie, Hal, Emery. Just those three, all when I was between the ages of 15 and 21.

I don't think Sadie ever realized she actually meant something to me. I know Hal realized he was sort of fleeting, a cover-up for something I couldn't begin to explain, but even now I hope he realizes I loved him, just in a different way that wasn't his fault. He went to college across the country in Vermont—maybe he survived. I could give him a real apology someday if I survive too.

I thought I knew where Emery and I stood. He was the Sadie I never got to experience all the way, someone who knew my secret, and my repentance for Hal and all the gestures that didn't mean to me what they meant to him. Emery was my first real love, in the way that I loved him, one hundred percent, and he loved me back in the same way. He loved me more than any of the scores of people he'd loved before.

Or so I thought. Maybe it's more complicated than that. Not quantifiable. I only found out love wasn't a solution, the answer to a bitter and looming problem, long after we had shared everything I had to give.

When he left, it felt like Sadie dropping me off in my rainy driveway after a sweet, confusing, blundering night, a half-failed attempt at epiphany. Like cold water soaking into my flats and sticking her sweatshirt to my skin. It felt like Hal telling me that, for some reason, *he* was sorry, and those words feeling like an accusation. A final kiss between us that I initiated, the Judas I am. Seeing him in classes, the last months of senior year, and avoiding eye contact. Hearing his friends in the hallways say I was a crazy bitch and they heard I might be secretly a lesbian anyway. Watching Sadie at soccer practice as I ran laps on the track and starting to realize there were things and people I'd never get over.

It felt like pithy cliches: *you're too much; you're not enough; it's not you, it's me, because I've learned not to tolerate psychos like you, because I have the breadth and depth of experiences you'll never understand. Because you'll never believe what's happening right in front of your face. Because you're naive and thought I'd never leave you for anything.*

It felt like Emery chose the world over me, and it felt like he was right when he did.

* * *

Frankie hit me, and I started screaming.

My mom rushed outside, Dad right on her tail. I fell back in the grass and kept wailing, holding my arm where Frankie punched me. Dad bent to scoop me up, and Mom grabbed Frankie by the arm before he could run off.

"Did you hit your sister?" she demanded. Frankie stared off into the dandelions in front of our blue house and muttered something. I was reduced to sniffling and hiccuping in Dad's arms as he held me to his black-and-red flannel. He rolled up the sleeve of my kitty-print shirt to examine the red splotch on my upper arm.

My mom wasn't having the nonsense. "Answer me, Frankie," she said, and turned his head so he had to look at her.

"She was annoying me!" Frankie protested, almost in tears himself. He tried to drop to the ground, but Mom held him up with one hand and pushed her glasses up with the other.

"We do *not* hit people, and especially not your sister." She let go of Frankie's arm, and he crossed it over his chest and stared at his light-up shoes. "Do you think hitting people is okay?"

Frankie scuffed his shoes. "No," he said, scowling.

"Do you want Cassidy to grow up thinking it's okay for boys to hit her?"

"No!" Frankie finally looked up and glared right at me. "But she's annoying!"

I started crying again. "Come on," my mom said. She grabbed Frankie's arm again and pulled him up the concrete steps to the front door. "You're going to time-out."

Once he went inside, my dad set me down on the steps and sat next to me. He picked up a roly poly and handed it to me. I held it, still sniffling, in my pudgy outstretched hand. "Boys are mean," I said, staring at the little black ball through smeared vision.

"Not forever, Caz." He leaned over and blew a raspberry over the fading red mark on my arm, which made me laugh. "One day you'll find a boy who's nice to you."

I watched the roly poly unroll and crawl across my hands. Its antennas wiggled and a hundred tiny legs followed behind. "Girls are nice," I said.

I let the roly poly fall off the edge of my hand onto the sidewalk. My dad pulled me into his lap. "Maybe," he said to the top of my head, "but you'll get what I mean someday."

* * *

AUGUST 2032

I don't know how it can be so simultaneously cold and bone-dry at night. I just expect snow when it's this blisteringly chilly.

I can hear Mom in my head now. *Well, Cassidy, if you're*

cold, just put on another layer. What are you doing outside without gloves on? Honey, I think you ripped your pants.

She would have said that last one with a jokey smile. Every minute I regret leaving the duplex in ripped jeans. The artfully distressed knees let in a lot of air, and the belt barely holds them up anymore. But I guess if I had anything better, maybe I would have thought to bring it. I really wasn't planning on this —"this" being, "getting jumped, losing my car, and walking south on a highway so boring it might kill me before the elements do." I *had* another few layers, a certain black soccer sweatshirt, but they're gone. I *had* gloves, but I wasn't wearing them that night because it was almost kind of nice out and I was distracted by the stars.

And now it's nighttime again, but instead of having stars, I have the smothering ash cloud, and the only extra possession I have left is the sleeping bag. It's warm, but not enough. That breeze that blew all day must have brought in a cold front. I can't stop shivering, even though the tension in my neck is giving me a killer headache. On top of the killer headache from the dehydration. And the starvation. And the concussion. Every time I move even a little, the cold seeps right through the burgundy cotton crewneck I've been wearing for almost three days, sliding frozen hands over my back and sides.

And that's not even mentioning the constant feeling that there are coals smoldering inside my busted wrist.

At the very least, I was able to find a jagged crack in the hard earth, deep enough to conceal me but shallow enough I can get in and out. It might be an old canal. It might be an earthquake rift. There's nothing growing on the sides, so maybe the latter.

Who knows. Who cares? I'd be worried about scorpions or snakes or whatever if I wasn't so damn tired. Desperate for water, I pulled up a tough old sagebrush growing at the edge of the rift. I yanked on it until the roots broke free and I fell backwards, a miniature landslide tumbling down with me.

Now I sittin the loose soil at the bottom, the sleeping bag wrapped around me, gnawing on a root. I don't know if this stuff is edible to humans, but there's jack-all else, and I feel like I've seen deer or antelope or something eating them in Montana. There was one big root growing straight down from the tangled network of smaller ones. When I get tired of chewing, I just suck on it. It tastes horrible. Bitter.

I can't get enough of it.

I don't feel better eating it, though. I can vividly imagine my stomach digesting itself from the inside out, acid eating through the soft, stretchy membranes and melting the muscles and ligaments around it. The thirst never abates either. There's a constant pressure in my throat that even one glass of water couldn't push away.

One tall, cold, sloshing glass of water.

With those little beads of condensation on the side.

Or a hot cup of tea, sencha, in a sassy mug I could warm my icy fingers on.

Or even room temperature water straight from the kitchen sink at the duplex, where I could taste the rusted pipes.

Fuck.

I should have stayed at Walker Lake. I don't know if it's worth the full day's walk back. I don't even know if I'd make it. My hands are so stiff I can't move my fingers. With my car gone, and everything inside it, I can't start a fire. I should have slept with a lighter in my pocket, not my useless phone. Then again, I shouldn't have left my keys in the ignition, and I probably shouldn't have even built a fire that time, drawing attention to my campsite between the lake and the highway. At least here, as my teeth chatter in the silence at the bottom of the rift, in near-total darkness, no one will find me.

The ground is getting more uneven here. Ridges spring up and steep valleys plunge around the ever-flat road. I might hit some low mountains within the next day. There might be water there, a barely-trickling creek or maybe old ranchland with full irrigation ditches.

I have to believe it, because otherwise I have to believe I won't find anything and there will just be more desert, except with hills, increasingly difficult terrain where even *my* endurance will falter, and at some point my numb legs will take a step and not lift high enough and I'll trip on a jagged rock, and I'll fall, and I probably won't get up.

Because by then, it'll probably be easier to just close my eyes and let the overwhelming failings of my body lift like fog on a fall morning.

* * *

OCTOBER 2030

My back and shoulders twitched, the muscles fatigued, as I set down the last box with a heavy clank.

"Careful," Emery said with a laugh and leaned against the kitchen counter. He wore a blue sweater, the same one, I remembered, from when we met three weeks before. It was a nice contrast to his blond hair. "What are those, dishes? You're gonna break them."

"It's fine, they're all shit anyway. Garage sale rejects." I cracked my knuckles. The insides of my fingers sported calluses from hauling reused cardboard boxes around all day. "Your eyeliner is looking almost presentable, by the way."

"What a lovely compliment," he said, tiptoeing through the mess to meet me in the living room.

He massaged my shoulders as I got a look at our new place.

He'd moved in the day before, bringing almost nothing from his nightmare campus apartment; I'd still had to settle things with Jeanine. She swore up and down the toaster was hers from home. I distinctly remembered buying it on clearance at Walmart. In the end, I let her have it. I didn't want to wait a second longer to get out of there, especially with her shady boyfriend already half moved in.

And I didn't want to spend another second away from Emery.

I surveyed the couple of rooms I could see from where I stood. The hardwood floor in the living room was good; unfinished, a little splintered in places, but a nice, reddish color. The white painted doorways were chipped but not hideous. A spacious sink in the kitchen, not much counter space but with a couple convenient outlets. Best of all, the walls were already painted. Not just a boring white or waiting room beige like the mass-produced McApartments all around town, either. The living room glowed with the softest magenta, the kitchen a warm yellow that reminded me of my grandparent's house.

And windows. Lots of them, all over. One over the sink in the kitchen and a couple on adjacent walls in the living room. Emery had brought an empty shelf with no back—perfect for potted plants. I could see it already: desk there, chairs there, maybe a cheap couch of some kind along the outside wall. Curtains to hide the cracks near the windows.

"This is great," I said as Emery carefully guided me around the labyrinth of boxes on the floor through the kitchen. His thumbs still unraveled knots in my shoulders. "I hope you don't have any opinions about the interior design, because if you did, they've just been revoked."

"Opinions are a privilege, not a right. Got it." He steered me to the long black curtain that covered the bedroom doorway from the other side, then crossed in front of me. He pushed back the fabric. "This way, m'lady."

"Peasant." I ducked under his arm into the bedroom. It was lit by a single window on the far wall, the low sun filtered in through a collage of autumn leaves. Painted a deep sea blue that almost matched Emery's sweater, it was nearly bare save for the pile of blankets and overflowing suitcase on the floor. His widescreen TV was propped against the wall by the tiny bathroom, plugged into an exposed outlet.

I turned back to Emery. "You didn't! All this, for me?"

"The finest bed in the land." He sat on the pile of blankets, thumped the spot next to him. I sat criss-cross, facing him. He gestured at the floor. "The highest-quality, mystery-gray carpet, the likes of which can only be found in sad offices and middle-school hallways."

His rusty baritone still gave me chills. I tried to look coy, peered out from under my bangs. "Dare I ask...?"

"Pillows," he announced, producing a saggy, caseless lump from the blankets behind him. "The flattest my coffers can buy."

He tossed it at me suddenly, and I only caught it after it had already hit me in the face. "Pillow," I corrected him, blinking. "One. Singular."

"Yes."

"Emery, this is sad. You are so lucky I'm moving in with you and bringing all my stuff."

"The stuff is why I agreed to it," he said, nodding sagely. Then his face turned serious. "You don't think this is kind of crazy, do you? Moving in together?"

My heart raged as wisps of his hair fell past his eyes, a paintbrush that dotted freckles over his nose. "With the room-mates we had before?" I swung the pillow at his head, catching

73

him off-guard. It thumped into his ear. "Maybe, but it would be crazier *not* to."

He chuckled. "Classic Caz, telling it like it is." Emery stood and extended a hand, helping me up.

"Classic Emery," I said, "relying on me for simple amenities." We walked into the kitchen. "A sleeping bag, Emery. How do you not have a sleeping bag?"

"I was thinking we could just get a real bed soon," he said and opened one of the white cabinets over the counter. A lone box of cereal sat inside. He looked at me over his shoulder. "Care for our deluxe dining experience?"

My phone was already out. "I'd rather starve," I said, dialing the closest pizza place.

Emery shut the cabinet and squeezed me around the waist. "Ah, Caz," he said. "Please don't ever change."

* * *

???

I wake to a darkness so dark it's hard to imagine there was ever light. I believe for a whirling moment that I've died, or I'm coming close. My brain is too numb to tell me how cold I must be, but I can still sense thorns raking the inside of my throat, and feel my rapid, wavering heartbeat. It patters unevenly, like raindrops.

The dying doesn't feel scary—it feels like melancholy disappointment, like when I've had something fun planned for months and months but my friends keep canceling, one by one, until I'm the only one left. And I either go by myself or just call the whole thing off. It feels like I've failed someone, but it doesn't seem like it's me.

Somehow, it's more disappointing to wake up to another grimy orange sky in the morning.

* * *

AUGUST 2032?

I walk all day. I'm getting slower, and I stumble a lot. Once my phone falls out of my pocket, and I nearly black out reaching down to grab it. Cars pass by once or twice, and I don't even flinch. I just walk. Suck the moisture out of the sagebrush with weak fervor. Sometimes emotion erupts in the pit of my stomach, rage and then despair, like the hot and cold pockets of air that clash to form a tornado. But even that doesn't have the force to give me energy.

Mostly I feel and think nothing. Words tumble in my head, bounce into each other and repeat almost without meaning: *Water. Water. Should have. Have. Let those ducks live. Should have. Stayed. Stayed with. At. Going to not. Make it. Anyway. Wasn't worth. It. Water. Not sure I'm even. Thirsty. Or anything. Anymore.*

I should have stayed. With. At. With.

I spend another night on the side of the road. A flat patch of ground, hard dirt surrounded by sagebrush, the same thing everywhere I look. I'm exhausted but somehow find it hard to fall asleep. My head doesn't hurt anymore, just thumps with a dull pressure. It feels like there's a marble in the hollow of my throat that I just can't swallow. Sometimes I start sweating like crazy and rip the sleeping bag open even though I feel the wind ripping my skin like plunging icicles.

Scenarios pass through my head and I get lost in them, forgetting for long moments where I really am. Some of them are memories and some aren't quite right, but I can't tell which is which. Most of them involve Emery, now that I don't have the energy to push those dreams away. I barely have the energy to re-zip the sleeping bag when I start shivering again.

75

* * *

???

We meet at the party. I don't make fun of his apartment, I tell him how I love the way he looks at me, his honey-amber eyes, his openness.

I tell him about high school, about Sadie, about Hal, and he tells me sometimes coming to understand yourself brings the burden of more questions.

His Jeep passes by me in the desert. We make eye contact. He doesn't stop.

My parents tell me they thought he was a nice young man, though they say something offhand about the eyeliner I told him not to wear.

* * *

Emery wriggles into the sleeping bag next to me. I can hear the rocks and sand grinding together underneath him. "I promise we'll get a real bed by next week," he says. "I may be an undeserving peasant, but you shouldn't have to live like this."

My tongue feels swollen. "I should have...stayed," I manage.

Emery repositions himself again. "With Jeanine? That would have been crazier than moving in with me."

He keeps moving around, and I feel so scared I get annoyed. "Stop," I say. I try to reach over and still him, but my arms won't listen to me. "You're letting all the cold air in."

"Classic Caz," he says, "always joking around."

I finally summon the energy to look over at him, but there's no one there. No matter where I look in the dark, moving just my eyes and not my head, it's empty. Faint movement only flashes in my periphery. My heart races. I feel a weight in the pit under my ribs and can't breathe. Emery whispers, but I can't hear him under the sound of my own shallow gasps.

The ground drops out from under me. I startle, my limbs jerk, but the feeling doesn't go away.

* * *

I haven't gotten out of bed all day. Emery has to go to work at the lab, but he stops in the bedroom before heading out.

"Hey," he says gently, sitting on the edge of the bed.

My eyelids feel like they're cracking as I force them open. I realize I've been squeezing them shut for a long time. "Hey," I croak.

"I can call in sick if you want," he says. "I really don't want to leave you alone."

I force myself to sit up. "Don't," I say. "It's bad enough I can't get my shit together. I don't want you guilty by association."

Emery brushes my scraggly bangs back from my forehead. His expression, as I've often found after almost a year together, is unreadable. I hope it isn't pity; my gut is already roiling at the thought that he might skip work for me.

"Why don't you come with me?" he says. "You can hang out in one of the classrooms near the lab. Bring a book." He smooths out the violently rumpled bedding that's twisted around my legs, stretching it out flat. "I can bring you tea from the break room down the hall."

"I hear their Earl Grey is marvelously subpar," I mumble and rub my eyes.

Emery smiles sadly. "It's the worst." He finds where my hands are tangled in the blankets and holds them. "But it's probably better than staying here alone all day."

My pulse stutters in my throat, and every breath catches. My eyes flicker to where my phone lays on the mattress next to the deep indent in my pillow.

I tap the screen. The time flashes. "You're already going to be late because of me."

"It's okay, Caz," he says. "I'll help you get ready to come with. You can just wear what you wore yesterday. No one will know."

I let go of Emery's hands and lay back down, staring at the same blank ceiling I've been looking at all day. "Just go," I say, rolling over, bunching up the blankets again. "It'll just be distracting if I'm there, and I'll be fine on my own. It's not like I'm going anywhere."

He doesn't move for a moment. When he stands, I sink a little further into the mattress. Slow falling.

"Okay," Emery whispers.

I squeeze my eyes shut.

* * *

Somebody lifts me, and the dropping sensation stops. I can feel my arms and legs sag. My broken wrist throbs with pain, the toes of my shoes drag over the ground, and then I'm lying down again, somewhere soft. Sort of stiff. Head propped up. I can't open my eyes; the effort is too great. It's hard enough to breathe, like hauling on a heavy pulley and trying not to let go too fast.

My entire body convulses involuntarily as I feel myself thrown into motion, sideways, up and down. The word *earthquake* loops in my mind, even though this seems different. I don't stop shaking. I hear voices, garbled underwater noises, and I strain to understand.

I catch only pieces. "Fluids," a voice says as if from deep in a cave. "One more...lucky we found...take this."

Something jabs the crook of my elbow. A weak sound I don't register as my own voice spills from my sandy throat.

The world lurches and rocks under me.

* * *

EARLY SEPTEMBER 2032

The hospital is nice.

Crowded and full of the sick and dying, ringing with the wailing of the injured, but nice. I have one of the last open rooms to myself, at least for now. A crinkly, thin hospital bed that feels like the softest marshmallow ever invented. And a window so I can see the outline of mountains beyond the haze.

The exterior is much cooler-looking than the bland yellow rooms inside. I saw a glimpse of it as the car carrying my half-alive body pulled up to the front right as dusk hit last night. Big windows, criss-crossed with narrow beams, sunny backlighting to contrast the smoggy gray sky. Blue mountain logo. A couple dead potted plants out front. Blocky and futuristic, maybe stucco, but I didn't get too close of a look. Something about rolling toward it on a stretcher with an intravenous needle stitching my innards back together makes things a little hard to remember.

The locals who drove me here, flooring it down Highway 6 while I seized and flopped around and generally suffered an unflattering introduction, found me just before sundown. Thought I might not be alive, and who could blame them? I'd been lying motionless in that sleeping bag all that day and the night before. Couldn't speak, couldn't move, and still can't remember being there that long.

Gabriela told me they almost didn't see me through the ash cloud, which has been particularly thick since yesterday. She was the one who spotted me and carried me to the car, putting the needle in my arm and letting my head rest on her thigh. Probably lost circulation in that leg for the rest of the day. Tiana, God bless her, cut an hour-long drive in half with her total disregard for the posted speed limit.

Gabriela also told me it's a good thing I didn't get to the Mexican border, because it's closed except to people who can prove they have family there. I would have gotten all the way there for nothing. So much for Tijuana beaches and sunshine. Somehow, though, I already knew it wasn't going to happen. The universe has a funny habit of taking my dreams and giving them a firm punt into oblivion.

This is, of course, the same universe that sends me a couple of pretty former EMTs when I'm quite literally in the worst state I've ever been.

I knew I wasn't doing great, not since the ducks and the road trip and especially since Walker Lake—but holy shit, was I lucky to not come across any mirrors in the six days I was on the road. There's a big one in the bathroom down the hall which spans the wall behind the no-touch faucets. I was too astounded by the running water to gawk at my reflection right away. But when I finally did look, I realized something.

I suck at survival.

Six days and I look like something out of a horror film. Not one of the hapless protagonists, either, whose scars and smudges somehow make them look more dashing in their desperation. I look like the haggard thing that crawls out of the sewers to devour reckless children every night while somehow continuously losing weight. Half my hair came out when I took it down from the topknot this morning. I still wear the crewneck and jeans, which look about three sizes too big and stained beyond redemption. My skin is corpse gray, maybe from the intense dehydration but also possibly from the ash, and black circles engulf my deepened eye sockets where my eyeliner smeared. The cleanest thing on me is the cast they put on my wrist to start healing that nasty distal radius fracture. It's a crisp, crosshatched white.

I'm getting a chance in the showers soon, once someone can confirm I won't pass out while I'm in there and, I imagine, waste a ton of water as it rushes over my limp form. Somehow the locals have kept the utilities running around here, working together to form this Promised Land of the desert mountains, but they're careful not to waste anything. So that means I have to stay conscious during my ten minutes in the shower.

I told Gabriela when she came in this morning that I feel fine, but apparently my blood pressure is still kind of a bummer to behold. She took out the IV, at least. Now I'm drinking water like a normal human. Well, mostly normal, anyway. I kind of freak out if there isn't a full glass either in my hand or within grabbing distance.

I might just stand in the shower with my head tilted back and my mouth open. And after that, I'm taking the crewneck and jeans and hurling them out the window in my room.

* * *

They charged my phone for me. I don't know when they got ahold of it. Maybe it fell out of my pocket in the car while I was having a seizure. I only realized it was missing when I got to the showers and noticed it wasn't in my pocket anymore.

Gabriela brings it in with my dinner, which along with breakfast and lunch is the first real food I've had in months. I'm almost annoyed when I see how small the portions are and have to remind myself each time that I haven't had more than, basically, two chicken wings every day for over a month. I'd drool over a bowl of rocks if it had enough seasoning mixed in.

I take the tray in shaky arms. "Thanks," I say, then see the full battery icon emblazoned on the screen next to the carton of milk. My teeth clench together, and I have to manually relax my jaw. "I don't need that."

Gabriela looks down at me with her big, dark eyes. Her curly black hair falls over her shoulder in a low ponytail. "You don't want it?"

"No." I grip the edges of the food tray, my fingers whitening. It agitates my wrist, but the adrenaline masks it.

"Are you sure?" Her eyebrows pinch in concern. "Someone must be looking for you. What about your family?"

The laugh is harsh when it erupts from low in my chest. "Yeah, I'll see what they're up to."

Gabriela's frown deepens. She doesn't say anything else, but she doesn't take the phone away either. Her gaze lingers on me a moment longer before she nods almost imperceptibly and leaves the room. Her white sneakers squeak against the tile floor, echoing down the hall after she's left.

I take the phone in my right hand, fingers poking out of the white cast, and drop it into the mini garbage can next to my bed. It clangs and falls silent.

Gabriela picks up my unfinished dinner a while later.

I can't sleep.

Someone started crying in the next room when it got dark. Sometimes they said a phrase or two, but mostly it was just wordless. I heard someone else talking to them in a quiet, soothing voice, but for a while it didn't seem to be helping. The sobs just got louder and less articulated.

The sound was grating. I wanted to knock on the wall like I did in the dorms my first year when the girl next door would bring her boyfriend over: *Keep it down, would ya? Your eardrum-shattering coitus is activating my fight-or-flight response.*

But when my neighbor at the hospital finally calmed down, suddenly *I* felt like sobbing. The hour before midnight fills me with the kinds of emotions that squeeze tight around my lungs and keep me thinking about everything I've done wrong. It's good my left hand is not as adept at pulling my hair out, because otherwise I'd be bald by now.

It feels like everything I did in the months and days before this, before Yellowstone, before Emery left, all of it—everything I did was a mistake. I never opened up to my parents, never told them about Sadie, about moving in with Emery after three weeks, about all these things that feel so trivial now that they're dead. I never told Frankie that he was my closest confidant through high school, the one person who could punch me in the arm and tell me when I was being annoying. Never admitted that I appreciated him being my older brother, even if he just told me things like how dumb it is to wear ballet flats in the rain.

Worse, though, is that I feel like, where I didn't tell my family enough, I told Emery too much. He knew me more than anyone, knew I felt like an impostor and kept trying to convince me I wasn't no matter how many times I wrote him off. He knew I struggled to be honest with people, with myself, and tried to find out who I really was anyway.

And it was too much. Just like it was for Hal and Sadie, everyone who I begged to understand me.

I squeeze my eyes shut, clutch the starchy hospital sheets. The thoughts keep flooding my brain, with one floating on top of the others: With how close I came to dying, I'm not sure if Emery survived.

And I'm afraid to find out.

* * *

I don't sleep at all, and before first light, I've lost the battle with myself. I lean over the edge of the bed. My loose hair falls to the floor as I reach into the trash can and fish around until I find my phone. I lay on my side and squint at the white battery on the black screen. It takes a couple of seconds before my eyes adjust to the light.

I power it on.

The loading screen spins for a long time before my lock screen appears. A younger, rounder-faced version of me smiles from behind blurry orange leaves. Emery stares at me with a similar frozen smile.

I hurry to put in my passcode and sigh in relief when the cherry blossoms appear, endlessly floating into the ocean of grass below. For a moment, nothing happens.

Then I get a text notification.

And another.

And another.

Six in total. All from Emery.

I have to look away. The bluish tinge of the screen glows eerily in the stark room, gleaming on the metal bedposts and reflecting in a rectangle off the dark window. I remember my nightmare of falling, but I'm definitely awake.

I wouldn't be this terrified otherwise.

I don't know how long I stare off into the dark, but it's getting light out when I finally look back.

My fingers tingle. I force myself to open the messages. They were all sent after my phone died, so they're marked with today's date. I scroll up to the last regular messages, something about groceries from before this summer, and read.

* * *

I'm sorry, Cassidy. I didn't know what else to do. Leaving you seemed like the only way to convince you to come with, if that makes any sense. I know you're sad and scared, and I wish I'd remembered that whenever we fought because I know you were trying to be strong for me. Even if it didn't seem like it, deep down I knew. There's nothing I can say to make up for that, or for anything else that's happened. But I hope you know I never stopped loving you, even when I left. And I hope wherever you end up, you're safe.

Almost to Penn. I don't know if you're getting these. Please tell me if you are.

Here. My parents are so happy I'm alive, it's almost like they forgot cutting me off for the past few years. I can just imagine all the things you'd have to say about that. It's making me wish you were here.

I feel like I'm in high school again, pretending to be things I'm not to keep them happy. Forgot how hard this can be. You're tough as nails, Caz. I know you're making it through all this.

Gov. help coming in soon. They're trying to rebuild the East Coast and keep D.C. under control. If you're still out west, I hope you're staying safe. It might be a while before help comes. Hopefully the phone lines are still working for you too.

· · ·

I know you're still out there, I can tell. I know you won't quit no matter what. If you ever need somewhere to stay, though, I'm here. Things are getting better.

* * *

The final text includes his home address in Pennsylvania. I read it over and over until the number is engraved in my memory.

I'm still rereading it when Gabriela comes with equipment and a clipboard to check my vitals. She stops in the doorway, her face lit by the window. "Cassidy. Did you get any sleep at all? You look exhausted."

I don't know how to respond. I don't feel exhausted at all. Sparks buzz one after the other through my entire body.

"Cassidy?"

"Are there cars around here?" I ask and sit up. I shut my phone off with my thumb and set it down on the bed. "Something I could borrow. Or, you know. Have. Somebody took mine."

Gabriela crosses her arms, shakes her head. "You're in no condition to travel around by yourself."

I laugh, and this time it doesn't sound harsh. Maybe a bit crazy, but genuine. "You'd be surprised how well I do on my own. I can get pretty far."

"Just because you can, doesn't mean you should." She crosses to the bed, wraps a blood pressure cuff around my arm. "Besides," she says, pumping it up, "I know firsthand what happened when you tried to get somewhere."

I kick the sheets off my feet. Gabriela has a change of clothes from the room of extras they keep at the hospital, and I put them on while she records some numbers on her clipboard. Plain blue jeans, no rips, and a white T-shirt like the one I wore over my mouth on the road. They're a couple sizes smaller than I used to be.

"Apocalypse: the best weight loss program since The Great Depression," I murmur to myself as I adjust the waistband around my hips.

Gabriela looks up sharply, taps her pen on my patient sheet. "You're in a funny mood today," she says, and I think she's going to criticize me for being callous, but then one side of her mouth tilts upward. She nods toward my phone. "What, your boyfriend text you or something?"

I smile too. "Maybe he did," I say, tucking in my shirt. "Maybe he invited me to come spend the night, and that's why I need to borrow the car."

"Ah." Gabriela sits on the edge of my bed. "Why doesn't he just pick you up?"

"Right?" I shake my head, sigh. "Sometimes boys are so much effort."

Gabriela studies my face and gets a knowing look. "I hear girls are nicer." I must look surprised, because she outright laughs at me. "I see the way you eyeball me. If you weren't such a mess already, I would have decked you."

I shrug, my face a little hot. "What can I say? Reverse Nightingale effect."

"Best give it up now. I'm taken." She holds out her hand, and for the first time I notice the simple silver ring on her finger. "Tiana's got a matching one. And she's also my age, kiddo."

I feel a hint of embarrassment even though I know she's just teasing. I turn to look out the window. "Nice day," I say.

It's true. The sky has only the faintest sheen of ash, the clear blue behind fighting through. The sun is brilliant on the horizon. Not too red. I watch a couple people walk on the street below. They wave at each other as they pass, tiny smiles on their tiny faces.

Gabriela comes to stand at the window next to me. "You know, if that boyfriend of yours is worth the effort, he'll want you to be safe, whether that's next to him or across the country."

I shift my focus to the faraway mountains. "Well then, he's definitely worth the effort." The fingers of my left hand drum on top of my thigh. A fluttering giggle escapes me. "The question is, am I?"

"Ooh boy." Gabriela takes my arm and guides me back to the bed. I sit, and she sits next to me, pointing the pen at my nose. "You're trying to pretend you're kidding, but I've been there. It's better to not ask that question and just believe you are."

I lock eyes with her. There's a depth to her gaze that tells me her sincerity comes from experience. "Yeah," I say. "You're probably right."

"I know I am." She does another half-smile and then stands with a groan. She taps the clipboard at her side, bends and straightens her knees. "Here's another bit of wisdom," she says, grimacing. "Once you turn thirty, you don't bounce back like this." She gestures broadly at me.

I laugh. "Thank you. I'll remember that next time I want to complain about how I almost died."

"That's right." Her sneakers squeak as she pivots. "Give me twenty. I'll be back with your breakfast."

I watch her leave, then grab my phone and turn it on again. The network indicator is visible in its usual spot at the top of the screen. I can't guarantee it's accurate, but I plead with every bit of hope left in me that it's working.

The sun climbs higher in the sky, brighter than I've seen it in months. It glitters off the dust motes floating between me and the window, and suddenly I can see why all the hospital rooms are painted this shade of yellow. It's beautiful, illuminated like this. Vibrant. It reminds me of the Easter daffodils in front of my childhood house, the aspen leaves at the park in fall. The kitchen of the duplex. Looking at it now, it feels like I've missed this color even though I never realized it was gone.

There are other things I miss too. Things I will never get back. Things I missed even when I had them. Things I will miss forever.

My cherry blossom screen starts to go dark, and I tap it to bring it back to life. I go to my messages, which are still open. Read the last six messages. Repeat the address in the last text. My lips move without making a sound.

Things are getting better.

My thumbs hover over the keyboard, and make contact.

END

DESTINATION VACATION

BY C. H. ROSENBERG

DESTINATION VACATION

Have Spacesuit? Learn About Our Seasonal Travel Packages!

Tracie swept the mess of brochures into a somewhat neater pile on the front passenger seat and pulled the sun visor down to block the early morning rays. All signs pointed to it being a beautiful spring day.

The kind of day that was *made* for souvenir photos.

Tracie smiled as she nosed into Union Station's main entrance and scanned the sidewalk. There they were—her Tuesday group.

Those just arrived off the space elevator yawned, stretching their pseudopods and vestigial fins; a couple grumpily sipped at caffeinated slime. A Rustacean family of six cheerfully munched a to-go breakfast; the colorful packaging brightly advertised yet another multiplanetary franchise. Tracie could see the two rugrats practically buzzing through their mottled grayish-red shells with excitement as they polished off their waffle-and-sardine breakfast burritos. The older juvenile slurped dourly at her shake, maintaining a carefully calibrated distance from the rest of the family unit.

Tracie inwardly chuckled—*teenagers*—as she continued down the roster, checking off next a Deesipod couple in their golden years. The ladies were frankly adorable in matching khaki harnesses, the latest-model holovid cameras dangling from their thoraxes. Tracie winced a bit at the safari-style hats —modified to permit antennae to poke through. *Probably on shore excursion*, was her guess. She'd heard yet another mega-cruise liner had docked in geosynchronous orbit last night.

Rounding out the group were three solo travelers. Two young adults, best Tracie could tell. *Students taking a gap year from university*, she quickly categorized the gelatinous Pungluroid and cephalopodian Xenatode. The ubiquitous backpacks were a dead giveaway. But the third...Tracie squinted. The male Pangalian didn't easily fit into any of the standard boxes Tracie had come to identify after four—*jeez, it has to be almost five—five* years of doing this.

She leaned over the steering wheel for a closer look. The Pangalian was quite a bit older than the two other singletons, the frosted fur indicative of early middle age. Tracie self-consciously ran fingers through her own dark hair; the silver had recently metastasized from a few isolated strands to outright streaks.

The Pangalian was dressed casually enough in pressed denim jeans—with part of the seat cut away to make room for the tail—a souvenir DC T-shirt, and hot pink fanny pack. But he held himself rather stiffly, a protective paw over a name-brand messenger bag.

Probably here on business, Tracie finally diagnosed sympa-thetically. She recalled those days of squeezing in the odd tour between one meeting and the next.

Craning her neck, Tracie double-checked to make certain

the passenger seats looked clean and inviting. The cupholders and compartments were stocked with all the basics, from tissues to water to strawberry-flavored bleach. *Good to go.* She sounded the horn—it cheerfully honked in all linguistic frequencies—and added a quick flash of violet from the head- and taillights.

The effect was immediate. Rustacean kids in the vanguard, they skittered, undulated, and bounced en masse toward the van. The vehicle was emblazoned with *Tracie's Terrestrial Tours*—in seven languages, including Interplanetary Standard – Written—along with an anthropomorphized rendering of the van itself, superimposed over the planet.

"Welcome to Earth!" Tracie called from the driver's window. She sang it in IP Standard – Verbal, followed by all five languages represented in the day's group. As always, the Deesipodian salutation clawed at her throat and she bit her tongue—*again!*—on the requisite tooth-scrapes. Xenatodish required the extra effort of pulling out a harmonica and a perfume bottle equipped with three sprayers, one each for vowels, consonants, and glottal stops.

But the beaming noses and chitters of startled delight made it worth the effort. *And the tips don't hurt, either.*

With a depressed button, the side door slid open. Tracie hollered: "Aaaall uh-*board!*"

It was the work of a few minutes to get everyone properly situated. The Rustaceans obligingly tucked themselves into the double-wide seats at the back—much like a row of pygmy elephants, each stuffed into a crab's shell and armed with the appurtenant pincers and walking legs. All six blinked at her expectantly from multiple eyes.

Tracie next lowered the ramp so the Deesipods could shuffle into the second middle row. She patiently waited as one of the pair obsessively wiped the seat down with disinfectant, and promptly secreted a layer of webbing over the pleather.

Tracie stepped aside for the first singleton to squish inside. The young Pungluroid gamely ingested her pack to make room. Next came shoving all the Xenatode's tentacles into the vehicle; Tracie determinedly put her back into it. The Pangalian nimbly leapt in after.

Having ensured everyone's assorted appendages were safely stowed inside the vehicle, Tracie gave a tap to close the passenger door. She hopped back into the driver's seat and settled more firmly into her role.

"All right, then!" she brightly chirped, turning around to face her audience. "Who's up for a full day of history, mystery, *maybe*"—*wink-wink*—"bumping into a Congressman or two— and just plain *fun?*"

The group obligingly cheered—all but the sullen teenager, who rolled up the sides of her ears like a window shade, and the Pangalian businessman. The latter opened his messenger bag and slid out a tablet made of a vitreous lavender material. He started swiping through it.

Tracie mentally shrugged and launched into her practiced spiel. It was practically second nature at this point.

"Welp, my name is Tracie, and I'll be your guide for today's American Highlights tour! I'm so honored to share my culture with such a terrific gang." She kicked off in Interplanetary Standard for the varied group. "We'll start out at the American History Museum, where you'll receive a quick backgrounder on this country's founding. Next," she continued enthusiastically, "we'll stop at each seat of this nation's three branches of government. Pay close attention, because later there *might* be a pop quiz—with prizes!" The kiddos jabbered excitedly.

"On our way to lunch, we'll make a loop of the major memorials and monuments—we're offering our comprehensive

Moonlight Monuments tour tonight, by the way—and you'll have a chance to record some holovid. Then—"

The Xenatode waved a sucker-studded tentacle, whacking the van's ceiling. "Yes?" Tracie said patiently.

"Will there be gift shops?" The Xenatode glurbed the question, echoed in his interpreter's mechanical tones. "I promised I'd bring back souvenirs." The skin beneath his mantle blushed a deep blue, making him look like an embarrassed cuttlefish. "My colony collects commemorative ornaments."

"Absolutely," Tracie promised. "And I'll pass around some coupons. Now, all that fun should work up quite an appetite!" she got back on-topic. "So, we'll stop at Freedom Fries for some grub—"

The Rustaceans visibly perked up.

"—as well as a variety of other palate-pleasing options," Tracie reassured the rest of the group. "Plus, I'll introduce you to *pizza*, a human delicacy highly beloved by my people." The Deesipods exchanged mystified expressions and immediately bent over their guidebook. "After lunch, we'll head on out to Mount Vernon, residence of the *first* elected leader of this planet's *first* modern democracy!"

"Where he lived with his one hundred and twenty-three slaves," the teenager interjected smugly.

"Right you are." Tracie didn't miss a beat; she winked and tossed the brat a tchotchke water bottle branded with the *Tracie's Terrestrial Tours* logo. Smoothly, she continued, "And we'll talk about the lead-up to the Civil War on the way back into town. In fact, we should arrive just in time for a behind-the-scenes tour of Ford's Theatre, followed by an authentic human performance."

The Pungluroid extruded four pseudopods and clapped them together in anticipation.

"We'll wrap up our exciting day with a buffet dinner,"

Tracie brought it home. "Then I'll drop y'all back off at your hotel—or at the station if you're waiting to be picked up by a tender." She nodded at the Deesipod couple.

"Now, some ground rules before we dive into our fun-packed day!" Tracie ran through the basics—"stay together and do *not* wander off on your own, don't touch or slime *anything* in the museum or the White House—sliming the Capitol Building is fine as long as you keep it to the public areas—please be respectful of others when recording holovids, and you *must* keep your small children by your side *at ALL times*."

Tracie shuddered, recalling the National Portrait Gallery incident from six months back. Sliegon larvae were constantly hungry, and they liked *anything* oil based. She shook off the borderline traumatic memory and forced a grin. "Now that we've gotten all that out of the way, let's *roll*. Buckle up!"

Tracie lowered her sunglasses and instructed the van to pull away from Union Station. A quick glance at the navigation screen, and she jumped right back into the script.

"Now, let's hear where all y'all fine folks are from!" She passed back a basket filled with blank labels and pens—modified for various appendages. "What brings you to our humble planet?"

The Rustacean teenager sighed dramatically as her siblings fumbled with the basket. Both pint-sized mischief-makers were already going to town on each others' exoskeletons with the sharpies. The family matriarch speared her offspring a warning glare with two of her eyes before introducing the nuclear family. Her proboscis proudly tapped in turn all three of her children—teen included—and affectionately caressed the shells of both husbands.

The senior Deesipod couple went next. "We're celebrating our anniversary tomorrow," one bragged.

Huh, Tracie thought. For some odd reason, it was rare to

see offworlders traveling as couples; they tended to vacation as families, singly, or in packs. She nodded when the other female added both were celebrating their retirement—one from a middle management position at a spaceship parts manufacturer; the other having just sold her accounting practice. The post-retirement cruise *was* a universal mainstay.

The two youths good-naturedly introduced themselves as —*I got it right*—university students out to "experience" the galaxy before classes started up again. Each slapped a nametag over their mantle or membrane, cheerfully swapping jokes in IP Standard – Olfactory. Tracie smiled good-naturedly, and discreetly cracked open a window.

"I'm just bumming around the Milky Way's Orion Spur for my gap year. It's way cheaper than the main spiral arms, with plenty of hostels along the way," the Pungluroid explained, forming a couple of pseudopods to gesticulate.

Tracie smiled again and nodded. *Enjoy your freedom now*, she thought. *You'll need to buckle down in school soon enough —and from there, to a full-time job.*

Not that any kind of job is guaranteed anymore.

The thought led to memories Tracie didn't much care to dwell on. Thankfully, the van pretty much drove itself, giving Tracie a couple of blocks to compose herself. She reaffixed her smile in the rear-view mirror, and then checked on the group.

Her gaze automatically went to the Pangalian. Unlike the others, he wasn't curiously pressed against the window— sunroof, in the Deesipods' case—or chatting it up with his fellow tourists. Instead, he sat with erect posture, tail coiled tightly around his waist—safely out of reach of the Rustacean toddlers' inquisitive mandibles. As she watched, the Pangalian studiously swiped through the tablet, the device capturing the light like a stained-glass windowpane. One talon stroked at his left whiskers—barbels, really, like a refined sturgeon.

The Pangalian had obligingly filled out a nametag in big, block letters, now pasted on that garish T-shirt. Tracie squinted —even hyperpolyglots had trouble reading languages in mirror image—and glanced down at the roster. *Let's see...*

She turned around again, lifting her sunglasses, and fixed the Pangalian with her brightest friendly-Earth-native smile. "Tee—uh, *Tine*, right?" Tracie sounded out the vowel as *aye*— damned Pangalese writing system wasn't exactly easy to decode. Her target dipped his ears in acknowledgement.

"Here for business or pleasure?" Tracie chirped.

"Don't know yet," was the curt response.

Ohhh-kay, then. "Glad to have you on-board!" she conceded lightly. The van's AI chimed—the first stop was coming up. Tracie resettled herself into the driver's seat, eyes facing front. Her faint reflection stared back from the windshield, outlining Tracie's rounded features, along with the crinkling lines making their debut at the corners of her eyes. *Don't let 'Taciturn Tine' get to you. His attitude is his problem.*

"Now, what *better* place to start our American Highlights tour than with the National Museum of American History?" Trace projected her voice to bounce about the vehicle, like a hyperactive ball.

"*History?*" The more outspoken Deesipod sniffed. She blew the word back out of her third and fourth nostrils. "This podunk little nation barely *has* three local centuries of history."

"Sweetie..." was her better half's weary rejoinder. But her spouse persisted. "I *told* you we should have signed up for the Marvels of Mesoamerica tour." Clearly, she'd forgotten *this* tour guide had greeted them both in Deesipodian. Or assumed Tracie knew only the basic salutations.

Well, it wouldn't be the first time.

"This shore excursion was half the price," her wife hissed

back. "It was a trade-off, remember? Or don't you want that hot stone massage?"

"Fine, fine..." her spouse muttered half-heartedly. "At least *this* tour comes with meals included."

Tracie again checked her professional smile in the mirror —*damn*, but her facial muscles were going to hurt by day's end. Still, she couldn't restrain a genuine grin for the two Rustacean rugrats gawking at the passing scenery with wide sets of eyes.

"Now, this nation *is* comparatively new to the scene." She improvised the script with casual nonchalance. "But we've sure crammed a whole lot into a short period of time!" Which led nicely into her patented—and sensationalized—nutshell summary of U.S. history. It was jampacked with cringeworthy phrases like *forged in the flames of revolution* and *pioneers seeking their Manifest Destiny*, along with *shameful legacy of genocide* and *original sin of slavery*.

That at least provoked some interest from the Rustacean teen. Tracie gritted her teeth and powered through the Civil War, the first two World Wars, and the rest of the twentieth century by the time the van came to a stop in front of the museum.

Tracie checked the time as she led the group past the information desk. The veteran docents saluted her over the heads of their own groups. Tracie nodded back respectfully, narrating as she chivvied her extraterrestrial posse from one exhibit to the next. She spoke mostly on autopilot, yet here and there she caught her voice lifting with passion, even after doing this ad nauseum.

She hid a chuckle at the Rustacean kids' innocent chorus of *why, why, why,* and patiently shut down the Xenatode's eager insistence on reading every single placard out loud. And whenever she had a chance, Tracie prompted conversations over how something was shockingly similar to—or sensibly different on—

their own home worlds. It was her way of shamelessly picking up whatever nuggets of knowledge about the rest of the galaxy that she could.

Well, it's not like I have a snowball's chance in hell of ever actually visiting those places.

Maintaining a professionally upbeat tone, Tracie checked the time again. *Let's wrap this up.* She herded the group into the popular entertainment collection, smiling wryly as everyone—but Tine—immediately exploded into a flurry of holovid-taking madness. Entertainment was the one area where humanity punched above its own weight. The big production companies had benefited enormously from First Contact, and now cranked out fresh content at massive scale, all geared for an interplanetary audience. Even recycled material could be marketed as "period" drama.

Fifteen minutes later, Tracie counted snouts and antennae as the group made a beeline for the vehicle, each one loaded down with a full suitcase's worth of *Made on Earth* crappola from the gift shop: "One, two, three..."

Somebody was missing.

Tracie's lips pressed together. *Oh, come on—at our very first stop?*

She admonished the group to wait and handed the Rustacean kiddos a set of *American Adventures!* coloring books and crayons before rushing back inside. Fortunately, Tracie didn't have to venture far: the Pangalian—*Tine*—stood right smack in the middle of the latest pop entertainment exhibit.

It was a life-sized diorama of a drive-in movie theatre. *Most Romantic Films of ALL TIME!* the accompanying placard boasted. Tine's tufted ears were fully perked, barbels sticking straight out with studied fascination as he stared at a series of images flickering against a miniaturized movie screen. The expression was the complete opposite of the Pangalian's earlier aloof manner.

A movie buff? Tracie was amused by the thought.

"Mr. Tine?" she braved a light tug at the T-shirt's sleeve. The Pangalian started, barbels twitching and tail bushing out. But his hackles lowered once he recognized the tour guide.

"Mr. Tine, we're heading to our second stop." Tracie tried for a sympathetic yet prompting smile. "We'd hate for you to miss out!"

"Oh." Tine blinked. "Of course." He followed Tracie docilely enough back to the waiting van. But his muzzle twice swiveled on the end of that sinuous neck, as he glanced back.

Tracie relaxed minutely once Tine was firmly ensconced in the van, his earlier, taciturn demeanor making a reappearance. For the rest of the morning, the Pangalian's eyes remained practically glued to his device, even in the middle of the Capitol Rotunda, barely aware his mauve sneakers were planted in a puddle of slime deposited by the holovid-snapping Pungluroid. He didn't even bother exiting the van at any of the monuments.

Tracie internally rolled her eyes and navigated the van down Constitution Avenue, toward the designated lunch spot. *At least he won't have anything to base a negative review on,* she noted with irony. *Unless he's turned off by my upholstery.*

* * *

Skip the crowded comets and overrated asteroids, and learn why Earth is the best under-the-planetary-radar destination for booking your next romantic escape.

Of course, the moment Tracie sat everyone down for lunch, she realized she'd misplaced a certain member of her group. Again.

"Doesn't even want to eat lunch with the rest of us, huh?" The Rustacean teenager fluttered an ear sarcastically.

One of her fathers flicked the youngling's shell with his upper claw. "Sweetie, that's not *nice*," he scolded. "Some people are just introverted."

The grumpier half of the Deesipod couple sniffed into nostrils two through five. "That's what self-guided tours are for." A The metal dining chair creaked alarmingly beneath the offworlder's weight as her mandibles tore into the stuffed crust. "Anti-social wretches."

The other wife *tsk*'ed, widening her compound eyes in concern. "But dinner isn't until the end of the tour, and that's a long time! Shouldn't we encourage him to eat *something*?"

Which prompted Tracie to experience a stab of guilt. "I'll go out and ask," she reassured the table. "The rest of you, please enjoy your meal." Tracie snagged a translated menu and ventured back out to the van.

Of *course*, Tine wasn't there.

And, of *course* she had no luck reaching out to Tine on his device—at least, not using the contact information he'd submitted with his registration.

Dammit!

Tracie inhaled a great big breath, trying not to panic. *If anything happens to him on my watch, I could lose my license! Or if he causes some sort of diplomatic incident...* She gamely tried *not* to think of all the ways an offworlder going off on his own could end in horrible, terrible disaster. *Like last year's 'incident' in the White House Blue Room. Not how I wanted to cut down on the competition...*

Calm down! Tracie's practical side snapped. *He was at the last stop, where you counted everyone. Twice. So, assume the idiot went off on his own. Where could he have gone?*

A lightbulb went off. *Of course!* Tracie immediately took off for the American History Museum.

The idiot was *exactly* where she'd intuited: squarely in the middle of the popular entertainment section. More precisely, the Pangalian had planted himself *inside* the exhibit—running February to May—on *The Great American Romance*.

Tracie wound her way around one display case after another, each containing pastel-bound romance novels. *An industry worth over a billion dollars a year!* declared a placard, posted right smack next to a life-size rendition of a bodice-ripper cover. Tracie paused briefly to admire the pirate-slash-Scottish nobleman's eight-pack, and then power-walked toward the recreated drive-in movie theatre.

Straight for today's problem child.

Tine had seated himself comfortably in the passenger side of a replica coupe—a powder blue, late 1950s model with exaggerated tailfins. The damn tablet was propped up against the glove compartment. But the Pangalian's attention was focused straight ahead, barbels slack beyond the occasional twitch, as he watched Deborah Kerr and Cary Grant moon-eyeing each other on the flickering screen.

An Affair to Remember, Tracie vaguely recalled the old film. *Wasn't there a famous scene, set at the Empire State Building? Never mind.* She firmly screwed a lid on her annoyance, glanced about—*where's a security guard when you need one?*—and slid into the driver's seat next to her pain-in-the-neck du jour.

"Mr. Tine?" Tracie wrestled her voice into a calm and level contralto. "We missed you at lunch." She couldn't help injecting acid into the next sentence. "Mr. Tine, you *might* recall the ground rules we set out at the beginning of the t—"

"Is that—that edifice—genuinely regarded as a *romantic* site?"

Tine interrupted, jabbing a talon-tipped paw at the screen. A nonplussed Tracie fell back as the Pangalian grabbed the tablet and stabbed at the screen. A few seconds later, he frowned, barbels drooping. "I see. This edifice *is* central to several derivative works set squarely in the romance genre. But it also features in numerous works of the 'action film' genre, as well as—" the muzzle scrunched with perplexity "—the 'alien invasion' genre."

Tracie winced, but refused to be derailed. "Mr. Tine, if we don't leave now, not only will you miss out on a *delicious* and authentically human lunch—" Tracie's stomach grumbled a disgruntled agreement. "—we'll also be late hitting the road for our tour at Mount Vernon."

"It's *Tine*," came the distracted response. "Not 'mister.' And I have *far* higher priorities than touring yet another political or war leader's place of residence," he added with superiority. The tufted ears twitched like miniature pom-poms.

Tracie bit her lip on the automatic retort. *Then why sign up to take the 'American Highlights' tour, you pompous sonuva...*

"Are there other such sites as these?" Tine looked up at her, attention finally shifted away from that damned tablet.

Tracie blinked. "What do you mean?"

"Locations with romantic connotations." Tine vaguely waved a paw at the screen.

Tracie blinked again. Part of her wanted to snap, *that's not part of the tour, dude!* But her more pragmatic side just shrugged philosophically and said, *What the hell.* Maybe, if she humored him, he'd be willing to get with the program.

"Well...you have some actual *buildings*, like the Empire State building and the Eiffel Tower," she began slowly, thinking through her answer as she spoke. "Then there are some natural landmarks considered romantic. And," she added after a few additional moments of reflection, "a few places have reputations as the best places for engaging in romantic *activities*."

"Oh." Tine sagely nodded. "Like your 'honeymoon suite.'" Of course, it was only *now* that Tracie realized Tine had been speaking all along in near-fluent American English. "Places where people indulge in—"

"Not exactly!" Tracie quickly grabbed back the conversational thread. "More like places considered ideal for, say, proposing marriage. Or destination weddings," she added.

Tine's ears nodded eagerly, barbels and ears at full alert as he bent once more to that tablet, tapping away.

The subject matter made Tracie feel mildly ridiculous. Self-consciously, she raised the bill of her baseball cap and brushed back a tendril of hair. It had slipped from her deliberately perky high ponytail—all part of a carefully curated image. "If you're interested in this sort of history, I'm happy to share more on the way to Mount Vernon. There's a *darling* love story between George and Martha Washington I'm sure you'd be in—"

Tine briefly flicked his eyes away from the tablet, ears flopped over in negation. "No, no; that's fine." He waved a desultory paw. "Go ahead and continue on without me. I have what I need."

While Tracie processed that perfunctory dismissal, the Pangalian added: "Do you have an—er—card?" Tracie bit her tongue, but handed over the rectangular piece of bioplastic readily enough. *Tracie Trang, President & CEO, Tracie's Terrestrial Tours, LLC.*

Tine stuffed the card into his fanny pack and pulled out a packaged eel-and-banana burrito, in blatant disregard of the multilingual *No Food, Drink, or Combustible Materials* placard on prominent display. The Pangalian began munching and turned back to the tablet, devoting all his attention to that jealous technological mistress.

And that, apparently, was that.

After a moment of hesitation—*leave no potential tip behind!* was the tour guide's mantra—Tracie bid Tine a resigned farewell. She rushed out to the van, fished a soylent bar from the glove compartment for her own, meager lunch, and instructed the AI to take an admittedly questionable shortcut back to Freedom Fries.

To her relief, the rest of the tour went off without a hitch. The more obstreperous half of the Deesipod couple ceased her grumbling after lunch, and began rhapsodizing nonstop about the pizza and plotting how to recreate the "human delicacy" in her own kitchen. The Rustacean teen similarly ratcheted way back on the sarcastic remarks. Mount Vernon was a hit, and the Lincoln assassination walk gave everyone a chance to stretch their appendages after the ride back. The play that followed also delivered a solid enough performance.

All in all, everyone was in a satisfied mood by the time Tracie sat the group down at Abe's All-You-Can-Eat. Tracie herself was relaxed enough to respond good-naturedly to the questions the Xenatode and Pungluroid peppered her with. It helped their curious inquiries weren't nearly as thoughtless or insulting as were so many she received on a near-daily basis.

I've read the average human family gets by on less than twenty-five zurons a month! What the hell are you spending all that intergalactic aid on, anyway? being a perennial favorite.

Still, Tracie permitted herself a sigh of relief when the van pulled up at the last hotel. The three Rustacean parents seemed a little ragged, but pleased. Even their teen daughter paused mid-scuttle through the van's passenger door. "Thank you," she said in halting but clear American English. "I had a really great time."

* * *

This tranquil blue-and-green gem, tucked away in the Orion Spur, has ranked among the top ten out-of-the-way destinations for carbon-based vacationers by Event Horizon Magazine *the past seven standard cycles running.*

Home—*at last!* Tracie smiled as the currency converter app added up all the tips. To her pleasant surprise, the Rustacean teen had transferred a separate—and very generous—amount. *Huh. Go figure.* The day's haul was impressive enough for Tracie to put Taciturn Tine completely out of her mind.

Tracie had just enough time left to take a catnap and bolt down a sandwich before the next tour. Her device started to clamor, just as she headed out to pick up her Monuments by Moonlight group.

"Ms. Trang?" Tracie permitted herself a few seconds to simply appreciate the speaker's accent. It was a particularly lovely vocal specimen—the cadence musical, the tone a little raspy—but in a good way, like velvet. It was also curiously familiar. Tracie's memory finally made the connection, and her upward-curved lips immediately flipped over in irritation.

The speaker on the other end tried again: "Tracie's Terrestrial Tours?"

"Yes?" she replied in guarded tones.

A chuff of relief. "This is Tinastic Hudheely—Tine. From today's American Highlights tour?" The Pangalian really *did* have a pleasant voice. Tracie must have been too pissed earlier to notice.

"A pleasure hearing from you so soon, Mr.—Tine," she warily said, checking the time with a measure of irritation. *He'd better not make me late.* Tracie yanked her hair into its usual, perky ponytail as she mentally ran through the possible reasons for the offworlder's call.

Had the Pangalian left something behind in the van? Tracie *always* went over the vehicle after every tour with a minivac, a fine-toothed comb, *and* Grade A disinfectant. She shivered, recalling an early episode with a client who'd misplaced his symbiont in the rear cupholder. *Nothing that small should have that many teeth.*

No; Tracie had unearthed nothing this time but a few dribbles of slime. And she clearly recalled Tine having his tablet with him when they parted ways in the museum—the only object he'd seemed particularly attached to. *I hope he doesn't insist on a partial refund for the second half of the tour—the half he cut short.* Tracie girded her loins to turn him down flat.

"How do I book a private tour with you?" Tine asked.

Tracie just barely caught her jaw from dropping. A private tour? *Odd request, coming from someone who* ditched *my tour just a few hours ago.* But she certainly wasn't about to turn down business. Especially the part of her business with such a high profit margin. *If he paid up-front.* Tracie cleared her throat and affected her very best customer-pleasing voice. "I'll need to check our calendar. What kind of tour? And when?"

"I want to see the most romantic locations on the planet," Tine immediately responded . "Full-day, lunch included. At a *romantic* eatery," he emphasized. "I want the full experience. And I want to do it by the end of the week."

"Um," Tracie prevaricated, recalling Tine's near obsessive fixation from earlier. *Huh. Maybe I was wrong about him being here on business.* "The end of this week..." Her mind raced. It *should* be doable, if an enormous pain. She'd have just a couple of days to craft a fresh itinerary, price things out, *and* make all the arrangements. Yet the challenge sparked some long-dormant interest.

Still, there *was* one overriding practical consideration. "You're talking about something *planet-wide* in scope, and we quite literally have a third world transportation system. For a single-day tour, I'm afraid my van won't—"

"That won't be a problem," Tine immediately dismissed. "I can arrange for a hovercraft rental. I'll also pay for everything in advance."

Jesus. The Pangalian certainly seemed committed. Still, Tracie hesitated. Not over-concerned about her physical safety —although one *did* hear sensationalized tales about less-than-savory forms of Earth tourism. But nothing about the businesslike Tine pinged her internal alarm. *And didn't I hear something about Pangalians being practically hardwired to mate for life? Or is that Pungluroids?*

"I'd love to arrange a personal tour—really, I would!—but I already have three tours booked that day," Tracie reluctantly said. Those were her most lucrative packages, too: the Democracy at Dawn brunch crawl, the Washington Walk and Potomac Sundown Cruise combo, and finally the Midnight Mall Mystery & Scavenger Hunt. "I can't disappoint all those folks who'd traveled light years just to visit our little, out-of-the-way planet..."

Tine named a price, one with a couple of hefty zeroes at the end. Tracie's inner accountant immediately converted the figure from zurons into dollars, deducted DC and federal taxes, and added back in the Jobs Promoting Interplanetary Goodwill self-employment tax credit.

"Done," she agreed. Her fingers were already tapping out cancellation notifications and arranging refunds—along with a generous promo code to rebook each tour at a twenty percent discount. *See, mom; see, dad? I can be practical. And, apparently, bought.*

The call ended with Tracie agreeing to meet Tine Friday

morning at his hotel. Tracie didn't know whether to smack her forehead or shake her head in sympathy for her newest client.

The most romantic spots on the planet, no expense spared. *Either he's popping the question, or the poor fellow must really be in the doghouse.* Or cat-reptile house, in the Pangalian's case.

Well, he's not too bad-looking, she considered. Tracie locked her apartment door and headed for the van. Unless Tine was a *complete* jerk, his mate could probably do a whole lot worse. *Either way, guess I'm playing Cupid, huh?*

Tracie pondered the challenge as she led her late-night group from monument to memorial. She shamelessly reached out to her old business contacts the next day.

"How are things at the Paris office?" she cheerfully queried one former vendor.

"Who's the best tango instructor in town?" she asked a bemused ex-colleague, now based out of Buenos Aires. "And where can I find a decent band, last-minute?"

"I'm pulling together something special for a new client," was her vague response to the inevitable follow-up question. "Hospitality-related."

By Thursday, Tracie had cobbled together a miracle: an itinerary she felt good about, complete with a spiel that was just the right mix of historical fact, clever zingers, and—*of course*—romance. At some point, doing the job right had become a matter of pride. *I pull this thing off, he damn well better leave a five-star review.*

Tracie ran through the script a few more times and headed off to bed, oddly excited about tomorrow's customized tour with Tine. Him and his special someone.

Abruptly, she felt a little less enthusiastic.

* * *

Come explore this third world treasure with access to all the first world amenities—when you book your romantic Earth getaway with T&T Terrestrial Travel & Tours.

It was a bit past dawn when Tracie pulled her van in front of the hotel. The Pangalian was waiting for her alone. No paramour in sight.

He also seemed much more energized today, alert and actually paying more attention to Tracie than to the damned tablet. *Less...taciturn,* she chuckled to herself, even as she cast about for her client's undoubtedly better half.

"Ready?" Tine all but tugged the mystified Tracie aboard the hovercraft. He impatiently tapped all twelve talons against the console as she gave a mental shrug and programmed in each location, settling down only when the hovercraft lifted off.

Here we go...

Tracie cleared her throat and launched into the scripted introduction. "Cleopatra and Mark Antony. Layla and Majnun. Lancelot and Guinevere. Romeo and Juliet. Human history and art are replete with themes of love and romance—at times tender, passionate, tragic, or inspirational..."

By late morning, Tracie was patting herself on the back. *Not bad for a single-day globe-trotting package put together on the fly, pulling every string I have.* Thank goodness hovercrafts could get to most places within twenty minutes—even if she'd had to play temporal Tetris with the different time zones.

First, they jetted back in time to greet the ass crack-of-dawn in Albuquerque. The Pangalian gamely crawled into the basket of the hot air balloon with all talons extended. Half an hour later, they placidly sailed against the blue bowl of the sky. Tracie loudly spoke over the sound of the burners, while the phlegmatic pilot pointed out Petroglyph National Park just to the north and poured them a pair of mimosas.

Half an hour later, the balloon bumped down and was met by the chase crew in their 4x4. Then they were off—to watch the sun rise *again* on Maui. The two walked hand-in-paw—figuratively speaking; Tine's focus was split equally between consulting his tablet and recording holovid—over what Tracie's research informed her was the best black sand beach on the island. Forty-five minutes after *that*, she instructed the hover-craft to make a slow pass by Waimoku Falls as they departed the island.

Thirty-five minutes later, Tracie coaxed Tine onto a gondola at Santa Maria del Giglio.

The Pangalian hissed briefly at the water, but obediently settled into the flat bottom of the wooden boat. The stripe-shirted gondolier made no comment; instead, he efficiently adjusted his banded straw hat and pushed off with the single oar. The jaded professional didn't even bat an eyelid at his offworlder passenger. And why should he? Venice had long been overrun by tourists, and Tine was probably just another variation on the theme.

But the gondolier's eyebrow lifted, ever-so-slightly, when Tracie climbed in over the rose petal-strewn deck after Tine and took a seat at his side. A chilled bottle of criz'theen rested between the two, along with two crystal flutes.

Deciding *to hell with it*, Tracie helped herself to a choco-late-covered strawberry, and munched away as the gondolier navigated the crowded main canal. Tine eyed the criz'theen, but refrained from pouring himself a glass. Instead, he muttered, *"hmm; a nice touch,"* and made a note on his tablet.

Tracie cleared her throat and nodded at the singer, on-call at a hefty premium. The portly man inclined his balding, gray-fringed pate at the accompanying accordionist, opened his mouth, and let loose with a powerful aria.

Tine's barbels twitched as he looked about—at the canal, the centuries-old buildings, the gondola, the accordionist—before he diligently bent to the tablet, and tapped away once more.

Feeling duty-bound, Tracie murmured a translation of the aria in Pangalian for a few minutes until she abandoned the effort. But not before she caught the gondolier's respectful nod.

Tracie winked, more an acknowledgement of finding common ground, rather than anything flirtatious. She cheekily helped herself to two more strawberries, plus half a flute of the criz'theen—only a mildly intoxicating effect on humans, and the bubbles tickled the back of the throat pleasantly—and sat back to enjoy the ride.

How could anyone *not* bask in a Venice dusk, serenaded by a crooning baritone, while the sun provided a perfect backdrop as it retreated behind the elegant skyline? The cool breeze ruffled Tine's fur and flicked a few tendrils loose from Tracie's ponytail. The setting sun cast oblong rays, making the green-gray dingy water glitter with a patina finish.

They passed beneath the Rialto Bridge, where the gondolier ducked with the smoothness of long practice. *Kitschy as hell*, Tracie sighed, leaning back. *Still, I always wanted to see Venice as a kid. Just like I'd do anything now to set a foot on any of my clients' home worlds. Like that's ever going to happen.*

She'd been more optimistic about her dreams as a child. Travel shows, online videos, podcasts, first-hand accounts direct from Indonesia's fusty jungles, the Antarctic desert, bustling São Paulo—she'd consumed it all. Sitting at her desk, lying in her bed, cross-legged in her playground hidey-hole, a young Tracie had tromped through the Amazon rainforest, camped beneath Saharan stars, meandered through the sky-touching lost cities of the Andes, sampled chocolate truffles in Brussels' Sablon district.

Each its own little world, with its own dress, its own food, and traditions. And its own language!—which little Tracie set out to explore, too. *When I visit all these places,* was her logical conclusion, *I'll need to be able to speak with the people there.*

Picking up languages was the easy part—Tracie soaked up each new tongue like a sponge. But as a practical matter, she'd been limited to exploring her own backyard.

At least I grew up in a diverse neighborhood where nobody really minded a nosy little girl. Tracie smiled at the memory of her precocious younger self. *Whatever happened to her?* Her eyes flitted briefly to Tine; the Pangalian's ears twitched as he gazed intently at the scenery, occasionally tapping at his tablet. Up ahead on a bridge, a trio of Xenatodes pantomimed for a holovid. *'Diverse' being a relative term,* Tracie qualified.

The gondolier expertly navigated the boat into one of the narrower passageways off the main canal. The comparative quiet perfectly reflected Tracie's introspective mood. Even the singer had taken a breather to gulp from a water bottle; after a brief respite, he drew in a lungful of air and exhaled a somber melody. The notes practically rolled down the damp walls rising on either side of the canal. Algae extended mossy fingers up that centuries-old brickwork and marked the high tides as they crept ever-higher, year upon year.

Tracie cast her eyes above the roofline, identifying the bell tower of yet another church. *The top of each hour must sound like a concert.*

There was so much to do and learn in this one city alone, but—alas—she had no time to linger. *All part of the job,* she sighed to herself, aware of the irony. Her career—both of them

—had allowed Tracie a closer peek at the alluring worlds her younger self discovered through those armchair excursions. Yet she'd never had the guts to be more than a wistful observer.

It would be so easy to place the blame on Mom and Dad. But Tracie's parents would simply have pointed out they were being *practical*. It worked out for them, providing the family with a solid, middle-class lifestyle. Tracie's travel fantasies just didn't jive with that mindset.

Teaching overseas? Too much work for not a whole lot of money. A diplomat? You needed all the right connections, plus a fistful of fancy and expensive degrees to boot. Peace Corps? That wasn't a *real* job.

And Tracie got it, in more ways than one—she'd lived through a recession or two, watched her parents grimly hang on. How many people had she witnessed blithely chase after their dreams—only to end up chipping away at a mountain of debt, joining the sharing economy's version of flipping burgers? At the end of those four years, she graduated with a major in business, plus a quintuple minor in five separate languages— her mild way of rebelling.

Her parents were proud enough to burst when a multinational firm recruited Tracie her senior year. *See? Now you'll get to travel all around the world, just like you wanted!*

Sure, mom and dad. Tracie embarked on a glamorous career that allowed her to sightsee in dozens of airports and bask in the interiors of countless hotels and conference rooms. Here and there, she caught a canned evening tour, or spent *maybe* an hour or two powerwalking through a museum before she had to catch the next flight out.

With twenty-twenty hindsight, Tracie realized the firm loved having an Asian-American female they could stick onto any negotiating team and achieve some nebulous diversity goal.

Cultural competency was the first bullet point under her company headshot.

Once I have enough experience under my belt, Tracie promised herself every year. She'd put out some feelers, maybe send in her résumé to the World Bank or the International Monetary Fund. Those careers were sufficiently *pragmatic.* She'd be able to do some good while traveling the world and without disappointing her parents. *What would they think of me now...*

"Tracie?" That was Tine, his full attention for once on something other than his tablet or making a mechanical assessment of the Venetian cityscape. The Pangalian's right barbels twitched. "It appears we have docked."

He gave her a searching look. Tracie had an odd feeling this client was, as a first in her experience, seeing *her*—an actual person, and not simply a reasonably capable, appropriately friendly local tour guide. A taloned paw gently tugged at the half-emptied flute of criz-theen, setting it down when a flustered Tracie let go.

The gondolier competently handed each of them back up to the dock. *Well, that was certainly one gondola ride down memory...canal, I suppose,* Tracie heavily thought. She gave the gondolier a substantial tip and repeated the treatment with both the singer and accordionist. *I sure hope Tine found the experience sufficiently romantic.*

The Pangalian wasn't precisely swooning, but he handed each of the three a thick wad of hard zurons before he expectantly turned towards Tracie. "Very illuminating. What is the next romantic escapade on the itinerary?"

Tracie had to smile. "Well...not so much an *escapade* as an *interlude.* Are you up for a stroll through Piazza San Marco? We can sample some gelato before we hop back into the hovercraft."

Tine's ears folded down in serious thought. His muzzle bobbled. "Yes; I suppose that sounds sufficiently—what *is* the local term?—mushy." A single barbel twitched.

"'*Idyllic,*' is how we'd describe it," Tracie corrected with a straight face. *Mushy as hell,* she silently agreed. *But I've earned my gelato.*

"Best you avoid the piazza," the gondolier unexpectedly spoke up. "It could be dangerous for your...friend?" He completed the warning with an upward inflection, accompanied by a quick flick of the eyes toward Tine. The gondolier spoke in Italian, apparently forgetting all about offworlders' ubiquitous AI translators.

He thinks—or at least wonders if—we're a legitimate couple! Tracie realized. The thought elicited more than a little amusement. *Well, at least he doesn't seem to be speciesist.*

But plenty of other humans *were*, and the grim tone underlying the gondolier's warning pinged every cautionary instinct. "What do you mean?" Tracie pressed. The young man hesitated. Tracie sympathized; she would venture the gondolier represented the latest generation carrying on a centuries-old family profession. *In contrast to a new kid on the block like me.* Who busted onto the scene with blatantly offworlder-friendly touring packages and shamelessly played up crowd-pleasing aspects of human culture to rake in the tips.

Tine, for his part, had gone eerily still. Neither the Pangalian's ear tufts nor barbels gave the slightest twitch.

Tracie shifted closer to the gondolier, changing tactics. "Look, you know I'm in this business, too," she confided in friendly tones. "More and more"—try, *all*—"of my clients are extraterrestrials. Whatever trends you're already seeing here, I'll probably see soon, too. *Some* warning about a storm on the horizon would be nice." Without shame, she added: "This is my *livelihood* we're talking about here."

The gondolier sighed and finally nodded. *Connection made.* Tracie permitted herself an internal fist-pump of triumph. Knowing how to speak somebody's else's language went far beyond linguistics.

"This isn't my grandfather's—not even my father's Venice," the young man explained. "It's changing too quickly. And we Venetians are at the breaking point."

"Changing into *what*?" Tracie asked, curious.

"An amusement park!" his eyes flashed. Flushing immediately, he lowered his voice to a fierce whisper. "For one thing..." The gondolier glanced again at Tine as he engaged in oh-so-casually observing the passing gondolas. "Offworlders are snapping up every available property for vacation homes. We had— what? Maybe fifty thousand *real* Venetians still living here twenty years ago. It's down to half that now. Some say—not I," the gondolier quickly qualified. "But *some* say that maybe it wasn't so bad when the tourists crowding the canals were all human. Now, well..." He nodded down the length of the canal.

Tracie's brow puckered. Sure: here and there she saw a Deesipod family, the odd gaggle of Xenatodes floated past. But extraterrestrials were hardly *crowding the canals.* She said as much.

The gondolier just sighed again and pointed. Downward. Tracie followed the gesture to the water's surface.

Just below, was that a flash of orange and silver fins?

Holy—that's one big fish! Or a school of fish? Tracie squinted to better discern the shadowy forms moving beneath the water. And immediately hopped back—*nothing* earthly possessed that particular combination of tentacles, double-lobed shell, and enormous pincers.

"Girni." The gondolier stated the obvious. He sank back onto the heels of his black shoes and rocked against the dock. "We *used* to get a bit of a breather from tourists during Acqua

Alta—that's flood time for us," the young man explained. "Now? It's just another boom period for the island. Mostly Girni and Tirillas. There's no tourist 'season' anymore—it's endless."

"I...don't suppose your aquatic sightseers have much use for gondolas," Tracie ventured.

The gondolier snorted. "No, but the national tourism agency landed on a *brilliant* solution. The government's investing in guided 'shipwreck' tours and underwater dining, for one thing."

Tracie blinked. "Oh. That's very, ah...entrepreneurial." She carefully phrased it, avoiding any hint of censure. *I'm self-aware enough to know that would be the pot calling the kettle black!* "And the locals don't like it?"

"Not only *don't like*. It's xenophobia and speciesism, pure and simple." The singer joined the conversation with a derisive snort. The accordionist looked up from where she was carefully packing up her instrument, and nodded in agreement. *Neapolitan*, Tracie immediately placed the singer's dialect— like his teeth sliced off every other ending vowel. "Or maybe not so simple," he allowed with a sigh. "But it *is* a problem when they're taking our jobs." The older man's voice shifted low. "All the technology they're flooding the planet with—who needs a human to do what a robot can do five times as quickly, and at ten times the quality, eh?"

The gondolier shrugged, a fatalistic gesture at odds with the outrage he'd expressed earlier. "At least *we* have job security." He quirked a lip. "All the offworlders insist on an *authentic human experience.*"

The four human professionals—gondolier, singer, accordionist, Tracie—exchanged sardonic smiles. *And so we give them authenticity. The very best we can manufacture.* She cast a quick look at Tine. The offworlder's muzzle was tilted in her direction, their eyes briefly met in a confirmation he had followed the conversation. But rather than give any indication of offense, Tine flicked an ear in the Pangalian sign of ironic acknowledgement and returned to innocently gaze out at the scenery.

"And that is why you and your—the two of you—should steer clear of the Piazza," the singer concluded. "Tourist traps like Piazza San Marco are practically crawling with young people out of work. I doubt any offworlder could make it halfway across the square without losing every single zuron on 'em—and that's getting off easy." His lips twisted. "Not everyone is up for serving espressos and gelato on the bottom of the lagoon."

Tracie bit her lip and nodded. Not that she approved, but she certainly empathized with finding oneself without a job.

Yet Tracie's layoff back then had nothing to do with First Contact and the subsequent flood of interplanetary aid. No; it had everything to do with home-grown, purely *human* progress. Specifically in new artificial intelligence technology that perfected the accurate and instantaneous translation of nearly every language. Available at a very reasonable corporate rate.

And once good ol' Hal relieved Tracie from her role as the firm's top interpreter, she was exposed to management as otherwise nothing more than a solid but uninspired employee. *And I guess 'cultural competency' didn't translate into all that much profit.* When it came time for the annual budgetary review, Tracie's position was among the first on the chopping block.

What was she to do?

Necessity wasn't just the mother of invention. Tracie could attest to that; it was the boot in the ass that finally got her moving.

Her options weren't good: UNESCO, the Department of State, USAID—they all still needed real, living personnel. But

Tracie was up against stiff competition—competition with the advanced degrees Tracie never attempted to earn and the key contacts Tracie never bothered to nurture. Hell, even teaching was out. There were still a few dedicated students willing to put in the work to acquire another language the old-fashioned way. But who needed a human instructor, when an AI could deliver a perfectly calibrated, customized learning experience?

The only *real* interest Tracie elicited came from the military. Her linguistic skills, her ability to navigate cultural nuances, could be a real asset in the intelligence business. Yet despite a rapidly deflating financial cushion, Tracie shied away from the recruiters. *I want to bring people together*, she stubbornly persisted—even as she dug into yet another ramen dinner and contemplated her dwindling savings account.

So, she sent out applications by the dozen and picked up a few gigs here and there with a local touring operator. *The market's gotten too saturated*, the owner clucked his tongue. *Or I'd give you more hours.*

Too late to do this, too late to do that. *Dammit.* Why hadn't she even bothered to *try*?

Then extraterrestrials made First Contact. And Tracie had one more chance.

After a couple of years on a consistent diet of noodles and supercharged language acquisition—*thank you, Sliegon missionaries and Rustacean maternalism*—her gamble paid off. The spaceports announced the first direct flights to Earth ahead of schedule, and two major cruise lines made Earth a regular port of call. Tracie's banking account started to plump back up.

And look at me now, came the inevitable, ironic reflection. *Globe-trotting and hobnobbing with aliens.*

* * *

Choose, from our extensive collection of lodgings and tours, the travel experience that's perfect for you—whether you're in a new relationship, just married, or part of a long-established couple, throuple, or cellular family (larger groupings of significant others and/or queen/colony relationships, please see our discounted options for booking an entire floor or even a full resort. Single supplements apply on all T&T cruise lines, to be refunded in the event of mitosis.)

Tine proposed over lunch; dinner, according to Paris time.

Tracie had arranged reservations at—where else?—the Jules Verne. Perhaps a quaint sidewalk café would have been more *authentic.* But a growing chorus of advice cautioned offworlders to stick to the main areas. Parisians were pretty pissed off at tourists, more so than usual. And so many people were out of work.

Tracie kept a wary eye out as the hovercraft touched down on the nearby Avenue de Suffren. Thankfully, she and Tine attracted no more than the odd look or two from the other tourists waiting on the elevator up. Given half were extraterrestrials themselves, that side-eye may have owed to the way Tine would intently fix on one aspect of the scenery, mutter something unintelligible in Pangalese, and scribble a talon tip over his damn tablet. Over and over and over again.

The maître d' greeted the pair with a blank-faced nod of approval for Tine's necktie and a derisive sniff in the direction of Tracie's attire. "Hudheely, party of two." Tracie resisted the urge to append a dutiful *sir!* and salute the man in his crisp uniform.

That supercilious fellow led them to a beautifully set table. Pride of place was given a vase filled with roses; matching petals were scattered across both place settings. The lace tablecloth hosted candles scented with ginger and eucalyptus—the closest Tracie could get to Surilan three-petal spice—and another chilled bottle of criz'theen. The stage was set for a magical romantic dinner, starring Tine and his supposed paramour.

It wasn't *all* wasted effort, Tracie supposed. She and Tine could still enjoy that breathtaking view of France's capital. Although the pair seemed to be the Jules Verne's main attraction at the moment. *They probably think we're on a bona fide date*, she thought with no little amusement. *Huh. My first 'date' since*—Tracie winced. *God, I can't even remember.*

The maître d' took leave, after he cast a final sidelong stare at Tracie's off-brand messenger bag. She ignored the snub and prepared herself for yet another stretch of awkward silence punctuated by the tapping of Tine's talons against that infuriating tablet.

Instead, to her surprise, conversation with the formerly Taciturn Tine flowed easily.

The offworlder shocked her by placing his tablet down with a soft *clack*. He waited patiently while the waiter switched out their cutlery for the first course—modified to meet Pangalian nutritional needs—and tilted his muzzle to one side. "Is it common for Earth-based tours to feature outdated modes of transportation?" he asked in a quizzical tone. "After the hot air balloon, followed by the antiquated watercraft, I am curious if a horse and buggy feature later on the day's itinerary."

Is he being facetious? Tracie couldn't decide if she should be offended. Pouring a flute of criz'theen—*hell, I've earned it*—she settled on taking the question at face value. "I *did* consider adding a sunset camel ride over the sand dunes just outside of Marrekesh," Tracie drawled. "But ultimately I decided against it—for one, very good reason."

"Ah." Tine tilted his muzzle to the other side. "And what is that?"

Tracie indulged in a long, slow sip. "Chafing," she responded with a straight face. "And not the fun kind, either."

Tine stared at her for five full seconds, ears pointing straight up. Then he made a chuffing noise. *Pangalian laughter*, Tracie realized. It wasn't unpleasant sounding at all. "No, I don't believe that *would* be very romantic, would it?" Tine finally got his mirth under control. He added, "and I earned that one. No: I mean to say that leveraging archaic vehicles to more fully situate tourists in local history and culture is yet another very clever human innovation." Tine smiled. "One the rest of us can learn from."

With a single ear twitching good-humoredly, he launched into a dry yet clearly enthusiastic recap of the day's activities, the people involved, and—yes—"human innovations in hospitality."

I guess he is paying attention to this bespoke tour, Tracie admitted halfway through the second course. *Well, at least I didn't spend all week running around for nothing.*

I can't remember the last time I so enjoyed going out on the town with someone, she realized with surprise half an hour later, during course number four. The Pangalian's observations were both entertaining *and* good-natured—not at all disparaging of the human locals. With Tracie's eager prompting, he shared a handful of fond reminiscences about his own home planet—his formative years in the forested city-state of Kay'entah, adolescent escapades scaling ancient Plefferoon ruins in express disobedience of parental directives. Tracie listened intently, reliving that sense of wonder that had been practically a constant state for her younger self.

They moved on from the fourth course to the fifth, featuring off-white lumps of something fried and covered with neon-green sauce. The conversation shifted, Tine relating a few humorous vignettes from his journeys; it was clear he was extremely well-traveled. Tracie was particularly struck by the Pangalian's apparent familiarity with the interplanetary hospitality industry—the way stations, the cruise lines, the resort planets.

"You're an insider," she finally accused. "You've been holding out on me. Admit it, mister."

Tine's barbels rippled self-consciously. "Yes," he said, making the Interplanetary Standard – Visual sign of surrender. "Accommodations and on-site amenities only, though; I've never worked on the packaged tour side."

Tracie frowned. Unease rippled through her. "And you're here on business?" Was Tine scouting for somebody with plans to move into the "packaged tour side"? Should Tracie start worrying about a multiplanetary horning in on *her* territory?

Tine's tail rapped the floor in a display of negation. "No. I'm recently retired from my firm, actually," he reassured her. "Burned out, you could say." The Pangalian's ears lowered in a sigh. "It's become a—how do you put it?—a race to the bottom. Cutthroat tactics to carve the narrowest sliver from each competitor's piece of the pie. At the same time, guest experience is homogenizing across the board while everyone still demands authenticity. And we both know what a contrived product *that* is."

Tracie nodded slowly. This Tine fellow was sharp—and that earlier exchange of glances on the Venetian dock now made sense. "I've seen what you're talking about."

"Yes. And after all those cycles in the business, I finally came to terms that nothing was going to change at BestGuest, no matter how many ideas I proposed. So, I cashed out," Tine said with relish.

"And then you decided to take that cash and go traveling," Tracie concluded, with deliberate irony.

"I decided I *needed perspective*," Tine corrected. "I'd been in the business so long, why not experience it from the customer's end?" Both ear-tufts twitched. "I used to love working in hospitality," he added, voice heavy with nostalgia. "Where did we go so wrong? Can't we do any better?"

Tracie blinked. She didn't need to be fluent in Pangalese to sense the *passion* in Tine's voice, a stubborn optimism that refused to die. Again, she was reminded of a younger Tracie, the teenager who would gesticulate excitedly as she babbled on about *traveling the world* and *bringing people together*.

"That's right," Tine emphasized with a forceful paw-clap to the table. "Hospitality and tourism have stagnated. We could— we *can*—do so much better! And..." The Pangalian leaned forward, barbels fully extended. Tracie couldn't resist the magnetic tug toward her dining companion. "*And*," he added confidently. "*You* can help me make that happen!"

The infuriating alien made Tracie wait until dessert arrived before he further elucidated.

"Romance!"

He grandiosely proclaimed the word, whipping a paw dramatically through the air. Right at the precise moment the waiter delivered their chocolate hazelnut souffles and deconstructed tarts.

The server nodded sagely. "*C'est Paris*," he agreed.

"*Plus de sauce au chocolat, s'il vous plaît?*" Tracie politely asked him. Once the waiter departed—with a long-suffering sigh—she echoed Tine's declaration with all the composure she could muster. "Romance?"

"Just look!" The cursed tablet made its long-anticipated reappearance. Tine spun the device about, so the screen now faced Tracie. She squinted at blocks of Pangalese claw-scratch text, each paired with a set of familiar images. *Most-frequented locations for—honeymoons, bachelorette parties, anniversary celebrations.* Tables and charts broke data down by year, location, and demographics. And by zurons.

Lots and *lots* of zurons.

"You and I," Tine pronounced with the absolute self-confidence most commonly displayed by straight white men and other idiots. "Can—*will*—market Earth as the galaxy's number one destination for romantic getaways." He proudly sat back in his chair, tail winding around an armrest in satisfaction.

Long seconds ticked by.

"What?" Tracie finally said.

"You're overwhelmed," Tine sympathetically interpreted .

"I'm nonplussed," she corrected with narrowed eyes. "What the *hell* are you talking about?"

Tine's ears and barbels both drooped; his tail thumped to the floor. "I thought you people were all about getting straight to the point," he muttered.

You people? Tracie's brow shot up.

The barbels swung high, then low in a sigh. "Look here." Tine pointed a talon at the central column of figures running down the screen. Each figure was paired with a zuron sign. "Now, look *here*." His sweeping gesture this time encompassed their fellow diners. "What do you see?"

Tracie was glad of the chance to prove herself quick on the uptake. "'Romance'?" she parroted. The word dripped with sarcasm.

"Precisely!" Tine nodded approvingly, his high estimation of Tracie clearly restored. "Of the *human* tourists, most here are enjoying a romantic outing. Now, would there be such a scene among tourists on other planets? Or even here on Earth, in a restaurant filled only with Girni visitors? Or Pungluroids?"

Tracie blinked. "I...don't know," she admitted. "I—I can't say I've ever really thought about that."

"Of course, there wouldn't be!" Tine answered his own rhetorical question. "*Nobody* has witnessed such a thing, outside of humanity. *I* hadn't. Until I came here."

After tendering his resignation, Tine explained, he decided he needed to just get away from it all. He dedicated a full cycle to finding himself, planning his escape to someplace bucolic and undeveloped. Somewhere he could just disconnect from all the noise, all the hustle and bustle of civilization. He needed a place where the pace was slower, where people lived closer to the land, where life was just...simpler.

So, he booked passage for Earth.

The trouble was, Tine admitted a little sheepishly, no matter how many light years he traveled, his mind just *couldn't* escape the business. It seemed the Pangalian wasn't quite finished with hospitality, after all. It was simply the current state of the industry that had driven him away in disgust.

Only a few weeks into his self-imposed exile, backpacking across the countryside and staying at no-frills accommodations —like the Ritz-Carlton and Four Seasons—Tine began noticing certain differences in local tourism, compared to the more sophisticated planets. At the same time, he witnessed the big players making early attempts to establish themselves on Earth as a potential zuron-mine.

"But!" Tine leaned in again and hissed with almost scandalous delight. "Those fools haven't the *foggiest* idea of the real potential here. Not that *I* knew any better, before I resigned," he admitted. "But as a *tourist* here, I started paying attention to my fellow tourists—my fellow *human* tourists. And it was so obvious, so clear!"

Tracie resisted tapping her foot in impatience. Her dining companion was clearly on a roll.

"I was completely confused at first," Tine confessed. "All those human couples following these native customs without any rhyme or reason *I* could discern—why *do* newlyweds spend gobs of zurons on their 'honeymoons'? And nobody could explain to me the phenomenon of physically mature—yet emotionally juvenile—cubs celebrating their 'bachelor and bachelorette parties.' Don't even get me started on retirees dipping into their savings for lavish 'vow renewal ceremonies'!"

He shook his head in sheer bemusement. "All this money expended on a very specific type of travel! And demanding the very best of everything, at enormous cost—'honeymoon suites' and 'banquets' and 'destination weddings,' and elaborate liquor-infused parties." His ear-tufts twitched. "Just think: if we could successfully market the same concept to everyone *else* in the galaxy, we'd be up to our crania in cash in no time!"

"And best of all?" Tine's voice lowered to a confidential volume. He gestured for Tracie to lean closer across the table. "All the major players have been scratching their carapaces, wondering how best to brand Earth, or even what market to target." He lifted a talon-tip in turn to list them off. "Rustic charm? Low budget family adventure? Off the beaten path?" *Bang!* went the paw again on the table; silverware jigged. "They can't even see what's right below their own proboscis!" Barbels and tail curled in derision. "Which just goes to show you how entrenched and unimaginative the industry's become."

"Wait a moment." Tracie seized a pause in Tine's soliloquy in order to clarify one very important point. "You're saying *nobody else* in the galaxy has conceived of the romantic getaway?" She *had* noticed—in an offhand manner—that curious absence. Practically all her tour groups consisted of harried family units, jubilant retirees, hostel-hopping buddies, and singletons of all ages taking a breather from their day-today grind. But *surely* that couldn't be the case across-the-board...could it?

Tine nodded in confirmation. "Humans really are pioneers," he applauded. Then he quickly backtracked, "not that people don't *appreciate* romance elsewhere. But commemorating those celebratory occasions—marriages, anniversaries, mating dances, and the like—is more about *intimacy*. Shutting out the world outside your den so you have the privacy to kindle—or rekindle—a romance, to get to really *know* one another, without interruption."

His muzzle twitched in annoyance. "What a lost opportunity for the hospitality industry. We could have been making a killing this entire time."

"*But*—we can redeem ourselves!" The Pangalian sat erect once more. He gestured again, expansively—at the Jules Verne, the beautifully—and romantically—set table, the Parisian night sky twinkling through the panoramic windows. "Starting here. With Earth. You and I."

"Starting with Earth?" Tracie tried processing that part first. She closed her eyes, attempting to order the bits and pieces of the last several minutes of conversation into something resembling a comprehensible whole. "You want to...start some sort of venture. Marketing romantic getaways to offworld tourists. *Affluent* tourists, I assume," she added. Tine bent the tips of his ears in affirmation.

"Starting with Earth..." Tracie frowned. "Why even bother with a—a third world? You could market this idea *anywhere*, right?"

"Earth's the best place to launch." Tine said, simply but firmly. "You're *already* set up for this kind of hospitality. The infrastructure is already here!" The Pangalian laid out his case. "And Earth's status as a developing world is a bonus! People are *tired* of the same-old-same-old. Nobody wants to go to a recreational planet anymore—who wants to be run over by a passel of brats on the way to the plasma pool, or crowded out of the buffet by a swarm of arthritic escapees from Shady Acres Asteroid? What people want is something real. Something authentic."

Authentic. There was that word again. Tracie battled a reflexive wince.

"And they all want *romance*," Tine continued. "Or they will."

"Once the advertising campaign explains that to them," Tracie concluded.

"Exactly," a pleased Tine agreed. "That's precisely what we'll do: promote the concept of the romantic getaway and market Earth as *the* destination of choice. We can scale up to other locales, once we're profitable."

Tine grinned, the facial expression revealing impressive sets of upper and lower incisors. Counterintuitively, the stiletto-sharp teeth—paired with the ears and the tail—just made him look like a naughty lizard-kitten, with a splash of koala thrown in.

"*Awww...*" The entire neighboring table practically cooed.

"But we need to strike now, before the big players I mentioned figure it out." Tine's tone took on a businesslike crispness. "Timing is everything in this business." He reclaimed the tablet. "You've given me a sense of where we can start."

"Start?" Tracie echoed.

"Which sites we should initially establish our pawprint in, how we can package tours for different target audiences," Tine explained. "*If* we put our noses to the hunt and court the right investors, it's not unreasonable to estimate we'll have sufficient runway to roll out a beta package within six tenth-cycles and then—"

"'We'?" Tracie had no compunction about interrupting this latest stream of consciousness. "*Our?*"

An awkward silence ensued.

"Oh! Ah. That's right." Tine, for the first time, appeared visibly embarrassed. "I completely neglected to pop the question, didn't I?" From his fanny pack, the Pangalian withdrew a shiny, circular object. Nearby diners gasped; Tracie distinctly heard a "*squee!*" The maître d' executed a tiny jumpy-clap in her peripheral vision.

"Here." Tine pushed the glittery item into Tracie's suddenly numb fingers. "My draft business plan. *Our* draft business plan," he corrected. His voice finally indicated a hint of uncertainty. "If you'll come on board as my human partner in this great, *romantic* adventure," he added more loudly. *Much more loudly.*

The maître d' fanned himself with a menu. Tracie ignored him.

"Why me?" she burst out, completely mystified. "You could do *so* much better."

"*Tch!*" Their server hissed, making his reappearance from an adjacent dimension. He set down Tracie's requested side of fudge sauce. "Do not sell yourself short, mademoiselle. You are a strong and confident woman with much to offer *any* man, *cheri!*"

"Could you please bring something alcoholic?" Tracie plaintively asked him in French. "Something really, *really* alcoholic?"

"*Oui,*" he nodded in understanding. "Champagne if yes; whiskey if no." The waiter gave the Pangalian a brotherly clap on the shoulder and took himself off.

Tracie inhaled a great big lungful of air. *Okay. Let's start with what I do understand here.* "You've been holding back from me. You're *clearly* some kind of big shot in the hospitality biz, aren't you?" she accused.

Tine's muzzle twitched in embarrassment, but he dipped an ear in acknowledgement. "*Former* 'big shot,'" he qualified. "Not big enough to change things in any significant way."

"Still, you obviously know the 'major players' and the 'right investors,'" Tracie leveraged her interpretive skills. "You also clearly have a vision—" *A crazy vision, so why am I so eager to learn more?* "—and I understand the rationale for finding a local partner. But why choose *me?*" she demanded, narrowing her eyes in challenge. "There are much larger operations out here, ones with much greater resources. Why ask—*propose* to a one-person shop like mine?"

"You're the best," came the artless reply. Tracie's jaw went slack. "I did my research before booking with you," Tine said with emphasis. "And believe me: I went on many, many tours with those 'bigger operations,' before hopping into your van. They're just as unimaginative and entrenched as the interplanetaries." Another shrug. "They don't have that entrepreneurial spirit I'm looking for."

"And I do?" Tracie skeptically asked. *Entrepreneurial spirit? Ha. And here I thought I was just being* practical.

"Oh, yes," Tine enthusiastically affirmed. "I told you I did my research. You were among the first to target the offworld consumer. Your operation has been around the longest. You're successful and, I'll wager, just a couple of cycles away from franchising. More *importantly*," he stressed that word. "I've seen you in action myself."

Tracie couldn't help a snort. *Seen? She* recalled Tine's barbels barely lifting from that tablet of his. *Unless he's been taking notes this entire time—notes on me?* Tracie shifted uncomfortably at the thought.

"I was impressed," Tine added. "The quality of the tour,

how you really *engaged* the group, as though you didn't run through the exact same spiel day after day. You built a real rapport with everyone by the end. Even if they were rude, obnoxious, or outright disgusting."

Disgusting was certainly a hazard of the job. Tracie grimaced, recalling the Pungluroid youth's slime incident at the Capitol building. *I told her the Senate Chamber was firmly off-limits.*

"You're flexible," Tine rhapsodized. "It didn't escape my notice how you adapted to new circumstances on the fly."

Tracie's cheeks burned. *I'm red, aren't I?* She forced a nonchalant shrug.

"Don't keep the poor schlub waiting!" a patron hissed. "Say yes!" another stage whispered. Their audience had expanded to the cooks, who hovered just inside the door to the kitchen. A few paces away, the server impatiently waited with a circular tray bearing a bottle and two flutes. Champagne, Tracie assumed. *What do I do?*

Procrastinate, of course.

She leaned forward. "It—It's a lot to think about. Give me, say, a week," she whispered.

Tine's muzzle dipped in disappointment, but he flicked both ears in understanding.

"Good!" Tracie brightly said. A mischievous spirit whispered into her ear. "Now—how about we put on a show? Maybe we'll even get a free meal out of it." She donned a huge smile and lovingly curled the fingers of both hands around the business plan. "My darling," she all but simpered. "You've made me so happy—*yes!*" And promptly threw herself across the table at a startled Tine.

The restaurant burst into exuberant applause.

The local hour was excessively late when the two were finally—firmly and politely, with a complimentary bottle of champagne—booted from the Jules Verne. They mutually agreed to forgo the rest of the itinerary, though Tine carefully made notations on his tablet.

Cherry-blossom viewing at Mount Yoshino—nature or culture track? Tracie shamelessly read over the Pangalian's shoulder. *Tango lessons and a show in Buenos Aires—dance-and-dine package?*

The hovercraft had just touched down half a block from Tracie's apartment when Tine cleared his throat. Tracie was beginning to recognize that embarrassed note. "We never got around to talking about *you*," the Pangalian apologized. "How *did* you enter the travel and hospitality business?" he asked, with what seemed genuine interest.

Tracie stared at him for several moments. Then she took a deep breath and started talking, narrating a thumbnail sketch of her life much as she would that of any of the Founding Fathers. *But with far, far less to show for it.*

"Your talents were wasted on those fools," Tine reflected when a hotly-flushed Tracie reached the part about being "excessed" from her last job. He stated the words with an immediate and self-assured conviction she would have found exceedingly annoying under any other circumstance. "You're something extraordinary, Tracie." He placed a paw awkwardly on her shoulder for a brief second or two.

She managed to produce a smile, albeit a sad one. "Thanks. I think—I think I needed to hear something like that, long ago."

Tracie pored through Tine's business plan the next day. She read it cover to digital cover and gave the idea serious thought. The proposal was sound; Tine's credentials seemed to check out. But she wavered.

What would be the *pragmatic* thing to do?

The whole proposal was preposterous on its face—wasn't

it? After all, if the idea was so fantastic, why hadn't someone already done it?

But *somebody* needed to be the first, right? *Why couldn't that "somebody" be us—me and Tine?*

Nervous pacing carried Tracie from one end of the apartment to the other. On her fifteenth pass, she glanced at the kitchen wall. Tacked there was a map of the world, lovingly hand-carried from her childhood bedroom to dorm to first apartment, and finally here. Tracie trailed her finger along the lines that denoted national boundaries and natural features, stopping at each pushpin. White pushpins for places she hadn't yet visited; yellow where she'd only briefly stopped; green for places she'd actually explored.

The green pins were depressingly few in number.

The star map next to it was a fairly new addition. White pushpins, again, denoted planets she yearned to visit. Orange stood for worlds her clients hailed from. Just a few days ago, she'd added another orange pushpin denoting Dendrobria, the Rustacean colony. There were no green pushpins.

Yet.

You'd be taking a big risk, that sensible inner voice cautioned. That prompted a look about the hard-earned, snug little home. Tracie could gain herself a more comfortable existence still—*if* she pursued her cautious, *practical* five-year plan in lockstep, slowly but steadily expanding the *Tracie's Terrestrial Tours* brand and reputation.

But big risks can reap huge rewards. Tracie ceased her perambulations and glanced back at the star map. *Little risks don't.*

What about all that resentment in Venice and Paris? that inner voice niggled. *And this is just the beginning; Tine said the interplanetaries were still just dipping their tentacles into the Earth pool.*

All that frantic pacing had loosened several tendrils from Tracie's ponytail. She brushed back a few strands; it seemed there was more silver every day.

Come on, Tracie, another voice urged; a little girl's voice this time. *Qué te gustaría hacer con tu vida?* And then, in Pangalese, a series of drawn-out vowels and glottal stops, punctuated by a purr.

Life's too short for regrets, my girl.

Tracie had negotiated time to mull it over. Taking the entire promised week to think it through was the *pragmatic* thing to do.

She reached back out to Tine the very next day.

"I'm in," she announced. "But this needs to be a *real* partnership—fifty-fifty. Sure, you might have an 'in' with the investors and know the interplanetary market like the back of your paw," she quickly added to forestall any immediate protest. "But, like you said, *I* have insight into human custom, *I* know how to work with a local staff, *and* I have experience putting together attractive tour packages." Tracie crossed her arms over her chest and waited with outward confidence and baited breath.

"That's fair," the Pangalian conceded. He sounded not at all distressed at the prospect of splitting their supposed profits down the middle. Tracie could visualize those barbels twitching upward as Tine parted his muzzle in a smile. "I still think I'm getting the benefit of the bargain."

Tracie's eyes fractionally widened, taken aback.

"I'll have my attorney draft the agreement and send it to yours for review," Tine was back to business, the switch chimera-like in a way Tracie suspected she would become accustomed to. "You can sign then, or we can meet in person to, ah—shake paws? That's how you do it here, right?'

Tracie grinned. "Sure," she said, and hearkened back to *An*

Affair to Remember. "And I know just the perfect spot. For launching such a *romantic* venture."

* * *

Planning a destination wedding? Bachelor party? Prenuptial agreement signing ceremony? Leave all the nitty-gritty details to our top-notch planners at Wed, Bed, and Fed,^{TM} T&T's one-stop-shop event management solution. We handle it ALL—from that show-stopping proposal simulcast to friends and family across seventeen star systems to the two-hundred-and-twenty-fifth anniversary extravaganza you and your partner(s) deserve. Schedule a FREE consultation today!

"Swag bags ready to go?" Tine paced back and forth, nervously checking each item off on his upgraded datapad. Tracie pointed at the table, practically hidden under rows upon rows of bags stuffed with branded tchotchkes. "Check."

"Do we have everything for making a toast?" the Pangalian fretted. Tracie nodded at the bottles of criz'theen chilling in buckets of ice. "Check."

"And we're all set for the behind-the-scenes tours?" Tracie waved at the trio of T&T resort staff, hovering nearby in their red, white, and pink matching uniforms, lanyards, and baseball caps. "Check."

"Scissors?" Tine tugged at one ear nervously. Tracie directed a reassuring smile at the floppy-haired intern in the corner, shifting nervously from foot to foot beside a cyclopean pair of ornamental scissors. Behind the kid stretched a red ribbon, each end tied in a gaudy bow around an ornate

Corinthian column. *C'est Paris!* the banner above proudly proclaimed. "Check that one off, too."

Her partner continued his obsessive pacing; the tail obediently followed in its owner's wake. Tracie tracked the tip: back-and-forth, back-and-forth, like a metronome. *It's almost hypnotizing.* "Tine," she soothed. "We're as prepared as humanly—as Pangalian-ly—possible. The staff did a great job. *You've* done a great job."

"Still!" Tine insisted. "What if we missed something important? What if everything gets knocked terribly out of orbit?" He reflexively twisted a barbel. "What if there's some *horrific* tragedy halfway across the continent, and every single reporter runs off to cover the breaking news—and leaves us with all this criz'theen? We couldn't *possibly* drink it all!"

"Wanna bet?" one of the uniformed tour guides muttered.

Tracie sighed as her partner agitatedly directed the *C'est Paris!* crew to shift *this* Grecian-inspired vase and adjust *that* gilt-edged portrait—all while consulting his datapad. She finally confiscated the device over Tine's yelped protests, much to the staff's profound relief.

Such drama. Tracie shook her head. But she understood where Tine's anxiety was coming from.

It's almost surreal, seeing six years of hard work finally pay off. They hadn't turned a profit right away; the very concept of a *romantic getaway* was, as Tine innocently put it, *alien* to the rest of the galaxy. But gradually, through creative marketing and word-of-proboscis, they grew. T&T started popping up in travel magazines —initially under "novelty experiences," and more recently ranking among the "hidden gems." From packaged romantic tours, T&T expanded to managing an impressive portfolio of beach cabins, mountain lodges, and sleek town homes. Business took off, and Tracie and Tine finally were ready to do something *big*.

Like announcing the very first, all-inclusive T&T resort and spa.

I wish my folks could be here for today's grand opening. Tracie bit back familiar tears. Despite her parents' sometimes lukewarm reception of their daughter's aspirations, Tracie wanted to do them proud. *And maybe*, she admitted, *there's also an element of vindication.*

That undoubtedly was the case for Tine. *He's finally trying out all those ideas he said his old company refused to take a chance on.*

"Shouldn't the press be arriving by now?" Tine anxiously muttered. He snagged their public relations director, currently engaged in at least five separate conversations over her device. "We *did* send out the press release—right, Bertie?" he demanded.

Bertie murmured an apology before tapping her earpiece off. She nodded. "We have confirmed interest from the industry press, plus a couple of the bigger mainstream outlets." This spoken confidently, even as she glanced about the room and bit her lip. "But it wouldn't hurt to follow up." Bertie tapped her earpiece back on and clacked away on fashionably anachronistic heels.

Tine returned to prowling about the lobby. His tail whipped about with a perfectly executed runway turn. *Swish-swish.*

Even with the Pangalian at the cusp of a nervous break-down, Tracie idly noted he cut a surprisingly debonair figure in his formal human suit. Too bad the fuchsia fanny pack struck a discordant note. *But it* does *match his tie.* "Bertie's done a fantastic job, hasn't she?" She tried for a calming tone. "Can you believe *Galactic Getaway* wants to do a spread on us for their next issue!" Tracie shook her head in amazement. "It's been one hell of a rollercoaster ride, hasn't it?"

Tine paused, furry brows knitted together. Tracie quickly translated the idiom into Pangalese, and his expression cleared. "It certainly has," he agreed, and then scrunched his muzzle back into a frown. "Are rollercoasters romantic?"

Tracie couldn't help it: she burst into laughter. "We are *not* adding a rollercoaster to *C'est Paris!*"

Tine's ears pricked in affront. Then the Pangalian began chuckling himself, a coughing sort of purr that emanated from deep in his chest. With a toothy smile, he turned and headed for the nearest bucket of chilled criz'theen. "On that note..."

We're both as nervous as a Rustacean at a clambake party, Tracie reflected with a grin. *But we always make each other laugh.*

Like when Tracie trained T&T's first cohort of tour guides, patiently explaining to the green recruits the *dos* and *don'ts* of keeping tabs on one's charges. Tine insisted on making "helpful" commentary, until Tracie finally hauled off and smartly told her partner he was absolutely the *last* person to supply advice on the matter. Pangalians didn't precisely blush, per se— but the tips of his ears did turn carrot orange.

Or when Tracie slid yet another green pushpin home into her much-creased map of the world, relocated to a place of pride in her new office. A perplexed Tine had scratched at one ear and innocently suggested *"knocking the rest out"* that afternoon. He'd ducked with true feline reflexes when Tracie faked lobbing the entire container of pushpins at his cranium.

Or when they were hiring pastry chefs for *C'est Paris!* The pair dutifully sampled one wedding cake after another, Tine's barbels dripping frosting like a cat going to town in a bowl of fresh cream. A baker had oh-so-helpfully stepped forward with a wet dishcloth which prompted the Pangalian to hiss and scramble onto the table, talons fully extended.

Well...Tine's brave when it counts. Tracie chuckled,

recalling her partner's single-minded determination as he climbed into that gondola in Venice, paws clenched and ears flattened against his skull.

One memory led to another, which chased her smile away. *Like the day we pitched T&T to the Polaris Fund's managing partner.* "What value, *exactly*, does Ms. Trang bring to T&T?" the venture capitalist had rudely glubbed. Her chromatophores released torrents of yellow-green pigment in an absolutely soul-crushing display of skepticism. Several tentacles gestured at Tracie dismissively. "I like the concept, Mr. Hudheely. But I'd feel better about investing if you cut the deadweight."

Tracie immediately wanted nothing more than to sink through the swirling brine of the conference room floor. But Tine had brashly waded forward, ears laid back in conviction. "Tracie is the lynchpin of the entire operation!" he'd stoutly said. "She's not just a local expert; she's brilliant at talent acqui-sition, and *nobody* outshines her when it comes to communi-cating T&T's brand proposition to our target audience."

He'd stood up for Tracie. *And we got the money!*

The sound of a cork popping jolted her back to the present. "Tracie?" She reflexively accepted the proffered flute. Wrap-ping the fingers of one hand around the delicate stem, Tracie reached out with the other to squeeze Tine's paw. Her partner started, ears twitching. Then his barbels lifted, and he conspira-torially squeezed back.

"We really should take the hovercraft down to Venice after this," Tracie mused. "We never *did* get our gelato at the Piazza San Marco that time, did we?"

Tine brightened. "Pistachio and jalapeño?"

"With cinnamon sprinkles on top," Tracie confirmed with a reflexive grimace. "Just don't try kissing anyone afterward." *Not that I would mind...*

Where the hell had *that* thought come from? *Travel*

couldn't have made my palate change that *much, right?* She brushed it off with a flippant chuckle.

"Oh! Are they reopening the plaza already?" The intern chaperoning the gargantuan scissors piped up.

"'Reopen'?" Tracie frowned at the apparent non sequitur.

"Yeah, everything's been closed off since the Big Melt." The intern regarded Tracie askance. "It was one of the places that got slammed. *Almost* as bad as Miami!"

"T&T made a very generous donation to the Gulf Coast relief fund," Tracie responded with automatic defensiveness. *Right after we backed out of that Florida Keys deal. But what's this about Venice?*

"Venice got flooded nearly as bad," the intern slowly informed her. *Have you been living under a rock?* said his incredulous expression. "The pictures were *everywhere*. They had to cordon off half the city."

Tracie hotly flushed. Sure, she'd been a *wee* bit distracted with T&T and getting *C'est Paris!* off the ground, but still...

Venice! The city would always hold a special place in Tracie's heart. The face of a certain gondolier flashed through her mind—a mind that her parents had trained so well to focus on the pragmatic. "Virtually their entire economy depends —*depended*—on tourism," she thought through the implications out loud. *Did he come through the floods safe and sound? What's he doing now?*

The intern shrugged with a spectator's disinterest, a switch in attitude that made Tracie blink. "I just know they're working with a big interplanetary to reinvent the entire city—turning lemons into lemonade or whatever. A buddy of mine is interning at BestGuest Galaxy Group," he added in a conspiratorial tone. "It's not public yet, but they're gonna build a *huge* new underwater resort."

"What?" That was Tine.

"I heard the Piazza's going to be a casino, mostly for Girni and Tirilla visitors," the intern added. "You think they'll still have gelato?"

Tracie barely prevented her jaw from dropping. "That's—" *Smart, I suppose,* she caught herself. *Maybe a new resort will help bring back jobs?* Her mind belatedly recalled the gondolier's warning about the Piazza San Marco. *"Not everyone is up for serving espressos and gelatos on the bottom of the lagoon,"* the singer had added. She swallowed. *Well, pragmatism may change some minds.* And it was a *good* thing this—BestGuest? The name sounded familiar—company was actually investing in the city, wasn't it? Intergalactic aid was drying up these days, what with the developed worlds insisting on measurable ROI for every single zuron they doled out like misers.

"*What?*" Tine repeated.

The intern puffed up with self-importance. "Yeah. My buddy says they're gonna tear down half the buildings and replace all the canals and bridges with underwater tunnels. Pretty clever, huh?"

"*What. Did. You. Say?!*" Tine stood stock-still; his tail simulated a bottle brush. The trio of guides traded worried expressions with the catering staff.

"That's *terrible,*" Tracie agreed, identifying with her partner's evident dismay. "All those centuries of history, demolished just like that..." She turned back to Tine, who looked as nauseated as Tracie felt. The Pangalian's muzzle worked. Finally, he hissed, "BestGuest Galaxy Group? Opening a resort on Earth? When?"

The intern halted mid-babble, confusion spread across his face. "Um, yeah? I think—no, I'm pretty sure my buddy said they're holding some big surprise press conference to announce it today. Right about now, I guess." He nervously scratched at the back of his neck and self-consciously brayed a laugh. "Some coincidence, huh?"

That was Bertie's cue to come jogging up on her high heels, face pale as the moon. She skidded to a stop, catching her breath before delivering the bad news everyone in the lobby already suspected. "We've been scooped," Bertie simply said, and shared the screen of her device with the group.

Tine's silver-frosted fur shivered with repressed fury as a BestGuest bigwig—the Vice President for Earth Operations, according to the banner—proudly announced the Venice Vacation Voyage Resort & Spa. *"The latest in BestGuest's proud line of five-star family-oriented properties!"*

Holding a press conference the same day as ours? Tracie's eyes narrowed. *'Some coincidence,'* indeed.

"...and how does BestGuest plan on responding to market disrupters like, say, T&T?" a writer with *Star Safari* asked. The vice president—a Deesipod—honked his amusement out of four separate nostrils. *"The 'romantic getaway' people? Well, we certainly encourage that type of gumption in the hospitality industry."* He emitted a mocking, high-pitched whistle. *"At BestGuest, we know what we shine at—providing one-of-a-kind vacation experiences for families looking to relax and unwind. And we always deliver."*

"I just heard back from *Galactic Getaway*'s spotlight editor," Bertie apologetically said. "They're going to 'stick with the tried-and-true' this issue—but offered to showcase us in next month's 'Offbeat Orbits' column."

Well, if that *isn't the cherry on top of this shit sundae...*

Tine completely lost it. The typically reserved, if neurotic, Pangalian abruptly morphed into a bipedal version of an infuriated jungle cat. He sprang into action, charging for the soaring double-doors of *C'est Paris!*'s grand lobby. *Presumably to engage*

BestGuest's Vice President of Earth Operations in mortal combat. Tracie started after him in alarm.

Unfortunately for Tine—and luckily for T&T's brand image—the Pangalian's ire blinded him to the ribbon blocking the way like a scarlet tripwire. Her partner went down with a startled yowl and immediately went on the offensive.

Tracie rushed forward to help and then halted, biting back ill-timed laughter. *He looks* exactly *like a spitting-mad kitten tangled up in a ball of yarn...*

She wasn't alone in drawing the comparison. The assembled T&T staff stared wide-eyed at their boss's predicament. Several suspiciously chewed on their lips.

I guess it's up to me, then. Torn between hilarity and concern, Tracie grabbed the giant pair of scissors by the handles and marched forward. Tine paused from the mismatched battle just in time to register his partner's determined approach, the gleaming blades yawning open at the ready. In a flash, the pair was engaged in a game of ring-around-the-rosie. Tracie chased Tine around one of the pillars.

"*Not* the tail! *Not* the tail!" her quarry yowled at the top of robust lungs.

Tracie grabbed for a trailing end of the scarlet ribbon; Tine jerked it away. Frustrated, she finally snapped. "Do you trust me, or not?"

The Pangalian came to an abrupt stop; Tracie barely avoided crashing into him, scissors and all. He took a deep, calming breath. "One hundred percent."

With that, he held very, very still as Tracie efficiently got down to business, ever-so-carefully shearing through the ridiculously stubborn span of ribbon holding Tine's lean, furry frame prisoner. She felt the nervous *thump-thump* of her partner's hearts, the citrus scent of criz'theen faintly detectable on his breath as he exhaled, tickling her ear.

Adorable. Tracie blinked at that unexpected thought. She took a firmer hold of the handles and concentrated on finishing the job.

Finally liberated from his adversary's colorful clutches, Tine stumbled to the nearest loveseat and sagged down onto the plush, champagne-dyed cushion. The Pangalian's barbels and ears drooped in tandem, the fight momentarily gone out of his body. Tracie waved away a handful of concerned employees —*sure; now they come to the rescue*—and took a seat next to her partner.

"So. Why the freak-out?" she bluntly asked.

"I used to work there," he said in a flat tone.

It wasn't difficult for Tracie to put two and two together. "BestGuest?" Her partner's barbels bobbed in acknowledgement.

"*'Gumption'!*" he snorted. "Sure, the C-Suite lauded my 'visionary leadership'—as long as I followed the old playbook. But whenever I proposed something that was actually *new*?" Tine gesticulated with frustration. "'Gumption' *definitely* wasn't the word they used. Instead, they always said I was being—"

"*Impractical,*" Tracie quietly inserted. *That's a wonderful hobby, Tracie. But, as a career? It's just not practical.*

Tine's ears flicked. "That's it, exactly." His muzzle parted in a crooked half-grin. "You always know just the right word." Heat spread across Tracie's cheeks, but her partner wasn't finished. "No matter the language, you always know what to say and the best way to say it. You always figure out how to get our message across, whether it's a—a targeted advertising campaign, or persuading loan officers into giving us a chance when we were starting out." His half-smile widened to full-on beaming. "Meeting you was probably the best thing to ever happen to me."

Tracie was certain she was red as a tomato by that point. *I've never really felt on equal footing with Tine,* she acknowledged. *But here he's saying I bring just as much to the table...*

She coughed. "Some might say it's *impractical,* spending so much time and effort on learning new languages."

Tine's barbels bounced upwards in startlement. "That's idiocy!" he scoffed. "Being able to communicate with anyone you want to is just as important—as *practical*—as faster-than-light travel. With both, you can go just about anywhere in the universe!"

That's when it happened. Or rather, when Tracie became consciously aware of it. The feeling didn't hit her like a sack of bricks. It wasn't something that unfurled, flower-like, deep inside her chest. Instead, it made her laugh. Tine quizzically tilted his head.

"Did you know," Tracie said, once she caught her breath. "That language is more than just communication?" She felt that old yearning stir. "Language is about how you interpret, how you *perceive* the universe around you. When you learn another language, you gain a new perspective, too."

Tine's teeth bared in a grin. "You've said my Human is becoming quite good," he noted, levering his lanky frame off the couch.

Tracie stood and extended a helping hand. "Your English and Vietnamese are excellent," she corrected. "Your French is passable. But the last time you attempted Arabic, you congratulated that newlywed couple on their burial."

"Progress is still progress," he maintained. "But does becoming fluent mean I'll start turning into you?" Tine affected a dramatic shudder. "I don't believe the galaxy is prepared for *two* Tracie Trangs."

You furry little... Tracie snorted and gave Tine's tail a hard yank. He yelped. *Jeez. I'm as bad as a little kid picking on her crush.*

"Are you hungry? I hear there's a darling little sidewalk café just a few blocks from here," she tentatively ventured. "*Authentically* authentic—not like the Jules Verne." Indeed, T&T's local staff described the eatery as *le café le plus romantique!*

"It's a date!" Tine enthusiastically agreed. Tracie's chest swelled. And immediately deflated when her partner added, "We'll gather our strength and strategize how to *destroy* the competition! Strike while the iron's hot, as humans say." His tail and ears stood at a warrior's attention.

"Ah," Tracie faltered. "Great?"

"I won't let my old employer win," Tine said, muzzle set in grim determination. "Or anyone else. Don't you see what they're doing, Tracie? They're trying to *squash* us. And do you know why?" Again, he didn't bother to pause before answering his own question. "Because they're *afraid* of us, Tracie! They know we have something great here, and they're fighting it tooth and talon."

The Pangalian's eyes and teeth gleamed. "And they're going to lose," he triumphantly said. "While *we* become the most successful hospitality venture in the galaxy. Together. Just you watch." He held out his paw in the human fashion.

It was, Tracie intuited, another proposal. T&T was gearing up to do battle in the name of romance. Which meant, oh-so-ironically, the quashing of her own nascent feelings. *For now,* whispered an absurdly optimistic voice. *For now.*

Well, Tracie had her own score to settle. Snippets of Venice floated through her memory, like a gondola placidly slipping along the Grand Canal, past the palazzos. The water glittered in the setting sun, church bells ringing the hour in glorious disharmony.

All slated for demolition. Unless somebody put a stop to it. *Why not us?*

She stepped closer and clasped Tine's paw. "Just you watch," she agreed.

* * *

T&T Terrestrial Travel & Tours specializes in romantic getaways for you and your special someone(s). Footnote: Earth is no more dangerous than any other third world, but we always remind our guests to take common sense precautions. Lock up or ingest any valuables before exiting your T&T hotel. Do the same for any important documents, but remember you may need your Interplanetary ID to access certain attractions. Know where your embassy is, stay sober, and rest assured that most locals are friendly and happy to give advice!

Tracie dropped her carry-on bag to the penthouse's hardwood floor with an emphatic *flomp!* and closed her eyes. It seemed like the frenetic activity of the past week was catching up with her, all at once.

She'd looked forward to sightseeing around Camazotz, the Balayang home world, and even purchased tickets to an aerial game at the Chiropteran Colosseum, followed by a concert at the renowned Echodome. But a demanding schedule once again took precedence, and Tracie ended up spending most of the trip cooped up in the corporate headquarters of Camazotz Worldwide Resort & Spa, which was headed for bankruptcy and looking for investors. Investors like T&T Travel, with its now-public ambitions to expand beyond Earth.

The suitcase popped open and commenced unpacking

itself with mechanical efficiency. Tracie longingly stared at her California King, piled high with embroidered pillows. Not that she would turn up her nose at a simple cot with a single, threadbare sheet. *Just wanna lie down for a few hours...*

A low buzz sounded. *"Incoming from Tweeden,"* the penthouse AI notified her. Tracie sighed and dragged herself away from the beckoning mattress to accept the incoming call. The image of a sturdy young man—impeccably dressed even at nine o'clock at night—resolved itself against the opposite wall.

"Welcome home, Ms. Trang!" her assistant—her new *executive* assistant, now that she apparently needed one, and with exemplary credentials that made her own résumé look depressingly thin—saluted, professional warmth infusing his voice. "I hope the trip back was comfortable. I took the liberty of arranging for a meal delivery service tonight; your dinner should arrive any moment."

Tracie tiredly smiled with the expected gratitude. *Wait for it...* Four seconds later, Tweeden launched into the next day's itinerary. "Tomorrow morning, you have the final round of interviews for the Polar Passion resort," he reported. "The hovercraft will meet you at eight o'clock sharp. Candidate applications are in your inbox, along with the quarterly profit and loss statement. The finance team has also narrowed down its list of potential underwriters," Tweeden added.

Underwriters. IPOs. Due diligence. Tracie pinched the bridge of her nose. *It's like learning yet another language.* She'd never felt so half-hearted about picking up a new vocabulary.

But it was a language Tracie *had* to become proficient in, if not fluent. T&T needed to raise a hell of a lot more capital if they wanted to "make that quantum leap," as Tine so enthusiastically put it. *"This will help position us to revolutionize the galactic hospitality industry, Tracie!"*

After all, what *did* one do after conquering Earth—or at least its tourism sector?

Apparently, the answer involved bringing in an investment bank to underwrite T&T's initial public offering on the Galactic Stock Exchange. *The GSX*, Tracie reminded herself. *This new language has far too many acronyms.*

"Everything's ready for you to review on the flight over," Tweeden brightly said. "Unless you wanted to get a jump on it tonight?"

Hell, no. "Why don't you do a deep dive into both and flag anything that stands out?" she tossed back. "Tine and I both greatly value your input." Tweeden went briefly speechless with the honor. The doorbell rang; Tracie grinned as she trudged to the door and accepted the waiting 'bot's delivery. *Food, pajamas, pass out in bed—crap; I need to review those applications.*

Tweeden regained his voice and picked up from where he'd left off on the next day's logistical gauntlet. "One more thing," he added. That perfectly coiffed countenance reappeared by the refrigerator. "The Inner Planet Hospitality Association gala wraps up in a half-hour. Is there any way you can attend tonight's after party? Scuttlebutt says Franu-La from *Cosmo Cruises* is looking for a local partner."

Tracie blinked, torn between responsibility and complete exhaustion. T&T had been tentatively courting Cosmo for over a year.

"Don't be ludicrous, Tweeden!" An oh-so-familiar voice cut in. The accompanying Pangalian muzzle manifested over the countertop. *Tine must also be burning the midnight oil—what else is new?* "Tracie's shuttle just came in—she deserves some rest. *I'll* attend." The tip of Tine's right ear twitched in a wink. "You enjoy a good dinner and an even better night's sleep. And, Tracie," his tone softened. "Welcome home."

It was foolish, but Tracie's cheeks warmed as she basked in Tine's near-purr. She completed her nighttime ablutions in a jet-lagged daze, robotically folded down the sheets, and bone-lessly collapsed onto the bed. But alas; sleep wasn't on the agenda—she had applications to review. Half-resentfully, Tracie instructed the penthouse AI to start a pot of tea. She propped herself up against the headboard and grabbed her tablet from the nightstand.

Quit grousing, she scolded herself. *Long hours and little sleep... that's just the price of success, isn't it?*

Success. *T&T sure has come a long way.*

The stymied grand opening of *C'est Paris*—*and rescuing Venice from an ignominious, watery end,* Tracie reminded herself with no little pride—had marked a turning point. They quickly scaled up to an impressive portfolio of resorts, elaborate tours, and dining experiences. Events, too; T&T handled every-thing from destination weddings and anniversary parties to the post-coital consumption of one's mate—that last required prospective clients to supply three waivers, four permits, and a fifty-page consent form to be completed by both parties *and* the groom's next of kin. T&T *always* kept itself at least three steps ahead of the competition.

And they were still growing.

Those days of just Tracie, chugging around DC with a vanful of offworlders, seemed a lifetime ago; she couldn't help the occasional feeling of nostalgia. *But life's better now,* Tracie forcibly reminded herself. *No more living vicariously through others. I'm finally seeing those far-off places for myself!* She'd already switched over every pushpin of her world map to green, and was making headway into the star map. The ice geysers of Jalifree, the plunging scarps of Hantilon, the singing flowers of Camazotz—she'd witnessed all those wonders with her own eyes.

Well, as part of evaluating candidate sites to add to T&T's expanding portfolio of romantic destinations, anyway.

What's wrong with me? I'm luckier than most—I've achieved my dreams, haven't I? Perhaps the raw *content* of those dreams, but not the spirit.

Don't think about it. Tracie let the tablet slip from her fingers to the counterpane. She closed her eyes, and drifted, drifted, drifted back in time. Back to a gondola, rocking beneath the countless suns sparkling overhead, a damp breeze carrying the sonorous notes of an aria. *Romantic.* Tracie smiled and snuggled into the companion at her side.

Still tapping away at his damned device, even in her dreams. But she smiled as he tugged her closer still.

Are you a nature lover? Go boating down the Amazon River, explore the African Serengeti, and experience snorkeling at the Great Barrier Reef ...before it's too late. Ask about our Beat Biodiversity Loss safari package. Six days/seven nights; breakfast and tents included.

Tracie yawned and stretched her limbs as far as the passenger seat would allow. The morning had been grueling, but the hiring committee was on-track to make the final staffing decisions for the Polar Passion project. Business Development was getting antsy; they were seeing early signs of a tourist boom in traditionally inhospitable areas—inhospitable to *humans*, that was—and T&T needed to capitalize on the trend before the competition ate their lunch.

Bertie and the public relations team were less enthused.

Tracie took their point; she'd side-skirted a crowd of demonstrators on the way back to the hovercraft. The activists were up in arms about offworld real estate magnates pressuring Earth's governments to open up protected regions in Antarctica. T&T's equity investors insisted the Polar Passion project was an entirely different animal. *We're not talking wholesale development—just the two resorts, plus a handful of excursions. If anything, T&T's actually doing a good thing in building awareness about the South Pole. Plus, we can always donate some of the profits—some!—to a conservation group or two.*

Tracie's device hummed, signaling an incoming call from Tine. She answered, glad for an excuse to shove the whole morning to the back of her mind.

"Tracie! How did the interviews go?"

"Well—"

"Wonderful!" The Pangalian interrupted his human partner's half formed response. "I have good news, too." He dramatically cleared his throat. "As of five minutes ago, T&T took possession of BestGuest's last remaining Earth-based property." Tine's tone was gleeful.

As it should be, was Tracie's first thought once she'd absorbed the update. *His revenge has certainly been sweet.*

T&T had gone after BestGuest's Venice Vacation Voyage Resort & Spa first. Tracie admitted to relishing that victory along with Tine. A split second after the takeover was made official, she'd started lobbying the Italian government to put a pause on the city's conversion into an aquatic amusement park. *T&T will bring in more local jobs and revenue by marketing Venice's romance—trust me!* she'd sworn. And immediately dispatched a team to make good on that promise.

Tracie *intended* to personally oversee the project. But her attention was taken up more and more with T&T's day-to-day operations, thanks to Tine's single-minded focus on making "that quantum leap."

Leaving Tracie to keep the trains running on time. And their investors happy.

T&T does things differently, she pressed the point at every meeting and on every call. *T&T is going to be the catalyst that changes the industry!* But more and more she found herself on the opposing side of a company increasingly fixated on profit and expansion at all costs. *We're going to beat the industry giants at their own game!* was the popular mantra.

But, I wanted T&T to start a new *game.* A fairer game, where the community had a seat at the table with the industry and their guests.

"Great news," Tracie weakly said, unable to tamp down an unfurling hope. *Maybe now that Tine's beaten BestGuest, he'll let go of this obsession, at least a* little...

"But we can't let ourselves get soft," Tine immediately dashed that optimistic fancy. "Especially now we're perfectly positioned to go public and step onto the galactic stage." Tracie's heart sank.

"On that subject," her partner cheerfully continued. "The finance team thinks we should go with Magnetar Investments as our underwriter. I'll send you the details." With that, he disconnected.

Tracie sighed and turned her attention beyond the hovercraft's window and the scene unfolding below. And immediately wished she hadn't.

The hovercraft wasn't far from T&T's headquarters now; already, they were passing over Manhattan's "Shamtytown." Even from the air, Tracie could tell the spic-and-span neighborhoods below lacked that distinctive New York City grunginess. The main thoroughfares were stocked—much like a supermarket shelf—with blandly restored skyscrapers, rehabilitated tenement homes, perfectly manicured parks, and cheerful storefronts. Sanitized authenticity was on blatant display, imbuing every restaurant, business, casino, hotel, and theatre. Tracie knew the stats—New York's tourist bubble was reportedly on its way to taking over a full fifth of the city by decade's end. Which the mayor credited for infusing millions, if not billions of zurons into the local economy.

But, at what cost?

Tracie scrubbed a hand over her face. She found herself returning to that question, every damn day. *What benefit, what cost?* So many cities were growing reliant on tourism dollars, even as traditional industries collapsed and offworlders competed with the human public for space everywhere—parks, streets, beaches, buses, and trains. Even outside Shamtytowns, businesses scrambled to survive with the interplanetary chains popping up seemingly everywhere.

And so it went.

But T&T is *different.* Tracie weakly echoed her argument to their investors. *Well, it's the truth! Their* guides showed guests *real* human neighborhoods, urged them to try *real* human food at human-owned restaurants, directed souvenir seekers to human-owned shops. *Look at the investment we've made in Venice!*

But are we—am I just fighting a losing battle? It certainly felt like it, when her efforts were increasingly challenged by practically everyone else at T&T. *At least Tine always has my back.*

Tracie's mood lightened and then turned dark again as the descending hovercraft passed over columns of sign-wielding New Yorkers winding their way down Fifth Avenue.

A headache built behind her temples. New York City, its Shamtytown, and its demonstrators, were hardly outliers. Venice's disaffected and under-employed young activists—pre-

T&T, of course—had been just the beginning. Religious leaders around the globe lobbed angry accusations against extraterrestrial looky-loos desecrating religious sites; civic leaders were furious over human-owned businesses closing up shop.

But T&T was different! When had that morphed into a desperate mantra? *We* hire locals at living wages, *we* contract with human vendors, *we* insist our guests show proper respect for the areas they visit.

Still, there was only so much one company could do, while still making a profit.

"How did the interviews go?" Tweeden stood to greet Tracie with a pleasantly starched smile as she passed by his desk on the way to her office. "Are you hungry?"

"Fine," she replied. Embarrassed, she softened the brusque statement with a smile. "I could eat."

"Perfect!" came the mechanically cheerful response. "Your lunch meeting starts in just a few minutes—and I understand fish tacos are on the menu."

Tracie brightened. "That's perfect. Tine *loves* fish tacos nearly as much as I do." No matter how busy they were, the pair had continued a tradition of testing out some new, prospective romantic venue every week. Although they regularly returned to a certain little sidewalk café, still doing brisk business a few blocks down from the flagship *C'est Paris!* resort. The little eatery was indeed *le café le plus romantique* and Tine was completely impermeable to the ambience.

That lunch was the one thing Tracie most looked forward to every week. She and Tine talked about *everything*—their plans for T&T, their respective childhoods, their hobbies and their dreams...

But no way in hell am I bringing up last night's dream. Or Tine's starring role in several more over the past few years.

Tweeden shook his head. "I had to cancel on your behalf.

The creative team *really* needs your input on next year's big Valentine's Day promotion," he hastily explained as Tracie opened her mouth to protest. "And like I said: fish tacos!" was delivered with a patronizing smile.

Tracie swallowed a disappointed sigh, politely thanked Tweeden—if through gritted teeth—and obediently toddled off to the conference room. *It never ends, does it?*

Halfway through a brainstorming session, the creative director cracked the inevitable joke. "Ever strike you as ironic that both our co-founders are single?"

Tracie refrained from rolling her eyes. *Aaaaand here we go again...*

The Chief Marketing Officer chuckled. "Well, Tracie and Tine are pretty much married to the company. You two spend enough time here to make any spouse suspicious."

Once again, the insinuation elicited a fresh round of guffaws and the tired old *Pangalians mate for life, watch out!* stereotypes. Tracie mercilessly steered the discussion back to the business at hand, doing her level best to ignore a pang in her chest. She was almost grateful for her assistant's interruption a few minutes later. Almost.

"Boss?" Tweeden's voice chirped from Tracie's device. "We have a...situation."

A *situation?* Tracie blood ran cold. The last time Tweeden stressed that particular word, she ended up spending three full days trying to convince an overly well-connected Tirillan guest that *no*, the Taj Mahal could *not* be purchased as a souvenir.

Tine, of course, took the entire episode as a sign that T&T should launch its own branded line of souvenir products.

"Excuse me, folks." Tracie quickly extricated herself from an argument over the wisdom of using a heart motif when Deesipods damn well *knew* the sentimental emotions resided in the pancreas and made a beeline for her assistant's workstation. "Is everything all right?" she demanded, on a futile hope the answer would be a casually puzzled, *yes, of course! Why do you ask?*

Tweeden shook his head apologetically. "Not exactly. The vice president for European operations just called in another scam. This one involving five of our guests." Tweeden's lips thinned, the movement stretching his pencil mustache into a straight line. "Pretty serious, this time. The scammer threatened them with harm."

"*What?!*" Tracie's eyebrows flew up in alarm.

Tweeden raised a hand in a belated calming gesture. "Relax, boss; no one was *actually* harmed! But the European office says the situation in the region is escalating and they want some direction from headquarters. Would you like me to draft a memo?" he helpfully asked.

Tracie frowned, rattled nearly as much by Tweeden's bureaucratic response as by his report. She knew about the spike in scams targeting offworlders, of course. A few years back, there were sensationalized accounts of extraterrestrial tourists *committing* crimes, but now most accounts were of crimes committed *against* offworlders. Including violent crimes. T&T's guests largely were spared, thank goodness. But this—*this* sounded serious. *Have we run out of our luck?*

"It seems like they had a pretty harrowing experience," Tweeden said. He frowned. "Just don't ask me why they waited until the end of the tour to file a report." He passed over a tablet.

Tracie's eyes darted back and forth as she reviewed the summary. Yes, five guests were involved; a young Rustacean couple and an elderly Plefferoon throuple celebrating their one hundred and seventy-fifth anniversary. All had signed on to the *Love's Legends* tour, a popular T&T package featuring some of history and fiction's most beloved romantic figures. The incident itself had occurred on the European leg of the tour, in Venice.

What? Tracie at first couldn't compute. *Venice is T&T's flagship model of corporate responsibility!*

The five guests had opted for the Casanova City Cruise, a four-hour motorboat tour of the lagoon. The motorboat operator—a local contractor and *not* a T&T employee, thank the Liability gods—had decided a little extortion was in order. He'd made his move when collecting payment at the tour's conclusion. Tracie turned to Tweeden with a raised brow. "Payment? Aren't those tours prepaid?"

Tweeden grimaced. "Yes, but the operator tacked on a bunch of fake 'extras'—a couple of snack bags he classified as a 'catered lunch,' answering questions about the glassmakers on Murano counted as a 'personalized tour'—you get the picture. And he put our guests in a position where they couldn't refuse."

'Couldn't refuse'? Hollywood-derived images of Italian mafia popped into Tracie's brain; she dislodged them with an irritated shake of the head. "How?"

The assistant pressed long fingers to his temples. *Probably thinking about all the paperwork this "situation" is going to produce.* "Instead of dropping the group off at the dock, the operator took them far, *far* out into the lagoon. He cut off the motor, and insisted everyone on-board immediately 'settle their accounts' before he headed back to shore. Specifically, he demanded they each transfer five hundred zurons to some cryptocurrency account—and strongly implied he'd leave them to swim with the fishes if they didn't pay up. Needless to say, Rustaceans and Plefferoons aren't exactly known for their swimming ability."

Tracie couldn't help a whistle. "Chutzpah."

"In spades," Tweeden confirmed. "And all caught on-camera." The Rustaceans, he gleefully explained, had surreptitiously recorded everything from the moment the operator began making threats. The five later sent in the footage, attached to their joint complaint and reimbursement claim, with a copy to the local police.

Good for them, Tracie mentally cheered. Far too many scam victims felt too embarrassed to file a complaint. "How are they doing now?"

The corners of Tweeden's lips pulled down. "From the report, the older three were pretty feather-ruffled. But all five are doing fine, physically speaking. The European office handled the situation satisfactorily and just want some reassurance that—"

"'Satisfactorily'?'" Tracie interrupted. She tugged down her blazer. "We need to do this *right*." *Why am I so upset? Because it's Venice? Or because Tweeden is acting like this is just about updating our internal protocols?*

True to form, her assistant rolled up his sleeves, ready to fulfill his duty to the firm. "Absolutely. There's still a chance they'll file a lawsuit. Shall I pull together a team from Legal?"

Tracie's facial muscles went rigid. "*No,*" she said curtly. "I want you to arrange for the company hovercraft to meet me on the roof in five minutes. Then, I want you to send me all you can find on the motorboat operator and tell Legal to go through his contract line-by-line for everything we can throw at him under the law."

Tweeden stared, nonplussed, but Tracie wasn't through. "And set up a meeting for me with Tine ASAP—just the two of us." She smiled thinly. "I don't care what you need to shift around."

Tracie had to give her assistant credit where it was due; the hovercraft was waiting for her on the roof in *four* minutes. Tweeden burst onto the roof as she climbed inside. "The negotiating team just finalized the engagement letter for Magnetar Investments!" he called, waving a datapad for emphasis. "We need your and Tine's sign-off."

"I'll look it over once I'm back!" Tracie shouted in response, and buckled herself in.

She opened the dossier on the Venetian motorboat operator as the hovercraft made its way to Ecuador. Tracie frowned after the first few screens; the background materials described a personable contractor who had been making good money working for T&T three years now. Yet he'd been revealed as a member of the local *ET, go home!* movement. A solid, dependable fellow like that...

The hovercraft set down at Mount Chimborazo just in the nick of time; Tracie put aside the partially-read file and caught up with the five guests not twenty minutes before they were due to head up the space elevator. She negotiated with security and huffed up to the gate, flats slip-sliding across the floor of the vast, domed chamber carved into Chimborazo's caldera. The pumped-in air was warm and thick across the exposed skin of her face, her nostrils filled with the acrid tang of the solvents used in maintaining the ribbon and its climbers.

Tracie immediately picked her targets out from the crowd at the gate; the shortest member of the elderly Plefferoon trio stretched at least two feet taller than the average human adult. The feathered crests—which added another foot—were bone-white, though the youngest's retained a hint of vermilion. The horns borne by all three appeared fragile, as though the tips might break off at any second, leaving the rest to crumble away. A stocky Rustacean couple waited with them; the female Rustacean subtly supported the eldest Plefferoon with an extended pincer.

Tracie shouted a *halloo* in Plefferoonese and burbled a salutation in Rustacean. The entire quintet turned as one—the

Plefferoons creakily shuffled their beaks about, while both Rustaceans swung their proboscis like flails.

"Tracie Trang, T&T's chief executive officer and co-founder," she gasped out the introduction. The moment she caught her breath, Tracie launched into an abject apology for the group's recent ordeal.

"Of course, T&T will not only issue you all a full refund for the entire tour," Tracie reassured. "We're also giving you a complimentary tour with us at the Epic Romance level—that's our top tier. If you're still willing to tour with us after such a clearly traumatic experience," she quickly added. "But we're happy to find alternatives. And—"

She paused before soldiering on. *Lawyers be damned.* "I want to be very, very clear: we take *full* responsibility for what happened. We're just glad you came out of the whole ordeal safe and sound. And I have to admit," Tracie's mouth quirked into a half-smile. "I'm pretty impressed with your quick-wittedness in recording the whole thing." *Though, why the hell you didn't report it right away...*

The eldest Plefferoon fluffed his crest in amusement. "Well, we have Charideeya to thank for that," he cawed. "She cautioned us to play along while Dendru recorded everything. I don't know *what* we would have done without you, my dear." The Plefferoon patted the Rustacean woman's foreclaw. "Charideeya encouraged us to file the complaint, too," he confided to Tracie.

"Really?" She started to thank Charideeya, only to realize two of the Rustacean's eyes were roving up and down Tracie quizzically. Tracie returned the inspection somewhat more politely. *Huh.* There was something oddly familiar about the young offworlder. From the introspective curling of the Rustacean's ears, she experienced a similar sense of recognition.

"Well, you've certainly earned *my* admiration." Tracie finally said. She spoke in deferential mode to emphasize sincerity and parted the fingers of one hand in an approximation of a pincer, the Rustacean version of a thumbs-up.

Another Plefferoon hobbled closer as she leaned on a cane. Her beak gaped open as she trilled, "These two salvaged our vacation! We were ready to cut the trip short and take the next shuttle home. But—" she loudly knocked her bill against the cane's knobby end. "Charideeya insisted we not allow one unpleasant episode to taint our entire experience of Earth. Impressive wisdom from a youngster."

The Rustacean paused her assessment of Tracie and indignantly clacked both pincers. "Well, it would have been a shame!' she rapped out. One set of lower extremities lifted and emphatically stomped back down. "You would have missed out on *so much*—the Taj Mahal, the French Quarter, the *exact spot* where Bonnie and Clyde were gunned down! Just think," the Rustacean added in a passionate staccato. "You never would have met those lovely people in Gibsland! Or learned the steps to the three-way tango, or how to say *'Shiawasena kekkon kinenbi,'* or..."

"*Happy anniversary.*" Tracie couldn't help the smile she felt spread across her face. *I just may have found a kindred spirit.* She tossed her head in amusement. The movement prompted several tendrils to fall out of her careful coif. Out of a long-ingrained habit she'd never quite shaken, Tracie raised both hands to sweep the entire mass of hair back and up into a perky ponytail.

The Rustacean immediately cut off the impassioned monologue. She stared straight at Tracie with every eye. "You!" she declared.

Startled, Tracie dropped her spare hairband and looked about. A few other passengers lounged by the gate, affecting the traveler's universal attitude of bored impatience. A sole Deesipod intercepted Tracie's glance and sniffed through every nostril in turn, mimicking an affronted harmonica. "Me?"

The Rustacean scampered two steps forward in a burst of excitement. "Yes! I almost didn't recognize you, with your cranial fur so different. My family was on your American Highlights tour, several years back," she belatedly explained, pincers clicking with embarrassment. *She speaks damn good American English,* Tracie registered in surprise. The Rustacean turned to her own partner with excitement. "This is the tour guide I told you about! Shells and shoals, I was *such* a brat about mom and pops dragging me on that trip. But I'm so happy they did!"

A single Rustacean family shouldn't have stood out among Tracie's recollections. But... *I remember that day, too!* Tracie barely needed to sift through memories of the countless tours she'd given. Because every detail of *that day* still stood out in her memory.

The day she first met Tine.

And—because of that—she *did* recall a certain, rather bratty Rustacean teenager. A teenager who, at the tour's conclusion, prettily thanked Tracie in stilted English and gave her an extraordinarily generous tip. *Here she is, all grown up,* Tracie realized, with a faint sense of shock. *Time flies by so quickly...*

Charideeya excitedly filled in those intervening years for the rest of the group, ignoring the flashing lights announcing the descending climber. "This is my third time visiting Earth. I wanted to introduce Dendru here—my favorite boyfriend," she nudged the purported videographer forward. "to my absolute *favorite* planet in the galaxy."

"It was you, and that tour, that made me want to learn *everything* I could about Earth," she all but burbled at Tracie. "It kind of became an obsession for me. I even decided to go into third world studies, and specialize in human culture."

Tracie felt her expression sour; Charideeya's ears sympathetically curled. "I *know*. Nobody truly appreciates just how rich Earth is in what *really* matters." The Rustacean's ears flopped down in a sigh. "The problem is that most people who even visit Earth in the first place are only here as tourists. There's no real *interaction*. So! I plan on devoting my career to changing that." She confidently flicked her proboscis.

"Ah—that's..." Tracie stammered, taken aback. Abruptly nostalgic—*envious? She's following* her *dreams*—she swallowed. "Good for you."

The loudspeaker's boarding call provided a welcome disruption. Tracie quickly settled matters with the appreciative throuple and rapidly extracted herself, though only after promising Charideeya to stay in touch.

Comfortably ensconced in the hovercraft once more, Tracie reached for the datapad. *All's well that ends well, right?* Tweeden would probably slap his hands together and move on to the next item on the docket. But the sight of demonstrators marching through Manhattan that morning remained fresh in Tracie's mind. She swiped back open the dossier on the motorboard operator, determined to give it a thorough read. Starting again from the first page. Featuring a mugshot.

Her eyes widened with shock. *I know him!*

The fact he was several years older—*aren't we all?* Tracie thought numbly—must be why she'd failed to recognize the face earlier. But the man was unmistakably the same gondolier from the day Tine proposed launching a business together.

He warned us to avoid the Piazza San Marco. Where tourists were being preyed on. Tracie closed her eyes. *And now he's the one carrying out scams.* She inhaled, opened her eyes, and rapped out a command to the onboard AI. *Clear my schedule for the rest of the day*, she then tapped a message to Tweeden. *There's been a change in plans.*

Tracie made an immediate detour to Venice.

T&T was the city's largest employer; Tracie shamelessly leveraged her influence with local law enforcement for a few minutes with the suspect. They left the pair in a nondescript room, after reassuring Tracie the station's AI would keep a leery watch through god-knew-how-many hidden cameras.

The motorboat operator-*cum*-gondolier warily took a seat. His eyes narrowed in immediate recognition. "So, you're some kind of big shot now," he drawled in the local tongue. "Here to take another gondola ride with your Pangalian?" The man chuckled, a humorless sound. "I can't promise you the same experience."

Tracie blinked, confused. She gathered her wits and pushed forward. "Why? Why are you scamming tourists?" To underline the irony: "Didn't you warn me and Tine *against* becoming easy marks?"

He smirked. "Got your attention, did I? Though it took longer than anticipated," the erstwhile gondolier drawled. He dangled both arms over the back of his chair. "I started to wonder if you cared as little for your offworld guests as you do for *all* the little people behind the scenes. Working to create— to *produce*—your romantic, *authentic* Venice."

"What do you mean?" Tracie sharply asked. "Of *course*, Tine and I care about Venice, and all the residents! Why do you think we worked so hard to toss BestGuest from the scene? Why do you think we lobbied the Agenzia Nazionale del Turismo to stop tearing down the city? Why do you think we poured *buckets* of zurons into offworld tech?" Her chest rose and fell in baffled frustration. "So we could bring Venice *back*, in all its glory!" *Well, that's why I worked so hard. Tine just signed off on pretty much anything likely to knock BestGuest down a peg or three.*

The gondolier burst out laughing, loud and sarcastic

guffaws. "Restore Venice to its 'glory'? Really? Oh, the city may *look* like 'olden times,'" he derided with a shake of the head. "No. You created a Venice World amusement park, and hired us as cast members to sing and dance on your *authentic* stage." The man's eyes narrowed. "Go for a gondola ride," he suggested, the suddenly mild voice at odds with the outrage of just seconds ago. "And tell me if I shouldn't be angry."

A normally glib Tracie had nothing to say in response. So, she stood up, quietly took her leave, and went for a gondola ride.

She returned not three hours later. *After all,* Tracie thought dazedly. *How much time do you really need at an amusement park, to realize everything's fake?*

Every place she'd passed on the way to the dock was sparkling clean, ordered, controlled. From the now-blatantly secure Piazza San Marco, to the designated holovid-taking slots on the Rialto Bridge, to the precise listings of calorie counts at each gelato stand where a uniformed vendor measured out perfectly calibrated scoops.

Tracie had waited in an orderly queue until a gleaming little 'bot in a natty red, white, and green poncho herded her into a spit-shined gondola with an equally sanitized gondolier. Both were indistinguishable from every other gondolier-and-gondola pair slipping down the grand canal. Hers stiffly narrated a curated selection of Venetian history as he poled along the prescribed route. Canned music played from a speaker.

No arias. No magic. No romance. Only the realization.

We *created the first shanty-town. Tine and I did this.*

And the inevitable progression. *Are we going to turn Jalifree's ice geysers into a honeymooners' theme park, too, complete with frozen waterslides?*

"I'll do what I can to convince our guests not to press

charges—though they're certainly entitled," she informed the gondolier flatly. "T&T will cover your fines and—if you'll accept the offer—we'll help place you in a new job. Any one you want that you're remotely qualified for." The man opened his mouth to protest; Tracie cut in with the practiced ease of redirecting recalcitrant equity stakeholders. "That's the deal, as long as you—and whomever I presume you're working with—don't do this sort of thing again," she told him. "Your grievance is really with T&T, anyway. Right?"

The gondolier's lips thinned. For several seconds, Tracie fully expected he would throw the offer back into her face. Instead, he took in a great breath and slowly released it. "Our 'grievance' is with anyone who thinks they're entitled to make money off any place they want—places where people are simply trying to make a living and enjoy life. Just because it's *charming*. No matter the cost to the people already there." Determined eyes met Tracie's. "Venice isn't a *product*. It is my home."

The man stood and straightened his shoulders. "We Venetians should have taken a bigger stand decades ago, before the offworlders ever arrived. But we're taking a stand now."

A stubborn Tracie waited in the foyer while the officers processed the gondolier and returned his personal effects. She fell in by his side as he headed for the exit. "Tell me: what can we do?"

The man barely deigned to look at her. "You can just all... go away."

Tracie should have let it go then and there, but her *pragmatic* side couldn't help but make a point. "Wouldn't that only leave you worse off? How are you going to replace all the revenue tourists bring in? How are you going to replace all those jobs in hospitality? Nearly every other industry is automated now," she bitterly added. The memory still held a sour tang. "Hell, how are you going to maintain the pumps, the floodgates? Who here's even trained to repair offworld tech!"

The gondolier stopped a few paces outside the station and turned on her. "You think we haven't considered all that?" he snapped. "Yes, it will be hard going. But Venice has experienced hardship before—from our very founders fleeing barbarian hordes, through war, decline, and occupation. We survived all that, and we will survive this, too."

They parted, amicably, under the circumstances. Leaving Tracie feeling guilty, dissatisfied, and utterly powerless.

Ridiculous! she chided herself. *You're the co-owner—CEO —of Earth's largest hospitality chain.* If she couldn't make a difference with that kind of clout, then how could anyone?

Tracie decided against taking the hovercraft directly back to the office, heading instead for her and Tine's favorite Manhattan coffee house. She needed to sit for a spell and just *think.*

The establishment rightly should have been a tourist trap, with its clear view of the Empire State Building. Yet somehow it remained a hidden gem for decades, there for the locals through the metropolis's many ups and downs. Its surroundings, however, certainly kept up with the times—as demonstrated by the clear message, *Bug-Eyed Aliens Can Bug Off,* spray-painted on the side of the adjacent building.

Tracie winced and pushed open the door to the coffee shop. A few minutes later, she collected her beverage and pastry at the counter and took a seat at a table—*their* table— prime real estate next to a window, but half-hidden by an ungainly potted plant. She and Tine often people-watched from this window, pretending to catch a glimpse of Cary Grant as Nickie Ferrante, rushing by to make his fated appointment.

These days, he'd be rushing by the Xenatode-owned pizza parlors and holovid repair shops that lined the other side of the street. Gone was the hole-in-the-wall Lebanese joint, the while-you-wait family-owned dry cleaners. As Tracie mourned the loss, now that she truly *saw* it—*just another casualty of joining the rest of the developed universe, right?*—yet another triple-decker hoverbus wobbled up to the intersection. Tirillan tourists inside the mobile aquarium pressed webbed hands up against the plexiglass windows and goggled at celebrity look-alikes posing at the street corners.

"What the hell?" she heard a customer exclaim from the counter. "Phlez and dumblederry danishes? You're *kidding* me!"

"They're from Dendrobria—in the Rustacean system," the barista calmly explained. "Very moist, and super-delicious sprinkled with cinnamon sugar and—"

"Not. Interested." The disgruntled patron cut her off. "Can't even get a cup of joe these days without a side of little green men," he grumbled. "Look, do you have any normal, *human* danishes?"

Tracie drew in a deep breath and nudged her own tazreen-and-ruffinnut scone off to one side.

Well, there goes my *appetite.*

Maybe I'm overreacting, and things aren't so bad every-where? Tracie knew she was fooling herself. But she accessed the latest industry reports on her tablet anyway.

We advise operators to factor in the risks associated with increasing anti-offworlder sentiment, the *Terran Travel Trends* warned. The rest of the article suggested strategies for miti-gating impacts on company profits and insurance premiums. But nothing addressed the actual *root* of the problem. *Probably because it would up-end the entire damn business model,* Tracie hopelessly thought. She couldn't avoid the hard truths anymore.

T&T—we—were supposed to be the good guys, the respon-

sible corporate citizens, blah-blah-blah. But in the end, are we so different from the rest?

Encouraging entire economies to rely on the whims of vacationers, selling tourists packaged "authenticity." The corporate promise of "building interplanetary goodwill" was a total crock, Tracie finally admitted. The only interaction most humans had with any of the galaxy's other sentient denizens involved bumping into some holovid-toting tourist on the metro.

Was it really surprising there was "increasing anti-offworlder sentiment"? That a hardworking gondolier, at the end of his rope, would end up shaking down an elderly throuple celebrating their anniversary? And how barbaric and backward would humans appear to the rest of the galaxy, as tales of scams and attacks circulated and grew in the retelling?

In the end, humans and extraterrestrials were no closer to truly understanding each other than the day of First Contact.

Tracie pushed aside the tablet and propped her chin in both hands. She thought about the idealistic Charideeya and ruminated on her own girlish dreams. *All I ever wanted was to open doorways between worlds.* Back then, Tracie truly believed language was the key.

I was naïve. Her lips shallowly curved upward in a sad smile. Even the advent of AI interpreters couldn't stop misunderstandings or overcome ignorance. *So, what's the solution? How can we show Earth is more than just some tourist trap— with unfriendly locals, at that? How can we prove extraterrestrials aren't just ugly offworlders or hustlers out to drain the planet dry?* Tracie considered the crossroads T&T found itself at.

Launch the IPO and, if they played their cards right, overtake BestGuest as a major interplanetary hospitality chain.

Or—pull back. Reexamine how the company did business, brainstorm how they could do—could *be*—better. Become the "good guys" in reality. *We've committed so many errors, but I refuse to believe T&T is irredeemable,* came the stubborn thought. *Yes, Venice is a loud wake-up call. I just need to make Tine hear it, too. We've worked together for years; I know he wants to do the right thing, too.*

Tine's obsession with expansion was just a detour; Tracie was confident of that. Her partner would get back on track, once it sank in that his score with BestGuest was settled once and for all. He would listen to reason.

A renewed sense of purpose did wonders for the appetite. Tracie scarfed down the tazreen-and-ruffinnut scone in three bites and swept out of the coffee shop.

She couldn't resist an ironic little smile as she strode down the sidewalk. *I'm about to make Tine a proposal.* Purely business, of course.

Her feelings hadn't changed. And it was clear Tine's *lack* of feelings hadn't budged, either. Tracie comforted herself that the Pangalian was truly married to the job. In her more insecure moments, she wondered if the possibility never occurred to him because he simply didn't find humans attractive. Or maybe it was just Tracie, after all.

And how uplifting is that, huh? She buried the self-defeating little thought and squared her shoulders.

Focus, Tracie, on making your case! Conviction carried her the rest of the way to the office.

Where, as though summoned, Tine stood waiting just outside her door. A stranger—a Pungluroid in vigorous middle age—squelched at his side. Tracie drew up short.

Tine's ears perked, and his barbels twitched with pleasure as Tracie cautiously approached. "Tracie! Wonderful—I said she'd be in soon." He beamed at his companion and turned back to his co-founder. "Tracie, this is Sboti—Sboti Vuvk-Vluvk. Sboti's firm runs a niche touring venture operating throughout the Sagittarius and Perseus Arms," Tine introduced the two in Interplanetary Standard – Verbal. "Their target market is high net worth, sophisticated travelers. They're looking to expand the brand into the Orion spur."

The Pungluroid extended a pseudopod encased in a firm, healthy layer of mucus. Tracie politely shook the proffered appendage, up and down, and withdrew as quickly as courtesy permitted. She discreetly wiped her palm off on the leg of her slacks.

Tine convivially thumped his tail against the floor. "Sboti's folks are proposing a partnership," he announced. "We give them thirty percent—"

"Fifty percent," Sboti cut in.

"Oh, Legal can hash out the details later." Tine's barbels lifted conspiratorially in Tracie's direction. "The point—the *vision*—is we provide all the logistical heavy lifting involving lodging, tours, and transportation, while Sboti's people supply name-recognition and a proven service model."

Tracie blinked. *What the hell is Tine trying to spring on me this time?* " 'Proven service model?' " She sidled closer and hissed in Pangalese. "What, precisely, *is* this guy's gimmick, Tine?"

"My partner wants to know your gimmick, Sboti!" Tine blithely repeated in Interplanetary Standard, carelessly shoving his partner into the *bad cop* role. Tracie resisted the urge to twist a pointy ear. Instead, she crossed both arms over her chest and projected extreme skepticism on all frequencies.

The Pungluroid took no outward offense. He widely grinned; the smile practically split the top third of his torso.

"Extinction," he said—no; *intoned*. "The end. Of days."

Tracie felt her eyes go wide. *I—did I hear that correctly? Is he even speaking IP?* "What?"

Tine excitedly bared his upper fangs. "Why don't you show my partner your proposal?" he suggested.

"Of course!" Sboti gurgled. He slimed backward two meters and drew from one moist pocket a device which bore a disconcerting similarity to a comic book ray blaster. To Tracie's relief, the business end did nothing more than project an image against the foyer's far wall.

Tracie found herself squinting at a logo, a pair of conjoined glyphs that emanated a tingly sound. Sboti launched into what was clearly a prepared presentation.

"*Extinction Expeditions* is a niche travel operator," he began. "We specialize in truly *limited-time* experiences. Just think!" Sboti extruded three pseudopods and waved them about theatrically. "Think of a planetary system about to be engulfed by a supernova, a one-of-a-kind ecosystem on the cusp of entering an ice age, a stunning vista in its final moments before a forecasted seismic event."

An appendage depressed the ray gun several times in succession. The far wall shuffled through a series of images, jaw-dropping scenes of beauty and astounding weirdness. "Here are just a few of our most popular attractions. Temporary, of course! The floating islands of Raiges Eleven—before it was demolished to make way for the interplanetary express. The coral forests of Clentron Three—before Hrliock & Co. got its mining permit approved."

"Our tours are *immensely* popular—and profitable," Sboti added, with an affected modesty designed to fool no one. "We're ready to take that next step, beyond mainstream extinction events. Given T&T's remarkable success marketing romantic escapes, we feel there's opportunity for a mutually beneficial collaboration."

Tine's ears vigorously wriggled in agreement. The Pangalian shot an encouraging look Tracie's way.

"And so, we propose..." Sboti drew out the transition. "the *Last Chance Romance* expedition!"

Tracie's jaw truly did drop at this. Splashed across the entire wall was a psychotic artist's rendition of a fiery supernova. Superimposed over the gratuitous destruction, a photogenic Xenatode couple was locked in a passionate embrace; the larger female's tentacles tumbled back with abandon, the smaller male's shell impossibly buffed.

"Our ultimate goal is a multi-planet experience," the Pungluroid boasted. "But step one is pilot testing the concept, taking advantage of the presence you've established here, on Earth."

"Here, on Earth," Tracie numbly repeated.

"Exactly! We'll leverage your experience to identify Earth's most beautiful, most meaningful, most *IR-ree-PLACE-able*," he bombastically stressed each syllable in glurby English. "and DOOMED sites."

"Doomed..." Tracie's voice escaped in a mangled croak.

Sboti's lower body expanded and squishily contracted, the Pungluroid version of a vigorous nod. "*Doomed!*" he agreed. "Doomed to destruction, at the tentacles of climate change, of war, of pollution, of encroaching development. And whatever else you suggest, of course," he added, rippling hopefully. "I don't suppose you still haven't moved beyond nuclear warheads?"

Tracie just stared, horrified. Sboti pancaked himself on the floor with satisfaction, apparently interpreting her shock as *struck dumb with awe.* "That's the five-point plan!" he confirmed, mounding himself back up, gob by gob. "We'll market a limited-time opportunity to experience—first hand!—Earth's most priceless heritage, in a whirlwind six-day, seven-night all-inclusive package. Plus add-ons for side-excursions, continuous holovid recording *and* editing," the Pungluroid embellished, "and an endangered species plushie of your choice, to commemorate the tour."

"Plushie," Tracie faintly echoed.

"And other co-branded souvenirs," Tine helpfully affirmed.

Sboti enthusiastically expanded and contracted, and then immediately segued into the logistics of staging wedding proposals at a melting ice cap. Tracie inhaled an enormous lungful of air—*breathe, dammit!*—and exhaled it like a leaky balloon.

"Would you please excuse us for a moment, Mr. Vuvk-Vluvk?" she calmly inquired. Exercising heroic restraint, she tugged Tine into her office, giving herself props for not bodily dragging the Pangalian in by the tail. She politely shut—fine; *slammed*—the door on the bemused Pungluroid.

Tine enthusiastically tilted his muzzle, barbels lifted in an upward curve. "So. What do you think?" He immediately tore ahead without waiting for Tracie's response. "Yes; it's definitely a wonderful opportunity to capture a new segment of the market! A terrific way for us to dip our talons into---"

Tracie *did* yank on his tail then. Over Tine's startled yelp, she gritted out, "Are. You. Out. Of. Your. Furry. *Mind?*" Tracie vigorously shook her head in disbelief. "No way in *hell* am I signing off on this!" To make her position absolutely clear, Tracie repeated that sentiment in the Emperor's Pangalese, and then in Interplanetary Standard – Visual. Hell, she'd repeat it again in Interplanetary Standard – Interpretive Dance, just to ensure not one iota of her meaning was lost.

Tine backed off, confusedly rubbing at his hindquarters. "I thought you would be pleased!" he exclaimed in injured tones.

"*Pleased?* At what?" Tracie hissed. "You do remember *I'm* human, right? Do you really think I'd be *ecstatic* at the 'opportunity' to exploit my own species' self-destructive tendencies? To make a tourist trap of our mistakes and our misery?" she snarled. "You think I'd be *thrilled* about turning humanity's failures into a-a *backdrop* for some bachelorette party?"

Tracie stalked forward as she spoke, the force of her glower alone sufficient to cause Tine to back away. Her partner's tailbone bumped up against the wall.

Business partner, an inner voice reminded her forlornly. *Probably just as well it isn't anything more.* "What the *hell*, Tine? How could you possibly think I would be 'pleased'?" Tracie's breathing was labored; her lungs bellowed in and out with barely contained rage.

Tine's tail, initially bushy in shock and distress, dangled limply in tandem with his barbels and ears. "Well," he said in a tinny voice. "You seemed to be fine with Venice."

Tracie stared at him, completely floored. Her partner regained his voice. "And this will be even *bigger* and *better*. Besides, collaborating with Extinction Expeditions will drive up the IPO price. Magnetar Investments completely agrees."

Tracie's eyes automatically shifted left, to the desk. There sat the datapad, the underwriter's engagement letter undoubtedly loaded and ready for her signature. Her eyes flicked up—to the only scrap remaining from her prior life. A map of the world, bristling with green pushpins.

Probably one for every shamtytown, by now. We ruin every place we touch.

She'd come prepared to convince Tine that T&T needed to reexamine the way it did business, but Tine was beyond listening and Tracie couldn't be party to this.

She couldn't help a sad chuckle. An "engagement" letter. Finally, a proposal Tracie had to turn down.

"I want out," she abruptly said .

Tine's ears shot up in shock. "W-*what*?"

Tracie didn't have a script for this. But who did? Her earlier fury drained from every limb, she canted her voice tired and dull. "It's over. I can't do this anymore; I can't continue being part of the problem." She let out a heavy sigh, let it all go. Everything wrong about the hospitality business, about T&T's high-minded, *wrong*-minded ambitions. About herself and Tine, and what might have been.

"I can't keep selling out my planet, my people as some—some scenic backdrop to pre-engagement parties," Tracie tried to explain, one last shot. She let slip a self-deprecating laugh. *Today's been all about honesty and self-reflection. Might as well put it all out there.* "Not that it's *all* about lofty principle. I'm tired of flitting from planet to planet and never meeting anyone outside of a conference room. I'm tired of being *practical* and I'm tired of moving further and further from building a legacy I'd be proud to call my own. I'm tired, Tine, and I'm through."

Tine stared, struck speechless, throughout Tracie's speech. A single barbel slightly twitched, and he opened and closed his mouth.

Well. While he's processing that... Tracie looked about the richly appointed office. Her eyes paused at a framed original movie poster advertising *An Affair To Remember*. A gift from Tine to celebrate their first year of profitability. She didn't care about the rest of it, but... *No. Taking it would reveal too much.*

"You can buy me out," Tracie added. "Don't worry about me playing hardball; I'll be more than fair, and I won't mess up your IPO." She paused, and the silence lengthened and stretched like a rubber band. "Speaking of being fair, I'll also admit I really don't want to profit off romance anymore." Tracie wryly smiled. "I—I think I just want to experience one of my own."

Tine's barbels froze in place, and then drooped as Tracie walked past her erstwhile partner. She opened the door and exited, striding past a confused Sboti without a single glance backward.

* * *

Enjoy the nightlife? You'll believe Earth is the galaxy's hottest spot, and only getting hotter under current greenhouse gas emissions projections!

Tracie tugged her ponytail loose with a sigh as she entered the midrise building. She ran her fingers through the silver strands and then e depressed the *up* button for the elevator. Tracie rubbed at both temples, completely exhausted—and very, very satisfied.

The latest cohort of Extraterrestrial Exchange Envoys had completed their three-day orientation without a hitch. The group—primarily Rustaceans, Pungluroids, and Deesipods, although the program expanded each year—were by now settling in with their human host families. Tomorrow, assigned mentors would introduce each protégé to their new city, and all would start their first day on the job by the end of the week. Tracie mentally ran through this year's roster. The three agricultural specialists would be deployed to train human farmers in the latest sustainable farming techniques. The fifteen educators would be dispatched to secondary schools across the globe to instruct students on the basics of interplanetary history and culture. The ten experts in artificial intelligence were each headed for incubator programs, where they would be paired with human computer scientists. A pair of civil engineers—Pungluroid, ironically enough—would join three colleagues from last year's cohort, already training their Venetian counterparts on operating and repairing the city's flood control system. The rest—biologists, doctors, poets, and more—were just as eager to get to work and begin making new friends here, in their home away from home for at least the next year.

Tomorrow would be just as hectic, because this year's cohort of *Earth* Exchange Envoys packed their own bags tonight. Tracie's team would see them off in the morning, when the group gathered at the Mt. Kenya station, ready to head out on their own year abroad. Far, *far* abroad. All were raring to start their training in high-demand fields and bring those newly acquired skills back home.

Looks like our Inter-Planetary Partnership Program is off to a third successful year!

Tracie grinned as she exited the elevator on the fifth floor. Too bad nobody else was around to exchange high-fives; like most commercial real estate in the neighborhood, the building had been hit hard by the pandemics and floods of the prior decade. At least half of the former tenants had cleared out— shut down, automated, or permanently shifted to remote work. One, Tracie noted without *too* much irony, apparently had been a translation service.

Consequently, most of the suites lining the corridor remained vacant, including the office directly across the elevator bank from IPPP. On the plus side, that meant rent was actually affordable. IPPP's leased space was small, nothing like T&T's sprawling headquarters, but Tracie found she preferred the cozier digs.

"*Bienvenido!*" Charideeya sang out as Tracie walked past her open door. The Rustacean made it a game to test herself with a new human greeting every day.

"Mahadsanid," Tracie challenged with a smile. Charideeya's ears rolled up tightly in concentration as she cogitated, refusing to be stumped. "Adaa Mudan!" she finally replied, triumphantly. Tracie stifled a chuckle.

"How did the last day of orientation go?" IPPP's Director

of Operations inquired.

"Excellent," Tracie reported, with a thumbs-up. "We're off and rolling in the new year!"

"Qué maravillosa!" Charideeya pushed back her rolling stool and clacked a pincer to indicate a change in subject. "Tracie, do you have a few minutes? We need to discuss recruitment efforts for next year's cohort."

"Already?" Tracie shook her head as she led the way to her own office. *It never ends, does it?* But these days, that thought energized Tracie rather than filled her with dread.

IPPP may still be in its infancy, but we're definitely strong, healthy, and growing! A happy fact due in large part to the popularity of its two core programs: sending Earth Exchange Envoys offplanet to receive a galaxy-class education, and welcoming educators and experts as Extraterrestrial Exchange Envoys to share their skills with humans on-site. Even with the recent crash in Earth tourism, the two programs didn't lack for applicants—which, Chiradeeya swore, was thanks to T&T's successful marketing of Earth as the galaxy's most romantic locale. Branding that survived even the industry's downturn.

More projects were already in the works, and next year, IPPP would launch its Cultural Ambassador program. Tracie had already received enthusiastic interest from a number of top-tier artists, actors, and athletes—all A-list celebrities, she joked to a puzzled Charideeya.

Tracie wasn't naïve; she knew these were small steps in addressing the root of the problem. Earth had more catching up to do than could be tackled by one non-profit. *But standing back and shrugging my shoulders—or worse, profiting off humanity's comparative disadvantage—isn't the solution, either. Better to take each win as we can get it, and then, as Ti—as some people would say—'scale up.'*

Realizing all those big visions cost money, of course. T&T's

buyout offer had set Tracie up with a decent amount of seed funding. Although her ex-partner insisted—through a company attorney, of course—she retain a percentage "in recognition of your invaluable contributions as co-founder." Tracie had silently acquiesced, wanting to avoid any more reason for communication.

She shook her head now, as though shaking away those memories, and pulled out a stool for Charideeya. The Rustacean settled all her lower appendages and began a quick summary of IPPP's latest fundraising efforts. Grants continued to roll in from a growing number of government institutions and private foundations—both offworld and Earth-based, she reported. The upshot was Tracie could add to her full-time staff, currently numbering three.

Tracie smiled. The inestimable Charideeya had been her first hire; the Rustacean had eagerly put down roots on Earth with Dendru—her former favorite boyfriend, now spouse—and soon after, her *other* spouse, Stenopo.

With Charideeya handling day-to-day operations, Tracie could concentrate on promoting IPPP's long term vision to potential partners across the galaxy, from the big multiplane-taries to elite universities.

I have more meetings than ever but now I get to actually open those doorways. No more racing from one stuffy confer-ence room to another. Tracie took the time to explore, strolling —or swimming or floating—through markets and chatting with locals, learning and absorbing all she could. Those same poten-tial partners were pleasantly surprised, if not outright shocked, with how easily they clicked with Tracie. And if they related so well to one human, why not to others?

In a way, Tracie had stepped back into her old role of tour guide. But now it was all about introducing those potential supporters to her home planet, both the bad and the good.

These hard looks at Earth—through not-so-alien eyes—showed Tracie that, for all her own species' flaws, there was *so much* humanity had to offer the universe.

And speaking of tour guides and tourism...

Around the same time IPPP launched, most of the big interplanetary hotel chains and tour operators started quietly closing up shop and exiting the Earth market. The industry had taken a massive public relations gut-punch from the swelling protests against offworlders, the swiftly accumulating reports of violence and scams.

But it was the bombing of the Girni embassy on the Gulf Coast that really sounded the death knell for the heyday of Earth-based tourism. *Thank goodness there were no fatalities.* The bombing nevertheless sent a very clear message, without need for additional translation: *ET, go home. Or else.*

We're lucky to be in the business of recruiting idealists. Applicants for the Extraterrestrial Exchange Envoys were undaunted; if anything, they had been galvanized by those events.

And what about T&T? The firm was one of the few, grizzled survivors, even though its profits had definitely taken a hit, the IPO stalled. Tracie couldn't resist keeping tabs; she'd heard through the grapevine that Tine had convinced the board of directors to transition out of Venice before taking a sabbatical for a year—or was it two? Industry gossip claimed the notoriously cutthroat executive had regrouped and was laying out a path for T&T to pick itself up, dust itself off, and move forward. *Tine's incorrigible.* If T&T had survived, Tracie was certain her ex-partner would find *some* way to realize his ambition to dominate the intergalactic hospitality industry.

As Charideeya waggled her ears over the proposed budget for the next fiscal year, force of habit pulled Tracie's eyes across the office wall. Straight to the framed *An Affair To Remember* poster; Tine had quietly arranged its delivery to his ex-partner's scrappy new office.

I should put it in storage, she admitted. *Having it around just makes it that much more difficult to let it—let* him—go. Tracie deliberately recentered both her gaze and attention on Charideeya, too enthralled by her lists and spreadsheets to register her boss's wandering attention. The Rustacean glanced upward with a grin. "Can't wait for this afternoon either, huh?"

"This after...? Oh!" A matching smile spread itself across Tracie's face. "Wouldn't miss it for the universe."

* * *

Unwind with your sweetie at T&T's on-site spa and salon. Lounge by the lava pool while our experienced therapists indulge you with a customized full-body massage, soothing the stress from tentacles and tails. Meanwhile, our licensed beauticians will fully detail and buff your shell. Don't forget to book an appointment with our hoof, horn, and nail technicians for a full mani-pedi—and, for those special occasions, our professionally trained stylists offer a full range of clipping, shearing, and dyeing services.

I wouldn't have missed this for the universe. Tracie hid an appreciative chuckle as she watched the scene unfold on the observation deck. She stood to one side, together with the rest of her staff and the carryovers from last year's cohort. All had convened at the Empire State Building to bear witness—as per Xenatodian custom—to a proposal.

More specifically, Blegripp, a xenobiologist on rotation at each of Earth's major biomes, was proposing to Jorge. The pair met the prior year, at an IPPP mixer. Blegripp now presented an awkward yet adorable picture as he sank to all four knees. The kiddo had gone the extra mile, his shell painstakingly waxed and cranial tentacles groomed to an inch. He carefully held a small box between both upper pincers.

The gawking crowd was mostly tourists; the majority human but with a respectable scattering of extraterrestrials—perhaps unsurprising, given the tales Tracie heard about *human* tourists fecklessly trekking about even actual, active warzones. They hooted their encouragement as Jorge hesitantly, blushingly, opened the box.

Tracie was prepared for the pang, but it still hurt. She flashed back on another "proposal," several years behind her now. *At the Jules Verne,* she recalled the now-bittersweet memory. *Although* here *is where the deal was consummated.*

Charideeya fluttered her left ear cheekily. "This is, what—our fourth or fifth proposal? Tracie, we *really* should think about just making it official and start a matchmaking service. After all," she continued, the skin around three of her eyes crinkled in a smile. "Didn't you introduce me to Nate?" She waved a pincer at her latest fiancé, deep in conversation with Dendru and Stenopo.

Casually, Charideeya added, "Have *you* reconsidered getting back into the dating game? And don't give the excuse that you're 'already married to your work.'" She made her sentiments clear with a rude gesture. "You're such an incredible catch—by all rights, you should have four or five doting husbands by now!"

Tracie desperately cast about for an escape route, but the Rustacean held her in place with a gentle but firm pincer. "In fact," she said in a considering tone. "Nate is close pals with a nice Plefferoon fellow. He's a physician-in-training, and—"

"We've had this conversation already, Charideeya," Tracie

interrupted. "And my answer is still the same. I'm really, truly, *genuinely* not interested."

Well, just not interested in any of the potential matches you keep offering up, like promotional giveaways. They all sound *great, but...* But the problem was with Tracie herself.

I wonder if Tine has found his mate-for-life yet... Tracie quickly pulled away from *that* irritatingly distressing idea, like fingers singed on a hot skillet.

"Or maybe..." Charideeya coyly said. "You already have someone in mind?" She withdrew the pincer and used it to give Tracie a—very careful—pat on the shoulder.

"What?" Tracie fended off an instinctive blush. "I can promise you, Chari, that I'm not keeping any paramour under wraps!"

"No. But you *are* keeping him waiting."

"Huh?" Tracie stared.

"Heh." Charideeya gave a flippant wave of her proboscis. "Well, why don't we just leave you two love-mollusks alone?" With remarkable alacrity, the Rustacean scuttled off stage left. Leaving the entire observation deck empty, as if the damn thing had been staged in advance.

Empty, except for Tracie...and Tine.

And I thought Blegripp *cleaned up nicely...* Tine's fur was groomed to the *millimeter*, that suit fit him so well—showing off those broad shoulders she started noticing, if she admitted it, three months into their partnership—and his barbels were, Tracie suspected, recently waxed.

The Pangalian approached; a slight twitch of both ears and tail betrayed his nervousness. He stopped a respectable two paces away. Tracie reminded herself to breathe.

"Tracie..." Tine swallowed and tried again. "Tracie, I'm sorry to waylay you like this. I know we haven't spoken for a long time. But I have something to say, if you'll just hear me out." He took a deep breath, ears flattening in determination. "I was wrong."

Tracie blinked. *Wrong?* She repeated the word aloud.

"Yes." Tine's muzzle dipped firmly. "Letting my obsession with BestGuest—yes, I *know* that's what it was—letting it make me push T&T into expanding no matter the cost. The IPO, partnering with those intestinal parasites at Extinction Expeditions..." He took in a deep breath. "I crossed a line. But at the time, I thought we were—that we were speaking the same language."

That shook Tracie out of her paralysis. "I didn't mean for Venice to become what we made it," She blurted out, recalling Tine's artless accusation. Tracie flushed, honesty driving her to add, "But it's still my fault. I took my hand off the wheel."

"Still, I should have realized you never would have—" Tine paused to ruefully chuckle. "When you left, I couldn't understand why. Like I said, it was like we were speaking two different languages at each other."

Tracie couldn't help a laugh of her own. "Maybe we needed an interpreter."

Tine nodded. "I found one." He reached into the fanny pack and removed—*not that goddamned tablet!* she thought, rather hysterically—a piece of crumpled paper. Before his nonplussed ex-partner, Tine slowly unfolded it with careful talons, treating it like a treasured manuscript.

My map! A dumbfounded Tracie stared at faded green and brown continents, outlined by washed-out oceans.

"I should have shipped this to you with the movie poster," Tine said, with a sheepish sweep of his tail. "But something made me hold it back. I'm glad I did." He crouched down as if embarrassed, and busied himself with smoothing out the much-abused sheet against the observation deck. "When you left, I couldn't understand *why*—or where you were even going. Fortunately, you left a map."

Said map was crinkled and battered nearly beyond recognition. But Tracie could see where all the green pushpins had been removed, and Pangalian hieroglyphs—checkmarks—were scribbled in their place. *Tine's leave of absence...*

"I've been traveling a lot lately," he murmured. "But not as a tourist. I've been learning new languages, too. Remember what it was you said? At *C'est Paris*."

"Language is about how you interpret, how you perceive the universe around you. When you learn another language, you gain a new perspective, too."

The two stood quietly for several long moments, no sound other than the wind pressing against the observation deck's transparent barrier, zephyr fingers trying to find their way inside.

"Translate all that for me, Tine," Tracie whispered. "What are you saying?"

Tine refolded the map and met Tracie's eyes forthrightly as he stood and tucked it back into the fanny pack. "We can do so much better," he said in the gentlest of tones. "Without exploiting anyone or serving up false authenticity. Maybe that means we won't be quite so profitable." Tine lifted and lowered his tufted ears in a nonchalant shrug. Then his muzzle parted in that old, familiar grin. "But not *necessarily*."

"Which is why we're considering alternative models!" Tine produced a tablet from the ether. *I knew it was coming!* Tracie thought with a familiar eye-roll. And a laugh, quickly extinguished. *Is he about to confirm the rumors?* "Is—is T&T really moving operations off Earth?"

"What? Of course not!" Tine's ears scrunched down in confusion. "No; T&T is making changes," he triumphantly announced. "Big, *big* changes!" And then the incorrigible

Pangalian was off and running. Tine swiped, tapped, and exclaimed over the tablet as he babbled on about "new paradigms in guest management," "collaborative partnerships with hosts," "community co-produced tour experiences with fair profit-sharing," and so on and so forth.

Abruptly, Tine cut off his soliloquy mid-sentence. He raised his muzzle and looked straight at Tracie. At some point, they had scooted close together, their heads barely inches apart. "And your IPPP..."

Tracie took a wary half-step backward. "Yes?"

"Is *brilliant!*" Tine exclaimed with barely contained enthusiasm. "Have you ever considered the potential for scaling up?"

"Well," said a nonplussed Tracie. "We're following a five-year plan that envisions substantial year-on-year growth, and—"

"Beyond Earth!" Tine excitedly burst out. "Why not bring your cultural exchange programs to *all* the inhabited planets? Especially third worlds."

Tracie blinked, caught off-balance. Truth be told, it was an idea she'd occasionally kicked around in her own head. *I just don't have a clue how we'd actually make it happen. Not that anything as minor as logistics or lack of money ever stopped Tine from trying to make a go of things.* The earlier exchange with Charideeya popped into Tracie's head, and she laughed. "Well, why not go further and merge our respective areas of expertise? Even my own Director of Operations suggested we go into the matchmaking business." She shook her head mirthfully. "At least three Fellows have paired up with humans, just in the last quarter."

Tine visibly brightened. "Genius!" Oblivious to Tracie's amusement, the Pangalian began feverishly tapping, already strategizing. "...and we could inaugurate that inter-solar system cruise line after all, but focused on matchmaking—among *all* sentient species. We'll call it...hmm." He turned to her in appeal. "What *should* we call it, Tracie?"

"How about the *Purple Passage*?" Tracie suggested with a straight face. When Tine approvingly nodded and began tapping away once again, Tracie threw her hands into the air with melodramatic exasperation.

"And for shore excursions, *definitely* Venus..." Tine trailed off. And gulped. He straightened, ears nervously flattened, paws clenched on gathered courage "But—but, that wasn't all I wanted to tell you," the Pangalian forced out.

Tracie raised a brow. "It isn't?" Her laughter faltered before Tine's serious demeanor. His barbels solemnly lowered.

"I told you I spent this last year and more studying human languages—especially *your* first language," he said in an oddly rough voice. "Trying to gain a better understanding of certain words. Words like—like *hospitality. Travel. Guest.*" He paused. "*Partner. Romance.*" Barbels and ears both twitched as he whispered. "*Love.*"

Oh.

"For a while there," Tine continued, looking anywhere but at Tracie. "I thought about recruiting another partner. Running the company myself was damned lonely, I admit. But just considering working with somebody else made me realize that there won't—there *can't*—be anyone else for me."

Well, Pangalians do *mate for life!* A quixotic voice gibbered at Tracie. *And he* did *travel the world in your footsteps, didn't he?*

"I know you're focusing on IPPP now," Tine quickly added. "And I completely support the work you're doing. But— and I know it's selfish of me—I hope you'll consider coming back. In any role. Partially because T&T can do so much good with you involved. But, also because—" Tine's barbels optimistically lifted as he inhaled deeply. "I miss you. And maybe—

you miss me, too?" He blew out that breath, all at once. "I'm not really talking about the company," he finally admitted.

Am I understanding this right? Had language finally failed Tracie, had she misunderstood what Tine—*her* Tine—was saying?

It was Tracie's turn now to gather all her courage. "Are—are you proposing another, ah, joint venture?" she tentatively asked. Tine nodded. A rising but wary hope shone in his eyes. That practical voice residing in Tracie's head—the one that sounded uncannily like her parents—chose that very moment to butt in. *You'd have to be* insane *to even consider this!* It scolded. *Hell, Tracie—you're two different species. How do you even know you're even, ah,* compatible? *Not to mention people will think it unnatural, they'll disapprove...*

No! I'm not listening to you anymore, she shot back. *I was "insane" to become a tour guide, I was "insane" to take up Tine on his proposal years back, I was completely insane to leave T&T at all. But those were the right calls for me. And what I most regret is never saying how I felt.*

With that, Tracie threw *practical* to the four winds.

She lowered herself to one knee and laughed a bit at finding herself in Blegripp's earlier position. Tine was by now sufficiently familiar with human customs of romance to understand the symbolism. His barbels quivered; those tufted ears twitched upwards.

Tracie grinned. "In that case, I have a proposal for *you.*"

Want to commemorate your T&T travel experience? Our 360-degree, 24/7 holovid package includes a premium 'bot team dedicated to recording your entire trip. Our discreet AI videographer will edit the footage, extracting a selection of social

media-ready clips—so everyone you know can follow your romantic getaway adventure. G, PG, PG-13, R, and X-rated options available.

The answer to the question of compatibility was an unqualified *yes,* Tracie was happy to confirm. She reflected on the events of the past several weeks with a smile as she approached the building which housed IPPP's headquarters. From her proposal at the Empire State Building, it flowed naturally to hold the wedding at a Las Vegas drive-through, officiated by an Elvis impersonator. The honeymoon was an old-fashioned affair, by intergalactic standards—just the two of them, holed up on Siluran's fifth moon.

Now they were back to reality, and back in business together. With significant differences: Tracie's first priority was IPPP, but she managed to carve out time to help Tine shake things up at T&T.

And we're really *gonna shake things up in the entire hospitality biz, too.* Tracie fiercely grinned as she exited the elevator. *Huh. A new neighbor?*

That certainly seemed to be the case: the vacant office just across the hall from IPPP finally had a tenant. Intrigued, Tracie approached a woman somewhere in her forties, cautiously supervising a maintenance 'bot. The latter hefted a sign into place, next to the suite's double-doors.

Tracie cleared her throat. The other woman turned. "Hello, neighbor!" Tracie introduced herself. The new tenant proved friendly enough, warmly shaking Tracie's hand.

"Camila Cohen," she smiled. "Just started my solo practice. Finally hanging out my shingle after *far* too many years at the firm!" She nodded with satisfaction as the 'bot drilled the remaining screw into place. "IPPP, huh? I'm a big fan of your organization." Camila waved a hand toward the other suite.

"Thanks," said a flattered Tracie.

Camila leaned forward confidentially. "You're building us ties with the rest of the galaxy. My folks think I'm nuts, but believe me: there's *great* business opportunity in a post-First Contact world. Especially now all the looky-loo tourism's simmered down, and we're seeing more offworlders coming here to settle down for good."

"Cohen Family Law," Tracie read off the sign with open curiosity. "You're an attorney?"

"That's right," Camila nodded. "Divorce attorney, to be precise—specializing in the brand-new field of interspecies divorce. A market *I* predict is about to...explode."

She winked.

END

BENNIE & THE EX

BY BRADY ROSE

"Wake up. We're dreaming," she whispered. Her voice was meek, but the words were ambiguous and horrifying.

Then, slowly and painfully, Ben returned from the darkness and woke up on a patch of grass that he never even remembered passing out on. The city's skyline was aglow with the first hints of dawn—a delicate blue behind heavy streaks of black cloud. Instantly sick, he hunched over to his side and vomited. Confused, with the dream slowly falling away to obscurity, he wiped his mouth with his sleeve and willed himself to his knees. He groggily took note of the park in which the night had apparently tossed him, and prayed no one was there watching. To his relief, nobody else was there.

...Not even Elton John, for which he was, strangely, very grateful.

SIDE ONE—A HALLOWEEN CRAWL.

Chloe was gone. That much was not in doubt whatsoever. Or at least it wasn't for those watching from the outside. For Ben, though, even months after their break-up, there still remained much that was in doubt. This is the story of Ben, and one fateful Halloween night, which occurred as he persisted in his efforts to pick up all of their broken pieces—both his and Chloe's. It would be a night of indulgences aplenty, through which the city would somehow come alive in fantastical ways: animals would speak, time would bend, and strange spirits would present themselves from strange places. It's a story of his longing and his selfishness; her beauty and her brokenness. It wasn't exactly right to say, however, that Ben was ever obsessed with *fixing* Chloe, more that he was happy to ignore that she ever needed any kind of *fixing* at all. But we've gotten ahead of ourselves...

* * *

It was ten to eleven, AM, Saturday morning, and Ben found himself day-drinking in some bar somewhere in the foothills of the city. He'd never seen the place before, even knowing his hometown as well as he did. It was a well-hidden dive and a comfortable distance from his apartment, where, for whatever reason, he didn't really care to be. Still a little early for the brunch crowd, there was only him and a few other parties-of-one: one working on a laptop, one watching TV, and another expectantly staring at the door. They each sipped their drinks and deliberated whatever had them in such a place at such an hour.

For Ben's part, he was sitting alone at the bar trying to get through a book that everyone seemed to love but he hated more with each page. It was oppressively Christian, with one-note characters that didn't seem to talk like anyone he'd ever met or heard about. But he didn't want to trash it until he finished it. About three quarters of the way through the book (and halfway through his second beer), he was confused by an author aiming to show God's ineffable mysteries, which could not possibly be contained in human conversation, while putting those exact words into God's mouth during His many conversations with the main character. The arrogance of man. Maybe he wouldn't finish it.

Empty as that bar was, there were still ample distractions to be had. None of them, though, were the text from his girl-friend, Chloe, that he waited for. No, she wasn't his girlfriend anymore, but it was still too hard to fully admit any different. They'd broken up months before, after she got sick—which was a term about which he had mixed feelings, but preferred to stick with anyway. Not because it wasn't true, but because the thought of there being any more to the break-up just hurt too much. Their friends said she was too afraid of commit-ment. They were surprised at how long he somehow did make it last. Contrary to how it may seem, he didn't want to think about it.

Three muted televisions hung in a row, above him and an ostentatious stack of booze. He let his eyes wander up to them. Baseball highlights rolled on the first. The batter sent one deep into right field. The crack of the bat and the roar of the crowd, despite the lack of volume, was crisp in his mind. Next to that was the scandal at the border, with some news crew touring some facility. Children were in tears behind grim chain-link barriers, separated from their parents. Ben couldn't imagine those sounds as easily as he could the sounds of baseball. On the last TV was hockey. The people in the crowd were on their feet, solemnly standing. The camera switched to ice level, where the players stood underneath Canada's flag, which was lowered from the rafters. The big Canadian scandal appeared to be all about how much funds the PM used towards a swing-set for his kids. That's what he read yesterday, anyway. *Point for Canada*, he figured.

He tapped his phone just in case anyone (Chloe) had texted. Nope. Radio silence. Resisting all urges to blow up her phone over the last few weeks, Ben had only sent the odd message here and there, to check in. He was just making sure she was okay, constantly telling himself that there wasn't anything more he was hoping for, but hoping all the same. Last night, a week almost to the day from his last, he'd given in and volleyed a fresh one before falling asleep.

"Going out tonight?" asked the bartender. They probably made her dress up, it being Halloween day, but she hadn't spared any expense. Her face was painted as a 'Day of the Dead' style white skull. Drawn purely in black was a hole overtop her nose along with two exaggerated circles surrounding her eyes, and a stitch-like pattern across her lips that extended from the corners of her mouth up through her cheeks. Modest paisley-like designs completed the look. She had pale skin and wore a tight black dress that Ben thought must have sucked to squeeze into in the morning. (It was perfectly late enough to be drinking though, he reasoned.)

"Don't know," he answered, unsure why he was lying. He knew full well that his best friend Jon was dragging him out later on. Halloween on a Saturday night, he wasn't going to take no for an answer. "You?"

"Nothing big," she replied. "Is it any good?"

"Pardon?" Ben asked, absentminded.

"The book," she clarified with a haunting smile.

"Oh. Yeah it is." Again, he lied. He wasn't sure why.

"What's it about?"

"Umm, it's about a guy finding God after his kid dies."

"Heavy," she said. "You like to read?"

After a second, he answered, "I think I like to be able to say I read more than I actually like reading."

She laughed. "Oh, really? Is that why you bring your books to the bar?"

He laughed back. "Maybe it is. I also just like to drink, but I like doing it alone as little as possible."

"Well cheers to that," she said and held up her glass of water. Ben grabbed his beer and returned the gesture.

Without much thought, he asked, "What would you say to hanging out with me tonight?"

"Can't," she replied in stride. "My friend and I are working on our resumes tonight. This place sucks."

Ben looked around sarcastically. "Are you supposed to say such things to the clientele?"

"Probably not," she sweetly replied and walked away.

Swing and a miss, he thought. All for the better though. He loved Chloe more now than the day she left him, but he had no idea what she was doing, and with whom. It was killing him.

Regardless, he knew what *he* was doing tonight, even though he didn't much care to go. Jon wasn't the kind of guy you said no to for a party you already—however grudgingly—said yes to.

Ben returned to his book to at least finish off that chapter. Christ, if he ever got the chance to challenge God on ripping away someone he loved, he hoped he wouldn't sound so robotic. What closed this ephemeral window of thoughts-that-did-not-include-Chloe, was the sound of her ringtone. He hadn't heard it in what seemed like ages. There on the screen, underneath a humbling stack of unanswered blobs, read:

Ben, I need you to move on and forget me.

Fuck.

He left the book on the counter along with a $20 bill. Leaving the bar, the sun was belligerent to his eyes and commanded the gap between the clouds and the buildings. A biting wind carried with it a message of winter's coming, which dug into his un-tempered bones. He put on his shades and attempted to re-examine the message, but found there wasn't any more to examine than there'd been a moment ago. And so he walked, with nowhere in particular he wanted to go.

Memories of drinking and laughing, and all the different ways that they'd opened themselves to each other, flooded his mind. He struggled to conjure a time together that they weren't having a blast—right up until she lost control of everything and was gone soon after. She was a completely different person then, someone Ben was told to expect but could never have fully prepared himself for. But, then and all the days since, he still believed that *his* Chloe was in there somewhere; that she still loved him and would find her way back. And he should be there waiting.

God damn, it was all so aggravating. Before she took that final turn, and she'd tell him that she was getting worse... once he could get to her, she'd brighten up. She'd kiss him and apologize and cry, and they'd screw and fall asleep in each other's arms. He thought he could be what she needed. Maybe he was wrong but he missed her dreadfully.

He kept on and tried his best to let the city be a distraction. The buildings around him were old and mostly brick, and they hadn't changed much over the years (although the company names and the corresponding colors overtop of them *were* constantly changing). He took note of empty windows, and 'For Lease' signs, and wondered why it was so hard to remember what had been there before.

Wherever he looked above him, the skyline was jagged against a cloudy sky. Below him, the sidewalks were cold and cracked, and littered with the golds and browns of crumpled leaves and cigarette filters. After a few blocks, he came across a homeless man who walked with a big stick while pushing a stroller that had three wheels and a spacious carriage. It was covered by a tarp and filled with who-knows-what. He locked eyes with Ben and slowed to a stop.

The man greeted him: "Hey brother. How's the battle?"

"I think I'm losing, my friend," said Ben.

"Yeah me too," he grumbled, dismissive but not altogether unfriendly. "Listen, what I need from you, brother, is just 76 cents."

Ben examined the old gentlemen, with his impressive but dirty beard and large hat, and wondered why he needed precisely 76 cents. Then he decided that he didn't care, and gave the guy all the change that he had in his pocket.

"God bless," said the man, and continued on his way. The sound of the walking stick and the stroller's wheels against the pavement was strangely rhythmic. Ben wished he was far drunker than he was, but he also found himself with a renewed interest in going out later. Yep, he'd hit the town and have a blast, and maybe the Universe would somehow relay that to

Chloe. Today was not the day to cut down his drinking (which was becoming a bit of an issue but he was okay). Though he did need to pace himself.

He continued on his undetermined path. He walked past shops and bars and fast food, and for some reason it felt like everybody was moving against him, as though he were headed towards a fire and they were running away. It was probably all in his head and he didn't feel all that heroic. He couldn't get his mind off of her. *What did she mean, forget me?* he thought. Well, he knew what she meant, but what did she *really* mean?

Their whole relationship replayed in his mind, over and over. Specific memories made him smile sadly. He remembered their first date, when the thought of really liking a girl was like an unexpected visit from a very old friend. Then there was them wandering the streets of Cabo: The time they accidentally got a little *too* drunk before blissfully losing track of the time and missing their flight. He dwelled on little love letters, and getting tripped up taking off her bra for the first time, and then how nervous he became like he hadn't done it a thousand times before. He thought about his fingers running up her thigh and hers on his, and feeling her wetness dripping down him and FUCK!

While he scavenged through all those thoughts, looking for something usable, his feet had brought him to where the city grew thickest and the skyscrapers all but formed a canopy overhead. Wood, brick and steel had at some point welcomed polished stone and immaculate glass panels voraciously into the fold. He could easily watch another version of himself walking alongside him, regarding him strangely as he moved, pristine within whatever surface he followed. Was there loyalty in those mimicked movements or was it more like derision? He wasn't sure.

He was well into the financial district now. Five days a

week, the bustle on 8th Avenue would be much heavier. There'd be a sea of white-collars to contend with, and they'd buy and sell amidst the chaos. And then, once they were done for the day, most of the establishments there would happily get them as drunk as anywhere else for twice the cost. But this was the morning of the sixth day (as God decreed), and though there were still people of all sorts scurrying about their business, it was relatively calm. So Ben found himself simply envisioning all that action, impassive and objective, almost like watching the empty field the night before a big game.

After a few more aimless blocks, it occurred to him that he was close to the casino where he used to work. Maybe that's where his subconscious mind had been taking him all along.

Sure, he thought. *Why not.* Luke, assuming he was there, would definitely have some thoughts on the matter of Chloe. Ben was curious to find out what they'd be, since he hadn't seen Luke for some time and had not broken the news. Regardless, Ben was always happy to bend Luke's ear. He was the kind of guy whose endless mirth and laid back nature made any situation seem less important. And so he cut south at the next block, and made off towards his old stomping grounds.

* * *

Twenty to twelve AM, on a day almost four years removed from Ben's last day of employment at *Big Sky Casino*. And there it was, in his sights: A sprawled grey building underneath grey clouds, planted on the edge of what could still be considered downtown. A familiar sign hung above the entrance and was easily visible from that distance—giant, red, scripted letters, and all of it flashed along every contour. He was so relieved once he'd finally built up enough clients to leave that place, where he worked security through college and then a few years after.

This was a few years longer than Ben planned, after a career in football proved itself more chimeric than he originally projected. He missed competing and lived in perpetual regret at not taking it seriously enough. If he was being honest, he also missed the casino a lot of the time. He later turned to personal training, and found that he was pretty good at it. When he left college he figured maybe one day he'd open a gym. Workout whenever he wanted; be his own boss. Sounded good.

Nowadays he found himself letting that possibility slip away. Mostly he lectured folks with varying levels of interest, but deep pockets, on how to do a rep, all the while giving nutritional advice that he himself had forgone a while back. The hypocrisy of it mingled with his dwindling passion and made him feel empty. Not like back in the day, playing ball and training with Luke, who'd started with him at the casino and now worked his way up to Security Director. He was a giant of an Aussie who came across the pond to train as a pro wrestler first, and do basically anything for a story second. The first he hadn't quite achieved yet; the second he'd accomplished in spades.

When Ben came through the main entrance he was greeted by a young, portly security guard who he'd never seen before. The guard wore a tilted cowboy hat and jeans that were far, far too tight. "Got your ID on you, sir?" he warmly inquired.

Ben dug out his wallet and handed the ID over. "Luke in today?" Ben asked.

"Not sure," the kid absently replied and turned the card over in his hands. He examined it as though it were a gold coin, and he, the buyer.

For a few moments they stood there in silence. Ben

patiently waited as his credentials were vetted. Finally, the kid looked up, but with a stern look on his face.

"All good?" Ben asked.

Suddenly his face brightened into something like a young, white, cowboy Buddha. "All good," he confirmed.

"Thanks," Ben said, a little hesitantly, and took the card back. He made his way inside and pulled out his phone to text Luke.

Working today?

He took a short walk around the casino floor, which as always was a cacophony of bells and lights and virtual dealers calling *him* a cowboy and asking him to sit down. The smell of it all was forgotten and once again strange inside his nose. Roaming the floor brought memories of twelve hour shifts spent watching gamblers and drinkers, partyers and loners, and, mainly, shooting the shit with his co-workers. It was a comfortable job, but comfortable like sitting on the couch, enjoying most of the days but always wondering when he would do something real with his life and what that might look like. Still early in the day, the only people there were seniors who had probably all arrived on the same bus. Eventually he took a seat on a progressive slot, thinking maybe the Universe might cut him some slack.

Thirty bucks in, with no slack to be had, he was joined by an elderly couple. The lady asked him if they could sit down at the empty machines beside him. The man, sitting on a scooter that he pulled to a stop beside her, looked surly and was silent.

Ben said, "No problem."

The lady moved the far chair aside for the man, and took the middle one for herself.

"Thanks so much," she amiably said.

After a brief few moments of silent button pushing, she

turned to Ben. Her face was beaming, and she asked, "So what's your name, Sunshine?"

Ben was taken aback, as that was the name his Grandma always called him. Was it less special than he'd thought? Did all old women call young men Sunshine? Something to ponder. "Ben," he answered.

"Benjamin," affirmed the old lady. Wonderful to meet you. I'm Daisy. This is my husband Jason."

"—Jay!" he cut in. His eyes were glued to the rows of spinning trinkets on the screen in front of him.

Ben took a moment before he mused: "Jay and Daisy? Just like..."

Looking confused, she put in: "Just like what, Sunshine?"

"Just like The Great Gatsby."

"Oh, we don't really watch movies anymore," Daisy dismissively declared.

"Fair enough."

Just then his phone buzzed.

Hey mate, on my way in now. You there?

Yeah I'm here, Ben replied.

See you soon.

"Is that your girlfriend?" Daisy probed, with a delighted grin that highlighted the creases of her skin and a copious layer of lipstick.

"I wish," he responded, before realizing that he should've learned by now to be careful what he wished for. Chloe didn't seem to have anything to say that he wanted to hear.

"Awe, Sunshine," she said and patted him on the back. "Handsome devil like you, you'll find someone soon."

"Thank you."

"Would ya believe Jason was once quite dashing? Weren't ya, hun?"

He grunted.

"And everyone loved him! I tell ya, he'd throw a party, half the city would show up!"

Was this old lady fucking with him?

"Wouldn't know it looking at him now though, would you?" she cackled.

"Dammit woman," he snapped, shaking his head.

She leaned into Ben and whispered, "He's so dang grumpy these days! Ever since the dementia started, I tell ya. At least when he can't remember things he's much more agreeable. Ah well."

Down to only a few credits, she spun the last of her reels. Nothing. "Well, I have to go to the bathroom," she announced, and stood up. "Don't go anywhere, hun."

Jay grumbled once more as she walked away.

"I only forget little things," he broached, once she was out of sight. "Turning off the faucet, the day of the week, something someone told me the night before. But that's how it starts though, I guess."

"I'm sorry, man."

"Not your fault."

Remembering his great grandmother who was senile his entire life, never knew who he was, and died at 102, Ben asked, "You ever forget who people are?"

"Like her, you mean? I wish I did! Ha!" he chuckled until he started coughing.

Amused and perturbed, Ben wished the old man luck and stepped away. He made his way to the bar at the center of all the goings on, which they'd creatively called the Center Bar.

"Hey Ben!" beamed the bartender, a young girl named Sandy who was tall and ultra-friendly, with dancer's legs and cat's eyes. Ben liked her a lot but also investigated her once for short-pouring customers and taking the remnant cash in tips.

He'd given the managers the ammo to fire her, but they chose not to. She didn't have to know that.

"Hey, what's up?"

"Same old," she answered. "I heard you, like, joined the army or something?"

Ben laughed, taken aback. "Joined the army? Who told you that?"

"I don't know. Just what someone said I guess."

"Huh."

"So you didn't?"

"No. No I did not." Strange rumors were known to spread in that place, but joining the army, that was a novel one. He wondered where it came from. "What's new with you?" he asked.

"Not much. Still here, obviously. Had to quit ballet."

"Oh, really?"

"Yeah. They say I'm too tall. There's nobody to pair with. So yeah, nothing I can do about that I guess," she concluded, shrugging sadly.

"Yeah, I guess not."

"Drink?" she exclaimed, a fresh smile on her face to help change the subject.

"God, yes."

"What ya having?"

"I'll take a Vodka and Tonic."

"—Make that two please, Sandy!" came an Australian voice from behind him. He turned to see Luke walk up to the bar. "Mate! How ya goin'?"

They hugged and it was like hugging an overgrown, but familiar and well-groomed, koala bear.

"I'm alright, pal."

"Just alright? That's no good!"

"Yeah, well."

Sandy cut in with their drinks. "Two Vodka Tonics, to set you on your feet again," she genially announced.

"Put it on my account please, Sandy," Luke said.

"Ok," she replied, leaving them with a skilled twirl that she was decidedly not too tall for.

The two of them took a seat overlooking a ring of empty blackjack tables. Dealers stood behind them, shuffling their feet and their cards restlessly, all awaiting their first action of the day. So far, the old-timers weren't biting.

"You're looking pretty down. Somethin' on your mind, mate?"

After taking a sip of his drink, Ben replied, "Well, Chloe and I broke up."

"Ah, no shit."

"Yeah. A couple months ago."

"Fuck. Well she was always a tough girl to hold on to, right? You knew that."

He said that as though it should make matters any easier. It didn't.

"Yeah."

"And you guys weren't together all that long. You'll be back at it soon."

About that: It was true. They had only been together a year and that was him graciously rounding up. And Ben knew that a lot of his friends had misgivings about her. She had a past, of which people weren't inclined to let go but we won't get into it here. Regardless, Chloe told Ben everything he needed to hear without him ever having to ask. She was a stunner, too—drop dead gorgeous—and nothing short of a wild child. The fun they were capable of together was inspiring. Ben knew that Luke, and others, suspected that the excitement of all that was what he held on to, more than anything else. But that never mattered as much to Ben as it seemed to for them. She had the purest heart of anyone he'd ever met. And he didn't know how to explain that he wasn't the first to say 'I love you,' or put into words for Luke the life that they'd planned for themselves.

In Ben's mind, it was all set in stone. But Chloe had her own seasons, and they came and they went, some harsher than others. Some were even harsher than anyone else knew. He couldn't deny, though, that holding on to her was sometimes like trying to capture light in a jar—so many signs whispered it wasn't going to work, all of them ignored.

"Yeah," was once again all Ben's brain could send to his lips.

"So what are you up to tonight?"

"Jon's dragging me on a pub crawl."

"Sweet! I miss that big, gay fucker!" exclaimed Luke. "How is he?"

Ben was familiar enough with his friend's vernacular to know that he meant no offence. In fact, Luke loved the guy. When he first started at the Casino, Luke would always call Ben a 'sweet cunt.' Ben wasn't sure how to take it at the time, but he soon began to realize that—outside of being grotesquely *problematic* to some—it was a supreme, Australian compliment.

"He seems good," Ben responded. "Still big and gay!"

"Excellent, excellent," said Luke, pleased. All 260 pounds of him held up a highball glass, and he was sipping the drink from a tiny straw. His long, blonde hair was untied—which was unusual, outside the ring—and dangled all the way to his chest. He was so literally a pro wrestler squeezed into a suit for a corporate role. It wasn't hard to imagine him walk into the ring a huge superstar, surrounded by thunderous cheers, but so far it just hadn't happened for him.

The two of them talked a little more about days gone by and how things hadn't gone exactly according to plan as they entered their thirties. But Luke still had designs on wrestling

stardom and the way he spoke about it, undeterred and passionate, reinvigorated Ben's own dreams. After not too long, though,
Luke said that he had to go. Apparently he'd come in early for
an investigation into who'd been spreading their own feces
across the walls of the upper administration hallways. Or
maybe it wasn't their own feces, but feces nonetheless. That
much didn't seem in doubt.

God, the more things change...

* * *

Twenty-five after five, PM, later that night, and Ben was back
in his apartment. After scrambling to tidy up the place—which
mainly required he disappear a sobering collection of empty
bottles and cans—he now sat on his couch and waited for Jon.
In an act of abject self-torment, and against all his better
instincts, he was also reading a note. Re-reading actually, for
the millionth time. It was the last of the notes that Chloe had
written him, and on this day, he failed to stop himself from
unearthing it. He did try, to be fair, but it was calling out to him
from the depths of the junk drawer—beating like the god-damn
Tell-Tale Heart. And it was a heart, too. A paper heart, valen-
tines style. The heart read:

To Ben,
Words can't express how much you mean to me. I didn't think
men like you existed and now that I've finally found you I don't
plan on ever letting go. I just really wanted you to know that. I
love you so much.
Chloe

She wrote that two weeks before she left. There were no
lies in those words—that much Ben knew for certain. But he

also knew that Chloe was getting worse when it was written. The unfortunate truth was that, though she meant every word, it was likely written for herself as much as for Ben. It was Chloe versus her urge to bail, reified and suspended in time. Ben's fingers followed her handwriting, trying to soak up the past through the ink. It was no use, obviously. Just then, finally, Jon called to be let in. Probably the garbage was the best place for that heart, but back in the drawer it went.

Moments after buzzing him into the building, Jon burst through Ben's door in a lurid display of yellows and reds, along with a chest full of hair that could not be ignored.

"Bennie!" he screamed, the highest pitch he could muster.

Ben laughed harder than he had in months. Somewhere, Jon had found himself the most garish yellow suit that Ben ever saw, the whole thing studded in red rhinestones from top to bottom. Already balding at 29, he'd parted what little hair was left up top, and carved out a set of long, bushy side-burns from the beard he'd been sporting when Ben saw him last. Along with a pair of gaudy, star-shaped pink glasses, the effect was pretty amazing. By day, Jon was a very tall banker with an affinity for weed and investment strategies. He'd effectively transformed himself into a young Elton John. With the afore-mentioned chest hair, the choice to go shirtless underneath the jacket also helped. He stood there in pose with a wide grin on his face while Ben tried re-collect himself.

"Wow. Nicely done, buddy."

"Damn right," said Jon as he closed the door and strutted towards him. "Wish I could say the same for you."

He wasn't wrong. Regarding costume, Ben hadn't been anywhere near as creative. He'd lost his taste for Halloween first after elementary school, back when his heart was set only on candy, and then again after a string of costume parties in college, back when his heart was set on equally empty things.

He was wearing an old, frilly pullover shirt which he'd managed to unearth from a thrift shop a few days before, with a blue bandana tied over his head. A pirate hat rested on the kitchen counter between them, waiting, calling out to him: *This is stupid.*

"You look like you're playing guitar in a Prince tribute band!" mocked his friend.

"I'm a fucking pirate dude," Ben proclaimed, defending himself. "See the hat!" he added, pointing to it.

"Right," Jon said. "Well, good enough. Just happy to get you out."

At that, Ben changed the subject. "So why Elton John?"

"So that I can sing BENNIE!" he bawled as he opened up a flask from his inside pocket.

Ben chuckled, and gladly took a swig that was offered to him. Jon sprawled onto his couch and landed with his arms behind his head and legs crossed. He seemed to be channeling his costume's bearer, and picked up a little extra swagger along the way.

"Place looks good."

"Thanks," said Ben, grateful he'd mustered the energy to clean. "What's the plan?"

"Bus picks us up from the gay bar at nine," he said.

"Oh. *Great.*"

"What, you have a problem with the partying gay community?" Jon accusingly barked.

"Fuck off," retorted Ben.

They killed time with a couple more beers and chatted over the white noise of the television. Jon lamented Ben's metabolism, which always seemed to treat alcohol as though it were water. He also continued to criticize the banality of his costume, but was taking it pretty easy on him all things considered. He said that they'd have to find him some eye-liner later on, about which Ben was mostly ambivalent. Ben skillfully avoided the subject of the breakup altogether. Jon was happy to oblige, but, knowing him, he probably wasn't sure if the avoidance pointed to Ben's positive acceptance or continued resistance.

Instead, Ben's morning meeting with Luke led him and Jon to re-live old stories from their casino days. Stories like the kid they arrested who took off running, hands cuffed behind his back, in sort of a half sprint / half hobble. He'd made it a good few blocks before they were able to chase him down. Or the one where Wayne, a five-foot-nothing lifetime card player, got hammered and hijacked their limo, only to drive it to the next closest casino and crash it onto their front steps. He claimed he was over-served, took a deal, and got a slap on the wrist. Then, of course, there was also the newly divulged mystery of who'd been shitting in the administration hallways. Jon, somewhat curiously, had some earnest theories on the matter. Before long they realized that they'd lost track of time, and they should probably get going.

And so it was off to the gay bar, for a Pirate and Elton John, to see where this Hallowed night would take them.

Seven O'clock, PM, and by that time the Halloween atmosphere had begun to impose itself on the streets of downtown. Dusk gave way to night and a general sense of oncoming hijinks was unmistakably in the air. They passed by witches and superheroes, minions and cross-dressers, sexy-this and sexy-that. The most clever dressers-up collected high-fives and fist pounds as they went. Jon was doing pretty well as far as that went. Despite the cold, or maybe in spite of it, scantily clad women were unavoidable no matter where he looked. They weren't doing anything for Ben, though, except reinforcing that none of them could hold a candle to Chloe—sweet Chloe. All the parts of their time together seemed to be getting brighter in his memory as the days mounted—the good and the bad. It sounded like a good thing but didn't really feel that way.

As they walked, Jon lit up a joint and inhaled deeply. "I can feel you thinking about her, man," he broached, accusingly, before exhaling.

"Yeah, well, I'm doing my best not to."

He passed Ben the joint and he took a couple drags himself.

"You just have to make a conscious decision to be over her," Jon explained, almost didactic in his delivery. "Take me, for example. My relationship just ended. No problem! Done and done, next chapter. And we were together way longer than you guys."

"Yeah, you caught him with his ex on Google Street View!" Ben reminded him. "It's a little bit different."

"Technology is a wonderful thing!" he responded, earnestly. He took the joint back before adding, "Careless motherfucker!"

As they continued, they began to hear a metallic voice that rose steadily above it all. Rounding the corner of the block, they saw a modest gathering set up at the edge of a grocery store's parking lot across the street. Above the heads, standing atop a milk-box, was a large woman who harangued into a megaphone. Behind her was a giant, makeshift cross erected with what looked like four-by-four fenceposts. She spoke with an impassioned, measured cadence. But amplified, it became a loud, indefatigable screech. Each word followed the next with its own heavy punctuation. All of it gave her words a disturbing, chant-like cruelty. An entourage of silent supporters, maybe a dozen or so, all nodded and cheered around her. Most of them held homemade signs, which were made with varying degrees of effort. Of the sparse collection of onlookers, many seemed less of an audience and more just held up from wherever it was they were going. Ben couldn't yet make out exactly what the woman was saying, but judging by the giant cross behind her, and the small book she clutched tightly in her free hand, he could probably guess.

"You've gotta be fuckin' kidding me," said Jon as he sped up his gait. Ben matched it, and wondered what exactly might happen but felt very much helpless against it.

Just as many of those who were still listening began to move on, Ben and Jon came to a stop on the opposite side of the road. The woman's words became clear. There they stood, a pirate and Elton John, taking in the sermon of a strident preacher atop her milk-box pulpit on 8ᵗʰ Street.

"In the Book of Leviticus, God clearly calls for the death of those living in sin who will not repent!" she crowed, to shouts of agreement behind her, groans and laughter ahead.

"Fornicators outside of marriage, you are living in sin! Homosexuals! You are living in sin!"

"I guess we're both fucked," Ben muttered. He looked up to his friend, who, although as gay as they came, took it all in without giving away much emotion. He only intently watched, arms folded, and absorbed the scene through pink, star-shaped lenses.

"Please, we beg you, do not consign yourself to eternity in Hell!" she bawled.

"Didn't Jesus say 'let he who is without sin cast the first stone'?" someone shouted.

As though the question were scripted in her mind, the woman didn't miss a beat. She went on: "Of course he did. But we are not here to cast stones! We are here to try to save these sinners before it's too late!"

Scattered laughter followed. Someone shouted, "What the hell is wrong with you?"

Then a thin man with long, straight auburn hair and a matching beard approached them with a small pamphlet. "Please, come to our mass tomorrow, hear what we have to say," he offered in a magnanimous tone.

Defiantly, Ben stated, "That's not going to happen." Annoyingly, the man only said "God Bless," and continued on to the next person.

"We can't let this stand, bud," said Jon with cool determination.

"Come on man, you can't debate these people," said Ben.

"I ain't debating anyone," he replied, and turned to look Ben in the eye. "I want that sign."

Ben's eyes followed Jon's hand, which was pointed towards one of the woman's supporters—a man in an ill-fitting suit that looked like he'd probably been wearing it since the eighties. He was waving a large, wooden sign back and forth as though it were a flag. In rainbow colors, it read: FAGS are BEASTS.

"Seriously?"

"Oh yeah," Jon confirmed.

"Alright. I can't wait to see this."

"You have to get it, man. I will run distraction."

"What? You want it! You go get it!"

"We need a distraction. You suck at that sort of thing. You're too shy and mopey."

"What the hell, man!" Ben cried, offended.

"Just grab the fuckin' sign, dude," Jon ordered before moving in.

"God dammit," muttered Ben, a strange flicker of guilt in his mind.

"...and grab my clothes," added Jon.

"Wait, what?"

* * *

With placid, almost robotic resolve, Jon carried himself across the street and towards that demonstration, disrobing further with each step. On pure reaction Ben followed, bending to gather each Elton style garment that Jon tossed behind him. Ben hesitated at the boxers, which were pretty nondescript compared to the rest, but he used the yellow pant legs to bundle them up without them ever having to touch his skin. As he did, a jeep came to a sudden stop in front of him and indignantly honked. Ben scrambled out of its way as shrieks and laughter came from all those around. Some fled, some pulled out their phones. Others sought some kind of cover.

There was no point in protesting when his best friend was this committed, and so Ben never even tried, as much as he would've liked to. Ass-naked ahead of him, there was Jon, crossing through a shallow covering of water on the edge of the road, atop which his feet splashed ever so softly. Then he stepped over the curb and onto the sidewalk, where he pulled a thin branch from a row of shrubs before continuing on his path. Ben watched Jon fidget with that branch, seemingly trying to tie its ends together, making a ring.

Fuck sakes.

Jon found no resistance as he stepped onto the woman's milk box. She staggered back, aghast, her microphone absently falling to her side. She surrendered her territory without any words at all; her jaw was on the pavement. Taking position above them all, Jon placed the makeshift, leafy crown atop his head and took a position against that cross, one leg overtop the other, his arms outstretched. Ben marveled at the audacity of his best friend—the balls that guy had (figuratively speaking). But he shook that away in time to charge that one acolyte with that one sign which he was tasked with snatching. Ben moved against that unsuspecting man so swiftly, so aggressively, and so without thought, that he later questioned the agency he ever even had in the matter.

But he got that sign.

There were screams and there was laughter, and several confrontations ensued throughout the scene. Photos were taken; video recorded. It was anarchy. All the while Jon hung above them, silent and stoic—the backs of his hands firmly planted against the wood of that cross, his nature laid bare, and his head held low in sorrow.

...Until, finally, they ran.

* * *

Ten to eight, PM, and the two of them had at last reached the gay bar. They entered triumphantly, with Jon thankfully clothed and with his trophy rested upon a shoulder. His suit was a little disheveled now; his skin was flushed and his hair was messy across his brow. It was evident something had gone down.

Jon brought that sign to the ceiling. "We're fucking beasts!" he declared to roars of laughter and cheers.

"FAGS ARE BEASTS, FAGS ARE BEASTS," they all chanted, as the kind of night that Ben had gotten himself into began to materialize.

Jon's entrance (and costume) had made him a de-facto rock star, and the two of them pressed through a mass of partyers that were eager to give props and take a share of the joke for themselves. Jon pumped the sign proudly, and each of them collected praise like they were politicians entering a rally, or the Rolling Stones taking the stage impromptu in some London dive bar—which, incidentally, Ben read once that they were wont to do.

"You see, I told you it'd be worth it," Jon shouted above the noise.

"Well, it wasn't worth seeing that distraction of yours!" Ben countered. "Won't get that out of my mind anytime soon!"

"Oh grow up!" he screamed and leaned into Ben's ear as they neared the bar and the music grew louder. "And let's do some drinking! You ready or what?"

"Always," Ben answered, and meant it.

The people had more or less dispersed, either back to their tables or to the dance floor. In a little more than an hour, a bus would arrive to ferry them off to the next spot. This meant their job was twofold: Find their wrist-bands, which Jon said they would need for the bus, and keep their buzz going.

The bar was tended by a tandem of a girl and a guy. The girl worked the far side. Dark-skinned with frizzy hair that was tied back underneath a policeman's hat, she managed several orders with ease. She wore aviator sunglasses and tied her button-down shirt in a knot atop her chest. She even had on a duty belt, complete with a gun holster and a baton, all of which looked curiously legitimate. Closer to them was the guy, who was shirtless and had his face painted like the lead singer of KISS. Ben couldn't remember his name—the one with the star over his eye. Surely a wig, his hair was thick, black and hung down to his lower back. He served a group to their left as they waited. Ben could just barely make out what they said over the music.

"Hey, maybe in the morning I'll wake up with a star on my ass!" shouted one of the guys as the bartender passed him his beer.

"Yeah, in your dreams!" he countered. He took the cash dispassionately and glided over to Ben and Jon. In a manner that was somehow both enthusiastic and disinterested, he asked, "What can I get you?"

Jon ordered four beers for the two of them and asked about the wristbands, which the bartender said they'd get from the bus. While they waited, the other bartender approached them, smiling.

"Very nice, Elton!" she complimented Jon.

"Why thank you!"

"*You* kinda half-assed it though!" she broke it to Ben.

Jon laughed. "I told him the same damn thing!"

"You definitely need some makeup!" she declared. "Don't move!"

She pranced to the far side of the bar and dug into her purse. Ben looked over to Jon, who was predictably delighted to meet such a congenial spirit. The guy slipped past behind her with their beers and placed them on the counter. Then, returning with a clutch of make-up, the girl instructed Ben to lean over the counter. He did as she asked, and she started with a stick of eye-liner.

"Since when did pirates start wearing make-up anyway!" Ben wondered aloud.

"Shut up and hold still!" she demanded.

When she'd finished with the eye shadow, she snapped the case shut, beaming. "There you go, all set!" she announced. With that, she seamlessly returned to her work.

Jon gave him a pat on the back, and they made off with their beers. As Ben took his first sip, though, he was bumped into and spilled half of it down his chest, which was barely protected by that thin, cotton shirt.

"Oh shit, I'm so sorry," came a soft, feminine voice along with an even softer hand on his arm. Looking up, Ben came face-to-face with Snow White—or at least a beautiful facsimile of her. He may not have put it together in his mind, her costume, had it not been for the file of dwarves who walked past her. One after the other they sauntered by, dwarf by dwarf, either indifferent to the spilled drink or simply oblivious. Ben guessed the latter, as they all wore enormous dwarf heads with enormous dwarf hats, each with very tiny eye-holes that he could only imagine made it tricky to see anything at all except what happened to be exactly in front of them. To Ben, they looked like bobble-head dolls brought to life. The beer dripping down his chest was unpleasant, cold and sticky, but he found it hard to be upset given the prettiness of the girl responsible and the hilarity of her posse.

"It's all good," said Ben. "Don't even worry about it."

"Are you sure," asked Snow White culpably. Her rosy cheeks failed to hide the dimples that bookended her smile. "Can I buy you a new one?"

Ben lifted his other hand. "It's fine. I have a back-up," he amiably said.

She countered: "No, no. I owe you one." With that, one of the dwarves grabbed her by the hand and pulled her away. "Find me later!" she yelled as she was whisked into the crowd.

Shouldn't be too hard, thought Ben.

After a couple more drinks and some top-notch people watching, it was almost time to expect their bus. Ben and his friend made their way downstairs to find the washroom.

"Are you gonna carry that thing with you all night?" asked Ben, referring to the sign that Jon still held over his shoulder.

"I don't know," Jon answered. "Maybe I'll take it home. We'll see."

The door marked 'Gentlemen' was politely held open for them by a lady with angel wings as she was leaving. Once inside, Ben made his way to the urinal and did his thing, but Jon went straight to the counter and set the FAGS ARE BEASTS sign against the wall. Once finished, Ben proceeded to the sink in time to watch Jon catalogue the contents of a small plastic bag.

"What you got going on there?" asked Ben, knowing full well the answer.

"Mushrooms, buddy," answered Jon enthusiastically.

This was a psychedelic bridge too far for Ben, but he was happy to watch his best friend trip out for the rest of the night. He washed his hands as Jon tossed a couple of the tiny, dried flakes into his mouth and Ben wondered with amusement whether the actual Elton John had done this very same thing in some other seedy bathroom of some other bar. He guessed that he probably had.

"How about that girl, Snow White? Pretty cute," Jon broached, chomping away.

"Sure," said Ben. Truth be told she probably was a girl he would pursue if he wasn't still so hooked on Chloe. Admitting as much to Jon was like admitting failure, though, and seemed oddly treasonous. Yes, Chloe left him, but only Ben knew just how much she was coming apart at the edges. He couldn't tell anyone the messy details without betraying her and so he never did. It meant hanging himself out to dry, a little bit. Everyone including Jon thought they'd maybe fought too much, or Ben wasn't attentive enough, or just couldn't handle such a free spirit. The truth was that Chloe was falling apart as a person and Ben didn't know how to keep her together, as hard as he tried. God he tried. But he also indulged in her wildness and happily matched her drinking, knowing how much it could mess with her mind and her meds but always pushing that from his mind. The biggest trouble was that he knew in his heart she still loved him.

As Ben's resolve to be the one to rein Chloe in was returning, Jon interrupted. "Come on," he teased. "I saw that big ol' pirate smile you gave her." He pinched Ben's cheek like he was his grandson.

"I didn't come here to pick up girls, man," Ben argued, and

then swatted Jon's hand away. "I came here to get messed up and forget about real life for a night."

"Says the guy that won't eat any of my mushrooms," retorted Jon, smiling. "Alright. Let's get going."

Walking up the stairs, Ben couldn't help but linger on a memory—a disagreement between him and Chloe that led to them bitterly leaving a party early. It was a house party on a T-shirt-at-midnight kind of night at the end of spring. Ben had walked out to the backyard of that house—a friend of a friend's —looking for her. He found her with her nose held a few inches above a carefully prepped line of white powder on the glass patio table. She looked up to him with a smile that he'd interrupted, but somehow still seemed meant for him and him alone. And he scolded her, a glare he intentionally left unveiled. He'd just watched Jon take a bump himself, not too long before that. But he judged *her*, harshly—quite the opposite sort of thing on which their relationship was founded. Storming off, he'd more or less left Chloe to her own devices, but at that point they were inseparable and he knew she'd follow. She wouldn't give in silently, though. Never silently.

Why was she judged so differently from his friends? He never partook in hard drugs himself but was always happy to watch others indulge. He told himself it was her mental health he was concerned with, but was that really it?

The craziness that ensued that night was difficult for Ben to describe, looking back. Just a barrage of irrational screaming (and flying kitchen utensils) that couldn't be fought, against which one could only take cover. Once they were finally in bed, each lying beside the other, drunk, pissed off and silent, Ben spent sleepless hours brooding on what may have been the right decision—at least the less volatile decision. Should he have given in, let her fall back into old addictions? Or admit to himself that the true reason for scolding her was because he'd found her opening a door that he couldn't follow her through. *Anger is the loss of control,* he'd once heard.

When they woke the next morning, they agreed to go on as if no argument had ever happened, much less been settled. Chloe rightly felt judged and controlled, but she also knew her behavior after the fact was past the point of extreme. She felt ashamed and the two of them called it a wash. The emotions that memory left behind were malleable: All the things between sadness, righteousness, and regret. He felt wronged by the Universe, which lately seemed even less fair than he'd ever before considered. He could separate all those emotions or mix them together, waiting for any combination to make sense. Returning to the bar from those stairs, he sloshed them around like a stress ball in his fist.

And then he invigorated himself with more alcohol and hit the dance-floor. He discovered that the girls there were all too happy to dance close to him, which helped to loosen him up and restore some of his ego, but he was forgetting in the moment that they more than likely thought he was gay. Jon took up a corner of the floor to himself and danced in a kind of subdued frenzy, spinning slow and continuous, with a beer in one hand and his sign in the other. His eyes were happily closed. Twice, Ben spotted the same guy—dressed up as a fireman—try to join him but fail to find an opening. He ultimately gave up.

Eventually there came a call over the sound system for all those taking part in the crawl to begin to exit the bar and find the bus, which was now parked outside. Jon didn't seem to have heard it, and continued to dance as though the music had never even cut out. When Ben tapped him on the shoulder he stopped at once, but only stared at him vacantly. His eyes seemed to look through Ben like he were on some other plane of existence. But then he snapped out of it and grinned, shouting: "What's going on, bud? Having fun?"

"We have to go, man! Bus is here!"

"Shit!" Jon exclaimed with muted surprise.

They left that bar and found the bus outside, almost fully loaded up. Presently, the last of Snow White's dwarves were squeezing their giant heads through the doors. Snow White was nowhere to be seen. Ben figured she must've already got on ahead of them. Beside the front of the bus stood a tiny old man dressed in black pants and a black vest, with a white shirt tucked underneath and a grey flat cap atop his head. With his hands comfortably in his pockets, he stood there and watched the people file past with little reaction to the absurdity of their appearances. Beside him there was a girl, shorter even than himself, who had a round figure. She wore glasses and an orange uniform that was much too big for her—a collared polo shirt and dress pants. On her head, to account for the Halloween spirit, she wore a set of playboy-style bunny ears. She had a fistful of long plastic bands in one hand and a clipboard in the other.

Just as they began towards that steel chariot, there came a very loud scream from across the street.

"Dad! What the fuck are you doing here?"

Everyone around heard it and a general commotion ensued, all turning their heads to attention. The yelling had come from the same young man dressed as the firefighter, who Ben had spotted earlier. Standing in the middle of the road, he screamed at an older man on the sidewalk. Evidently his father, the man was very dapper, proper looking, and conspicuously out of place in that crowd. He had close-cropped, salt-and-pepper hair and wore a blue golf shirt above a pair of khakis.

At the top of his lungs, unconcerned with the crowd, he

reviled his son. "Like hell I'm letting you do this tonight! You're coming with me!"

Compelled, Ben and Jon slowly moved closer to the action. Inside the bus, many disparate faces pressed against the glass, all of them fighting for a decent view.

"Do what?" challenged the son.

"Lead this fucking lifestyle, with these people! This isn't how you were raised!"

With that, the crowd was confirmed their villain in the show, and vigorously booed.

"Oh fuck you, Dad!" screamed the faux-firefighter, and the boos turned to raucous cheers.

"What did you just say?" bellowed the dad, his eyes wide and disbelieving. He removed his reading glasses and stepped onto the street.

"You heard me!" his son shouted. There was a slight tremble in his voice but he held his ground.

"Oh shit," muttered Ben.

And Jon beside him: "They're gonna..."

And with that, sure enough, the son shoved the dad and they both started swinging. It was a full on fist fight in the middle of the street, and nobody was really sure if it was appropriate to interfere or simply stand by and let the two of them work it out. A cab screeched to a halt as the dad had his son in a headlock and fed shots to his midsection. The driver began honking, which was enough of a distraction for the kid to break the headlock and deliver a haymaker straight to his father's chin. The dad went down, and hit the pavement amidst the hazy glare of the cab's headlights. The crowd bellowed; the son immediately bent down to check on his father. Most were ambivalent viewers, but some moved in to try and help the situation, somehow. At that moment, though, there came a dull voice from behind them, which the two of them barely registered above the disturbance.

"Alright! Last call for the club crawl. Let's go!"

It had come from the tiny girl beside the bus—the one with the bracelets. The driver had already taken his seat inside. Ben took one last glance at the intersecting road, on which more cars had stopped and more people joined a growing circle that helped the father to his feet. He noticed then that the firefighter had slipped away and staggered towards them, under the aid of two others. Apparently, he was still intent on defying his father's orders. As he passed by Ben could see the tears that were built up in his eyes, despite his obvious efforts to hold them back.

Jon said, "This is going to be a fucked up night."

With that, they collected their wrist-bands and followed the firefighter aboard.

Inside that bus was a party, and every jostle of it bent Ben's ear and whispered that he was already a little bit drunk. Beside him, Jon's head absently nodded to the electronic music that played. The lenses of his glasses hid his eyes and reflected the passing lights of the city, like shooting stars within the stars. His prized anti-gay sign lay propped between his legs and against the seat ahead. All around them there was screaming, laughing, dancing and general drunken revelries. Everyone was someone else, but still themselves somewhere underneath.

Ben checked his phone. Nine Twenty-Four, PM. The battery was at only seventeen percent. *Shit.* He forgot to charge it.

They came to a stop outside a bar called 'Ranchers.' Ben knew it well; it was a popular spot with his friends after high school. Time had passed since then, as it does, and removed some of the luster from the memories. Seeing it now, it was just a grey, brick building with a shabby red awning above the only entrance. A place you'd hardly notice walking past, until it came alive at night with sober people trying like hell to get in, and then devolved gradually to drunk people trying like hell to get home.

A sharp whistle blew across the hubbub and silenced the inebriated passengers. It was a piercing, shrill sound that seemed to bounce around in Ben's brain even after it'd stopped.

"Alright everyone, listen up!" shouted a deep, male voice.

A few rows ahead of them, at the very front of the bus, two guys dressed in dark uniforms and aviator glasses stood up. Clearly fake, overly large badges were pinned to each of their shirts, and they glittered in a way that police badges shouldn't.

At that moment, Jon shuddered and nearly fell out of his suit. "Oh, shit dude!"

"What? What's wrong?" asked Ben, alarmed.

The guy with the whistle continued: "We're going to be chaperoning this affair—"

Jon frantically snatched the plastic bag from his pocket, and searched for the opening with jittery fingers.

"What the hell are you doing, man?"

"Not getting arrested tonight, bud. Nope! Not happening."

"Let's have a responsible night, but let's keep the party fuckin' going!" With that the bus roared and shook, and Jon quickly gobbled the last bit of mushrooms he had in the bag.

"Are you kidding me, man?" Ben cried, incredulous, slightly above a whisper. Only in that moment did Ben realize just how worse-for-wear his friend was: Jon was clearly mistaking those two party-bus bros for sworn officers of the law.

"Those aren't actual cops, you idiot!" Ben barked.

Jon fiercely grabbed Ben by the lapels of his jacket and reiterated, "I'm not fucking getting arrested!" His face was flushed, and what little hair that remained atop his balding head was soaked and disheveled. As far as Ben could imagine, it was a shockingly convincing portrayal of what a demanding, entitled (and quite intoxicated) rock star might look like up close. Jon tossed the empty bag out the window, and munched away on the last of his mushrooms with a rapid, paranoid cadence.

"Let's fuckin' do this, people!" bellowed one of the 'cops.' Then their whistle rang out one last time and everybody began to file out.

Once outside most made for the door and dutifully lined up like ants—loud and intoxicated, but otherwise well behaved ants. Others formed small cliques and laughed at each other's costumes. The two of them maneuvered to the fence-line beside the building so that Jon could have a smoke and gather himself before going in. He wasn't looking as healthy as he'd started out that night. The muscles in his face seemed to be losing their strength and were weighing down his cheeks. And his skin had lost more shades of its color than he could afford. Ben set Jon's sign against the fence and then forgot about it almost immediately.

FAGS Are BEASTS.

Ben let Jon fiddle with the cigarette box for about a minute —he was fruitlessly looking for the pull tab on the plastic wrapping—before he stepped in and opened it himself. Ben asked him if he was going to be okay, to which Jon only replied by demanding to know who'd been talking shit about him. Ben just said, "Never mind," and watched as his friend then attempted to light the cigarette, which, finally, was successfully in place between his lips. But Jon was taking long drags of nothing as he held the lighter a good half-foot away from its target. Gently, Ben guided Jon's hand and the flame towards the cigarette. Without much reaction, except ordinary contentment once smoke finally began to enter his lungs, Jon put the lighter back in his pocket. This might be a shorter night than either of them had anticipated.

At some point the night's air had turned from crisp to near frigid. Many of the partyers began to shift from one foot to the other, and whoever actually had pockets buried their hands into them. The line-up became more orderly though, conveying slowly forward as each of them, one by one, satisfied the two bouncers at the door—the gatekeepers of modern times, the pawns of the bar-owners and the enemies of underage drinkers and adult over-indulgers alike. Presently, as Ben watched the crowd and wondered about the odds of Jon getting through the doors, he heard a sudden dry, kind of rustling, crash behind him. Looking back, he noticed first that his friend was no longer by his side. He then immediately solved that question, as well as the source of the sound, as he observed a pair of gold-panted legs writhing out from a row of shrubs planted along the side of the club.

Discreetly, Ben darted around the corner. "Jesus, man! What the hell are you doing?" he demanded in a muted shout, his arms searching for enough purchase around Jon's waist to pull him out.

"He took my smoke!" Jon screamed from somewhere in deep.

"What?"

"My fuckin' smoke!" Jon repeated. "He snagged it!"

Here, it is necessary to stop and speak to Jon's size. Perhaps the most accurate description of him was indeed 'big and gay,' as Luke had said. The guy was 6'4" and though he had a natural build and hadn't worked out a day in his life, he had to be well over 200 pounds, conservatively. Many people they'd met over the years, they would invariably call him 'Little Jon' and laugh, as though he hadn't heard that a million times before. And at present, aside from the sheer mass of him, he seemed to be actively working against Ben's efforts. If he didn't want to be pulled free from those bushes, Ben likely wasn't going to be able to do it.

But then there came a voice, which called out, "We got you, man, don't worry," and Ben was joined by two men in thick, flannel winter coats. Each of them calmly reached into the shrubs, as though experienced in matters such as this, and grabbed a chunk of Jon's outlandish suit. The three of them swiftly hauled him out, and back onto his feet.

He came out even more of a wreck than he'd gone in. No way Ben was getting him in now. Jon nonchalantly brushed off what he could but the suit was irrevocably stained and torn in more than a few different places. His bare chest was marked with several faint, red scratches. Ben hastily scanned the area, and to his relief it seemed that nobody had come around to notice what had happened. Nobody, of course, except for the two flannel-wearing Samaritans who helped him dig Jon out.

Those two assisted Jon in brushing himself off, and one of them was even kind enough to light him up a fresh cigarette. Each of them wore their twin jackets of grey flannel overtop skin-tight spandex body suits that Ben only then noticed. One was red, the other was blue. The one in the blue spandex had shoulder length, wavy hair with a modest beard that was sparse from the corner of his lips outwards. The other, the one in red, was taller and thinner than his partner, with a bare face, pointed nose and a narrow, square jaw.

"What were you up to in the bushes, fella?" asked the one in red, with more than an air of facetiousness.

Jon took a moment to reply. "The raccoon," he blankly stated.

"Raccoon?" the one in blue repeated, with a wide grin full of perfectly white teeth.

Jon was silent. He only stood there with his cigarette in hand, burning away. His face, were he not up on his feet, would have one believe he'd passed out.

Those boys, the newcomers, clearly found the whole event hilarious and weren't letting it go. "What'd the raccoon do, pal," urged the red one, flashing a wink and a smile to Ben.

They waited another moment before Jon spoke. "He stole my cigarette."

"He stole your cigarette?" repeated blue.

"I bummed him a drag, and he ran off with it," grumbled Jon, and a long stick of ash faltered and fell to his feet. "Damn Raccoons."

The two guys heartily laughed, but silently, so as not to offend Jon and ensure he keep talking. "Oh, man! What a scum-bag," red declared once they'd regained their composure.

"Scum-bag," affirmed Jon. His large frame swayed now, just a little, like a tower in a storm. "You're absolutely right."

"Hey, thanks for your help guys," interrupted Ben. "It's looking like this is the end of our night."

"What are you talking about?"

"Well, look at my friend here," he explained. The three of them examined Jon, who in that moment could have been described by a lot of different words, but 'sober' was most definitely not one of them. "I'll never get him into the club."

"Naw. Fuck that, buddy," announced the shorter one, ditching his smoke. "You and Elton, come with us."

They led them around the corner and back to the entrance, explaining on the way that they were in the band and that they would get them in no problem. Ben thought that calling it a night was clearly the better decision, given the state of his friend and the fact that the more he drank, the more densely his thoughts had focused on Chloe. But Jon, without words or expression, followed them happily and so Ben didn't have much of a chance for dissent—or if he had, he hadn't taken it. As it turned out, hardly a single word was needed. They followed their guides straight past the bouncers and what remained of the line-up, and entered through unobstructed to the next stage of the night.

Inside, it was bursting at the seams with people and the people danced and mingled under cobwebs and gothic ribbons, which festooned across the walls and spiraled down from the ceiling. Lights of many colors danced along every surface. Ben was struck by the atmosphere of it all, feeling as though he had stepped into a new world, complete with a new culture and new rules. Certainly, there was a theme, but it was less one of simple dress-up and more a palpable sense of everyone escaping who they actually were, if only for a night. Somehow, the total number of minds in that crowded nightclub seemed to be one—at least it did to Ben in the moment.

Elevated above them on the far side of the club was a main stage. Also above them, were a handful of small platforms, distributed evenly throughout the space, atop which dancers danced with freed, loose movements that seemed to be setting a licentious tone for those below. Instruments were set up on the stage, lying in wait.

Making their way through the crowd, the man in red leaned into Ben's ear and shouted above the music: "We should probably get your friend some water, bud!"

"Yeah, no kidding!" he agreed.

They pushed through the bodies towards the nearest bar. The other guy in the band, the one in the blue spandex, had one hand clutching Jon's jacket—though in an unambiguously friendly kind of way—leading him forward.

Red continued: "Name's Paul!"

"Ben. He's Jon."

"Easy to remember!" he yelled. "The hipster looking one there is my brother, Miah!"

"Maya?"

"Miah! Like the girl's name, yeah!" he confirmed with a grin. "For Jeremiah! When we were little I couldn't say Jeremiah, went with Miah instead. And it stuck! So now he's left with a chick's name!"

"Does he like it?"

"Well he's been trying to ditch it for years! He'll never say so, but he actually likes it!"

They reached the bar and leaned Jon up against the side wall, where he seemed content to remain. Ben introduced himself to Miah, but when he shook his hand he said 'Jeremy' instead.

"We got a pretty decent tab here," said Jeremy/Miah. " What are you drinking?"

"Spiced rum and coke, man. Thanks."

"Spiced rum for the pirate... A little on the nose but I like it!" He turned to the bartender, a heavily built girl with a glittery face and butterfly wings, who was simultaneously frightening and frighteningly beautiful. "Hey Chrissy! Can I please get two more pilsners, and a spiced rum n' coke for my friend here, and also like a big jug of water!" He mimed his hands together to emphasize the amount of water he wanted.

"Sure, Sweetie!" Chrissy cooed, and began working her bar with swift, delicate movements that belied her size. This had the fascinating and slightly comical effect of making her wings flutter behind her. Once finished, she took a final calculating look at all the drinks she'd assembled between them. Then, as if to congratulate herself, she shouted, "Yeah!" and danced away.

Jon too was dancing—again. This dance was more

restrained than his last, however. At least he was still where they'd left him. Ben came to him with the jug of water. "Here, get this in you!" he ordered.

Jon took the jug in stride and sipped from the straw without protest, saying nothing and continuing to dance.

"Alright, buddy!" Paul shouted with a hand on Ben's shoulder. "We gotta get ready for the set! You guys enjoy your night!"

"We will, man! Thanks a lot!"

With that, the brothers made off towards the stage. The place was awash in flashing lights and brought noticeably above room temperature by the sum of the bodies. The vague mix of sweat and perfume was sweet and unmistakable in the air. Sipping his drink, Ben watched the goings on. He saw a Batman on the dance floor, basically having sex with what looked like a scantily clad, female 'Where's Waldo.' He saw The Joker, paying Batman no mind, stopping to photo-bomb a group of girls dressed as Ben-didn't-know-what. He saw fairies and zombies, a Reaper and a Hulk Hogan, a vampire as well as a giant PAC-MAN followed by a file of PAC-MAN Ghosts. He didn't, however, see Snow White (or her dwarves), who he'd been looking for on a level he didn't quite admit to himself.

A remix of 'Living on a Prayer' was playing, and when the chorus dropped Jon came over Ben suddenly and captured him with an arm. He gleefully roared: "Whoooooa, we're half way there!" The straw in his water jug was a microphone. "Whoa-yeah! Living on a prayer!"

"How you feeling, Buddy?" Jon asked, his personal volume cranked to the maximum.

"Me?" Ben retorted. "What about *you*?"

"I'm excellent!" he replied, seeming to have spent the last few minutes getting a better handle on himself. "I'm always excellent!"

"That you are!" agreed Ben.

Just then the music died and the speakers delivered a booming voice: "How's everyone doing tonight?"

The crowd squealed and Ben looked over to see two face-less figures taking the stage, one in a blue spandex body suit that covered him completely, head to toe, and the other in matching red: Paul and Jeremiah. Behind them was a third who took a seat at the drum kit. He was dressed all in leather, a vest and tight pants, with long black hair and what looked like a pilot's hat. He had a definite 80's metal, biker kind of vibe. Curiously, Ben had the distinct impression it wasn't exactly a costume. Obscured in shadow at the far end of the stage was a fourth member, who stood between a keyboard and a drum machine. The blue man whipped a bass guitar around his neck and took his position beside his brother in red, who continued on the mic, a guitar slung over his shoulder.

"We're from beautiful Regina, Saskatchewan and we're called The Invisible Hands!"

This was met with tempered cheers. *The Invisible Hands,* thought Ben. Not what he would've expected. The red man rang out a few chords from his guitar and the drummer followed suit and they were off. It was an electronic-fused kind of new-age beat that took Ben by surprise, but in a good way. All of it was a surreal painting before his eyes: The music, the costumes around him and the two lithe, human-like figures— one red, one blue—bobbing to the beat on stage. People under-neath ate up the heavy down-beat and resumed dancing. The red man stepped back to the microphone and began to sing. As much as Ben could make out, the lyrics were:

> Promised what we hoped,
> We got what we expected.
> Behind closed doors,

Both sides rejected,

The promises, promises.

All of them broken,
The closer I watch.
Robbed of a memory,
Too many times through the wash...

The promises, promises.

Think you had your say?
They're selling you their ruse!
So face-to-face,
Just tell me the truth...

Ben felt an unmistakable wave of political angst from the song, which he would never have expected from the pair he'd met moments prior. But he couldn't help but hang onto a lyric and somehow think of Chloe (yet again). *Promised what we hoped, we got what we expected.* Something about that line carried a picture of her up into his mind's eye. She lay atop him, telling him how much she loved him and how scared that made her, basically taking the words right from his mouth. Each of them promised the other that they weren't going anywhere, but maybe they knew deep down it was probably a lie. If there was connective tissue between politics and love, he mused, it would probably be broken promises.

"These guys are fuckin' good!" declared Jon, ripping Ben from that line of thought.

"Not bad," Ben agreed.

Just then there came a high-pitched voice over his shoulder. "Hey, I think I owe you a dance!"

Ben turned to find Snow White, standing there all pretty and demure. "Oh, hey," he timidly said. "I, um, I'm flattered but my friend and I—"

Jon cut him off. "Oh, go dance with her you stupid bastard!" he blasted. And then looking to the girl, he continued in slurred, drunken words: "He'd love nothing more than to dance with you!" He shoved Ben towards her and she laughed and led him away.

Through a sea of bodies they pressed, her pulling him through. "Why so shy?" she asked.

"It's not that," he replied, looking back for Jon but he'd already been washed away by an undercurrent of drunkenness. "My friend's just kinda fucked up."

"He seems fine!" she answered as she came to a stop in the thick of the dancefloor.

"For now," Ben countered, uneasy about leaving Jon. "He was digging in the bushes chasing a raccoon a few minutes ago!"

She laughed at that and he found himself once again caught up in her beautiful dimples and snowy-white smile. "Relax!" she shouted. "He's big and glittery! You won't lose him!"

He supposed that was true enough as she put her hands above her head and began to dance as though there was no never-mind whether he joined her or not. But he decided *to* join her, and she moved closer and closer into him. Soon, he was lost in her and the music, no thoughts of Chloe or Jon or clients or schedules or life goals. Her thighs pressed against his and he found himself purely attracted to her. He wanted her and no one else. His fingers found no resistance as they explored her body and he felt hers doing the same.

Held in his arms, she at some point stopped dancing and turned to face him. Her green eyes met his and remained there for a time. Then, she raised her hand to her mouth, slipped a small tablet onto her tongue and swallowed. There was still another between her fingers, and she brought it over to Ben's lips. For reasons that were not completely lost on him, Chloe was back in his mind. It was the night of that house party—the cocaine and the craziness and the only night he'd ever judged her.

Owing to some culmination of nature and nurture, Ben had developed over time an odd duality when it came to drugs. On one hand, he gleefully kept with crowds that partook here and there; on the other, there was always an underlying sense of superiority towards them. This unfortunate piece of Ben's psyche led him, that one night, to lash out at Chloe, who was caught quite unsuspecting. So when Snow White offered her mystery pill, Ben reversed course and opened his mouth.

She placed the tablet on his tongue and let him suck on her finger as he swallowed. Without knowing the future, his impaired mind comprehended it as a definite turning point in his life. But he'd think about it later.

On the stage, the red man and the blue man—Paul and Miah—were well into their third, or maybe fourth song. Ben wasn't exactly sure. Regardless, they were still up there, swaying in unison and waving their hands in the air as the drummer drummed overtop the electronic melody. The crowd ate it up and clapped to the beat until the song ended. Assenting cheers followed.

"Hope you all are enjoying your Halloween!" roared the red man. "If you remember nothing else, remember how awesome the band was and remember to go out and vote!"

With that, Paul started a funky rift with a helping of reverb, and the drum machine kicked in leading into their next song. All four in the band belted out the words: "Against the tide!" and then hit their instruments hard.

Snow White grabbed Ben's shirt and pulled him into her. The kiss was forceful and fluid, and there was a strange but not altogether unpleasant taste on her tongue. Abruptly, she ended it and patted him twice on the chest, saying, "I have to pee. Find me later!"

She floated away, and vanished for the second time. Above the crowd, Ben's eyes were drawn to what would become the indelible sight of Jon, in his full Elton garb, up on a vacant dancer's platform busting more than a few moves. Below him, a very conflicted bouncer was both enjoying the sight while also trying to coax him down. Ben made his way over.

"You know this guy?" asked the bouncer.

"Yeah I do!"

"As funny as it is, you have to get him down, bro!"

"No problem," Ben said. "Hey, Jackass! Get down!"

"This is my jam, man!" he protested.

"You've never heard this song in your life!" retorted Ben.

Jon stopped and listened intently. "Oh yeah," he shouted, and then stepped down without a fuss. "What's up, man?"

"I need another drink," Ben replied, equal parts amused and exasperated.

"Amen," said Jon.

They had to brave their way across the dance floor in order to get to the bar that looked somewhat accessible. Jon led the way, and the very size of him helped to clear them a path through the bodies. Just short of the bar, though, he looked up to the stage and became suddenly frozen. In addition to the almost otherworldly sight of the red and blue men writhing to their own music, a rank and file had formed of those big-headed dwarves, orderly making their way up a narrow platform adjacent to the stage. Once on top, they faced the crowd and began to move their bodies to the music, and their bobbling heads jerked eerily from side to side. Their eyes were big and black and almost alien, and they were unavoidable, seeming to draw in one's very soul. At least, that's how it seemed to Ben's impaired eyes. He wasn't even on shrooms. Jon, though, *was* on shrooms and he was a statue in front of him.

"Jon?" he cautiously shouted. "Jonny boy! You good?"

Nothing. His face was ice.

"Jon?"

Finally, Jon looked to his friend and said, with dreadful sincerity: "I can't be here right now."

With that, he was off and running. Ben followed as quickly as he could react, but after a few strides he collided with a big, yellow disc and hit the floor. The yellow thing crashed beside him, followed by a few other things which he couldn't yet make out. Once he gathered his wits, he was able to identify the guy dressed in the giant PAC-MAN costume, the one he'd seen earlier, and the others that subsequently tripped over them were the ghosts. Apparently, they'd been recreating the video game while someone else filmed it. Ben had ruined the fun, running right into them—or they ran right into him, however you wanted to look at it.

"Sorry, dude!" shouted the PAC-MAN, who struggled like a turtle caught on his shell. One of the ghosts offered a magnanimous hand and lifted his enemy onto his feet. Another helped Ben up as well.

"My fault!" Ben replied as he tried to rub a disgusting stickiness from his palms. The PAC-MAN bodies were hilariously big, but right now Ben didn't see the humor and only struggled to try and see past them and spot Jon. No sign of him. "Sorry, again!" he yelled, and pressed on.

He jogged through the crowd and out the exit. The autumn night's air blew through his shirt and bit into his skin. Scanning the area, he found no sign of Jon. He spent what seemed like so long searching for him. Around the corner and in the bushes, in the taxis and at the hot dog line. Nothing.

Just then there came a voice from behind him, with a heavy Australian accent: "How ya going there, mate?"

He turned around.

Standing there in front of him, to his great shock, was a raccoon. But it wasn't a normal raccoon at all. It was human sized and wearing human clothing—blue jeans and an AC/DC t-shirt to be precise. Leaning against the fence, he puffed away on a cigarette that he greedily held between two clawed fingers. Immediately, Ben realized that he'd forgotten all about the pill he'd taken from Snow White and understood that it was probably just then kicking in. But it didn't make the matter any easier to address. He could only stand there gawking at the thing.

"You look like you could use a hand," said the raccoon.

* * *

At a table tucked away on the upper level of the club, sat Ben and the Raccoon. They hadn't yet spoken another word. It was ten to eleven, PM, according to the clock that hung above the raccoon's head.

Physically at least, Ben was feeling ok at this point... all things considered. Light had taken on a more profound intensity for him, though. And the light from the fixtures that hung from the ceiling was all changing colors to his eyes, seemingly dependent on who was underneath. The bartender, for example, seemed to be awash in a comforting blue hue. He and the raccoon sat within a harsher red. Mercifully, though, they'd found a spot that wasn't quite so loud as it was below. Ben could actually hear himself think. But the bass of the music was in his bones. It rumbled throughout his entire body and made his extremities tingle in a bizarre way.

Ben sipped on a fresh rum and coke that the raccoon had graciously bought for him. His eyes were without pupils, instead big and uncomfortably dark orbs were suspended in the center of his black, raccoon patches of fur. They were piercing and inscrutable without meaning to be—his manner up to then was undeniably pleasant. He had helped himself to a bag of free popcorn from a machine set up beside their table, and was gobbling it up with his tiny, doll-like raccoon hands. Popcorn remnants formed a messy trail down his shirt; a fresh beer sat untouched beside him. Ben didn't really have any words that seemed relevant, and the raccoon seemed content with just the popcorn.

But eventually the raccoon did ask, shouting enough to be heard over the music below: "So, what's your name then, mate?"

For a moment that Ben couldn't measure, he was silent. He could only keep staring at the thing in front of him while trying his best to reacquaint his senses with so many new and strange inputs. Eventually, he must have given his name because the raccoon said, "It's a pleasure, Ben."

He continued: "Listen, I'm sorry we couldn't find your friend. I'd seen him earlier. Nice enough to give me a smoke before you guys went in. Like I said, though, I didn't see him leave." The raccoon said something else that Ben couldn't understand, whether because of his accent or the drugs ...or both. Ben said that it was fine and thanked him for the help, likewise making himself heard over the music below.

"Not a problem, mate," the raccoon assured him. "Not a problem whatsoever!" He'd finished with the popcorn and took a couple vast gulps from his pint of beer, securing the mug between both his hands.

Following another silence, in which Ben diligently scanned the surrounding area for potential threats and viable escape routes, the raccoon said, "Well, my name's Rick."

Rick the Raccoon, thought Ben.

"I gotta say," Rick continued, "you seem a little messed up."

This was the first thing he said that made any sense. "I think you're right about that," replied Ben.

"So what's your drug, then?"

"I don't even know."

"Never a good sign. A little acid, maybe. Or maybe a bad reaction to some ecstasy? Hard to say, mate. Important thing is to keep you awake, keep you talking."

Taking advice from a raccoon was terrifying, indeed, but also strangely reassuring. And the latter seemed to outweigh the former; Ben became a little more at ease.

Rick went on: "Not normally a hard drug user, are ya?"

Ben said no.

"Might I ask why you did tonight?"

"Snow White," he answered.

"Ah! Beautiful women," Rick declared with a chuckle. "They'll get ya every time! They give you a little attention, and you're in their grasp! Especially coming off a breakup, huh?"

Ben was confused at this. He didn't remember telling Rick about Chloe. He guessed that he must have, at some point.

"Easy to forget who you are," said the raccoon pensively, before helping himself to more of his beer, some of which trickled through his sharp teeth and dripped down to the floor. He wiped off his mouth with his furry forearm.

Ben could sense a Chloe-related prodding, and he had very little interest in that right then. So he asked, "What's your story?"

It did the trick.

"Me?" asked Rick. "Well there's not too much to tell, mate."

"How long have you been here?"

"What, in this bar?" he asked.

"No, I mean—"

Rick snickered. "I know what you mean. I been here ten years, mate. A little more than that now, actually. How bloody fast time goes, hey?"

Ben could agree with that. "What brought you here?" he asked.

Rick sighed and his eyes seemed then to fall into themselves, losing all of the severity they had prior, becoming less feral and more human. He pulled a small tin canister from the pocket of his jeans and began snapping it up and down in his hand. Then he removed the lid and Ben recognized what it was. Rick took a pinch of chewing tobacco from inside the can, and placed it neatly under his lower lip. Then he put the tin back into his pocket and spoke, with a new weariness about his raccoon countenance.

"Well, mate, that's a long story," he began. "But if you do wanna hear it..."

"I do," said Ben truthfully.

"Well then, there was a storm back home," he explained, "a monster of a storm! We did what we could to shore up the place but it wasn't near enough. The wind was insane. And the water! You wouldn't believe the water, mate! Flooded our home completely. Everything was destroyed."

Ben's emotions were under a new level of gravity—weighed down tenfold, ready to buckle and experiencing time much differently from the way he remembered. He felt tears well up in his own, human eyes and struggled to fight them back.

Rick went on: "And our business, mate. Home and business, they were one and the same, you reckon? Everything gone in a night. And my mom—"

He dipped his head and tried to compose himself. When he was ready, he finished: "—My mom didn't make it."

"Oh my God," said Ben.

"Yeah."

Each used the ensuing silence to sip their drinks and rein back in their emotions. Soon, a server floated by dressed in a long, ghostly white sheet with two holes cut out over her eyes, drink tray in hand. Ben thought that it was maybe the most frightening thing he'd ever seen in his life, and shot back in his chair. She asked if they were both doing okay. Ben could only remain frozen in place, wishing for an escape, as those cut-out eyes cut through him. Rick awkwardly assured her that everything was fine. She turned unnaturally and floated away, passing through the far wall as though it weren't even there. With her gone, Ben began to regain a bit of his ease.

"Anyway," Rick said, carrying on with his story, "the old man and I, we never really saw eye-to-eye. And it was tough after the storm, for both of us. I don't think it was all his fault, really. Still, though, making ends meet got harder and harder and it got to the point I couldn't stay with him any longer. And I got an uncle; he's lived over here my whole life. Let's just say he's much better off, financially. I came over to live with him in his penthouse... ten years back, like I said. Been here ever since, making my way, working as much as I can, playing my music."

"Oh, you're in a band?"

"Yes, mate!" he said, appearing to brighten up. "You heard our set earlier, I think!"

"Oh, right," said Ben, hiding his confusion, having not recalled seeing a raccoon on stage with the band. "With, umm, Paul and Miah, right?"

"That's right! They're good old boys, mate. Met 'em both shortly after I came over! Farm boys, just like me!"

"They had a cool sound," Ben muttered, as though talking to someone else.

"Come again?" asked Rick.

"Oh, you guys had a cool sound, man. I really liked it!"

"Awe, thank you so much, mate. I appreciate that!"

Just then there came a crashing sound from below, followed by screams and a general tumult. On the upper tier, several people gathered at the railing to get a look. Rick and Ben joined them, and saw a chaotic cluster of people on the dance-floor below. At the center of it, two figures—one red and one blue— were throwing punches at some other person and their punches left streaks of their respective colors in the air. Those streaks were breaking apart and dissipating into the atmosphere like some kind of hot gas. It was a difficult sight for Ben's incredulous mind.

When Rick peered over the railing and saw his band-mates in distress, his eyes instantly regained that animalistic fierceness Ben had seen before. His lips snarled and furled back, revealing ferocious, jagged teeth. Without warning, he shot up and hunched atop the railing, his claws deftly securing his balance. He then threw himself down and landed on a light fixture before gloriously diving, limbs spread wide, dead center into the fight. Ben watched with amazement as he found his target, and his raccoon claws frenetically slashed at whatever poor souls had started shit with his friends. A couple bouncers fought through the melee and attempted to separate all those involved.

Ben was now too far removed from doubting what his eyes told him. He'd forgotten about drugs and gay bars, about Jon and about club crawls. All he knew was things were weird and getting weirder, and that he was scared and still missed his girl-friend. While everyone else either crowded the railing to get a better look at the fight, or fought their way downstairs to join it, Ben ran for the washroom.

Once there, he puked into a disgusting toilet that he tried his best not to touch, and then he unsteadily carried himself to the sink. He took all the cold water he could hold and splashed it onto his face, and then took some more and brought that straight into his mouth. There, examining himself in the mirror, he tried his best to re-collect himself. Of course he knew that talking raccoons and ghosts that served drinks didn't exist, but he was having trouble reminding himself as much at the moment. In the reflection, he found that he looked foggy and flushed and ridiculous in that stupid pirate's hat. He snatched it off his head and threw it behind him.

"I thought that looked rather nice on you, darling," came an unexpected voice with a gentle English accent.

Ben looked behind him, and there, standing confidently with a foot up against the wall, was Elton John.

Not his best friend Jon, mind you. This wasn't a matter of dress-up or make pretend. This was undeniably, unmistakably, modern day Elton John. His suit was somewhat more subdued than the one Jon had found, yet still fittingly eccentric in its own right. It was blue with gold threading that outlined its edges. A pair of sunglasses covered his eyes—rounded gold frames complete with lenses that Ben's eyes could only just penetrate. His shoes and his belt and the cross that hung from his right ear, were also gold.

Ben's feet slipped out from underneath him before he could even think to shut off the faucet. Crawling frantically atop that bathroom floor, he retreated to the far wall and took care not to let his eyes off the aging rock star who had so inexplicably appeared in front of him. The music had been shut off after the fight and the hiss of the faucet, along with the dull shouting that reached through from underneath them, were the only sounds. Calmly, Elton walked over to the sink, pumped some soap into his hands and began to wash them. Once finished, he turned the water off and his footsteps echoed as he moved to the hand dryer beside Ben. The sound of it was deafening. As he worked the hot air through his fingers, he'd let his shades fall a little down his nose and his eyes took a long, calculated look overtop them and down towards Ben.

Once his hands were dry and the machine hummed to a stop, he said, "I'm sorry darling, I didn't mean to give you a fright. I was only waiting there to wash my hands, but you seemed to be a little jumpy over something. I didn't want to rush you."

"You... You're—"

"Oh, you're a fan, then! How lovely!" he delightedly said and helped Ben to his feet. "But listen my friend, I'm just a bloke like any other. You mustn't hit the floor when you see somebody that's a bit famous, right?"

"I, umm—"

"That's quite alright though," he remarked with a grin and a hand on Ben's shoulder that unknowingly cut him off, "you're hardly the first!" Elton John laughed at that, and gave Ben a somewhat condescending, but not unfriendly, pat on his cheek.

"What are you doing here?" asked Ben, perplexed.

"I've been here all night, darling," he responded, stepping around Ben and towards the door.

That was true, Ben supposed.

Without any more words, Mr. John left the washroom and Ben watched as the door slowly pulled itself shut. Just then, a toilet flushed and a disturbing clicking sound followed. The stall door opened. Ben turned his attention to find that whoever it was that had first gone into that stall, they had since been transformed into a gigantic insect. The thing crawled out, its hardened shell squeezed through the opening and scraped along the metal frame; its feet chattered against the tiled floor. For a moment, the disturbing creature turned its head to Ben—who was positively petrified. He couldn't bring himself to turn away though, nor could he even move at all.

Jesus!

When that creature's eyes locked on his own, what was in those two giant, black domes, more than anything else, was despair. Its pincers twitched hungrily, but Ben had the distinct impression that it was an involuntary action. With it came that same clicking sound he'd heard before—something like a thousand snapping fingers somewhere in the distance.

Is it going to talk? Is it waiting for me to talk? Dear God, what happens now?

Then it simply disregarded Ben, crawled past him to the door, and rose onto its hind legs. Wrapping its arm around the handle, it swung the door open, fell to its feet and scampered out. Once more the door slowly creaked to a close.

It didn't even washed its hands...

When the door finally shut, the sound of it snapped Ben out of the gloom the creature had brought with it. With all his courage, he crept cautiously towards it.

Opening it only a crack, he couldn't see anybody there, but found that the music had resumed. The bass and the lights were seemingly working together towards some sinister goal. What that was, he couldn't imagine. But the coast looked clear enough—void of monstrously large insects, at the very least. All of them must still be downstairs. Or maybe they'd left entirely. *Could it be trusted?*

There was no choice in the matter. He crept out, watchful for danger, his back pressed against the wall as if the ground below him gave way to some perilous fall. Inch by inch, he progressed in that manner, until he'd come upon a dead-end where the wall turned ninety degrees and quickly descended down to the main level. Across the stairs was the railing—his best shot. If he wanted to get out of there, he'd have to jump.

God dammit.

On the other side of the room the bartender regarded him strangely, as if he were somehow behaving oddly. He was certain he was not, given the circumstances. This didn't concern Ben, though; he barely registered her at all. He kept his focus where it needed to be. She never said anything.

He had to muster most of his courage to do it, but he made the jump, wrapping his arms tightly around the railing upon landing. It was a heroic leap. If he'd messed up at all, he could've been done for.

Making his way down the stairs, he kept himself pulled tight to the railing. He really had no idea where he was going or what he should expect. All he could do was keep one foot ahead of the other, and hope—hope for a friendly face or, failing that, for some sign that could give him an idea of what to do next. Where to go. The crowd seemed to be just as they were before the fight interrupted the party. That was good.

Numbly, he wondered how much of what had happened up to that point was actually real. Whatever happened next, he didn't really care, so long as he could be sure that it was. Maybe that was too much to ask, though. Life isn't fair, and he was pretty sure that it wouldn't go out of its way to assure him of what's real, even during a brutal trip.

Ben had no idea how true this would turn out to be...

It wasn't until he finally reached the bottom of the stairs that the strangeness of the scene dawned on him. Sure, they all danced and they were all dressed more or less like he remembered. But the way they danced, it was too organized. Each of

them paired off with another and respectfully took their partner's hand, ample room between them for the Holy Ghost.
Then they stepped and twirled, stepped and twirled, switched
hands and did it again in the opposite direction. It was a scene
out of time, a bit of Victorian England in a modern nightclub.
But he couldn't figure any of it out, and though he knew it was
strange he wasn't sure exactly why—he couldn't put his finger
on it. Panicked, he frantically made for the exit, and darted out
the door.

Outside, he hunched over and gasped uncontrollably until
he was able to calm himself. Once he did, he was actually able
to enjoy the fresh air he was taking in. It smelled of a particular
dream but he couldn't say which dream, exactly, only how it
made him feel. And then he heard his name and it ripped him
from that expedition towards a memory.

"Ben! How you doing, buddy?" it said. "You get kicked out
too?"

There, standing in line for hot dogs, was Rick the Raccoon
and the rest of his band—Paul, Miah and that leather-clad
drummer, who despite the cold was still happily shirtless. Only
Paul looked injured, with the beginning stages of a decent
shiner over one eye.

"Oh, hey," Ben said tentatively. "No, I just... just needed
some fresh air I guess."

"Fair enough," said Paul. He was still in his red body suit,
but without the mask and once again wearing his flannel coat,
as was his brother.

"Can you believe they fuckin' kicked out their own band?"
protested Miah. "They haven't even paid us yet!"

"Haven't paid us for last week either," mumbled Rick, spitting a dark blob to the ground beside him.

"Drop it already," said Paul.

"Whatever, mate," Rick slurred.

BENNIE & THE EX

They eventually got their hot dogs and each of them hungrily chomped them down—Rick especially (after he took the dip out of his mouth). They discussed what happened leading up to the fight, detailing what each of them had done and when, but Ben had more or less tuned them out. He was cold—so cold—and leery of giant bugs, or God knows what else that could come out of nowhere at any second.

"You guys see anything weird out here?" Ben asked warily.

"Like what?" one of them replied.

After a quick consideration, Ben said, "Nothing. Never mind."

No reason to scare them, he decided. Better if they kept a clear head.

As they talked and he kept watch, he became immersed in everything around him and the way it reminded him of something else. Something that he couldn't quite form in his mind, not completely. *Déjà vu.* He'd stood outside this club and others like it enough times, but that wasn't it. He took note of the buildings, the streets, the chill of the air. None of it told the full story. But when he turned around he saw something that seemed to bring the temperature down even more.

Standing across the street, alone and unwavering, was a dark figure—hooded and cloaked. He could just barely discern it but whatever it was, it was undeniably there, standing like an ominous statue except statues don't flutter in the wind. Though there was no way to tell for sure, he knew that it was watching him. He felt his skin harden and his muscles tremble. He chose to ignore it and managed to turn back to the band, but it didn't leave his mind.

"We're hitting a bit of an after party, bud," said Paul as he finished his hot dog. "We'll be a little earlier than we figured, though. Wanna come?"

"I think I just want to go home," Ben answered.

"Shame," said Miah.

"Well, we'll stay and get you in a cab, anyway," Paul added as he scanned the area, but no cabs were in sight.

"Thanks," Ben said and pulled his phone from his pocket. He had to fight with his eyes for the screen to make any sense. Eleven thirty-three, PM, it said. The battery was on its last legs: Ten percent.

Doing his best to hide his fear, and stop his fingers from trembling, he called the first number he knew. But the message on the line said that demand was high, and the wait would be forty minutes. He tried another. One hour minimum.

"No luck?" asked Rick.

"No."

"Alright, mate," he said. "Well we're getting out of here. Sure you don't wanna come with?"

"Yeah, I—" Ben began, but was stopped by the sight of that same figure he'd seen before. It now stood under the hazy cone of a street light that was a little ways away over the raccoon's shoulder. How could it have moved there, to the opposite street, so fast? He had no idea but there it stood, motionless still, inscrutably watching him. In the light, Ben thought he could make out a bit of its face and a hint of its legs underneath the cloak, both as purely white as its garments were black.

"Yeah, you know what," he stammered. "I'll come with."

The five of them made off down the street. Whatever that figure in black was, it definitely turned to watch them go. To his relief, it remained where it was. Somewhere down deep, Ben had the sense to chalk it up to the drugs and decided it was best to disregard it. But the familiarity he felt as they walked away, the sense of deja-vu, hadn't gone away, and he couldn't quite shake the unease it left behind. Nor could he ignore the unmistakable feeling of being watched, though he didn't dare look back again. If he had, he might have discovered that figure in

BENNIE & THE EX

black hovering above, inexorably stalking him, and the ends of its cloak which dangled above the group's heads.

But nobody noticed, and the surface of Ben's mind eventually convinced him to go with the flow. He could catch a cab from their place, and stay warm in the meantime. Hopefully Jon was doing better.

As they walked, he tried calling him—a couple of times actually. No answer. Meanwhile, the band was still re-living the brawl, particularly laughing about Rick's dive off the upper balcony. Rick, for his part, was fairly modest about the whole ordeal. The drummer never said a single word, enjoying his hot dog, making it last.

Parked in front of an empty lot a few blocks down, was a black pickup truck with tinted windows and a cover over the bed. As they approached it, lights lit up and the doors unlocked. The band started to file in. Paul stopped at the driver's door and turned to Ben. "Hey, man. So listen, a bunch of our equipment is still in the back seat, and we're short on room," he explained. "You mind riding in the back? It's not far."

"Yeah," said Ben as he rubbed whatever warmth into his arms that he could. "Sure."

He was so cold and just wanted to find some shelter ASAP. Paul dropped the tailgate and Ben shuffled himself in, feet first. The topper above would completely seal him inside, but he hadn't anticipated the full consequences of that until it was too late. Watching Paul vanish as the door snapped shut, he was left alone with nothing but the darkness and the cold steel of the truck bed underneath, the two of which making for an intolerable combination. Deeply uncomfortable, he did his best to control his breathing, but wasn't so sure that he could manage that drive. He didn't know how long it would be and, it occurred to him, he didn't even know these guys at all, did he? *Where the fuck were they taking him!?* A wave of panic came upon him, and his heart was suddenly as bent on escaping his chest as he was on escaping that truck.

Just then, though, as he resolved to somehow kick that tailgate down, there came a gentle voice with an English accent. It told him: "Relax, darling."

"Jesus Christ!" Ben bellowed and begged his eyes to break through the darkness.

"Don't panic. Breathe, darling. I've been taken to parties in shittier ways than this," the voice said.

Then there came some light from a tiny flame and Ben discovered Elton John huddled beside him, lighter in hand.

"Just breathe," he said once more, before beginning to sing 'Rocket Man,' which was actually quite soothing.

> She packed my bags last night, pre-flight.
> Zero hour, 9am.
> And I'm gonna be high,
> As a kite by then...

SIDE TWO—A HALLOWEEN CAROL.

Candy and Ronnie,
Have you seen them yet?
Oh, but they're so spaced out!
B-B-B Bennie and the jets!
Oh, but they're weird and they're wonderful!
Oh, Bennie, she's really keen!

At some point after Elton stopped singing, Ben was pretty sure he'd asked him for the time.

"Quarter to twelve," he thought Elton replied, from somewhere within the opaque blackness of that truck bed. His voice was disembodied, impossible to place.

Otherwise, that entire ride was bumpy and claustrophobic, but on the whole it wasn't *too* terrible. He wouldn't remember much of it anyway, and was just grateful that it didn't turn out to be too long of a drive. Even still, the truck stopped several times throughout, and each time it did Ben lay there in the dark, anxiously begging the gate to *just fucking open*. When they mercifully did come to their final stop, Ben felt the engine grumble to a halt. All he could hear was footsteps and muffled chatter outside. The gate opened, and standing above it was Paul and Rick. Ben felt liberated by the light that was returned to him, which revealed that he'd been alone in the back of that truck all along. No Elton John after all.

Such a timeless flight.

He slid himself out and the raccoon helped him to his feet. All of their breath became tiny, delicate clouds that disappeared instantly into the night. They stood at the foot of their destination, quite an old house which had a very large front porch that took up half the yard. On the porch was a frayed couch on one end and a hammock on the other. The lights were on, and through the curtains Ben could see the whisked silhouettes of many people inside, moving about. It was such a holdout from time, that house. The boards of its walls were split and cracked with age, and losing paint in broken, dried up flakes. Much newer, post-modern looking dwellings surrounded it, with shiny stone facades and striking, glossy edges.

"Gonna be a good time, mate!" proclaimed Rick with a slap on Ben's shoulder that returned him to the moment.

"Looks like it's well underway," Paul observed, as Ben followed him and his band-mates through a surreal, white-picket membrane.

Perched atop the porch was a small statue of a cat. But when Ben reached the last step and came upon it, it turned its head to meet him. He watched as the cat regarded him curiously, seeming to take stock of him. Ultimately, though, it turned away disinterested. It unfurled its body, breaking free of the stone and shaking off the dust. Then it jumped to the ground and landed silently beside him. It curled itself around his leg before it pranced into the house. (Ben hadn't even noticed that the front door had opened.) The cat darted underneath a pair of dainty, bare legs that stood inside the entrance.

Looking up, Ben found that the legs belonged to a very petite girl who looked about his age, but that was belied by some intangible maternal vibe. She wore a black skirt with frills that billowed out and away from her thighs, below a sleeveless cream colored blouse. Her hair was parted in the middle and fell to her shoulders with subtle curls. Cat whiskers were painted on her face along with a dot of black on the tip of her nose. Behind her hung a tapestry of music and revelry.

"Oh," she said. "Hi guys. You're back early I think, right?" Her voice was timid but exceptionally lovely.

"Yes we are, my love," said Paul, capturing her in his arms and lifting her off her tiny feet.

"No, no, no," she protested. "Put me down, put me down."

"Alright, alright," said Paul, setting her and her slippers back on the floor and heading into the house. "Ronnie!" Ben heard him shout before he disappeared around a corner. The rest of the band filed past, each stopping to give the girl a quick hug. When Ben reached the door behind the raccoon, she smiled, and her smile was like an unfinished painting that he thought couldn't possibly get any better.

"Who's your friend?" she asked.

"Oh, sorry," said Rick. "Ben, this is Candy. Candy, Ben."

"It's a pleasure," Candy said sweetly, holding out a delicate hand.

Ben took it in his own and said, "Thank you," without realizing the awkwardness of the reply.

She giggled, beckoned him inside, and shut the door behind him.

Once the door clicked shut the entirety of the atmosphere changed in an instant, though the transition was lost on Ben. A small corridor with a tiny closet opened up into a great room that was full of people who might well have been transported from the club. The age of the place was apparent, and though it looked modest from the outside, inside the house became its own kind of mansion. The walls were hard plaster and humbly, but tastefully, painted. Sofas and tables and miscellaneous furniture were placed throughout. It was all so old, but also new—somehow brought forth in time. Entropy hadn't ever been welcome. A gorgeous piano of glossy wood lay in the corner. Nobody played it. Everyone simply sat or stood around in silent, tempered conversation. He got the distinct impression that they were all indifferent to his presence, if not opposed to it. The music had died.

The guys he came with had somehow all disappeared, leaving Ben unsure of what to do next. As he wondered he caught a glimpse of a very old boxed television sitting on a cart beside him, to which nobody else paid any attention. The sight of it filled him with an unexpected dread. It took all of his strength but he had to get a closer look, to be sure. Crouching himself against that TV, he confirmed with fright what was on the screen: That cloaked figure he'd seen earlier, outside the club. Its eyes were still buried and hidden under its hood but as Ben lifted himself away, its head inescapably followed his own. Its black-and-white, staticky milieu, Ben knew well and couldn't deny—Chloe's apartment. Now he knew his next move. He was getting the hell out of there, and fast.

He turned and made for the door, forgetting entirely about Candy and colliding with her, sending her tiny body sailing to the ground.

"Shit!"

She lay in the corner by the door, rubbing her head. Feeling awful, Ben leaned down and helped her to her feet. "Oh, don't worry about it, Sweetie," she said with a meek flicker of a smile. "Were you leaving?" she asked, confused, as she fixed her skirt.

"Oh, umm," he began as he apprehensively scanned the room behind him. But whatever it was that seemed to be haunting him was gone and the TV was off. He turned back to her and continued: "I, umm—Listen I've drank a lot tonight, and I took a pill I shouldn't have, from a girl that I lost, and I have no idea what it was and yeah, that was pretty stupid but it's not really me, you know? And I think I'm pretty fucked up 'cuz I keep seeing things and I'm scared."

Candy's eyes moved along with his words and enticed them from his mouth.

"...And I smoked some pot too," he finished.

"Oh, Sweetie," she said, stroking the side of his face. "You shouldn't go off alone in the cold after taking some strange pills from some strange girl."

Then she eagerly took his hand and said, "Come on, you need a crepe!"

Before he could think to resist, he was led through the living room and into the kitchen. Nobody turned any of their attention.

Once in the kitchen, she let go of him and pranced to the refrigerator. Only then did he recognize how cold her hand was, as though *she* were the one who'd just stepped in from the autumn night's chill. It wasn't an unpleasant hand to hold, though. It was inviting, almost vulnerable, and he was happy to share what little warmth he'd regained.

The kitchen was much like the room that led to it—old but new. The colors were vibrant, but had gone out of style decades ago, and the paint was somehow like makeup on an elderly woman. It was very clean, though, save for a great big island counter that divided the room, on which there were mounds of fresh desserts—cookies, pies, and yes, crepes. Dishes wet with batter and sprinkled with flour lay piled high in the sink. Candy danced back from the fridge with a jar of golden syrup, which she drizzled indiscriminately onto the various plates on that counter. Then she began shuffling them aside to make room for a pan of something else from the oven. Behind her and to Ben's right was a modest passage where narrow steps disappeared up into darkness. To his left, across from the island, was a small table with four chairs and only two were empty.

Sitting on one of the chairs was the raccoon, and on the other was a very old man who sat with a presence that opposed his weakened appearance—his frame gaunt, and his skin as cracked and as pallid as was the outside of his house. He was dressed in his Sunday's best: A white cotton button-up and dress pants that were held up by black suspenders. His suit jacket rested behind him on the back of his chair. Atop his head was a fedora with the brim pulled low. The hairs on his face were white and well-trimmed, sparse but as sharp and as digni-fied as the suit he wore. Looking at the man, a picture of Leonard Cohen came into Ben's mind.

On the table in front of the man was a very large house of cards. Curiously, it looked a lot like that very house in which Ben had found himself. With bony fingers that slightly trem-bled, the man placed a final card atop the house, completing the chimney. Behind him, the room seemed to extend further than it had any right, and it too eventually gave in to the dark.

The old man leaned back in his chair, arms crossed, pleased with his creation.

"How ya goin', Ronnie?" asked Rick.

"Oh, not so bad," replied the old man gruffly, his voice hoarse. "You?"

"Yeah, not bad," Rick perfunctorily answered, as he rattled his claws against the table.

"Don't do that!" snapped the old man. "You'll ruin it!"

"Oh, sorry Ronnie."

"Oh damn," said Candy from the island, soft and sad. "I think it burned."

"You said that about the muffins and they were amazing," assured Rick.

"They're fine, love," said the man, still admiring that house of cards. There was kindness in his voice but his face hadn't softened.

Licking icing sugar from her finger, Candy reminded Ben of the crepes she'd offered. "Well, come on Sweetie! Have one! I promise once you eat one, you'll feel much better."

Ben made his way to the counter. His steps were tentative owing to the alcohol still in his system and a lingering sense of unease that, given the night he'd had, wasn't unreasonable. But he picked up a crepe and took a bite. It was so delicious his mind let go of nearly everything else.

"Oh my god," he said, chewing blissfully. "This is unbelievable!"

"Yay," cried Candy, elated, clapping and dancing on the spot. He helped himself to a second.

Then there came a melody from the room behind him— soft, confident strokes of the piano, key after key in a haunting combination. Some familiar tune hid within them, but Ben couldn't quite pull it from his mind.

"So. You seem like a strong young man," Ronnie posited from the table, his head tilted up slightly so that his eyes could find Ben from under his hat.

"Umm, I guess," replied Ben, who was already on his second crepe.

The old man's chair rattled against the linoleum as he shot up from it. Vitality that Ben couldn't have thought possible in him revealed itself in an instant. There was an excited grin on his face now.

"Oh, love. Please don't," begged Candy half-heartedly. "The poor child has had a long night."

"It's harmless fun," said the man, rolling up his sleeves.

Rick muttered, "Oh, boy."

Confused, Ben asked, "What are we doing?"

"Candy, clear some space!" he trumpeted. With careful, labored steps and his arms outstretched, he slowly found his way to the kitchen counter. If he wasn't fully blind, Ben guessed he must have been pretty close.

"Oh, dear," she tsked. She quickly but carefully removed plate after plate of her baked goods off the counter. "Boys. Never change!"

The old man followed the edges of the counter until he'd rounded it and found the other side. With a frail, yet excited hand and a grin that missed several teeth, he beckoned Ben towards him. "Arm wrestle, son!" he declared. Errantly, his eyes were focused ahead of him and missed Ben entirely. "Think you can beat me, heh?" His last word was more like a cough.

"Seriously?" Ben asked.

"Oh he's serious, mate," said Rick from the table.

A beautiful voice that was unmistakably Elton John's joined the piano keys from the other room:

Ain't no sunshine when she's gone,
Only darkness every day...

Ronnie had taken an eager arm wrestler's stance and slapped the counter, which sent a whiff of flour or maybe powdered sugar into the air. Thinking *why not,* Ben joined him.

"Don't let him intimidate you, Sweetie," said Candy, as she leaned against the refrigerator and lit up a cigarette.

Each of their elbows rested strategically opposite the other's, hands at the ready. Ben replied, "I'll try."

"One thing, young man," cautioned Ronnie. "Don't you hold back!"

"Okay," Ben answered, unable to hide a bit of a chuckle.

"I mean it, now!" he gasped. "If I think you're holding back, I'll kill you!"

His next word echoed, filling the silence: "Dead."

Ben faltered a little in his stance, noticeably rethinking the match and where the night had taken him in general.

But the man broke down laughing. "I'm only teasing, Son! Now come on!"

Their hands neared—Ben, unsure; the old man, ostensibly zealous. He quickly added: "Seriously though, don't hold back."

Their hands met and clasped together. The old man's laughter became uproarious.

"Are you ready?" asked Ben.

Once Ronnie's laughter somewhat settled, he looked Ben dead in the eyes. Ben discovered then that the old man's eyes were opaque clouds of grey and white. Somehow they'd still found their target. The old man crowed, "I can see you now!"

At once, Ben felt pressure from the old man's hand, though it wasn't near enough to catch him off guard. He honored the request and put all his force into winning the match, which he handily did. Ronnie's frail hand pounded against the counter and another cloud of baking product rose into the air and began to settle. Ben wasn't sure what would come next.

Then, once again, the old man laughed and his laugh grew more sinister.

From the next room the song continued:

And this house just ain't a home,
Anytime she goes away.

. . .

That unnerving laugh mercifully subsided. "Well done!" he hollered. "Let's go again!"

"I really don't see the point," Ben admitted.

"Oh," began Ronnie. "That was a practice round! We feel each other out! Don't you kids know how to arm wrestle these days?"

The song went on:

I know, I know, I know, I know, I know, I know...

"Alright," said Ben, resigned, getting back into position.

*...I oughtta leave young thing alone,
   But there ain't no sunshine when she's gone.*

The old man stopped just short of taking his hand and added, "Let's make it interesting this time, heh?"

"Umm, I don't think I have any cash," said Ben.

"I don't want your money."

"Well then what do you want?"

"It *is* Halloween!" he declared. "How about a trick, or a treat!"

Ben, exasperated, sighed, "I don't know what that mea—"

"Good deal!" Ronnie interrupted. He forced his hand into Ben's and pushed on it with all of his might: This time more might than Ben could have possibly prepared for. But he was able to recover before the old man could take the rematch.

"Oh, now," Ronnie taunted, "is this the man that Chloe fell in love with?"

Blood abandoned Ben's extremities and left behind a barren cold in each of his limbs. His heart went numb at hearing her name but it was also pounding in his chest. Why the fuck would this old man even know Chloe's name, let alone what she meant to him. *What the hell was happening?*

Ronnie gained another inch and Ben struggled against him. "Come on, Ben!" Rick cheered while chomping on a cookie.

"I can see you!" the old man proudly announced. His dead eyes were lit with glee and peered straight into Ben's own without difficulty.

Shuffling on his feet, Ben struggled to regain both his strength and his composure. The old man's decidedly not so frail arm wasn't budging. Ben could feel every muscle in his body strain for purchase. It must've been a pitiful sight.

"Sweetie, don't let him bully you," recommended Candy but it barely registered. He struggled far too much.

"Sometimes, you're not even sure she really loved you at all, are you? Not really sure you ever really loved her!" Ronnie goaded.

He gained another inch and Ben was in dangerous territory.

"What the fuck is this?" Ben desperately demanded.

"Arm wrestle, son!" Ronnie re-iterated. "You damn kids!"

Ben let out a strained gasp and gained back a little ground, but as quick as he did his opponent continued his taunts: "You can't help her... You never wanted to! She's just a pretty face and a broken soul for you to possess!"

There was nothing Ben could do, he was going to lose.

"What are you, a demon? Incapable of love so you find a soul to possess until it's withered and died?"

"Fuck you!" cried Ben. He fought against the old man with all of his strength—physical and mental, and maybe even spiritual.

"You're wondering if it was you that broke her? That she realized that wherever he was, the man she loved, there was somewhere else he'd rather be!"

With that it was done. Ben's arm faltered and his hand pounded to the counter with a convincing thud.

The old man laughed once again. "Not so strong as you look, hey young man!"

Ben was left panting and crying atop the counter, unable to comprehend or even define what had just happened. He reminded himself of dreams he'd had in the past, dreams that were going south from which he was able to wake himself once he realized the truth. For a moment he became convinced that he'd passed out at some point after the club. But it was no use. Every time he opened his eyes he was still there, and so was Candy and Ronnie, and so was the raccoon.

That old man's cold, boastful laughter mixed with the ending of the song:

Every time she goes away...

Still laughing and doing a little victory jig on the kitchen floor, he asked, "Will it be a trick, or a treat, then?"

Ben turned to leave but as soon as he did he heard the raccoon shout: "Mate! Don't!"

He stopped. Candy and Ronnie were still behind the island. She was inhaling a puff from her cigarette and he was beside her, sternly staring back at Ben. Rick had stood up from the table and had a strangely desperate look on his face, which, being a cute, furry raccoon face, was very effective. But it was something more than that which compelled him to stay.

"Trick or treeeat," the old man sang, derisively, as might a child looking for candy.

Ben wiped the tears from his eyes. "Well I don't have any fucking treats!"

"Trick then!" shouted Ronnie, and expectantly leaned against Candy.

Unsure what exactly the old man was hoping for, the only thing that came into his head as far as tricks was an old gag his grandfather used to pull on him when he was a kid. So he stood up from the counter and placed his hands underneath it, so that they couldn't see them. With a jerk, he feigned being in pain and brought his hands, cupped together, back into sight. He bent his fingers appropriately and pulled them apart so that it appeared that a finger had been cut in two. He slid it back and forth across the finger below it.

Nobody was impressed.

"You call that a trick?" barked the old man.

"Very uninspired, Sweetie," Candy agreed.

"Jesus Christ!' exclaimed Ben. He leaned into the counter with both hands atop it. "I don't know! I don't even know what the hell is going on!"

"I'll show you a trick!" the old man proclaimed as he grabbed a butcher's knife from behind him. With a disastrous smack he brought it down on Ben's right hand, dividing all four fingers in two.

Blood erupted across the counter and Ben let out a hellish, uncontrollable shriek.

"Ah, God damn," muttered the raccoon.

The old man laughed until he started coughing, so much that he had to brace himself against the stove. Ben was panicking. He cradled his injured hand against himself, howled, and danced in torturous circles. Blood had already saturated his shirt and was dripping to his feet.

"Sweetie, Sweetie, Sweetie," he heard, but it was like a few raindrops in a violent thunderstorm.

Then two hands grabbed him by his shoulders and he met Candy's eyes. They were wide and sweet and pleading.

"Sweetie," she emphatically repeated. "I told you not to let him bully you, didn't I?"

"He cut off my fucking fingers!" Ben whimpered.

"Look again," she instructed.

He gazed deeper into her eyes. They were so lovely; his must have been desperate and scared and bewildered and so much more. But he willed himself to remove his hand from his shirt and take a look. His hand was intact, and the shirt that had been drenched with his own blood was once again untarnished, as though nothing had ever happened. Apparently nothing had.

"I—I don't understand," he managed to say, through gasps of relief.

"That's a fuckin' trick!" exclaimed the old man, filled with glee.

The room fell silent. Even the song and the commotion from the living room had disappeared. From the corner of Ben's eye he thought he spotted something looming, watching him, but it turned out it was just a dark curtain covering the window. It delicately swayed. Must've been from the furnace, or maybe the window was opened a crack, he convinced himself.

Then there came a howl from somewhere outside in the distance. And then another soon after that.

"Lousy mutts," groaned Ronnie.

Candy's hands were clasping Ben's and it was equally chilling and soothing. He wanted to leave but she pulled him in and there was something about her that wouldn't allow him to resist.

"Sweetheart, he's just a crotchety old man." Her voice

sounded re-assuring but there was nothing re-assuring about the situation. Smiling wide, she told him: "You can beat him!"

Candy reached high on her toes, gave Ben a soft kiss on the cheek and let go of his hands. As she did Ben saw a flicker of something unpleasant on the old man's face—anger, disgust, jealousy maybe? Whatever it was, it was clear that the kiss had struck a nerve. She rounded the counter and gave Ronnie's backside a playful smack and he jumped a little.

"Old Spook," she admonished him, giggling, and her giggles echoed through the kitchen. It seemed to Ben that there were other voices that had joined in the laughter, just as the echo began to fade. When it faltered, a chill was running down his spine and carried through to his toes.

"Rubber match then, mate," encouraged the raccoon.

"That's right! We need a winner!" Ronnie agreed. He plopped his elbow back on the counter and dug his feet into position. His fingers writhed with greedy anticipation.

Ben couldn't find the words to express how desperately he wanted them to allow him to just leave—he'd given up all desire for answers by this point. All he could do was make sure that they could all see the look on his face, and hope that would convey the message.

"Come on, son," Ronnie said with a calm and earnest voice he hadn't used before. "I'm sorry about the finger business. Just a friendly gag between us guys, heh? Don't get many visitors these days. Let's have a winner and we'll send you on your way."

Couldn't he just leave?

Ben deliberated it for only a second or two before he turned and ran. But once he did he found that what had earlier been a simple passage through to the living room was now a closed door. He opened it only to find an ordinary pantry full of ordinary things. His flesh was stiff; he had no choice but to turn

back around and shuddered at what he may see. He found only
that the three of them had remained just as they were. They
were regarding him in a striking manner, as though he were
being obtuse or dramatic.

"What is this?" Ben pleaded and his voice quivered.

"Just an arm wrestle, son," said the old man with that
greedy smile still on his face.

Ben looked to the raccoon, who he didn't like quite as much
anymore. There was more howling outside now, and he was at
the window guardedly peering through the curtains. "Just an
arm wrestle, mate," he concurred without turning his attention.

Finally, Ben looked to Candy, who was his best chance at
reason and somehow seemed able to end all of it if she so chose.
But she only rolled her eyes, exhaled a plume from a fresh
cigarette, and asked: "Is it ever *just an arm wrestle?*"

Bereft of a better option, Ben found himself back to the
plate, as it were. He came to the counter and plopped his own
elbow opposite the old man's once again. He was freezing cold
and terrified beyond anything he'd ever conjured in his worst
nightmares. It escaped his notice, but the darkness had slowly
crept in, further and further, until everything outside of its
circle—the three of them—was impenetrable. Somewhere
outside the dark, it was as if every wolf, every dog, and every
coyote that could be heard had joined in the cacophony.

"Kick his ass, Sweetie!"

With that, Ronnie grabbed Ben's now undamaged hand
and the final match began. Ben felt drained in every sense of
the word. The sensation couldn't easily be explained, but he
wasn't so chained to reality that he couldn't glean that whatever
he'd lost, Ronnie had taken. It was as though Ben were being
robbed of his very soul, piece by piece, and the culprit was the
once frail old man before him. Ronnie's entire manner was
more spirited now—healthier, more vigorous. Even his skin had

more color, less wrinkles too. Whatever this bizarre game was, it was zero-sum. (Verging on that realization almost pulled Ben away to another place, but it slipped away.) Each of their hands remained clasped to the other's. Their combined fists trembled between their faces, at a ninety degree stand-still.

Blowing out another puff of smoke, Candy playfully mused, "You know, many, many years ago, Ronnie was almost as handsome as you are, Sweetie."

Ronnie appeared to falter a touch before regaining himself. He grumbled, "Damn you, woman!"

Just then Ben remembered the look the old man betrayed when she kissed him. "You love her, don't you?" he asked.

"Of course I love her!" he snickered, as if to say *that's the best you got?* "What of it?"

On some level deep down, Ben was figuring out the old man's game. He said, "You just seem a little old for her."

Ronnie grumbled long and flat and then chided: "Maybe I will kill you. Witless boy, can't even see what's right in front of his eyes."

He wasn't exactly sure what the old man was talking about, but for the first time he felt like he had an in—a chance at winning. And there was something else, something in his mind that fought its way to the surface. Whatever it was exactly, he wasn't sure, but he knew that it was important. He could feel it struggling for air.

"You're looking for something, heh!" Ronnie spat. "Something to come along and give you the win. Your whole life, spent waiting for the miracle!"

Again, the match began to turn the old man's way.

"Never willing to put in the work, dedicate yourself, your mind!"

Ronnie had a hold of Ben's insecurities, as fiercely as he did Ben's wrist. Ben was in danger of losing.

"What happened to football, Bennie?" he ridiculed. "Lost your spot and didn't care to fight to win it back. Too many parties to go to, too many girls to chase."

It was almost over and Ben had no weapons to pull.

"And then there was Chloe. The girl that chased you!" he sneered. "Whole lot of good that did her. Worse off now than before! Did you listen to her?" The old man had become visibly angry, but he went on: "Did you give her the time she needed? No! You harassed her!"

Something was happening. Ronnie, lost in his rant, was losing strength and Ben was able to slowly regain position without his opponent seeming to even notice.

"Maybe if you opened those eyes to what you were afraid to see, you could've helped her! Afraid to lose her, afraid to let go! You could've understood you weren't what she needed, when she needed it! You could've changed!"

With that, Ben had retaken all the ground that he'd lost. They were back to a draw.

The raccoon cheered, "There you go, mate! Yes!"

Ronnie regained his focus and was instantly annoyed with himself.

"You old grouch!" laughed Candy. "Can't get out of your own way!"

As Ben was reminded of her, the thing that had been clawing its way free from the soil of his mind emerged. When it did, he turned his gaze and found her changed into an old woman. Still Candy, mind you, but with many decades added on. Her hair was frail and silvery, and her skin was as weathered as her lover's. She'd lost none of her sweetness.

The thing that his memory had struggled to give him was a lyric from the song that Elton had been singing earlier, from the other room:

. . .

I oughtta leave young thing alone,
  But there ain't no sunshine when she's gone.

"Can't let go... Maybe we're not so different." Ben whispered to himself. Pensively, he concluded, "You left her behind somehow."

Ben was winning. Just slightly, but it was something to finally feel good about.

"Opening your eyes finally, are ya?" snickered Ronnie. "Well look over there!" he cheerfully added, gesturing to his right.

Ben took the bait and there, between Candy and the raccoon, stood Chloe—a drained, lifeless version of her which wasn't completely unfamiliar, but Chloe all the same. All feeling escaped his body and the house sank behind her as his vision tunneled. Somehow, he was able to hold his grip before losing, his hand held maybe a couple inches off the counter.

Just then, precisely as Ben needed something to save him, the entire kitchen began to tremble as though there'd been an earthquake. Crumbs of the walls and the ceiling came free all around them. The cupboard doors all rattled against their shelves. A plate of muffins fell to the floor and smashed. Candy was fighting for her balance with one hand holding the shelf and a leg pressed against the island counter. She looked devastated as another plate of her desserts shattered across the linoleum below. Chloe, as quick as she had appeared, was gone.

Ronnie was distracted by all this. In fact he seemed utterly dismayed that such a thing could happen in his house. Ben weathered that storm and was then able to seize the opportunity. He took the old man's hand 180 degrees, decisively smashing it to the counter.

The house began to calm. For a moment, Ronnie struggled

to understand and identify what had happened. When his eyes found the kitchen table, though, he became enraged. "You son of a bitch!" he bellowed as his face stretched and tightened to a ghostly form that chilled Ben to his very bones. Though he wouldn't always remember it, he would see that very face in his dreams and struggle to endure it many times thereafter.

When Ben turned his attention, he found a heap of playing cards scattered across the table and spilled onto the floor. Rick had brought down the house of cards and stood over them, knowing there was no hiding his guilt. All came to be still in an instant, like someone abruptly pulled the cord which powered the quake. Now Ben found that the house was no longer what it had been before. Color had abandoned all of its surfaces and everything was rough and cracked with age—not quite as alive as it had been, as though many years had suddenly passed and in the intervening time it had gone without repair. Ben missed that the darkness which had hidden much of the room had abated, and the places it shrouded turned out to be empty and mundane.

"Fucking raccoon!" Ronnie blasted, and proceeded to grab a broom that had fallen to his feet during the quake. Rick circled the table and Ronnie gave chase, errantly swatting but unable to land a blow. He chased him into the living room, which was once again as it had been when Ben first entered. There was a smash of piano keys followed by the sound of breaking glass. Something solid made a loud thud and the barking and howling of dogs returned. Now Candy too had vanished and Ben was left alone, unsure whether it was smarter to get the hell out or not move a muscle.

In a horrific instant, it became dark; all the power in the house went out. He could see only a sliver of light from the window, veiled somewhat by the fluttering curtains. Ben brought his body on guard, but had no notion of what he may be defending himself against. Something as cold as ice pressed against his eyes and into his back. Everything disappeared. He may well have died of fright.

* * *

When Ronnie took his hands from Ben's eyes, he found himself in a bedroom aglow with too many candles to count. Hanging by the neck, uninhabited and swaying gently ahead of him, was Candy's body. She was young again, but blue in the skin and bluer in the lips. Ben's breath panicked and abandoned him, going off on its own wild path.

"This is how he found her," said Ronnie as he stepped past him from behind, regarding her sadly. He lovingly ran his frail fingers across a strand of her hair, moving it from her cheek and resting it behind her shoulder. His voice, his words, his face, were altogether different. With a voice that was full of regret, he finished: "Same clothes, same sorrow... much younger man."

Ronnie seemed reluctant to leave her. But he did, and took a seat on the bed across from Ben. Opposite the bed, sitting on a small ottoman, is where Ben found himself, frozen and fearful. Ronnie took off his hat, and Ben was taken aback by an altogether changed face, one strained by an unnatural amount of years and fraught with pathos. His eyes were sad and sunken deep into their sockets; his skin was loose and pallid. Ronnie placed the hat beside him on the bed, which was primly made and perfect. Despite his fear, Ben could only sit, listen, and fight off the pressure of tears behind his eyes.

He continued: "They loved each other more than they could explain, but love isn't always enough. When they were together they were in bliss, but when they were apart they were missing something—her especially. And what was missing haunted her, until it became that when they *were* together, she could only remember what was missing. "

A fleeting message, just then, arose from Ben's subconscious: if he and Chloe could ever just lay it all on the line, those last words were probably pretty close to what she'd tell him. At least then Ben could rest, knowing that he was right all along, and a part of her *was* still his. This helped to soften Ben's terror just a little.

Ronnie went on: "The man worked, and he worked, and at some point that he missed, he got lost in the work. Meanwhile, the girl was sick, and she had no work to get lost in, and the man thought it was strong of him to keep it that way." With his head held in despair, he finished: "It was weak."

Ben now found himself lost in both the old man's story, as well as his own subliminal calculations—the parallels between Ronnie's story and his own (vis-a-vis Chloe) required a visceral, ineffable formula that used emotions rather than numerals.

"But the girl *was* sick and had nothing other than her own thoughts, which became darker and darker. She disappeared further and further into herself."

Ronnie stared at Candy's body longingly, lovingly, and he began to cry. His voice remained stoic, though, as he continued: "The man sent her to doctors, and took her out wherever he thought she'd like, but it only got worse. Eventually, the girl locked herself in their bedroom and the man thought selfishly that the rest would do her some good...

"...But the girl never left this room," he lamented.

The old man paused and there was an agonizing silence. Ben thought better of interrupting it. He couldn't bear to look at either of them, and so he stared at the carpet. A haunting pattern turned about like clockwork and made him dizzy, but it was still easier to look at than either of them.

"It wasn't long after that," Ronnie resumed, "the man

started seeing her again. First there were noises, strange noises in every part of the house. Footsteps in the night, a tap on the window. Things began to shift when he wasn't looking, and move on their own. Then, one cold night, the girl revealed herself in a mirror. The man wasn't scared, never scared. Desperate, more like. But soon they were able to communicate, and not long after that he could be with her all the time. Things that were once so important were now foolish and insipid."

Compelled, Ben found the courage to look up to her body once more. Even he, having known her for so short a time, found that he missed her. He fought away an image of Chloe in her place, and in that instant he lost control of his tears.

"Every night after, the Lady in Black would come. Each of them would see her, across the street, at the window, or in the house. She'd grimly beckon the girl, onto the next place. Come with her and leave this struggle. But it wasn't a struggle anymore for the girl, and she felt as though she'd already left the man alone once before. She couldn't do it again, and he remained too selfish to let her go.

"One day the Lady stopped coming. They kept expecting her, for days and weeks and months. The man would open a door, or turn a corner, and he'd be sure that she'd be there to greet him but she never was. The years went by, as they do, and he grew older than he should have: Strained, worn and unhealthy, but alive and breathing. One day, he knew that *his* time would come. The Lady in Black would return and the two of them would go with her, together, and let go of their hold on this life that failed them. The man wasn't even sure when it happened. But there came a time it was undeniable—he *had* passed on.

"Only sometime after, when the people altogether stopped coming and they'd lost track of the years, did the Lady return. The man and his bride let go of their cares and made off towards her, but she turned away, cheated. She wouldn't take them. They'd made their choice and became prisoners of this house, in death as they were in life."

There was a slight change in Ronnie's manner. He seemed a touch amused as he said, "She still comes, the Lady in Black. Every so often. Reminding them both of what they'd held on to and what it cost them—taunting them."

With each man now crying, and Ronnie's story concluded, Ben found it a little easier to look upon him. Behind the thin haze of the old man's tears, his eyes were still clouded and dead.

"...Now how's that for a fucking trick?" Ronnie asked.

"You have questions," Ronnie finally said, after he'd collected himself. He was still sitting on the bed across from Ben. Candy's body still hung between them. "I can't answer them all. I can only start you on a path and tell you—show you—that you have to change. Holding on to what isn't yours is a road to misery, which you won't like as much after a while."

Defiantly, Ben rationalized that this was overstating things. Yeah, he was in a lot of pain and consistently drinking at whatever hours suited him, but it was just a bad break-up, he told himself, and he had it all under control. Chloe would be okay too—but this he couldn't quite push past the point of being a hope.

His thoughts were not safe from Ronnie, who snapped: "Heed my warning, boy! Chloe may or may not suffer the same fate as her!" He motioned to his own lover, her end met however long ago by suicide. "But your obsession will surely doom you as it did me!"

Ben couldn't keep fresh tears from falling. Imaging Chloe hanging like that. He wasn't sure it could happen, but it *was* something he had considered, try as he might not to. Did he ignore Chloe's sickness as Ronnie had apparently ignored Candy's? No! No he didn't think Chloe would do such a thing. She'd call for him before that ever happened...

"You think your love was more pure than ours, boy?" quipped Ronnie, sardonic and accusing. He reached a hand into his pocket and pulled from it a deck of playing cards. Ben felt violated but had nothing to say in response. He thought, probably, the answer was no. Ronnie shuffled the cards. Ben examined the backs, and believed them to be the same cards as the ones from the kitchen, some time earlier.

Once satisfied, the old man cut the deck and fanned the cards out in his hands. "Only she can save herself," he said with a cough. "Now pick a card and turn it over."

Ben wiped his eyes with his sleeve and did as he was asked. When he turned the first card over he found that it wasn't an ordinary playing card at all. On its face was a picture of a man who looked like a typical joker, with a jester's hat atop his head. But he also wore a modern blue suit with gold stitching, and was seated at a piano, appearing to play it raucously.

"The Piano Man," said Ronnie. "He'll be your first spirit."

"I think I've already had the pleasure," said Ben, his voice faltering.

"Another," barked Ronnie as he held the cards up higher.

Ben examined the deck and slid the cards back and forth before deciding. When he picked the next card and turned it over, he found on its face a man in a raggedy, grey cloak-looking garment and a pointy hat. He held with him a large wooden staff and had a proud look behind a bushy white beard. Behind him were two bolts of lightning.

"The Wizard," Ronnie stated. "Your second spirit."

Ben, still so haunted by the thought of Chloe succumbing to the darkness, as Candy had, couldn't think. Beyond that, this all was too surreal to even acknowledge so he simply didn't. He went for a third card. Counter-intuitively, he felt compelled to take the very first card that would have been atop the deck. Flipping it over, Ben found another he'd already seen that night, but had refused to admit it and kept it out of his mind. Until now.

On the card was a beautiful woman, but with a grim skull atop her shoulders. She was dressed in black from top to bottom: A cloak, a corset, a tight skirt that ended well above her knees, and a set of lace stockings that descended towards a pair of deadly high heels. Below the neck, her skin was as ghostly white as the skull that was atop it. The Lady in Black.

The old man grumbled deep in his throat as he held back his rage.

"Tell her she's a right bitch for me," he said.

And then they were gone—Candy and Ronnie—never to be seen again outside of his own dreams. Once again he could hear the howls and the barks of the dogs outside. He dropped the cards to the floor and ran out the bedroom.

Something climbed up from his stomach and the world around him had begun to twirl. Bracing the railing for support, Ben made his way cautiously down the stairs, soon finding himself back in the kitchen. Outside, something clawed at the walls, trying to get in. The howls grew louder. The playing cards that the raccoon had spilled still lay scattered across the table and the floor below it—ruins for future study. Otherwise the house was dark and empty. He peeked tentatively into the living room. Still nothing. No more people, no more music. Still, he couldn't shake the unmistakable feeling that someone was still there watching him.

Just as he'd made up his mind to break for the front door, he heard heavy, quick footsteps coming at him from the hallway to his left, and a desperate, screaming voice along with them. He swung his head to find Elton John running towards him with a baseball bat held high, cocked and ready to swing. Ben staggered back against the wall and brought his hands up in defense. But Elton, recognizing him at the last moment, came to a sudden stop.

"Bloody hell!" he shouted. "It's only you!"

"Yeah, it's just me, man!" gasped Ben, cautiously lowering his guard.

Elton panted and his face was painted with fright. Scratching and clawing at the front door stole their attention. Each of them jumped back as the feral silhouettes of whatever beasts wanted in could be faintly seen through the frosted glass of the door. The barking was frenzied and desperate and hungry.

"They won't let us leave, darling," whimpered Elton. "They think we're one of them."

"One of them?" asked Ben.

"Oh, dear Lord!" erupted Elton, ignoring Ben altogether. He'd spotted an old landline phone hanging beside them. He picked it up and the relief was unmistakable on his face. "It works!"

He tucked the baseball bat under one arm and began to dial. Along with the rabid sounds from outside, Ben could hear the front door rattling against its lock.

"Who are you calling?"

"My bloody manager! Who else?" cried Elton John. "This whole nightmare is unacceptable!"

Ben couldn't disagree.

"Johnny Boy!" shouted Elton into the phone. "Yes of course it's me. This gig you've booked, it's a bloody nightmare! Beyond a nightmare!"

It was starting to seem more and more possible that the

front door would give way. Ben grabbed the bat from under Elton's arm and stood in defense.

"Oh, well where do I Begin?" screamed Elton. "Let's start with the bloody ghosts, how about! Yes ghosts! The after-party is fucking haunted, darling. That's right! Haunted! Ghosts! I don't have to tolerate this kind of thing! No I will not slow down!"

Random keys of the piano played in slow succession, but there was nobody there in front of it. Then they heard a faint laugh from somewhere above them.

Elton cradled his body against the wall, frightened nearly to tears. He sobbed into the phone, "I don't know what they want. They left, but then the wolves came! Yes wolves!" he bawled. "They're at the door now! Call the cops?! What the fuck are the cops going to do?"

Just then there came a soft tapping against a window across from them. Ben could see Rick the raccoon behind the glass, waving to him, calling them over. Silently, he grabbed Elton John by the suit and gestured to the window. Elton left the receiver dangling by its cord, and together they crept across the room. Rick carefully slid his claws under the frame and pushed the window open a crack.

"It's alright. These wolves, they aren't after you," Rick whispered when they reached him. Then, pointing to the ceiling inside, he said, "It's them."

Ben willed himself to scan the area above him, but didn't see anything.

"They can sense them, I reckon. Help me open this," added Rick.

Ben helped him but once it was open Elton shoved him aside and pushed himself through, head first, and he landed on the grass with a thud. Then Ben felt something run itself along his back, from his neck down to his waist. Daring not to look, he dove for the window. But whatever it was that had him, it didn't want Ben to leave and had latched onto his legs. Ben pulled himself with all his strength and the raccoon helped, grasping his jacket tightly. Finally he was freed, and came crashing hard against the ground, landing square on his head.

His thoughts hadn't left him entirely but comprehension of time had, and for some reason his eyes wouldn't open.

* * *

Detached and ethereal, Elton John's voice bounced around in the darkness. *"No, no, let the poor lad dre*am," it gently instructed; to whom was a mystery. *"Just a little longer, if you would. For in dreams, things have a way of revealing themselves —things that might otherwise be just out of reach."*

The Light wavered.

"Thank you, darling," said Elton.

* * *

It was the night before Cabo, and not a creature was stirring... except for Chloe and Ben, who were each of them hammered, passing a bottle of wine back and forth between them and blissfully dancing about her apartment. Ben was completely naked; Chloe had on a tiny pair of underwear but had lost her top somewhere along the way. Their state of undress was curious as the thought of sex never occurred to either of them that night. They only talked, drank, danced and laughed, and somehow found themselves less clothed as the night went on. It was well past midnight and their flight was at eight, but they didn't care. They kept the music blaring, Chloe's neighbors be damned.

The wine came and went between them but the final pass occurred as they were hand in hand, dancing away. Ben put to action a thought to twirl Chloe. She obliged and left him the bottle before she went. It was more of a drop than a pass, though, Ben would argue. She didn't give him much of a chance. The bottle tumbled to the carpet as Chloe's foot caught on the leg of the coffee table underneath her. Now she was falling along with the wine, and Ben was forced to make an unfortunate decision between the two. He chose the wine.

He managed to capture the bottle before it went end-over-end completely, but he never let go of Chloe's hand and just as he was confident he had the bottle secured upright, he was jerked downwards himself. Merlot rained upon them both. Neither was upset in the least. They lay on Chloe's suddenly stained carpet with their bodies dripping red, each of them overcome with laughter. Chloe eventually rolled herself atop him and began kissing the wine off his body. "You know how much I love you, right?" Ben asked her.

"Yes," she answered between kisses. Then she asked him: "But will you always?"

"Of course," Ben replied.

"You don't know that."

"Yes, I do."

"What if I didn't have my crazy pills?" she posited. "Would you still love me then?"

"You know I would."

"But you've never seen me without my crazy pills," she reminded him. "So you can't say that." Her chin rested on her hands which were resting on his chest. Her face betrayed a woeful hint.

"Yes I can," Ben assured her. She seemed to accept that, else she skillfully made it appear like she did. She gave him one last kiss before lifting herself to her feet. Wine dripped down her body and to the floor. She staggered a little, drunkenly, before she reached the kitchen table. There she collected herself for a moment before using a tea towel to wipe herself off. She asked Ben to turn off the music and so he did.

Then, Chloe sat herself down at her piano. Beautiful notes came along with each stroke of her fingers and soon she began to sing. This was the first time Ben heard her play—really play. Not just a cursory chunk of some tune to indulge him when he first asked (and probably other guys before him). His eyes soaked in the sight of her bare back, and the gorgeous hair that was draped overtop it, as her fingers danced over the keys and her voice filled the room. Something was in that performance: her investment in the melody, the passion in her voice. Here, Ben came to fall as deep as one *could* fall.

Chloe sang:

> ...I know it's not much but it's the best I can do.
> My gift is my song, and this one's for you.
> And you can tell everybody, this is your song.
> It may be quite simple but now that it's done,
> I hope you don't mind, I hope you don't mind,
> That I put down in words,
> How wonderful life is, while you're in the
>   world...

* * *

A perfect dark swiftly fell upon him and ended the song. Ben very gradually became untethered from himself. Beyond the blackness of unconsciousness, this was a step away from nothingness. But eventually there did come something. Ronnie's voice was like a roll of thunder in the distance. *"Heed my warning, boy,"* it said. *"And learn to let go."*

* * *

Nothingness abated as time took an immediate leap, and we come to find Ben and Chloe on a decidedly less lovely night. Ben was home with the flu and Chloe was out with her friends. She'd driven them all downtown and left the car outside Ben's place so that she could crash with him and not have to worry about how much she drank. Which, as it turned out, was a lot.

Playful texts went back and forth between them that night. Eventually Chloe wanted to leave her party and be with him. Ben was in rough shape but he wanted the same. She said she'd walk over and Ben said OK but asked her to be careful. She told him not to worry so much.

Not long after, there came indistinct screaming outside Ben's apartment. With his head spinning he carried himself outside. There he found Chloe banging on his neighbor's door.

"Babe, my key isn't working!" she bawled. "Benjamin! I miss your handsome face open up!"

"Chloe!" barked Ben and she swung her head to find him. Instead of realization, however, there was only confusion.

"Babe?" she whispered. And then she returned her eyes to the neighbor's door and wondered aloud: "No. No I could hear your voice inside."

"Chloe it's one AM, get over here," urged Ben.

At that moment, the neighbor's door opened. The austere face of an older gentleman emerged. Ben had seen him many times in passing but never really met or said much to him. The mistake finally appeared to dawn on Chloe, but she was the opposite of apologetic. "Oh calm down, man!" she spat.

"Excuse me?" the man grumbled in reproach.

Ben made to remove her from the situation, pulling her by the wrist. "What are you even doing home, it's Saturday night!" she shouted—unfortunately not at Ben. The poor old man scoffed but thankfully said nothing more and retreated back inside. His door slammed and the lock clicked behind it. Chloe didn't relent. "It's Saturday night, buddy, get a life!"

Ben managed to maneuver her through his door—the proper door—and pushed it shut behind her. He wanted to say a few different things but there was no opening through which to get a single word. He was caught in the grips of a massive hug as Chloe frenetically recounted her night. Her energy was strange and severe and off the charts. As much as Ben did, in the moment, chalk it up to a night of drinking, he knew deep down that something wasn't right.

"You're sick!" she proclaimed, tossing her purse to the floor. "You need soup! Let's make soup!"

"Chloe—" began Ben, but she was already at work rummaging through a drawer of pots and pans and the sound of that drowned him out. "Chloe!" he repeated louder.

She was filling a pot with water now. "Yes, babe?"

"Is everything alright?" he asked, nervous that it was not.

"Yeah of course," laughed Chloe. She brought the pot to the stove and a blob of water escaped and splashed to the floor. She didn't seem to care. She turned on the heat and made for the fridge. She swung the door open and became distraught at the dearth of soup-like ingredients. Actually there weren't really any ingredients to speak of at all. "You have nothing! You know I wanted to make you soup!" she bemoaned.

"I, umm—" he stammered. She'd mentioned it in passing but he couldn't see how this was his fault.

"You know what, never mind!" she stated and danced back to him. "It doesn't matter!" She had a smile back on her face, and Ben back in her arms.

"Just have sex with me," she gasped. "Just please have sex with me!"

Here, two things were going through Ben's mind. One: he was overwhelmed and frightened by the way Chloe was behaving. She was a wild girl at the best of times but this was wrong. Two: he still had the flu, remember. It was kicking his ass and he was exhausted and genuinely did not want to make his girl-friend sick. Because of these two things working in tandem in Ben's brain... he turned his cheek. This was not a deliberate choice, but a near involuntary action.

When Chloe's lips unexpectedly found his cheek, she was devastated. The face that Ben was confronted with as she pulled herself away was a sobering mixture of rage and sorrow. It looked as though she'd been betrayed by the one man she trusted most in the world. All the days after he'd have to constantly convince himself that this was not what he'd done. Sometimes it wouldn't feel that way, though.

"Fine," she barked. "I get it! I'll go home."

"Chloe, what? Listen, please..."

"Just stop," said Chloe as she retrieved her purse from the hardwood. She strung it across her shoulder and swung open his door.

"Chloe?"

"I know what rejection looks like, Ben," she snapped. "It hasn't happened to me a lot, but I know!"

"Chloe, you wouldn't let me talk," Ben pleaded. He chased her through the hall and into the stairwell. She fled down those steps as quickly as she could manage, conspicuously using the walls for balance. "Come on, I just don't want you to get sick!" he cried.

She couldn't get herself far enough away from him. "Save it!"

"Chloe!"

She erupted out the lobby doors and stormed to her car across the street. "Chloe what are you doing?" Ben demanded. "Chloe!"

She wouldn't answer him, and was in the car before Ben

could reach it. His body crashed against the driver's side door as it slammed shut behind her. He tried the handle but it was already locked. "Chloe!" he screamed. He banged his palms to the glass but it was no use. With her angry eyes resolutely forward, the car left the curb. Her steering was erratic and the car veered wildly left. Steering it back to the right, she overcompensated greatly. Her car took off the side mirror of a parked Jetta before she managed to get a better hold of it. Then she sped off and disappeared around the bend.

Fuck, thought Ben to himself. He didn't know what to think. Sunken and lugubrious, he sat himself on a concrete flowerbed outside the main entrance. There he remained until he remembered about the boiling water atop his stove and ran back inside.

This was the beginning of the end. Three more volatile weeks, and Chloe would walk away. She would tell him only that she thought she was ready, but actually she's worse than ever, and she's sorry but she couldn't do it any longer. Lastly, she would ask Ben to leave her alone and he would lie and say that he would.

And then, once more ...fade to black.

Muffled bickering grew in Ben's head, which concluded with a loud, strangely abstract smack. Then he heard another, and there came a burning sensation along with it that he couldn't quite place—removed from himself, like pain from a phantom limb. But then a third smack came, and all that pain rapidly assembled across his cheek. His eyes opened.

He found himself lying atop pavement with gravel pressed into his skin. Crouched over top him was a man with long, greasy hair that was tied back save for some strands that dangled from his brow. With a single hand held above him, that man, whoever he was, was ready to lay down another swat should it be necessary. Ben noted the lightning bolt across his t-shirt, between the letters AC and DC.

"Holy shit, mate!" the man gasped—an inexplicably familiar Aussie accent. "We thought we'd lost you!"

The man in the AC/DC shirt pulled himself from overtop Ben and offered his hand. About to take it, Ben suddenly felt that vile feeling crawling up his stomach once again. With no choice in the matter, he rolled to his side and vomited. Once he was finished he felt several hands on his body, comforting him and pulling him to his feet.

A woman passed by walking her dog, quite innocent in the whole matter. She pulled back the dog from trying to lick up the puke and offered them all a heavy scold.

"He's got the flu," one of them explained.

"Yeah, he's got the fucking flu, lady! Keep walking!"

Ben barely registered the spat. His vision was working hard to return to him. Firstly, he saw the moon. Big and brilliant, it hung full just below the clouds, which had all settled in a peculiar way above everything else, as though the top of the globe were the bottom of a bowl.

Secondly, he was able to discern a couple of familiar faces. Miah and Paul stood before him, bracing his body, concerned still but mostly relieved. Along with them was the man he first saw, with the long hair and the AC/DC shirt. Behind them was the black pick-up that he'd almost forgotten he'd ever gotten into.

"I think that did it, Rick," said Paul.

"I reckon so," he answered.

Rick, thought Ben, recalling a raccoon only vaguely in his mind.

"You don't look so good, bud," Miah said. "Better than a minute ago though."

"What happened?"

"We had to pull you outta the truck, man," Paul explained. "You were passed right out."

"Thought you were dead, for a minute there," Miah dryly added.

Passed out? Before Ben ever even stepped foot inside that house? Ben let his eyes take in everything around him, as if to confirm reality. They eventually fell upon that house. *That house... what was it about that house?* He was too fucked up and out of sorts to register the missing time. The haze that covered all that had just happened was thickening, obscuring the memory from his renewed consciousness. The harder he fought to remember, the further away it slipped.

He asked them for the time.

"11:45," said Paul.

He thought he remembered someone just telling him that. None of it made any sense.

Across from them, that same bum Ben had seen earlier in the night, wanting his 76 cents, was creeping along the sidewalk, slow as could be. His walking stick and stroller rattled overtop the concrete. He didn't seem to be paying anybody any mind, only keeping forward at whatever pace he could manage. Did he actually have a destination, or was he just wandering?

Not all who wander are lost...

"Well, you probably shouldn't be alone for a while," Paul said. "Why don't you come in with us and chill out for a bit."

The night air had suddenly calmed and the sky was beautifully aglow by that moon that was so gorgeously full, and shockingly apparent, as though someone had pulled it closer to the earth. The house itself was modest and pretty enough. From what Ben could see, the people on the porch and the ones behind the windows were altogether innocuous and seemed to be enjoying themselves. Nothing about the house should cause anyone unease. All that notwithstanding, when Ben gave it a closer look he encountered a rush of anxiety. For some reason, he couldn't stomach the thought of even taking a single step onto the lot. The thought of going inside, however irrational, horrified him. When the three of them headed towards it, guiding Ben along by his arms, he resisted.

Each of them stopped and turned to Ben, whose anxiety was so conspicuously apparent. "What's the problem, man?" asked Miah.

Ben couldn't even find the words. He only backed away from them and the house, gawking more with each step. Truly, on some level, he *was* aware of the foolishness of his fear. But it didn't matter.

"Buddy?" prompted Paul. And then: "What the hell's his deal?"

"Shut up, mate!" admonished Rick. "Can't you see he's had a bad trip!"

"Oh, like that time you locked yourself in your closet reciting Shakespeare?"

"How many times I tell you to shut the fuck up about that?" Rick barked in return.

Miah and Paul both laughed.

"It's not fucking funny! You know how dark that night was for me!"

"Yeah I know, I know" conceded Paul, but continued to laugh. "To be, or not to be..." he mocked, to bursts of laughter from him and his brother.

At that, Rick stepped to Paul and shoved his chest. "You mother-fucker!"

"Calm down, it's funny."

"It's not fucking funny, I've told you that!" Rick screamed, shoving him again.

"You touch me again, we're going," Paul warned.

"Come on guys, not this shit again," pleaded Miah.

They had a brief stand-off, which was concluded by Rick smacking his band-mate across the cheek. It was a half-hearted swing, nothing that would itself inflict any damage, but it did the trick. The two of them started swinging and soon each grabbed the other and pulled themselves to the ground. There they rolled about, throwing punches wherever they could while each struggled to overtake the other.

"Dammit," muttered Miah as he moved to pull them apart. "Think about the band!"

"I'm through with the band!" announced Rick, wrestling out of a head-lock.

Both back on their feet and ready for more, Miah stood between them and endeavored to keep each man at arm's length.

"Don't be a baby!" Paul shouted.

"Fuck you, mate!" Rick retorted. "I'm done. I'm sick of this city. I'm sick of the band. I should've stayed on the farm! I should've listened to my old man!"

"Yeah, we've heard that before!" Paul mocked.

Ben still couldn't force himself to move, even as he spotted a pair of blinding headlights emerge from the bend in the road. They grew bigger and brighter as the car neared. The shape of the vehicle revealed itself and came to a stop, and the headlights were joined by the flashing reds and blues of a (silent) siren atop it. The doors opened and a cop stepped out from the passenger side.

Oh no, thought Ben. Were they on to him? He wasn't even sure what he did.

"Hey!" snapped the officer. Ben could only see a silhouette

against the headlights, but it was a woman's voice. "Knock it off, let's go!"

The car's engine fell silent and the lights of the sirens abated as her partner stepped out. He pulled a flashlight atop his shoulder and shined it their way. His other hand was resting on his gun. Ben and Miah shielded their eyes; Paul and Rick remained still and for a moment seemed to deliberate the merits of seeing the fight through to the end. But it was only a brief moment, and ultimately they allowed their better senses to prevail. Each of them stepped away from the other, and Miah released his grip of them both. The one cop switched off his flashlight as the pair of them stepped towards the band. They were altogether fairly non-descript, the officers—he was a little shorter and rounder than his partner, herself quite tall and fit.

"What's going on?" the woman demanded. She came to a stop and crossed her arms, effortlessly projecting that she needed her gun much less than did her partner. He still had his hand on the holster.

After a pause, Rick said, "Nothing, Officer."

"Bullshit between friends," added Paul.

"This your party?" the woman asked.

"Friends of ours," answered Paul.

"Let's see some ID, guys," said the man.

"No problem," Miah put in, and the three of them reached into their back pockets.

At that moment the front door opened and more partyers stepped out onto the porch, all peering at the commotion.

"You two, stay where you are!" the male officer ordered. He left his partner and moved towards the house, which incidentally was the last on that block. "Where's the homeowners?"

His partner remained behind, stoic, beckoning for ID cards and expecting little to no nonsense involved. Rick, Paul and

Miah handed them over and she examined each card, one by one. None of them had Ben in their attention. Realizing this, and desperate to get away and find refuge in his bed, he took a step back. And then another, and then another. It appeared he'd escaped all of their notice, by some miracle. If he could just reach the corner, and get around a large conifer in the yard, he could successfully make his retreat.

"What's this about, Officer?" Paul asked.

Ben kept on, step by delicate step.

"We got a few calls," said the woman in a manner that was at once chipper and impatient, as she continued to scrutinize each of their IDs.

Almost there, thought Ben.

"Too loud?" Paul dared to venture.

Ben had reached the corner without notice. Grateful, but careful not to celebrate just yet, he began around the tree. The last thing he heard before leaving their sight and running for his life, was the cop's reply: "That, yes. And also we got a call from some Englishman, saying his client was trapped inside."

Ben never looked back.

* * *

After a while, when he absolutely couldn't run any longer and had to stop to reclaim some breath, it became clear that Ben had no idea where he was. The surroundings were familiar enough—intermingled narrow houses and tiny apartment buildings —but it could've been any of a hundred bits of the city. The drive wasn't very long or so he remembered, which couldn't exactly be trusted.

Hopefully Jonny Boy is okay, he thought to himself. But his phone was now dead and he had no way of finding out. He doubted Jon would even answer; this wasn't the first time they'd been separated by his antics. It never really bothered Ben. Knowing there wasn't much to be done at the moment, he allowed the yearning to get back to his bed to conquer everything else. He kept hope and, once he was ready, he kept walking. One foot ahead of the other. That was what mattered. In that manner he continued, just hoping he'd find something he could recognize.

Ben found himself far more paranoid than he ever imagined he could be. Someone was definitely watching him, though. He could sense it. God only knew who they were. The hipsters and the Neo-Nazis, the scammers and the saints, all the people caught in the grind and all the ones pretending they're not—them and all the rest in between. They were all around him, somewhere. *Could be any of them,* he thought. Countless roofs with countless different worlds underneath and he moved between them like a cosmic outsider, just trying to pass through unnoticed.

Don't mind me.

At some point the skyscrapers mercifully presented themselves along the skyline, jutting above and overseeing the smaller buildings beneath. The arrangement marked him North of downtown. A decent way from home. Truly, his apartment never seemed like 'home', particularly since Chloe left just as she was discussing moving in. In this moment, he'd call it 'home' in his mind. *Get home.* That was his one and only mission now.

Making his way towards the towers, he pulled his jacket—woefully inadequate, chosen more for the costume and less for the weather—tight across his body. A beautiful park was across from him: A flat bit of land sprinkled with stale leaves and various pieces of garbage, in which a lonely ballerina twirled. She must've been insanely cold, but you wouldn't know it from her movements, which were graceful and alluring.

He kept on, along an endless offering of narrow houses. There were tiny balconies on each, and on one of them was a stolid brown cow, chomping away on a collection of grass. It didn't seem interested in Ben as he walked by. Soon after, there came a run-down high school, where the words 'AIN'T NO SUNSHINE' made him feel as though he'd forgotten something. They were spray painted in big, gold letters over the school's façade—stylized graffiti, shining bright. A giant tree in the courtyard towered over him. It was a tangled nest of grey, leafless branches. *How could something that looked so completely dead ever start anew?*

Eventually, he found a street that he recognized and followed it. Knowing where he was now, he was finally able to make progress towards his mission. The entirety of downtown had opened up to his eyes as the road descended along a modest valley which led to the river. A bed of trees lay underneath his destination, a mix of green conifers and more dying, grey oaks. A delicate fog had settled in the air and the windows of the skyscrapers were set ablaze by the light of the moon. Beyond the yellow brick road, which now moved steadily under his feet, Oz neared. In his world, the edges of the towers were much sharper than the rounded towers of Oz. They gave way precipitously to the sky behind them, however far away that was.

At the bottom of that valley, over the river, was a bridge covered in lights and on this particular night the lights were all orange. The mist in the air glowed against the steel, making it look as though the bridge itself tore through the world from some other place. Nearing it, Ben realized that the flurry of traffic, to which his ears had subconsciously grown accustomed, had vanished. Along the venture home, he'd come across the odd passers-by and stragglers, likely making their own pilgrimage towards their front doors. But he suddenly found himself alone, and the only sound was the reticent chatter of frigid water overtop the rocks below.

He came to a stop and ran his fingers across the bridge's beams, as though there was something that the steel could tell him. There wasn't. As he admired the view, a pair of voices emerged from below. They seemed so close, but turning his head, he saw nobody there. Unable to make out their words, he crossed the street at the foot of the bridge—two narrow lanes; footsteps echoing—and gazed down the opposite side.

Burning on the rocky shore below, between a pair of empty camping chairs, was a small fire. A couple approached it from a house along the river. It was dark and he couldn't make out much about them, except that neither of them were dressed for the weather. But they didn't seem to be cold. The two of them sat down at the fire with their backs towards Ben. He could hear their voices but, still, couldn't quite make out their words. They sounded so young.

"So very young," a voice broached from behind him.

"Jesus!" Ben cried as he swung to find Elton John standing there on the street.

Elton placed his hands on Ben's shoulders, who was hunched over and staring at the grass in disbelief. "Oh, dear," he said. "You really must stop being so jittery, darling."

Ben, unable or unwilling to look up, only muttered, "What the fuck?" over and over again.

"Just breathe," said Elton pleasantly.

"You're not real," Ben proclaimed, each word clear and distinct in an attempt to convince himself.

Suddenly pain shot down the side of Ben's face. Straightening his body, he found that Elton had a strong hold of his ear, as though Ben were a child throwing a tantrum. Howling in pain, Ben swatted the arm away and gave a reproving scowl to the rock star in front of him.

"Well, you didn't think I was real," explained Elton John.

"I still don't," Ben spat. "But I should kick your ass anyway!"

"Oh, bugger off!" laughed Elton. "I knocked out Keith Moon in '75 over an 8-ball he stole from me … and you, darling, are no Keith Moon."

Absurdity notwithstanding, the pain was quite real. Rubbing it from his ear, Ben was once again reminded of the voices from the riverbed. Somehow, the commotion hadn't interrupted them. They didn't seem at all fazed, going on as though, in that moment, the Universe was theirs and theirs alone. Something about them held him from turning away.

"Let's go get warm, shall we?" said Elton, already moving past Ben towards the fire.

"Wait!"

Elton stopped. "For what?" he asked, in earnest, as if to convey that there was nothing to wait for. Ben couldn't think of anything. And so, Elton continued down the bank with his arms outstretched and bobbing for balance. Ben followed. The night still had its hold on him.

He joined Elton by the fire. Compelled, despite the blatant intrusion, he stretched his hands to the flame and gathered its warmth. The couple were opening a bottle of wine and still in conversation, and did not pay him or Elton John any mind. Ben couldn't help but interrupt them and apologize, but they weren't interested. They completely ignored him, carrying on as if no one else was there.

Just then, familiarity struck Ben as the fire revealed their faces, and their voices broke through his remaining incredulity. The fire, the chairs, the couple, the way it was all set up… it was all out of place—removed—but everything else he remembered exactly. And the girl: The way the flames bounced off her glasses and her cheeks, the sound of her voice, the words she said and the way she laughed... Once, a long time ago, he was sure she'd be the girl he'd marry. Her name was Laura. And there *he* was, too young to know any better, sitting across from her once again, filling her glass with wine.

"What is this?" asked Ben, his fingers still unconsciously taking warmth from the fire.

"A moment in time," answered Elton.

"I've always loved it out here," Laura said before taking a tiny sip of wine. Ben, the younger Ben, poured some for himself. "So far from the city, nothing but the mountains and the stars," Laura finished.

Ben turned to ensure that the city was still there. To his relief, it was. But then he gazed upwards, and found that the stars were no longer the stars above downtown. Magnified, their brilliance glittered everywhere above the horizon. They were the stars of the open country. Constellations were obscured in the mess of them, and the milky way seemed to cut open the entire night sky. All stars are from the past, but those... Those stars were truly theirs.

Ben (the younger Ben) answered: "Me too."

But his voice lacked something. He seemed distant. More distant even than Ben remembered being. They sat silently for some time. Behind them, the river endlessly echoed, and a horn rang out in the distance. Ben understood that the young couple couldn't hear any of it. For them, there was only the crackling of the fire and a conveyor belt in each of their minds, delivering word after word, many of them discarded before reaching their lips.

"I told you nothing happened," Laura said at last.

He didn't answer.

"Are we going to get through this?" she sighed.

"I still don't even know what *this* is," he answered.

Again, there was silence, and Ben didn't have to try too

hard to conjure the tension he remembered back into his mind. *Tell her you deserve an honest answer. Tell her that you went through her phone and you know more than she thinks. Tell her what Jon told you.*

Tell her you'll walk...

"I told you," began Laura, "I've been confused. I mean, we're both looking at leaving here, for college..."

He wasn't.

"And we have whole new lives ahead of us," she continued. "It's been a lot."

"I just wish I knew where we stood."

"All I can say is that I love you."

Ben wanted himself to say so many things, all the things he wished *he* had. But he knew none of it was coming. Ben told her only that he loved her too, which despite everything else, was true, and the young couple sat in silence once more.

Only this time the silence lasted far longer than he remembered.

"So very much unsaid," Elton John mused.

"Why are we here?" asked Ben.

"We're all responsible for where we end up, darling."

"That's not really an answer."

He sighed. "We're here because it is a place you feel you should re-visit."

"I feel?" asked Ben, accusingly.

"Of course. I wasn't there, was I?"

That much, Ben was fairly certain, was true.

"Only you could've created this for yourself," Elton explained.

"But what's the point?"

"I suspect, this is something of a parallel."

"A parallel?"

"Yes. A similar source of pain, maybe, to what you're going through now?"

"I think that's exaggerating."

"I'm sure you do," said Elton. "But tell me, how many nights have you spent alone these past months? How many of those spent drinking yourself to sleep? How much of life have you actually been experiencing?"

"I fucking miss Chloe!" shouted Ben. The young couple paid no mind, still sitting in silence, letting the flames be a distraction. "Laura has nothing to do with that!"

"I agree," said Elton.

"So why, the fuck, are we here? Tell me!"

"Because it's Halloween!" he proclaimed, which made no sense to Ben. "And because another chapter has ended, and you're just as unable to turn the page from this girl as you were the last."

That did make some sense, he couldn't deny.

"Look at those stars, mate," said Elton, with a more solemn tone of voice. He had one arm up to the sky, and the other around Ben's shoulder.

Ben obliged.

"Look at the beauty of it all! The cosmic fucking divinity, shining down from hundreds of millions of years away. Many of 'em have died and gone away long before we ever got here. Others have been born that we will never get to see."

Ben didn't know where Elton John was going with that, but his mind *was* lost in the sky—the organization and splendor of the Universe, displayed so plainly above.

"Providence, darling," chuckled Elton. "Cosmic discernment, the idea that whatever you have was meant for you, it's bloody seductive. And you my friend, not so very long ago, were just as enamored with the idea that the Universe brought you Laura, as you are today, that it brought you Chloe."

Their eyes met at a near uncomfortable distance, Elton still had an arm tightly wrapped around Ben. "If you stubbornly keep your faith in those stars, you'll keep losing grip on what's in front of you," Elton concluded.

Ben ruminated on the words of the rock star, letting his eyes fall back to the flames. "You think I'm trying to learn how to let go?" he asked.

"I do," said Elton.

Ben stepped out from under his arm and asked, "And you're here to teach me how?"

"Oh, I don't know about that, exactly," laughed Elton. "But I had the same troubles. I thought I'd solved them with drugs and alcohol. Then I had to learn to let go of that."

After a brief consideration, Ben earnestly asked: "And how'd you do it?"

Elton answered, with thrashing flames reflected in his sunglasses: "I realized how good of a time I could *choose* to have without them."

Just then Laura broke the silence: "I know those eyebrows."

Ben, in a sudden tumult (feeling those same eyebrows on his face) flashed his attention back to her. But she wasn't talking to him this time.

"What?" asked the younger Ben, similarly shaken from his own thoughts.

"Those eyebrows. You're upset," she replied. "There's something you want to say."

"I wish I knew what to say," he answered sadly.

"You never want to let me in on what you're thinking."

"I'm sorry," is all he said.

Elton stepped away, towards the river. Ben, not wanting to be there anymore anyway, followed.

"I'm guessing you thought there'd be an apology in that

conversation," he said. "Bet you didn't think it would be from you though, did you?"

"No," he admitted.

"You'd have buried your head in the sand and married that girl, if she didn't leave," said Elton.

Ben conceded: "Yeah"

Elton put his hand on Ben's shoulder. "Go home, darling," he said amiably. "And remember that not all things are meant for you to keep."

With that he was gone, as was the fire and those young, doomed lovers. Ben examined the sky and found it hard to spot a single star through the clouds and the light pollution from the city. In that moment, though, that was actually comforting. He stood there against the river for a few minutes, watching the water race away and the light that was sprinkled atop the ripples.

He found himself deep in thought. Chloe was so different from Laura, and in so many ways. But he couldn't deny that he was at certain points equally obsessed with fixing both relationships. Suddenly perplexed by the reminder of how all-important another relationship seemed once upon a time, and was now so distant and trivial, everything came into question.

As special as Ben knew he was to Chloe—she'd admitted it enough times, at her most vulnerable and her most honest— maybe he just wasn't *as* special as he liked to think. Probably nobody was. Ben was clinging so fiercely to the idea that he was exactly what she needed, and forcing out the reality that, at least for now, nobody was. He was genuinely worried about the dark places to which he might be abandoning her, but, yeah, he could probably move on if he allowed himself to.

Along with this pensive realization which he began to allow, he was also curiously envious of his younger self, because he knew that the next thing that happened that night was the incredible sex that he and Laura had under those lost stars.

* * *

Much headway had been made and, finally, Ben found himself back to where the skyscrapers were once again giant walls erected all around him. He still had to make his way through them all to get home. His body was so, so cold but his intoxicated mind had subjugated it into obedience. Forgetting already that his phone was dead, he pulled it from his pocket. *Shit.* Still dead. Without his watch he didn't know the time, but judging by the sparse crowds filing out from the establishments around him, it was probably pretty close to cut-off. He kept on.

Was the love between him and Chloe so powerful that it could only have been fated, designed cosmically like the stars above? Ben thought so, lame as that sounded... at least he did. Whatever concoction was still in his system, it had all combined in such a way that made logic and memory increasingly difficult to hold on to. But the memory of Elton and Laura was still there somewhere, and it had Ben questioning everything.

He did believe in fate, but a question he'd never considered until now: Was he so in love with the idea of it that he inevitably discovered it in every relationship? If he and Chloe *were* like the stars, then he should fight endlessly, for however long it took. If they weren't like the stars, then he would just be wasting days, months, years, basically banging his head against a wall.

The conundrum of it haunted him as he walked. *Fate couldn't be trusted, then, whether it exists or not?*

Physically speaking, he moved mostly on instinct, with little mind paid to exactly where he was yet still following the best possible path through the city. He tried his best not to pay too close of attention to the people around him, all still in their costumes, lest he freak himself out. He felt invisible after his third attempt to wave down a cab. But then a group of Power Rangers asked him for a cigarette.

No smokes, sorry. He asked them for the time.

"Twenty-five after one," they said. AM.

Ugh. He pressed on.

Forced to stop at an intersection not long after, Ben took his hands from his pockets and blew some warmth into them as he danced a little on the spot. It wasn't far now—twenty minutes at worst, he figured. Next to the curb below him was an abandoned pair of high heels, which rested neatly side-by-side as if the lady wearing them had vanished while waiting for the light.

As Ben mused about the shoes missing their lady, or the lady missing her shoes, he heard what turned out to be the rattle of a wheel against the sidewalk beside him. Coming towards him was an old man in a grey cloak and an absurdly large, pointed hat. He pushed along with him a wooden, wheel-barrow-style cart that was modest but well crafted—Its only wheel forged from iron. Its condition was impeccable but it looked positively ancient, as though it were pulled out from its own time. Whatever was inside was covered by a tattered cloth, but atop it rested a large walking stick that was twisted and carved into an elaborate pattern.

He came to a stop at the intersection beside Ben and set the cart down on its pegs. There, he pulled out an old, wooden pipe that reached from his lips down to his chest. Shielding the bowl with his free hand, there appeared a glow from a flame. He puffed on the pipe a few times until satisfied, and then the light of the flame disappeared. Ben found it curious that the man didn't seem to have a match or a lighter to put away, but he'd had enough of curiosities for one night and dismissed it almost instantly. Still, he couldn't help but stare. Exhaling a tired breath of smoke, the man regarded Ben only briefly with a fleeting, commiserative smile that came through his considerable beard. He turned his head, smoked, and waited for the signal to cross.

After a moment the man's eyebrows jumped and he let out a sigh that was equal parts pleased and impatient. The crossing light had switched on and, with that, the man clenched the pipe tight between his teeth, picked up his cart, and began across the street. The lonely wheel of that cart was smooth and flat, decidedly light on friction, and he had a little bit of trouble starting off over a lip where the curb met the asphalt of the street. But just as Ben decided to help the old man out, he gave it a couple extra shoves and worked it onto the road without much more trouble. From there he was off, albeit at a crawling pace. And so Ben made his way past him and continued on with his own journey home. He was focusing hard now on walking in a straight, sober line.

On the next block, he passed by a group of men—who weren't dressed up at all as far as Ben could tell—chatting up a couple of girls who were dressed in Thing #1 and Thing #2 onesies. To Ben, the girls didn't seem too interested, but neither did it seem like they were being harassed. He kept walking. A pair of crows swooped across his path and landed on a bike rack beside him, each cawing in turn as if continually affirming what the other said. He wondered what that might be. It seemed important, whatever it was. As he walked by, one of them dove for a discarded wrapper on the road before his partner could notice. Snagging it in its beak, he flew to the top of a pub and began pecking away whatever morsel of nourishment remained inside. An echo of squawks went back and forth.

Soon after, there came some other commotion behind him —something hollow crashed against something much harder,

317

along with several voices which shouted indistinctly. He turned around and saw that the old man's cart had been tossed onto its side. Bottles and cans lay scattered across the street.

Ben was too far ahead to hear exactly what was being said, but one of the guys shouted at the old man with a threatening finger that jabbed the air between them. Soon enough, he stepped into the old man and shoved his chest. Ben took a couple hesitant steps forward and watched as the two girls pressed in to intervene. They held the guy back from the old man, who'd already humbly begun the task of setting his cart back upright and collecting his bottles.

One of the others joined in, and shouted loud enough for Ben to hear: "Why don't you get a fucking job and mind your own business!" That jerk then blew past the others and kicked the old man's cart back to the ground. More bottles and cans exploded onto the road. One of the girls gave him a shove in reproach but he bounced back and captured her in his arms. With her body held tightly, her legs struggled to kick herself free. The other girl became similarly ensnared by the first guy she'd been holding back.

That was too much. Ben started towards them. "Hey!" he yelled. Even with that single word, the intoxication was plain in his voice, which he recognized and hated. They didn't seem to have heard him, above their own clamor. The disturbance seemed to have stirred the crows as well. All of them joined the raucous—incessant shrieks from the rooftops.

"Get off me!" the girl wailed as she continued to struggle out of the guy's arms. The old man moved to pull him off of her, but he was held back and thrown to the ground once more. He lay there defenseless in the gutter, trying to gather himself. His attacker jumped on the opportunity. He let go of the woman, flew across the sidewalk and delivered a kick to the old man's stomach. When Ben reached the scene he didn't think. He just pushed the first guy out of his way and landed the best fist that he could manage to the next one's jaw, which freed the second damsel. Ben put so much into the punch that he tumbled to the pavement along with his target.

"Motherfucker!" he heard right before he took a few kicks of his own. Ben lay there on the curb, coughing desperately, with pain radiating throughout his insides. The concrete was rough against his cheek, and cold, so cold, against his body.

"Leave them the fuck alone, Terry!" he heard a girl's strident voice howl.

Ben wasn't sure what his next move would be, but he knew that he had to get himself back to his feet. While attempting to do so, he noticed that the old man, on the ground beside him, had sat himself against a streetlight and was reciting some foreign words in a strange cadence under his breath. A moment later, the frantic clamor of birds erupted and rapidly grew more intense. But then Ben received another kick and collapsed once again.

A tumult exploded among those left standing as crows descended upon them all. Still collecting himself, all Ben could glean was a shadowy mess of tiny black figures. But he clearly heard the thrashing of their wings against the air, beaks against flesh, and the baffled cries of the birds' quarry.

"Dude, what the hell?" exclaimed one.

"Get them off me!" demanded another.

Finally, everything in front of Ben coalesced into actual vision, and he saw one of them make contact with a crow, mid-air, with a swat of his hand. This only served to further anger the others, who all wailed indignantly and attacked more mercilessly than before. More of them flew in. There must've been a dozen of them or more. One of the girls ran off for cover, and pulled along a crow behind her that had a chunk of her hair in its beak. The other girl followed her as frantically as she could manage in her heels. The two guys continued, quite fruit-lessly, to defend themselves.

As Ben labored himself onto one knee, the old man had already turned his cart upright and replaced most of the recy-clables he'd lost. Ostensibly, he wasn't concerned at all about the poor bastards in front of them, who'd staggered a little ways over but were still unabatedly under attack.

Ben stood and tried his best to ignore the pain. He gazed at the group incredulously. "Jesus! Can you believe that?" he mused.

"Oh yes," said the old man, his voice a baritone with a hint of an accent behind it that Ben couldn't place. "Crows are loyal creatures. I feed them whenever I'm able."

He placed one last, crumpled Pepsi can back into his cart and replaced the cloth overtop. With some effort, he then hunched over and reclaimed his walking stick. Lastly, he re-lit his pipe and inhaled a few puffs. With that, he continued on his way, regarding Ben only with a quick nod of his head. Mostly because he was going the same way, but partly out of curiosity, Ben followed.

Though he was still in pain and somewhat hobbled, Ben quickly came up beside the old man and took a closer look. His face was nearly entirely hidden behind his beard and the shadow that was cast under the brim of his hat. He was still puffing on the pipe that he secured in the corner of his mouth. Ben saw small flickers of light in that beggar's eyes, and found them to be so very blue, like the sky before sundown. He kept those blue eyes aimed ahead of himself.

"Is there something I can do for you, young man?" he asked. His tone verged on annoyance.

Shaking a thought from his mind, something or someone he was told to expect but couldn't quite comprehend when or why or how in that moment, Ben replied, "No, sorry." Chloe's face

BENNIE & THE EX

came upon his mind's eye, but that was hardly unusual and so he disregarded it. He continued on his way and said, "Goodnight."

But after Ben had put a small distance between them, the old man called out: "Do you mean to wish me a good night..."

Ben stopped and turned. The man continued towards him.

"...Or do you mean to say that this is a good night in particular?"

The old man brought his cart to a stop in front of Ben and removed the pipe from his mouth. Smiling, he asked, "Or do you simply mean to say that this is a night to be good on?" He suddenly seemed quite friendly.

Through a vague sensation of unreality, Ben responded: "All of them at once, I suppose."

The old man let out a guttural chuckle. Then, he said, "I wonder, my friend, if you would be willing to help me out?"

"With what?" Ben expectantly asked, numbed against the conventions of real life, now so far out of reach.

"I wonder if you have just 24 cents?"

Ben was slightly disappointed. But he checked his pockets and turned them loose, showing the man that he, genuinely, had no change whatsoever.

"Shame," he said impassively. "Then we're in the same boat, as it were."

Ben could feel his own face still gawking at the man, but wasn't quite aware of it at the same time. Though he'd recall it all vividly later on, Ronnie—the first strange old man that he'd encountered—and his tarot cards were at this point an inaccessible scene covered in haze, like a chapter in a book he hadn't read in years. Yet the archetype in front of his eyes wasn't lost on him. Still, the words '*Heed my warning, boy*' rang out through his mind—said in some gravely, haunting voice. Passing traffic, and a burst of laughter from a group running across the street, shook him out of it.

"Who are you?" is all Ben could say.

"Only a wanderer," the old man said. "A vagrant and a bum —to those who've turned their hearts away." His voice was so much warmer than his words.

"What's your name?" asked Ben.

The old man paused at this. His head fell slightly and his gaze seemed to loosen. Pensive and mournful, he answered, "You know, I've quite forgotten my name."

After a moment's deliberation, in which he seemed to be searching the depths of his memory, he added: "*Wisdom*, I was sometimes called, though not in your tongue."

"Wisdom?"

"Oh, yes. One of the four great Wizards!" he proudly proclaimed. He seemed to have gained a couple inches in height.

"*Wizard*," Ben admiringly whispered, though somehow not surprised the word was introduced.

"Oh yes. Do you not believe it was so, looking at me now?"

"No, I do."

"Well I am glad," he said. "Tell me, friend, what is *your* name?"

"Ben."

"*Ben*," he repeated, dragging the name from deep in his throat. He raised a hand to Ben's chin and clutched it between his thumb and his fingers, which were thick and cold and marred with dirt. Ben had no thought to resist. The wizard pulled Ben's face into his own and examined it closely. His head tilted with scrutiny. Then, in an instant, his eyes widened, pulling free the wrinkles underneath them. Hearty laughter followed and he turned to retrieve his cart. Wheeling it towards

Ben, he declared, "Why didn't you say so from the beginning! Come, I've something to show you!"

Something to show me? thought Ben. "Is it about Chloe?" he asked.

"Chloe?" replied the wizard with an absent tone. And then, dismissively: "Oh, yes, yes. Chloe! Of course! Sure as rain."

The wizard hobbled further into the night and Ben followed.

* * *

They'd come to 9th Avenue and were at a stand-still waiting for traffic to abate at an intersection without lights. Drivers were not heeding the crosswalk which was clearly marked in reflective paint. Ben, still feeling quite well, wasn't all that concerned. The wizard, however, was positively vexed.

"Gods!" he bemoaned. "Great conjurer! A Quarter of the Soul! Wielder of the *Star of Mímir!*"

Ben had no idea what the wizard was saying, but thought better of asking just then.

"...And now, motorists do not even think me worth stopping for," he grumbled.

"I think I see an opening coming up," said Ben in a placating voice.

"Nonsense!" he scoffed, grabbing his staff.

The wizard ordered Ben to watch his cart as he outstretched his arms and strode onto the road. Ninth Ave was one-way, and cars flew across it from their left to their right. The wizard didn't break stride, even as a truck that would've taken his head clean off roared past, mere inches in front of him. Undaunted, he continued, bawling out words that Ben couldn't understand but sounded like they'd come from the heavens. He found a safe area in the middle of the avenue, faced the traffic, and slammed the bottom of his staff against the asphalt. Ben felt the ground rumble beneath him.

In the same Godly voice, he declared: "You cannot pass!"

Some cars continued past him, but the ones ahead began to slow. He repeated more emphatically, more forcefully: "You cannot pass!"

They all came to a stop.

"Come now, Ben!" he instructed, waving Ben over. His other hand was still firmly grasping his staff. "Mind the cart, now!"

Ben didn't delay. He grabbed the handles of the cart and pushed it onto the road, trotting it across 9th, behind the wizard whose arms were held as if supporting some great, invisible wall between him and the vehicles. Once Ben was across, the wizard lifted his staff with indignant triumph, and resumed his path across.

"Witless oafs!" he admonished.

The rumble of engines resumed as they carryied the vehicles through the intersection and back to speed. Inside each of them, the drivers never seemed to regard them at all. They barely seemed real.

"So where are we going?" Ben asked as they resumed walking.

"Hmm?" grumbled the wizard, leaning his ear to Ben.

"You said you had something to show me?"

"Oh! Well then, come along, by all means!" he proclaimed, no longer the disgruntled pedestrian, but the amiable old man he was prior. Still, there seemed to always be at least a hint of impatience in his voice. "Oh, could you be a lad and pick up that bottle just there," he added, pointing to a discarded mickey of vodka in the gutter.

Ben did as he was asked and placed it under the wizard's cloth with the rest of his haul.

"Thank you," he said, and the sincerity in the words was unmistakable.

"No problem," said Ben. And then, prodding him again, "So, what is it?"

"What is what?" asked the wizard.

"You said you had something to show me? Something about Chloe?"

"Oh, yes! Chloe! Beautiful girl... caught in the middle, pulled at by the light and the dark, never at peace."

"What," Ben blurted out. "What does that mean? Do you know where she is? Is she okay? Are we going to her?"

The wizard only chuckled in a way that assuaged Ben's sudden anxiety. "My lad, Chloe will return in time. But for now, we must look elsewhere!"

"Where?"

"Well, only the finest place in all the city, at this time of night!" replied the wizard.

Sounded good.

Hastily, the wizard added, "But we've a longer journey to make than time available. Best make haste. This sort of thing isn't easy."

Again, Ben had no real recollection of the cards that Ronnie had pulled earlier, the spirits who each supposedly had some message to deliver—The Piano Man, The Wizard, or The Lady In Black. Hadn't he been passed out, after all? Had he even entered that house? But he wasn't passed out now, of that he was fairly certain. And Elton John had endured afterwards, too, hadn't he? Still, some hints of that vision lingered, and whatever it was that lingered had Ben following this old man, who commanded birds and spoke of journeying through time, without question.

The drugs and the booze probably helped.

* * *

And so they continued on their path, the wizard leading with Ben at his side. The wind had subsided and Ben wasn't so cold anymore. In fact, he was quite content. Everything was brighter somehow. And instead of feeling haunted, as he had through the night, he felt as though he were being guided—and not just by the old man to his right, but by the Universe itself, which was once again fascinating and lovely. All thoughts of everything else—Jon, Clients, Indie bands, Snow White, Elton, and even Chloe to some degree—had dissipated, for the time being at least.

Sometime ago, it seemed to Ben, they had entered a park which he knew well. Between 12th and 15th Avenue, it was a sanctuary thick with trees and gardens built up with cascading stone walls. A cobblestone pathway cut diagonally through it, which they'd taken. Nobody else was on the path with them— no one in the park at all it seemed, by the sound of it (or lack thereof). Enjoying this respite from the bustle of the city, Ben and the wizard travelled in silence.

The trees thickened as they walked into a growing darkness. Soon it became that the two of them were sequestered from the city lights entirely, and Ben found that he couldn't see anything at all—not even the shape of his hands right in front of his face. Just then the sound of the wizard's cart atop the path ceased, and Ben heard its pegs fall to the stone. He'd set the cart down and must've stopped, and so Ben did the same. But the old man hadn't said anything at all. Ben could only hear him fumbling with something, and the sound of it echoed all around him and carried strangely. Uneasy, and feeling something potentially worse underneath, Ben asked: "Wizard? Are you still there?"

"Yes, yes," assured the wizard. "Stop where you are for a moment."

Ben didn't want to panic; the beautiful high he rode into the park was still alive, but fading fast. "Wizard?"

"One moment, one moment! No need to fret, it's only the dark of night. Believe me, there is nothing else here but you and I."

"How can you know that?" asked Ben. His eyes pleaded with the darkness. How could he possibly account for what lurked out there in the wild? A single terrifying thought emerged: Winter was coming, and the bears were getting ready to hibernate!

Oh no.

He began to hear them. They were all around: Ferocious, hungry, helpless against their biology. They couldn't be blamed, of course, Ben was in their territory. But that wouldn't matter to them.

"Wizard," he gasped, each of his senses on high guard. "What about the bears? Can you hear them?"

"Shut up!" the old man barked. After an agonizing pause, he finally spoke again: "Here we are!"

With a snap of his fingers there was suddenly a bright white light atop his staff; it defined the wizard's face in a way that the city's lights never could. To Ben's great relief, he could see no sign of any bears. Under their feet was the same cobblestone path that he recognized from that park, with trees planted to either side, equally spaced from each other. But there wasn't as many of them as there should've been, and they weren't quite as dense; they rose up higher and on thinner trunks. Through them, Ben saw the light of the wizard's staff reflect in the ripples of waters that were seemingly endless in any direction. The path had become a bridge across some ocean, dividing it while somehow apart from it.

In awe, Ben looked back to the wizard, who gently blew the light on his staff into the sky and that light grew and became the moon. It was a stunning full moon that was half as near as it should be, and it covered the path in a gentle, silvery hue.

"Wha—Where are we?" Ben stammered, amazed.

"On an ocean of time," he answered, once again lighting his pipe, which he'd freshly packed.

An ocean of time.

Where had Ben heard that before?

Exhaling a plume of smoke and looking quite satisfied, the wizard began once again along the path. He had the look of a man who'd regained a part of himself he'd long ago lost. Ben thought that was probably the case. "Be a good lad and take the cart, would you? My arms have grown quite tired."

Ben did as he was asked and followed.

* * *

The wizard pensively smoked as they walked, while Ben took in the sights and sounds around him, incredulous yet astonished. Off somewhere in the distance, the horizon was hazy and softly aglow, but the light quickly faltered as it reached up to the moon above, which hung in an opaque sky void of stars. He wondered about Jon a little, and about Chloe a little more than that. But ultimately he trusted that the wizard knew the best course forward regarding everything. He was a wizard after all. At some point, something he'd heard the Wizard say earlier came into his mind.

"Why did they call you *Wisdom?*" he asked.

"Because I am very wise," laughed the old man. And then: "It is the facet of the soul I represent."

"Facet?"

"*Wisdom, Wit, Courage and Love,*" he explained. "Four

facets of the soul, and four Great Wizards sent to represent each." That line was more recited than spoken. A hint sarcastic even.

"Sent?"

"Mhmm," he grumbled an affirmation.

"From where?"

"Paradise," he replied bluntly.

"What was that like?" Ben asked next, the words sounding so stupid only after they'd left his mouth.

Sorrowfully, the wizard said that he couldn't remember.

Ben repositioned his hands against the cart's handles. Its iron wheel bounced delicately along the stones beneath. The sound of it was steady underneath the whoosh of the wind against the top of the water.

"What about the others?"

"The other wizards?"

"Yeah."

"I wish I knew, Ben. The four of us went our separate ways during the Last Great Battle, each our own tasks to accomplish. I never saw them again."

Ben thought he could see the outlines of a set of buildings in the distance ahead, but he wasn't sure. The more he squinted and tried to extend his vision, the less he could make anything out. He wanted to ask the wizard why he'd resorted to roaming the streets collecting bottles, especially with such great magic still at his command, but he didn't have the heart.

The wizard went on: "The evils besetting Man were finally conquered, but I was never called back."

There definitely were buildings ahead. Ben began to discern the shape of them, their edges were modestly defined by the light of the moon against the sky. He noticed something else, though. Some dark figure was on the path ahead. Whether it was coming towards them or moving away, Ben couldn't tell.

Ben asked, "Do you see that?" He pointed to where that figure loomed.

"See what?" asked the conjurer. His eyes were squinting in an attempt to match Ben's younger vision.

"Someone's coming."

"Here? No, No—Nonsense."

By now Ben could unequivocally say that it was coming towards them. "I'm telling you, man. There's someone there."

The wizard stopped and instructed Ben to do the same. With a hand pressed against Ben's chest, he now examined the road ahead with a severe look on his face. Ben set down the cart and watched with him, making sure to take his lead from the old man.

"You see it?"

"I see it."

As it neared, the moonlight began to settle on the surface of the black garments it wore, which covered it head to toe. Whatever that thing was, it didn't seem to be walking at all, rather it glided smoothly, unnaturally along the path.

"Wizard? Wisdom? Whatever—what the hell is that?" Ben demanded, sinking into terror as it neared. It wasn't far now—throwing distance for sure. If he'd had the nerve he could've whipped one of the old man's bottles at it. The cloak was ripped and tattered at the edges, which floated unnaturally like the air around it was liquid instead.

The wizard didn't immediately answer.

"What do we do?" pleaded Ben.

"Quiet!" he snapped. And then: "We do nothing. Pretend she isn't here and let her pass. She's no power unless you give it to her."

She?

More of her was revealed as she drew closer and a gust of wind peeled away some of her cloak. What wasn't concealed by her garments—which were all as black as if made from pieces of the night that were somehow torn away—revealed pallid, white flesh. Ben was struck by the dichotomy between the two. Her face was still hidden, but a tiny neck emerged from the shadows and led to a delicate chest, with a pair of breasts pressed up under a black corset, which was laced up its length and tied off in a bow. Her legs reached high from her boots to her skirt, aided by perilously high heels. In a terrifying way, she was quite beautiful.

"The Lady in Black," Ben muttered, unsure exactly where the words originated. They came up suddenly from somewhere deep down, the way forgotten memories sometimes do when they seem like the opposite of memories.

"Shhh," ordered the wizard.

The two of them parted as she came upon them. Another inch and Ben would fall into the water. He braced his arm against one of the trees for support. Ever so slowly, she slid between them. The toes of her shoes dragged along the path below her, just barely touching. As she passed, her head tilted towards Ben, and though he couldn't see them, he knew that somewhere in that darkness her eyes were locked on his own. Whoever and wherever that Wizard of Courage was, Ben could've used him then. But ultimately, the Lady turned her head back to the path and continued on her way.

"Well then, come now. Steady on," the wizard beckoned, and nonchalantly resumed their course.

Ben had not wanted to take his eyes from the Lady, but she'd drifted away impassively into the distance and disregarded them entirely. So he grabbed the cart and ran with it, catching up to the wizard.

The buildings ahead were dark and solitary, lifeless and strange. Towards them, the pair continued. The wizard's resolve remained unchanged, inscrutable, and as before Ben found himself following him without any of the thoughts that might otherwise seem reasonable. In truth, there were not many other options which Ben might consider, caught on that narrow road over that bizarre *ocean of time.* His mind continued to take this predicament at face value, and he could either turn and face the Lady, who he had no interest in ever coming across again, or go on with the wizard—who had promised something about Chloe.

Chloe!

"Where is she? Is she okay?" Ben pleaded, remembering her so suddenly, which was surreal given that his thoughts had never drifted away from her like this. But thought wasn't functioning like it was supposed to, and all the things that were divorced from the '*there and then*' of it were untenable moving targets.

"Who?" asked the wizard.

"Chloe."

"Goodness, boy!" scoffed the wizard. " She will be just fine without you."

This made Ben sad, but the cause of it fell to obscurity and only a confounding sorrow was left behind.

The buildings neared. Ben looked up to the row of them— an ordinary city block of otherwise ordinary structures, save for just how... dead... they all seemed. Almost like some sort of negative image. (That wasn't quite right but it was as close as Ben could get.) Even with that blinding moon hanging above, his eyes could only just distinguish the ends of them against the night sky. The path of small stones atop which they'd traveled now allowed for a sidewalk and a curb, which rested against it as though the path were actually a city street. But there were no cars, no people, no signs of life outside of themselves—none whatsoever. Only an island of buildings atop the ocean, which branched out from a cobblestone path that until then had been so narrow and inertial.

Ben stopped at the entrance of the first building. They all looked like run of the mill inner-city structures, but placed as more of a way-station on this surreal road and at some point abandoned. Looking up towards decaying brick and impenetrable windows, he asked the wizard, "Why are we here?"

"What?" he answered. "Oh no, no this isn't it. This is nothing." The wizard seemed only to have stopped to pack his pipe. He was struggling to get it lit against a sudden breeze.

Still, Ben was compelled to look inside. He approached the glass and it grew more transparent the closer he got. Inside was a flurry of colors, all of which appeared muted yet vibrant all the same. He could make out a dance-floor and a DJ behind it. Only a handful of people were dancing, while others were dispersed throughout—all in costumes that Ben didn't even care to figure out at that point. Some were at the bar waiting for drinks towards the far end. Others stood in conversation, laughing, drinking. Such was one pair against the dancefloor, right behind the glass. Ben's eyes somehow passed over them initially. On the girl's face was a big, beautiful smile that Ben knew well. She was looking up expectantly to the man she was pulling close with a handful of his shirt. It took a moment to confirm, but yeah, it was Chloe.

Ben was furious. He barreled his fists against the window, screaming her name. It made no difference and now their lips were locked. *So I guess she's doing okay?!* Ben vented to himself. He ran to the front door and frantically tried to make it open, but the door would not budge. He pulled with everything that he had. It rattled against the frame, louder and louder, but would not open. He resorted to several attempts at kicking it down. Still, nothing. He went back to the window. Scanning the entire bar, person to person, he couldn't find her.

Fuck!

Just then, a large man in a tight black shirt opened the front door, and Ben ran back. He tried to run through the guy, but he was thrown down to the concrete with strength that, even despite that dude's size, Ben could not have prepared himself for. He brought himself to his feet, dusted himself off, and tried reason.

"Please, there's someone inside I have to see. I'll be quick," he explained.

The bouncer said nothing. He only crossed his arms and shook his bald head.

Ben tried once more to run through the guy, and again he was tossed to the gutter. At that point the wizard came over and helped him to his feet. Ben watched as the bouncer opened the door (without issue) and retreated inside once more. The door came to a slow, yet oddly definitive close behind him. Ben tried for it once again but was held back by the wizard.

"Please," said Ben. "I have to get in there."

"My boy," began the wizard, still holding him, "you could entreat that man with the most flawless logic, or the purest cause, ever known to man, and he still would never relent. You could launch boulders against that glass, and it would never break. It is not our destination."

"What the fuck are you talking about?" shouted Ben.

"There can be only one destination," Wisdom explained.

"And this isn't it?" Ben demanded.

"No" said the wizard, and continued on, taking back his cart and pushing it to where the path bent into obscurity. "Come, there's little time."

Modest waves were coming upon the path now—tiny laps along its edges. Ben, desperate as he was to reach Chloe and demand answers, still found himself altogether sure that, as the wizard said, he'd never get into that bar. Despite all of his instincts, which were on fire, he gave in and followed.

The mania that forced a wedge between him and Chloe had abated—at least somewhat—since she broke up with him. He knew that because she confessed it on a clear minded night in which she showed up at his door and left the morning after. That was actually the last time he saw her.

Thoughts of pressing the advantage of that night came only later on. But Chloe's mania left behind a terrible depression, and that depression persisted past the point of Ben being able to reach her at all. He could never be sure how much of her ignoring him was because of *that*, or because of *him*. This was the state in which we found Ben this morning. But now, thoughts of her with someone else flooded his imagination.

What the fuck is she doing? She's supposed to be sick! She shouldn't be out! Shouldn't she be sitting by a fire, reading a book, taking her meds, following some plan laid out by some psychologist? And if not, shouldn't she then be with him again? He was the one that made her feel like nobody else ever had!

With that Ben was finally confronted with his own selfishness, laid bare, and he didn't like the feeling. Snow White came across his mind's eye. Might Chloe have been peering through a similar window, some time earlier? What would she have seen? She would have found him in an equally provocative situation. How did Ben know that she hadn't? But, he reasoned, she left him! Did that even matter? It was all so maddening.

With Ben thusly brooding, they'd come to the corner of the block, around which the pathway bent. Rounding it, they found another crop of derelict buildings, planted perpendicular to the others. There was a spattering of ineffectual street lights along the path now as well, and all around them the waves seemed to be picking up, thrashing against themselves. Ben could see bits of light bouncing off the white-water, which pressed higher and higher towards the moon.

There was grass between them and the buildings now, but the grass was... not dead... but somehow not really alive either. As for the buildings themselves, they were as the others—dark, dead, brick and glass. None of them had caught Ben's eye, but he did see that the last one, only a stone's throw away, actually had a bit of light coming from its front entrance. Above it, there was what looked like a neon shop sign but the lettering was dim and obscured by a growing haze about the air. From that distance, he couldn't discern any other details.

It was then that the wizard dropped his cart and removed his staff from its resting spot atop the handles. Then he whispered something into the night and pushed the staff to the sky. The moon was pulled towards him, shrinking as it came down until, finally, it became a small spark of light once again and settled atop the staff. There, it simmered for a moment, like a wayward ember, and slowly dimmed to nothing. Once again, Ben was left in the pitch black.

Voices grew louder in that darkness, several different voices in conversation and laughter. They weren't frightening, though. It was all much too ordinary, prosaic—commonplace banter you'd hear around town on a busy night.

A sliver of light opened up in front of them—a vertical tear in the world. Ben recoiled a little, allowing his eyes to adjust as it widened to reveal bright lights of many different colors. The wizard had pulled open the darkness as if it were a curtain covering the world from which they'd came.

"Come," he said. "The cart too, please."

Ben walked himself and the cart back into his world, his city. The wizard stepped through also and his staff was once again a walking stick that tapped against the concrete. Ben let the curtain close behind him, which now appeared to be an orange tarp that covered the entrance to a stalled construction site. Across an ordinary road stood the building that they'd apparently been journeying towards, though it was now alive and part of the city, rather than standing derelict and alone as it had been. The blinding neon sign which Ben had trouble with before, he could now easily read.

On a bright yellow backing, with blue neon letters, it read: *Uptown Liquor: Beer Wine & Spirits.*

Underneath was a crowd of people, coming and going. Mostly everyone was still done up in their costumes, though many of those were a little worse-for-wear from the start of the night, presumably. All of them were there in time to procure enough booze to keep their party going, from one of the few stores in the area that stayed open as long as they were legally able.

* * *

Before two AM, then? What the fuck?

It seemed like hours since the Power Rangers told him it was... what did they say? One thirty, he recalled. Here, Ben let the series of events replay in his mind. All the time he'd spent walking, and all the people he'd come across, the ones he'd watched straggling out from the bars not so very long before... Was his brain really so fucked? That disjointed from the reality of time? He guessed that this was probably the case. Or had he truly crossed an *ocean of time?* Was the wizard's magic really that powerful?

None of it made any sense. Ben bawled in furious exasperation. When he'd finished, and opened his eyes to find everyone around staring at him, much of the strangeness somehow subsided, surreal as that is to say. Now, left with the enduring reality of that wizard still before him, and that open liquor store (which he knew well) behind them, his bewilderment fell to the sudden realization that he'd inexplicably found himself at the complete wrong end of town.

"What the fuck are we doing here?" Ben whimpered.

"Best place in the city at this time," the wizard replied, smiling. But his smile was bereft of all his prior sincerity. "Just as I said."

"As you said?" he bemoaned. Ben was on the verge of an all-out freak out. "You took me on a journey across time and space... to a fucking liquor store?"

"Now, Ben, calm down, please," begged the wizard.

Ben didn't say anything, but ran over to a newspaper box and kicked it as hard as he could. Then, panting angrily, he marched back to the old man.

"What are we doing here, man?" he demanded.

"Well," he began, appearing unsure of himself for the first time, "I thought, perhaps, you would purchase us a drink? Finish the night off properly, you know?"

Ben gasped. "I thought you had something good to show me, man. Now I'm halfway across town in the wrong direction!"

"Oh, well, I showed you wonders! Did I not?"

"Fuck!" screamed Ben, at the top of his lungs. Again, everyone was staring.

You know what though, one last beer, after the night he'd had... *Fuck it.* Under protest, if only in his mind, he stormed across the street and into the store, turning his body and side-stepping through the crowd. He was plenty drunk enough already, in truth. Despite everything, though, he still liked the wizard, and he honestly felt bad for the guy. One last beer and then he'd make his way home, and hopefully never see anyone else that shouldn't exist ever again. Chloe could do what she wanted, at that point. All the plans they'd made, if it's how she wanted it, he'd figure it out with someone else. In his mind, her mental health was a storm which he could blame for everything —for her walking away. It was fucking Yoko Ono, breaking up the band just when the music was at its best. Hurricane Yoko, they'd call it. If she was out with other guys, well, maybe he was wrong. Maybe the band *was* doomed to fail. He felt like an idiot.

"We close in eight minutes," he heard as he entered.

Inside was a rush of inputs to his senses, and he was miserable hauling his thoughts through the aisles. The lights were white and blinding—from the ceiling above and from the coolers all around. People were everywhere, wandering from shelf to shelf, beer to wine to harder stuff and back. They all looked as messed up as he felt, and more than likely looked himself. Within all that light, he felt truly awful. Still, he grabbed a random four-pack of beer from behind a random cooler door, and stood in line to pay. In front of him was a pair of girls dressed as what he could only describe as *Goth Fairies.* He kept his head down until his turn came.

"Hello my friend," erupted the clerk, a middle aged Asian man—Korean, Ben guessed. He rang through the beer with a big grin on his face, which Ben couldn't help but resent him for. "$11.99."

Don't judge me, you bastard, Ben thought, as he tapped the machine with his credit card.

"Very good!" the man announced. With that same smile and an inscrutable laugh, he skillfully bagged the beer in one swift motion, and slid it across the counter. "Happy Halloween, Sir!"

He wasn't sure what the guy's deal was. Anyone that mirthful, while shit had gone so sideways, couldn't be trusted. But he was just happy to get out of there. With the beer successfully in hand, he staggered out of the store. Without warning, a girl to his left began violently puking into the gutter and the sound of it hitting the pavement caused Ben nearly to leap out of his shoes. He had to re-collect himself, and ensure he wasn't going to puke himself, before continuing across the street. He found the wizard where he left him, sitting next to his cart on the newspaper box that Ben had kicked over.

Ben ripped off a single can for himself and dropped the rest onto the wizard's lap. "Here's your damn beer," he chided.

Undeterred, the old man ripped a can from the plastic. "Thank you, my friend," he said. He was amiable and cavalier, and seemingly removed from the relationship Ben thought they had built. He simply opened the can and drank.

Ben set off angrily on his way.

"Wait," urged the wizard. "Please."

Ben turned.

"Please, young man," he said again. "Have a drink with me."

Ben remained where he stood, unsure.

"Please. I'm sick of drinking alone."

Ben acquiesced. "Fine," he said. "One beer. Then I'm going home."

"Of course," the wizard replied.

Ben came back, opened his own can and took a seat beside him. There, against the chain-link fence that blocked off the construction site, they drank. Unsure what more there was to say, Ben said nothing. He only dwelled, still quite indignantly, over Chloe.

The wizard ultimately broke the silence. "I'm growing tired, Ben," he said. "And time stands still before me." He finished the first can and skillfully tossed it onto his cart. Without hesitation, he opened another.

"What do you mean?" Ben asked, though still quite annoyed.

"I completed my task. The only evils amongst Man now come from within Man himself. Magic is all but dead, and of little use anymore. I shouldn't be here.

"...Maybe there's something I missed," he ruefully added.

Ben wondered at that, and said what came into his mind: "Maybe there's something you're holding on to?"

The old man seemed to consider that genuinely. "Maybe," he agreed.

"...Maybe."

To that, they finished their beers, and Ben carefully considered all the things of which he'd ever had trouble letting go. Not the least of which, was Chloe.

* * *

He'd been walking for a while, making up a lot of ground in the process but now alarmingly drunk, or high... or both. Ben wondered if Jon has having his own adventure, in some other piece of the city. That guy had no cares to speak of, though—no lessons that needed learning. He was sure Jon was fine.

In any case, Ben had bigger problems at this particular point in time. Keeping even a somewhat straight line was a heavy task for both his mind and his body; each now felt connected by only a thread. He knew he was heading in the right direction but wasn't exactly sure where, between A and B, he was.

At a certain point he'd never recall, Ben placed a foot too far to the right and the next one came up from behind it and overcompensated immensely. A few rapid, desperate, futile steps later and he had collapsed into the grass.

He tried to push himself off the ground but it didn't work very well, and he found the feel of the cool grass to be quite nice, actually. Maybe he'd lay there, for just a minute. He rolled onto his back. The sky and the clouds and everything else around him continually came and went, but there was nothing out of the ordinary until suddenly he opened his eyes to find something dark and unfriendly hovering above him. There, it haunted him silently. It chose not to move for some time, but it didn't matter because Ben's every muscle was no longer under his control. He couldn't move, he couldn't speak, he couldn't even blink. He could only breathe, watch the thing above him in terror, wait for something to happen and hope that it wouldn't be too terrible.

Hands that were only chalky-white bone came up to remove the hood from its head. The Lady in Black finally revealed herself.

"The worst is yet to come," she said, and pulled shut the lids of his eyes with her cold, dead fingers.

When his eyes finally *could* open, he found himself standing in front of his apartment building—though he felt no sense of accomplishment or relief. It was dark out still, but he wasn't cold anymore even though he knew that he ought to have been. To his left, he discovered with fright, was the Lady in Black, standing oppressively. It was as if wherever she happened to be, that territory would suddenly and inexorably be marked as her own by some unspeaking force.

Again veiled from head to toe, Ben could only discern a sliver of her face underneath the hood, and what he saw was like a white desert floor—lifeless, chalky. The memory of seeing it prior had never taken root. Silently, she loomed. Her cloak eerily fluttered all around her as though it were being tugged upon by some strangely deliberate, sinuous wind. But there was no breeze at all, at least there wasn't one that Ben could feel.

If the Lady was aware of Ben beside her, or concerned with him in any way, there was no way to tell. She only gazed at the door. Eventually, with a slow, bony hand, she pointed to it. He was truly scared of her, but for whatever reason she felt less like an enemy as she had before. At this point, all logic, all reason, all cause to think through what would otherwise be so clearly strange... it had all entirely abandoned him.

Without the need for a key, Ben opened the front door, and then a second set which led into the familiar lobby. It was darker inside than it should have been. The regular lights were turned on, and they even seemed bright enough, but their bulbs weren't able to reach as far into the darkness as they usually could. On top of that, the air seemed thicker than ordinary, and it made quick movements difficult, maybe impossible. Somehow, even though he hadn't accounted for her when he came through the doors, the Lady was still at his side.

Numbly, Ben asked, "Why are we here?"

She didn't answer.

Across from them was the elevator. She pointed to it, and Ben obeyed. He didn't feel *right* by any means, but he did feel relatively alert and sober. When the elevator door opened, though, he saw in the mirror opposite him a tired, worn-out, drunk version of himself whose skin was a pallid flush of bone white and raspberry red. Again disgusted, he turned away. The lady glided past him and into the elevator. Compelled, he followed her. The door slid shut and, as fast as this place would allow, he lifted his arm and pressed the button to his floor.

Had time even existed in that elevator car? Ben wasn't exactly sure. It may have taken ten seconds to get to his floor, it may have taken ten years. All that he knew was that he'd gotten lost trying to find the Lady's face within the shadow of her hood. When the door finally opened, he was left with the strange certainty that something had happened inside which he wasn't allowed to keep for himself.

A dull thwacking sound came from somewhere in the corridor. It came once, and again a few seconds later, and again after that. Despite Ben's curiosity, he could only stand there hoping that the Lady would take the lead (he didn't especially like the feeling of her behind him). But the door remained open and it became clear that she wouldn't be the first to exit. So he stepped out.

The lights in the corridor were as ineffectual as those below. Under their weak glow, he discovered the source of the sounds. There, facing his apartment door, her back to him, was a girl and he knew by the shape of her that it was Chloe. But her clothes were tattered and grimy, and her hair didn't have its usual shine—some of it looked like it might have even been missing, but he couldn't be sure in the darkness. She walked into the door repeatedly, absently. Each time she did she'd bounce backwards, and stagger into it again. *Thud, thud, thud.* The third time, her purse slipped from her shoulder and fell to the ground. She didn't seem to notice or care.

Desperately, he asked the Lady in Black, "What's wrong with her?"

Again, no reply. She remained at Ben's side, coldly watching Chloe.

Thud.

This time, when Chloe bounced off the door, her foot awkwardly bent from her high-heel shoe. Ben heard a snap before she crumpled to the ground. There was no cry of pain, no reaction from her at all other than trying to force herself back to her feet. From across the hall, he wanted so badly to run to her. This place though, the air, it wouldn't allow it. He might well have run across the bottom of a lake to get to her. As he ran he watched her silently struggle, her hands scraping against the wall, searching for something to grasp. It was still so dark, and her disheveled hair obscured the face he wished so badly to see again.

When finally he did reach her, and crouched low to help her, he became horrified at what he saw. Behind dangling strands of hair that was once peerlessly soft and beautiful—but now was decayed and indeed missing in patches atop her head—was a gruesome sight which he could hardly bear. Her skin was frightfully anemic, even fringing on green. That's where there was still any skin left, for it had rotted away in several places. Through a hole in her cheek, he could see her darkened tongue and some discolored teeth.

Aghast, he stumbled back and began to cry.

"Oh," she said in a fatigued voice that was both lovely and unfeeling. "Hi, baby."

Ben whimpered through his tears, "Hi, love."

Composing himself, he crawled over to her. He brushed the hair from her eyes, which left much of it tangled between his fingers. Letting the strands flutter to the ground, he asked her, stupidly, if she was okay. *Of course she's not okay, you idiot. Look at her.* But what else could he say?

Her lifeless eyes found his and held on. They were so achingly vacant and desperate, which made looking into them harder than he ever could have imagined.

"It's okay, love," he assured her. "Can you stand?"

Without words, the face she gave him said something like, *why are you saying such unimportant things?*

"I just meant, with your ankle," he explained, as she wordlessly followed his eyes towards the injured foot, which was bent at a grotesque 90 degree angle.

"Oh, shit," she sighed dismissively, and proceeded to reach her hands down, grab it tightly, and force it back into position. There was no pain in her face (nothing in her face at all, really), but the sound of the bones and tendons grinding against each other sent a shiver down Ben's spine. Placidly, she asked him to help her inside, which he did without question.

"What are you doing here?" asked Ben.

"I missed you, baby," she answered, which warmed his heart.

Forgetting all about the apparition who brought him there —that spirit, his guide—he brought Chloe into the apartment with her arm around his neck, and shut the door behind them. He must have left the TV on; he could hear voices overtop strident music. But it had that distant quality to it, seemingly coming from a far-away somewhere, the way that sounds sometimes do as we're waking up, or drifting asleep—that amorphous in-between.

He carried her through the kitchen, which opened up into the familiar living room. Familiar, except for three great chandeliers that now hung above it which didn't belong. Their golden, glowing bulbs were caged by iron and glass, and each was suspended by chains as thick as Ben's arms, and the chains ascended far above him until they disappeared into the darkness. If the ceiling was even up there at all, it was so much higher than it was supposed to be. Ben only noticed this superficially, though, hardly stopping to think as he placed Chloe gently on the couch.

"We don't have to talk," he said, stepping around and taking a seat beside her. "Whatever you want, it's okay with me."

She looked at him with those same vacant eyes, but still she was silent. Chloe—the real Chloe—was buried somewhere deep down, but he *could* still see her. (Barely, but she *was* in there, somewhere.) He lay there quietly beside her, mindlessly watching whatever was on the TV, but actually focusing all his peripheral sight to her. Ben was hoping she'd show him some sign. He wasn't even sure what it would be but he'd take anything.

Commercials had been running for some time when Chloe, dispassionately still, broke the silence. "Oh, I brought wine."

Eagerly, Ben responded, "I'll grab glasses."

He quickly got up, but before he could move into the kitchen her hand found his wrist and clutched it tightly. He stopped. She looked up into his eyes and Ben found that she seemed to have recovered a little bit. A more natural color had returned to her skin and the sickly wounds on her face had begun to heal. The real Chloe was fighting back. Her lips even looked half-way kissable, and it was a good thing too, because the next thing that she did was pull Ben into them. There was no dispassion in that kiss, and even though her mouth was dry and tasted... strange to say the least... he kissed her right back without hesitation. When he pulled his head back, she wasn't miraculously cured, but he was still convinced she was coming back. With a sad look on her face, she reached into her purse and produced a bottle of wine. Ben went into the kitchen and brought back two glasses, which he set on the coffee table in front of them.

Anyone watching this scene play out would have been fixated on the evil looking thing perched in the corner watching them, dressed all in black, obscured in the shadows. Ben completely forgot about the Lady, and didn't notice her at all. *He* was fixated on Chloe.

"Want some?" she asked.

"Please," replied Ben, holding his glass up to her.

Chloe twisted off the cap—she never had anything against cheap wine—and tipped it into the glass. Nothing came out, not even a drop. The bottle was empty. Still, she held it tipped as if delicious wine filled the glass. When she was satisfied, she stopped and brought the bottle to her own glass, doing the same. Again, nothing came out. But, content, she placed the bottle on the table, laid back, and delightedly sipped at nothing at all. Ben willed himself to ignore it and set his empty glass on the table.

"Oh, good!" she beamed, brightening a little more. "I love this movie."

On the screen, a young girl walked apprehensively down a staircase and into a dank, old basement. He knew the movie—the demonic, horror type thing. They'd watched it together some time ago.

When?

Each of the little girl's steps down those stairs were long, drawn out ticks of a clock.

"I know," said Ben. "I remember."

Tick. Tock. Tick. Tock.

Voices entered along with the ominous tones in the background. Was it from the movie? Again it was coming from that far-away-somewhere.

"Are you sure your ankle is okay," Ben asked.

"It was no big deal," she answered, leaning over and squeezing it as evidence. "Don't overreact, babe."

"Okay."

"I'm such an idiot, though. I can't believe I fell like that."

"You're not an idiot."

"I'm sorry I'm so off," she said softly, still sipping air from her wine glass. "I think it's these new meds."

"Don't be sorry."

"Well, I am. And I probably look horrible. I wasn't able to do myself up for you."

"It's fine, love," he said, smiling, lost in another time.

"I think I'm feeling better now, though," she whispered.

"You look better," he replied. And he was being honest. Next to him, she looked like a living, breathing person again.

Tick. Tock.

In a flash, the demon revealed itself on the screen. The girl was possessed, and the movie could begin.

Chloe giggled and happily burrowed her body into the corner of the couch. Ben preferred to watch her rather than any movie, and, blissfully, he did just that.

By the time the movie ended, Chloe was Chloe again—body and mind. "Let's go to bed," she said.

Ben didn't protest. He put his hand in hers—which was soft and warm and alive—and allowed her to lead him into the bedroom. It had been so long, but she still knew all the ways to make him forget himself and think only of her. Constantly, they rolled each other this way and that. When one got sick of the bottom, they'd roll themselves on top. It was a well-practiced dance that worked well for them both. With Chloe clutching the headboard in euphoric desperation, they finished, and she collapsed onto him, each of them a sweaty mess.

Ben never remembered falling asleep, but he awoke in terror with the Lady in Black hovering above him and her hand pressed into his chest. Insipient rays of sunlight came through his curtains and told him that the night had at some point ended. In the morning's light, the face she'd kept hidden underneath her cloak was bare and unavoidable.

In point of fact, she had no face at all—only an inscrutable, bleak skull. Eyes that were so big and empty and impenetrably black stared down at him without emotion. He didn't think it could be possible for that face to hold any emotion. All the same, he didn't care to find out. Instinctively, he reached beside him to wake and warn Chloe, but his hand found nothing but bed-sheets and a cool pillow. She was gone.

The Lady in Black slid away from the bed, and with her dead finger made a slow 'come with me' motion. Dreadfully scared, but overcome with the understanding that only she could lead him to Chloe, he knew it was already written that he'd go with her. She'd come to a stop underneath his bedroom door. He approached her cautiously and grimaced at the thought of the myriad of things that might happen next. Without warning, she outstretched her arms and pulled him into her cloak. The world went black.

> Wonder this time where she's gone,
> Wonder if she's gone to stay?
> There just ain't no sunshine,
> When she's gone.

* * *

Next thing he knew, he was inside a moving C-Train. The car jostled here and there, and he had to fight to keep his balance. Dangling above him was a rubber strap for support. He grabbed it, noticing only then that he wore nothing but his boxers. The Lady hadn't given him a chance to put something on before she took him from his bedroom. And there she was, beside him, fixed to her space. The train bounced and swayed but she was unaffected—some kind of constant.

Others were on the train, too. Many others, in fact: All manner of people of different ages, different backgrounds, different walks of life. As diverse as they appeared, it seemed to Ben that there was something common about them. In the same kind of way everyone seemed unified on Halloween night, so too did these people, but in a much gloomier way.

As to the fact that he was half-naked on the train, standing beside a ghostly apparition with nice legs, nobody seemed to care. Only a little girl without any hair looked at them, perched over the back of her seat. The moment she caught Ben looking back at her, she panicked and swung back around. Everyone else had their heads in their phones, or a book, or out the window, or to the floor or wherever. There were no conversations.

He looked out the window opposite him. All there was to see, as far as the horizon, was ocean. Out the window behind him, it was the same: Just water, topped with gentle, choppy waves.

"Where are we?"

The Lady in Black turned her head down to his. He recoiled and looked away. Looking into those eyes was so unpleasant—down to the core.

She never answered.

Holding his head away from her still, a wash of shame came over him—the feeling of not physically being able to do something you think you should.

Ocean of time? he hazarded, knowing that it was right.

The train made several stops before he and the Lady would eventually get off. Passengers made their way on and off the train. It was a strange sight as patches of land or places without walls (in one case, what appeared to be an empty funeral service) would emerge out of nowhere, islands in the distance until they reached it, and then disappear behind them. None of the oncoming passengers particularly regarded either Ben or the Lady in Black, except maybe in the fleeting, perfunctory ways that people do on public transit.

Eventually, another stop began to emerge ahead—a platform on the water—growing larger as they neared. Once they got closer, and Ben could make it out, he saw dozens of chairs that were half filled with people, seated, waiting. There was a walled section on the far end of it. Three windows with three desks stood before a sliding door that went God-knows-where. The train hissed to a stop.

The door opened and the Lady slid off the train and onto

the tiled floor. Ben followed. Clearly, it was a hospital waiting room. Waves lapped against the floor's edges, but standing on it you'd never think that this was a place that was floating on water. There was a lineup of people at the triage desk, and a general bustle of people throughout. The woman at the far desk patiently asked for the next person, and the line crept forward.

He and the Lady in Black took a few more steps inside, and as they did walls began to materialize around them and, generally, the whole place just seemed to become more real. He found the courage to look up to his guide, but she was still giving him nothing. And so he let his eyes scan the crowd. Soon they inevitably discovered Chloe, who was alone, sitting sadly in a corner chair beside a vending machine. She'd begun to deteriorate again. Her skin was sickly white and dying. Her lips were the lips of a corpse. He ran to her.

"Chloe!"

"Oh," she said, surprised. "Hi."

He clasped her hand tightly in both of his, dreading ever letting go. "What's wrong?"

"I think I'm getting worse," she answered, and she turned her palm to the ceiling and that revealed a horrid row of slices down her arm. The cuts were shallow but deliberate; it was hard to tell how fresh they were because of just how dead she was all over. It didn't matter. Ben started crying, and then so did she. The Lady in Black loomed over them still.

"How did you find me?" she asked.

Through tears, Ben replied, "I crossed an *ocean of time.*"

"Oh."

"I'm sorry," he sobbed.

"Babe..."

"I get it. You just can't be in love right now. I need to let go. I've been so selfish."

"Babe, listen..."

"It's just so hard."

"Babe," she cried emphatically, jarring him from an outpouring of thoughts.

Then, lovingly, she said, "Wake up. We're dreaming..."

* * *

Slowly and painfully, Ben returned from the darkness, waking up on a patch of grass that he never even remembered passing out on...

END

DEATH VALLEY

BY JODIE KEENAN

It was a narrow path along the beach, the same path that had seemed so vast to Mary when her mother had taken her in one of her earliest memories. And then there was the breakwater, those massive slabs of big ugly rock, porous and pockmarked with bits of scum and the pungent smells of the cracked and brittle crab shells wedged within the crevices. It had seemed simultaneously as solid as the presence of God in her toddler mind and as ready to fall to pieces as that same concept almost three decades later.

"Aaaaaaaaaand jump!" her mother had said. She held firmly to her daughter's little hand when they came to any particularly large gaps on their way down those huge dark rocks that seemed to be the only solid things in the world. The silvery spray of the waves crashed down on either side and the mist hung thick and heavy, as though the breakwater was a path to the end of the world. But it didn't lead to the end of the world, rather a stubby white lighthouse. This too had seemed towering and awe-inspiring to her way back when she had been a child and the world was just one great new wonder after another.

Coming back to the present, the ocean was calm and the sky was clear. She could see all the deep green hills of the surrounding shore and islands jutting out of the jagged coast-line. The water lapped, calm and gray, against the breakwater.

Aaaaaaaaaand jump! Mary said in her mind as she and Alec walked down the rocks, not looking at one another, not talking to one another, and pretending with everything they had for those fleeting moments that the two-inch cardboard box she held wasn't there, or that that breakwater on that clear summer day didn't, as it turned out, lead to the end of the world after all.

Up an uneven handful of roughly chopped stone steps, through the lighthouse gift shop, up a claustrophobic corkscrew of creaking metal stairs to the observation deck, and there they stood, side by side, looking out at the tourist's on their sailboats and jet skis.

"Okay," she said, and that was all.

"Okay," Alec agreed.

Mary looked down at the small box in her hands. *More than anything in the world I wanted to come here with you ... but not like this.*

Together they fumbled a bit with opening that little cardboard flap, then released barely a handful of powdery gray ash into the wind.

* * *

The New Mexico desert was three-thousand miles from Camden, Maine, but to Mary it felt like another planet.

Days before, when she and Alec got home from their somber trip to the lighthouse, she figured she might as well enjoy the fact that she'd be able to indulge almost three months earlier than she'd been planning. She'd stripped out of her black dress in favor of washer-soft paint-stained jeans and a band tee shirt, ordered a ton of sushi, and drank so much that she'd hardly have been surprised if the milk that still leaked from her tender nipples came out tasting like a white Russian. But nothing seemed to make a drop in the emptiness she felt within.

Not wanting to sleep in the bedroom where all the baby shower gifts were still stacked up, she'd passed out in the living room. Days later, she'd barely left the couch, her face as blank as the TV screen. Finally, Alec had confronted her.

At the climax of the awful fight that ensued, she had screamed at him.

"You heartless fucking bastard! Why the hell can't you just let me grieve?"

"Because you're not the one who died!" he'd shouted back. "And neither am I. We're still alive, Mary!"

Flustered, she hadn't been able to articulate what she was feeling; that she didn't feel alive at all anymore, that the whole world just felt like a mass of walking corpses to her. So instead, she'd just cried "fuck you!" and grabbed her car keys.

"Where are you going?" Alec had demanded.

"For a drive!" she'd snapped.

Peeling out of their winding gravel driveway, she shut her phone down at the first beeping text alert, and with no particular destination in mind, she'd just kept driving. At that point, she wouldn't have thought she'd be able to wrap her mind around life getting any stranger. She had been wrong.

* * *

"Hot out there."

"That's the desert," the sweaty smear of a man behind the counter muttered absently as he stared in horror through the dust mottled store window to the lot where Mary had parked her Prius, once shining silver, now the same desert sand color as everything else.

With a smile she placed one perspiring liter bottle of water after another on the counter, leaving streaks in the dust as she slid them over to the clerk. Eyes still fixed on her car through the window he began to run the vitals she'd gathered over the scanner.

"Don't believe in air-conditioning?" she asked, running her fingers through the mass of sweat and snarls her hair had become.

"Air-conditioner's running full blast," the clerk said. "Desert blasts fuller. Will that be all?"

"Just a sec, actually."

She perused a rack of knickknacks, filed through the rows of Mad Libs and Travel Scrabble, then picked out a classic poker deck.

"For my friend," she said, nodding to the window at the small, slight, dark figure huddled shotgun beyond the windshield of the Prius. "He doesn't need any food or water."

"I'll bet he don't," the clerk said, not taking his eyes from the window.

"But I feel bad not bringing anything out for him. We've still got a long way to go."

"Where you heading?"

"Me? Nowhere. He's heading to Death Valley. I guess they all are."

For the first time the clerk took his eyes off the window, fixed them on her, wide, intense, burning as hot as the desert sun.

"Death Valley?"

"Irony's not lost."

"You know what that thing is?"

Mary looked out the window. That slight dark figure, though clearly a desiccated corpse, browned and mummified by the parched heat of the desert, perked up when he noticed them looking and waved. Mary smiled and waved back.

"Yeah," she said. "That's Jett."

"It's a damn zombie!"

"I don't think that's technically accurate," she said. "In the movies zombies are pretty much just mindless corpses, and it's usually on account of a virus or radiation or something. Nobody seems to know what the hell caused this. And trust me, that kid out there is hardly mindless. He's kind of a smartass if anything."

"It's holding you against your will?"

"Nah, he just needed a ride. I picked him up a few miles back."

"These are dangerous times," the clerk told her. "End of times."

"Trust me, I've felt like that before," she said.

She remembered the moths dancing on the screen of the hospital window. It had been deep into the summer but she didn't want to breathe AC. She'd had to beg them to open the window for her. That was way back in the cool moist place she'd never be able to think of as "hot" after experiencing the desert.

"It'll be seventeen-seventy," the clerk said, and she handed over her debit card. Mary never handled cash if she could avoid it. It was swarming with disease.

Stepping out into the desert sun she knew the clerk was right. The air conditioner in the convenience store really must have been running full blast, because past the threshold the heat licked her like a tongue of fire. She could almost hear her skin sizzle.

Though she'd left all the windows in the Prius open, settling into the driver's seat only seemed to intensify the heat. She'd drained the entire contents of one water bottle before she could even turn on the ignition and start up the futile blast of AC.

As the engine roared and they sped down the highway she passed the cards over to Jett. He seemed immensely pleased. The skinny crispy lattices of bone and human jerky that were his hands flipped and shuffled the cards adeptly.

Mary smiled and picked a card when Jett prompted her. He didn't let her show it to him before sliding it back through the deck. He shuffled the cards and she let out a gasp of genuine amazement when he fanned the deck again, only the three of spades she'd drawn face up against the scrolling blue cherubim backs. She even took her hands off the wheel a moment to clap. It wasn't like there were twists and bends in the road or wandering deer and moose like back home. It was a beautiful desolate expanse of bleached blues and browns made even more beautiful and desolate by the fact that she had long since been the only car on the road. Most people were going hard and fast in the opposite direction of the way the dead were walking.

None of that had entered into Mary's calculations after they'd scattered the ashes off the lighthouse in Rockport. It had been early morning, less than a week after she'd refused to breathe AC, only three days after the hand almost too small to close around her thumb had squeezed with such fragile strength when she reached into the incubator.

She'd promised that choking, gasping, little miracle that she'd give everything, right down to the barest nuts and bolts of her soul, if he would just keep breathing. She'd made herself believe in a future with him. He'd have a big smile, lots of friends, and all the girls would press lipstick kisses against their signatures in his yearbook. And if the world ended on his watch, he'd John Conner the survivors and they'd never bow down, never be broken, they'd rise up from the ashes and thrive, prove that there was no force great enough to scatter the human spirit. Maybe he'd be some brilliant introvert obsessed with the stars. She and Alec could buy him a telescope. He could have discovered unknown wonders in the cold dead depths of space, and made first contact with an alien race. Or a musical prodigy, maybe? Premature as he was, it was likely he would always be small. Maybe he'd be one of those frail boys who was always carrying an instrument case that was bigger than he was, but nobody would notice how small he was when his fingers pressed the frets and sliced the bow across the strings eliciting celestial fire. He could have been anything, anybody.

And then she scattered his ashes on that bright cold summer day on the breakwater. They didn't make urns small enough, just a blank sterile cardboard box no bigger than a fist. The wind blew the handful of dust northeast, so she started driving southwest. Simple as that.

"That was amazing!" she told Jett as he folded up the deck of cards. "How did you do that?"

Jett held up one desiccated claw of a finger then took his little dry erase board from under his seat and wrote "Trade secrets," then crunched his bony hands into a finger gun salute.

Jett had a lot of personality. That was obvious from the start. She met him after almost two days on the road.

Mary had only been driving a few hours when she heard the first cries of terror in the podunk New England town she was passing through between expanses of tall pine forest and rocky foothills. She smelled the dead before she saw them, an aroma like autumn leaves and old garbage hanging thick in the air.

Her mind had gone blank with panic for a moment, then she recalled the little gray cloud floating north over the ocean and she pressed harder on the accelerator. On the other side of the highway the lanes began to jam, and anyone not fleeing north was on their knees shouting in tongues and spouting evangelical proclamations of the rapture nigh at hand.

But the horsemen didn't break their seals. Fire and brimstone didn't rain from the heavens. The dead didn't swarm and attack, hungry for blood and brains, they just continued on their steady trek southwest and eventually the living, still praying hard and fearing the end, went on with their lives as well.

Many of the dead seemed well enough aware of their

circumstances to avoid the sunlight like a plague. Further east where the air was thick and heavy with the heat and moisture of the summer and the smell of rot, you wouldn't see the dead walking until the sun had fallen low beneath the horizon. Mary had been afraid the first night. She'd pulled off as soon as the sky went red and huddled in a roadside motel. But eventually she'd learned that the lurching and moaning silhouettes of dead men, women, and children that shuffled through the dark made better company than the terrified zealots shouting biblical passages ceaselessly through the night. And so, when night fell on the second day she just drove on.

Well after the forests and swamps had given way to wide grassy prairie which had given way to the the bright burning desert she had stumbled upon Jett. He had been a desert person, had lived, died, been buried, and risen in harmony with the hard, dry, burning beauty of this place. When she first saw him, he looked like Tutankhamun in a hoodie and jeans, though he'd probably been interred in a respectable suit. After Mary had gotten over her fear and aversion enough to actually take a closer look at the dead, she'd noticed that the suits and dresses of even the freshest corpses had been traded for more casual fare. It made sense enough. They'd already looked nice for their funerals, why hold onto pretenses any longer?

And as the heat didn't seem to bother Jett, he'd opted for a sweatshirt so big and bulky Mary hadn't even realized he was one of the dead until she slowed down. She had thought it was just some kid hitching in a desperate but laid-back attempt to escape the end of days. Getting close enough, though, she saw that the little dark brown hand was not just slender, but a desiccated amalgamation of leather wrapped carpels and flaking talon-like phalanges. The eyeless face within the low drawn hood was warped and stretched into an eternal grimace, accentuated every now and then by a gust of wind moving lank clumps of long stringy blonde hair over the mummified leer. And this gruesome specter from the beyond, clad all in comfy denim and French terry, was holding the kind of dry-erase message board she used to have on her dorm room door. It simply read "Death Valley."

Though Mary had still been a little on edge where the dead were concerned, the image had stricken her with such a surge of gallows humor that she couldn't stop a choked and desperate laugh from escaping her. And somehow that laugh trickled down her nervous system all the way to her feet. Her toes let up pressure on the accelerator, she flicked on her blinker, pushed on the break, and as the car stopped moving her heart started racing.

When the north wind had taken Johnny C from her, she felt something deep inside dying. Alec felt it too. But after the wind took his ashes there was nothing left to bind them. Perhaps their love rode north on a gale as well. Mary hadn't looked back at him as she got into her car and turned off her phone. They hadn't spoken since.

But if the capacity to feel love or fear in her heart was dead it was still alive and kicking in her body. As the leathery corpse approached Mary's breath had come harder and harder until her chest burned. It took a concerted force of will to turn her head and look at the message board he'd pressed into the passenger side window.

"Are you afraid?" it read.

She'd felt her head nodding.

The French terry sleeve of his sweatshirt wiped the letters away and the withered claws penned new ones.

"Don't be," they read. "I'm nice."

She'd felt her head nod again. Fingers trembling, she reached over to flick the unlock switch. Jett had raised one bony claw to thin stretched out lips as though to indicate he meant to smile reassuringly. Then he reached down, opened the door, and climbed in shotgun.

Though the highway was bare for at least ten miles in either direction Mary had signaled again before pulling out. She had to really pool all her reserves to get herself breathing in and out until finally she could bring herself to speak.

"So ..." she said, dry and breathless, "you're heading for Death Valley?"

Pushing his hood down the mummified corpse nodded vigorously, then cocked his head to one side and pointed to her.

"Me?" she said, "I'm heading nowhere. Might as well get you a little closer to somewhere in the process."

The corpse wiped his sleeve over the board again, wrote something new, and held it up.

"I'm Jett."

"Mary," she replied.

So together they rode on for miles and miles while the desert changed and stayed the same. As the miles elapsed the sleeve of Jett's hoodie grew thick with black residue as he wiped the board clean again and again to make room for new messages. Before too long she'd been able to piece together the long and short of his tale.

When Jett woke up, he'd known he was dead. He wasn't given the luxury of a glamorous exit while drag racing or hang-gliding. He got a nice, slow, chronic demise and plenty of time to come to terms with it, to savor it when it came. So he was really confused when he opened his eyes again. But he figured if he could come to terms with dying, he could come to terms with anything, so he shrugged and started to feel around the aesthetically arranged but not super comfortable folds of satin over and crumpled newspaper in the darkness of his coffin.

He thought at first that maybe that was how it was supposed to be. The gift of death was an eternity of peace and solitude with which to contemplate his thoughts. After a few hours he got bored contemplating his thoughts, though.

The satin seemed way too easy to rip through, the wood way too easy to break. It took no effort at all to squirm up through the dense fine-grained earth and when he met the surface somehow he knew the right direction and started walking.

* * *

"Any more tricks, Jett?" Mary asked as he shuffled the deck, "Wow me with the good stuff!"

He shrugged and took up his board again. When he held it up it read, "That was the good stuff."

"Never lead with the good stuff," she said. "You're supposed to save that for the grand finale."

Another wipe and write.

"'Grand finale' rings hollow for a dead guy," it said. "Gotta make each moment count."

"A sentiment that might be lost on the living," she said.

The next message he wrote simply read "?"

"Sometimes we just need to get through the moment."

"Dead are smarter," he wrote.

A few more dozen miles brought on a few more respectable card tricks. Despite her map and GPS Mary somehow managed to get them lost once or twice but Jett always managed to guide them back to the right path.

The desert teamed with life; hard, beautiful, and tough as the leather that made up her companion. Carrion birds glided as dark silhouettes against the glaring sunlight. Snakes poured and looped over themselves rutting sideways trails in the dust. Gnarled hares and rodents scuttled through the brush and rocks. But despite all this hard, easy, life the next person they encountered was another corpse.

It was Jett who spotted him, tapped a mummified claw to Mary's shoulder and pointed to the reaper specter patiently trudging against the horizon, no doubt with the same destination in mind. What made Mary double take was the message on his board.

"Dead?"

While an absolutely fresh body, dead less than a week, and worked over by an undertaker of Salafia caliber might at first deceive the less perceptive, there could be no shadow of a doubt of the departed status of the walker up ahead. Clad in a bulky ankle-length duster and honest to God old-school cowboy, the hands, neck, and face were all that could be seen of the man up ahead. But even at this distance it was plain to see that not a scrap of flesh remained on him. He was nothing but bleached gray-brown bone, the ropy shreds of ligament, and hard worn clumps of earth cemented into the spongy cracks and crevices between.

"Very dead," she said. "What do you see?"

"Guy in a cowboy hat," he wrote. "Dead don't look dead to me."

"Good to know," she said.

"Don't tell me how I look," he wrote. "Don't want to know!"

"You look just fine, Jett," she said with a wink. "But if you can't see ... what I see then how did you know he was dead?"

Instead of writing Jett tapped a bony finger at the LED thermometer on the dashboard reading 115°, then tugged on the collar of his hoodie.

"Gotcha," she said. "Heat doesn't bother you guys so you can wear heavy clothing."

Jett tapped his finger to the collapsed Jack-o-lantern cavity that had been his nose, then started writing.

"Think he needs a ride?"

"I don't know," she said. She'd gotten used to Jett's appearance by that point, even begun to reconstruct him in her head. She imagined he'd been about seventeen, but looked younger. Slender build and long shaggy hair his mom must have always been nagging him to cut. But the thought of that grim skull staring at her from the rear-view kind of gave her the heebie-jeebies. Instead of saying this she gave the more diplomatic excuse that it wasn't really safe to be picking up hitchhikers.

"You picked me up," he wrote.

"Yeah," she said. "Because it's not safe for a kid your age to be hitching."

The way he moved his head had Mary feeling certain that if he still had eyes, he'd be rolling them.

"I'm already dead!" he wrote.

"Good point," she said.

"Help another dead guy out?" he wrote with a shrug.

"Fine," she said. "But keep in mind; if he turns out to be a psycho killer or something, we're not *all* of us dead already."

He cleaned the board and started writing.

"I'll protect you!"

Mary had to smile. Jett was a sweet kid, there was no denying it. As she flicked the signal and pulled up alongside the skeleton cowboy, she found herself thinking about Jett's mom, what kind of a wreck she must have been, might still be if she were still alive somewhere out there.

She rolled down the window and Jett leaned out. Then quite unexpectedly he emitted a dry hissing wheeze like a broken rain-stick, the moaning desert wind, or the fringe of a carpet jamming up in a vacuum cleaner. Mary found herself crying out in alarm and when Jett turned around with an inquisitive cock of his head she shrugged and smiled apologetically.

"Sorry," she said. "I guess your voice sounds different to you too."

He shrugged back, but then his attention was commandeered by the skeleton man who, upon witnessing their interaction, had begun to jerk his hands about in furious gesticulations to which Jett responded by doubling over and letting that horrible wheezing escape him with the unmistakable rhythm of laughter.

"What?" Mary asked, feeling quite left out.

Jett pulled up his board again and scrawled a message.

"He thinks I kidnapped you! Chivalrous guy!"

Mary laughed a little as well.

"I appreciate your concern, sir," she said, leaning over Jett and doing her best to treat the fleshless man to her most carefree smile. "But honestly I offered him a ride. I'm Mary and this is Jett ... I guess he already told you that, huh?"

The skeleton tipped his hat with casual grandeur and offered his hand for her to shake. She did hesitate a second at the thought of touching the dry weathered mass of bone and knotted tendons, but that would have been supremely impolite, so she wrapped her hand around his and, careful not to squeeze too hard, they shook.

This formality concluded, he motioned for Jett to hand over his dry erase board, laid it out on the hood of the car, and took his time writing out a message with slow deliberate strokes. When he handed back the board it was covered with the small careful writing of one who had attained literacy later in life.

"It is my supreme honor to make your acquaintance, ma'am. I am Nathaniel Goodridge, known to my friends as

Natty, which you are welcome to call me. As your young companion has no doubt informed you, presumably all of us share the same compulsion to reach Tümpisa, the meaning behind which sadly alludes us."

"I'm going nowhere," Mary said. "Jett's heading to Death Valley. If you're heading that way anyway, you're welcome to join us."

Mary was a bit amused to find that even with his complete lack of flesh she could see full well how uncomfortable Natty was when she looked in the rear-view mirror. He predated automobiles entirely, Jett had explained through the dry erase board as the older man's slow and fastidious handwriting would take much longer than any of them had the patience for. It was a real "mind fuck," Jett explained (and was promptly scolded for his language), to see what he could best describe as locomotives without rails zipping about. To actually ride in one was something he certainly was not prepared for.

As Jett transcribed the story that Natty conveyed through what Mary heard as a series of hisses and clicks from his dry and broken brown teeth, the cowboy kept one skeletal hand pressed against the top of his hat as though, despite the sealed windows and blasting AC, the wind of their 70 MPH momentum would carry it off in the desert wind, and several times ventured to peek out the window beside him just long enough to turn away again with a nauseated bob of his skull.

"Nat was a cowboy for real!" Jett, wrote before a smack in the back of the head from the skeleton in back had him rolling his absent eyes and wiping out and re-writing "'cattle-driver.'"

"Is that so?"

"He fought bandits!"

"Bandits, huh?" Mary asked, raising an eyebrow.

Natty leaned forward once more to whack Jett in the back of the head. Mary had to take a breath and remind herself it was only a good-natured reprimand when it dislodged a patch of the boy's mummified scalp, complete with a lock of scraggly blonde hair. Again, Jett reluctantly cleared the board and started writing again. "Once, okay? Some rustlers came after his herd once and he fired a shot in the air to scare 'em off."

"Very modest of you, Natty," Mary said, and in the rearview mirror she saw a tip of the hat.

"Still badass," Jett wrote. "Know how he died?"

"How would I know that?"

Jett rubbed the rapidly blackening sleeve of his hoodie over the board and started writing. "Mudslide up in the mountains," he scribbled. "Crazy dude rode right into it, threw himself against this big-ass rock to divert the path of the avalanche. Saved the whole herd and all his men."

He wiped off the board and began to write again.

"This is *so* much worse than texting while driving," Mary muttered before reading the next message.

"They buried him right out there on the trail. Next thing he knows he's awake and just kinda feels like heading out to the valley."

Then Natty began to hiss and click and Jett began to dryly wheeze back at him. After a few seconds of this casually unsettling conversation Jett once more handed the board and marker back to the skeleton. It was a good five minutes of Mary and Jett staring out to a horizon that wavered like an ocean in the blistering heat before Natty passed the board back to the front.

"The lad is inclined to paraphrase," Mary squinted, slowed to thirty, and moved to the breakdown lane to read the tight script of his archaic handwriting, "but on the subject of Pearl my own words will suffice. She was a most excellent Quarter, and brave as any hero to charge into that cataclysm with me. I have seen to animals all my life, ma'am. I am not at all surprised that Pearl would have gone on to paradise without the need for a journey such as this. She was a creature of most pure heart and profoundest loyalty. I hope to ride with her again at our journey's end."

"I'm sure you will," Mary said with a smile.

Jett wiped the board clean and wrote, "Pfft! Doesn't talk like that 4 real. Only writes fancy."

"That's okay," Mary said. "It was quite poetic."

Jett cleared the board and wrote.

"Wish I got to die cool like that. Went to sleep in the hospital hearing Ma pretend not to cry."

Mary read this and went quiet. She knew that sound only too well. She remembered lying, bleached and sterilized in crisp paper gowns and clean cold hospital blankets. They'd turned off the incubator hours before, and it was down to her and Alec, and soon the cheese would stand alone. But on that first night he sat by her side while she pretended to sleep and every few minutes, she heard a cough or a clearing of the throat to camouflage his silent sobbing.

"Yeah," she finally managed to say, and she couldn't stop her voice from breaking as she considered all those baby-shower onsies and tiny sneakers currently gathering dust in her apartment back north.

And perhaps sensing the inherent weirdness of the moment, Natty's teeth began to click behind her. And despite Jett's casual gestures and wheezing protestations the cowboy in back lurched forward to grab the dry erase board. After what seemed like eons later, he passed the board back.

"There were voices I would have heard, hands I would have held. I do not begrudge the fact that I died upon the trail. I had a job to do and I did see it done. The fact that Pearl was the only one to breathe her last with me does not make my death any more worthy. I cannot imagine it is easy for those we left behind to see us walk upon the good earth once again, but we, the departed, see to one another when our paths should cross. Every one of us, I can assure you. Whomsoever you may have lost does not walk alone."

Even if he was alive for barely a week? she thought, *Before being reduced to a handful of fine ash and scattered across the cold gray ocean almost an entire continent away at this point?*

Mary's eyes looked seconds from tears even to herself when she glanced up to the rearview mirror. She let her focus shift to Natty, but before she had to try and figure out the words to thank him he simply nodded and Jett didn't seem to notice the exchange at all, though he did immediately attempt to change the subject, wiping away Natty's sweet message and writing simply "Can I drive?"

"You know how to drive?"

"Got my permit before I got sick."

"So you *know how* to drive?" Mary repeated a little more earnestly.

With a shrug he turned his mummified face to the miles and miles of empty highway stretching out before them.

If Natty had been uncomfortable in the "locomotive without rails" while Mary drove the tough old bastard entered full on panic mode when Jett got behind the wheel. And despite her forced calm and attempts to coach him supportively, Mary was right there with the cowboy. At first Jett stalled so many times the engine had begun to smoke. But once he managed to shift up to overdrive, and no matter how many times she reminded him of the speed limit and reflexively shoved her break foot down to the empty carpet of the passenger side, it just didn't seem to take. At one point, going around a slight bend in the typically unwavering desert highway, Mary could have sworn that she felt her side of the car go airborne. Needless to say, the instant a service station came into view she put her foot down in a more figurative sense.

"Pull over!" she practically shouted, and Natty emphatically punched his bony fist against the roof in accord.

* * *

"You guys!" Mary rushed back to the car while the gas was still pumping. "It's a proper truck stop! It might be the last one before we officially enter the middle of nowhere, so we're gonna have to stock up on gas, food, and water ... I mean I am. Anyway, they've also got showers. Showers! Would you mind it if we hung around a bit? I mean, I'm beyond gross at this point."

The dead guys clicked and wheezed at one another for a second before Jett scribbled onto his white board: "Knock yourself out."

"Why don't you come in?" she asked. "Get out of the car for a bit, stretch out your bones?"

In the back seat Natty cocked his skull, clearly none too appreciative of her sass. In the front seat Jett put up his hands and omitted a wheezy "Ooooooooooh!" that clearly needed no written interpretation.

"You're not going to scare anyone; the place is deserted and mostly looted out," she said, and in response to the big question mark he drew on his board she looked back to the highway where, just visible through the desert haze, a half-dozen corpses in varying states of decay casually shambled along. And seeming to notice the strangers' eyes on them a few even looked over and waved. "I think the living have started to realize where you're going. I bet I'm the last person with a pulse for miles. Come on, let's go souvenir shopping."

. . .

Inside the truck stop was the remote desert version of the Mall of America, stripped down to its bones. Mary gazed sidelong at Natty and hoped that the dead cattle-driver hadn't somehow telepathically picked up her second bad pun, but the congenial skeleton, emitting a feint cloud of ancient brown dust with every step, had found one of the few remaining bottles of Jack Danial's from the liquor aisle and was in the process of settling into a tattered bright red pleather corner booth, heedless of how the swigs he tossed back spilled down his bare spine to soak into his ancient rags.

Jett, for his part, had found the old school arcade situated among a veritable graveyard of taxidermized desert wildlife and cute little cactus gardens. With the scattered quarters from a toppled Pac Man machine, he quickly made short work of Liu Kang with his video avatar's sinister cries of "Get over here!"

Content that her companions were enjoying their pit stop, Mary made her way to the shower stall. She stripped down, abandoning her white cotton panties and the heavy beige labyrinth of her maternity bra along with the paint-stained jeans and Throwing Copper tee-shirt that she had been wearing since she'd first passed out on the living room sofa days and days ago.

She washed her hair with the thin chemical pink soap from the hand dispenser by the sink, and scrubbed away the paste of sweat and desert sand that caked her, then used a Grand Canyon tee-shirt from one of the stripped and tumbled racks in the gift shop as a towel. And after a few seconds of browsing she grabbed a tribal patterned maxi dress from the section catered to tourist women having a hard time dealing with the intense desert heat.

It was when she had ambled on to the crusted goop and

shattered glass that had been the "cosmetics" section to find some dubious *ode de toilette* to dab at her wrists and earlobes that she heard the gulping, gagging, and weeping coming from the dark corner that had been a checkout booth once upon a time.

"Though I walk, though I walk, though I walk, though I walk," she heard a shuddering whispered chant. "Shadow of death, shadow of death, shadow of death."

"Valley of the shadow of death," Mary said softly as she approached. She leaned over the counter and let her damp hair fall free. He was just a kid, if a worldly twenty-one or twenty-two. Still, every other employee had fled by this point, so you had to give him credit for his fortitude.

"I think that's how the psalm goes anyway," she said with a shrug.

The kid turned his head to her, but his eyes didn't seem to focus.

"All dead," he muttered, fatalistically catatonic. "They're all dead."

"I'm not," Mary said with a little smile.

Very slightly his eyes seemed to focus, then darted in a paranoid rush over her freshly showered and touristy attired façade.

"You promise?" he asked. "You swear? See, they all look a little different, don't they? This one chick came in ... this chick was hot. Blonde chick. With an accent. She goes to pay, for like, bleach and stuff ... her fucking eyeball falls out! There were maggots. Spilled out like winning big at the slots. All dead. All rotten. What was it that movie said? When there's no room left in hell ..."

Mary looked over her shoulder, way across the big looted truck stop, to where a clearly furious Jett was punching the scratched-up Plexiglas cover on the old school Mortal Kombat arcade game after Sub Zero turned his wicked ninja into a statue of living ice. Meanwhile Natty had begun to play Five Finger Fillet with a big rusty bowie knife and his own barren carpals.

"Yeah," she said, her voice dripped with sarcasm. "That makes sense."

Staggering like Natty hadn't been the only one to loot the liquor aisle, the young clerk in his sweat stained polo shirt pushed himself to his feet. It was about then that Mary noticed the eight-millimeter glimmering in his hand.

"Hey, buddy ..."

"What to do?" he stammered. "What to do?"

"Oh shit," she put out her hands as he raised the barrel to his own temple.

"But if I fucking do it will I just turn into one of them? Ha! Will I just ramble on while I'm all dead and rotting? Will I? Fuck it, they don't seem to care. Maybe I'll fucking risk it."

He pulled back the hammer, and on an impulsive and awkward burst of heroism Mary lurched over the counter to tackle him.

It was about an hour later that they all sat at a corner booth playing Cards Against Humanity. Natty was killing it, and Jett grew increasingly confused and angry at his lack of success. The clerk, who had calmed down quite a bit and introduced himself as Jason, was tied at second with Mary.

"You know there ain't nothing there," he told them after winning a hand with the multiple combo of *When you get right down to it _____, is just _____, An unhinged ferris wheel rolling towards the sea,* and *A windmill full of corpses.* "It's just desert and more desert. People die out there."

Natty and Jett exchanged an eyeless, albeit meaningful glance. And Mary could almost see them smile.

"Well, I don't know if there's anything there," she admitted, and Jett and Natty shrugged their accord. "They just *have* to go. And if I can help them ... well, I will."

On the road again Natty sat in the back with an unfolded map over his lap trying to wrap his skull around the fact that, in a day, they'd covered a distance that would have taken him over a week with Pearl and the herd. Up front Jett, quite enamored with Mary's Spotify, had created a playlist heavy with his favorites from his flesh and blood days; *The Smiths, Guns n'Roses, Metallica*, before moving on to discover the jewels of the twenty-first century.

Mary let her vision slip out to focus on the towering wind-swept pillars of rock scattered across the softly undulating air of the horizon. The sky began to turn red with the encroaching night, making the world a blur of dim ruby and gold. Jett's high-octane playlist notwithstanding, it was a comfortably tranquil place until the boy hit them with a spike of nervous energy. He rapidly dove low under the dashboard, slapped at Mary's shoulder with one mummified husk of a hand while frantically pointing out the window with the other.

"What?" Mary asked, letting a nervous giggle escape her. In the back she heard the rattling click-clacking she had come to recognize as the skeletal cowboy's laugh.

"Girl," Jett hastily scribbled onto his dry erase board. And, taking her eyes off the horizon, Mary saw a silhouette, dark against the fading sunlight, swaying gracefully as she pushed along the bleached asphalt on a pair of old-school quad skates, long black hair whipping back and forth across her narrow waist. Mary had seen stranger things.

Jett poked frantically at her ribs and she slapped him away impatiently as she read his next message.

"Alive???"

"It certainly looks like she is," Mary said. "But she *is* roller skating down a desert interstate smack dab in the middle of the rapture. Why would a living girl be on your path like this?"

"You are," Jett reminded her.

"Touché."

"Needs help?" he wrote.

"We can ask," Mary said, and immediately Jett sank lower beneath the dash. "For heaven's sake, Jett! *I* can ask, okay?"

The dead boy offered a hesitant thumbs-up, still bent double in his seat, and Mary sped up a bit to overtake the skater before slowing down again to pull over in the gravel twenty feet or so ahead of her. When Mary stepped out of the car the girl executed a graceful pivot and popped up on her toe-stops to spin to a halt.

"Hi," she said, her voice was hesitant, and sounded young. As Mary stepped closer, she saw adeptly applied, if rather obvious contour makeup. Despite the twilight she wore a pair of thick white plastic-framed sunglasses behind two heavy curtains of thick black hair.

"Hi," Mary said, and the two of them stood sizing one another up for a few more seconds, the only sound to disturb the silence being the whispered *whurr* of the passenger-side window of her car sliding down an inch, no doubt so that Jett could listen in. "It's a bit late for shades."

"What can I say? They make me look cool. Is ... is there any chance that you're headed towards ... you know?" Mary raised an eyebrow and the girl leaned in to whisper, "Death Valley?"

"Yeah, that's the plan. I'm with a couple of friends."

"Okay," she said with a heavy sigh. "Okay."

In her defense, Mary felt extremely bad. She really should have known, after all. The makeup was so heavy for one so obviously young, a desperate attempt to hide her hallow cheeks and sunken eye sockets. And when she pulled the sunglasses away those sockets were not quite empty. It was the pincers of a scorpion poking out of one corner followed by the creeping of its stinger, and that sugar-sweet of the Baby-Gap-perfume commingled with the underlying rot that had Mary turn aside to retch.

"I fucking knew it!" the girl snapped, her voice broke as she shoved her sunglasses back over her face and kicked her skates off. Almost in the same motion she threw them over her shoulder and took off, stocking-footed, at a sprint across the desert, frantically perpendicular to that lonely asphalt.

Almost immediately the passenger-side door of the much-abused silver Prius was kicked opened and Jett took off after her, pausing only briefly to shoot a look, hands thrown wide, that unmistakably read "What the fuck?" Mary was about to follow after herself when a pointed, almost weightless hand came to rest on her shoulder. She turned to see the fleshless brown skull beneath a cowboy hat, and patiently he held out Jett's dry-erase board scrawled over with his slow, deliberate script.

"It is time to make camp, ma'am."

"You've got to be kidding me?"

But clearly he was not. Sauntering over to one of the rocks he spread his duster out against it and, in tattered vest and shirt-sleeves, he lay his bony frame down, pushed his hat low over his sockets, and folded his arms.

With an exasperated sigh Mary went back to the car.

As it happened, Jason made a pretty penny from commissions (or would have, had the truck stop not degenerated to total chaos by that point), and in the end that made him a pretty decent salesman. Still, citing the end of the world, he had stead-fastly refused all offers of payment, though he was happy to share his expertise, regardless, with the one living member of the travelers' party. The desert was cold at night, he assured her. He'd saddled her trunk with a thermal sleeping bag, a flare gun, fool-proof kindling and matches (although Natty had assured them, and been as good as his word, that he could get a blaze going with any scrap of brush they might find in the wilderness), a simple compass that seemed to be broken upon closer inspection as a few miles down the road its arrow just continued to spin and spin with no inkling of True North, several packs of dehydrated food, and of course, gallons and gallons of bottled water.

At Natty's suggestion, Mary pulled the car off-road to close off the site and give them shelter from the wind. All the while she kept her eyes to the horizon where the two dead kids continued to circle one another, gesturing animatedly, carrying on in heated conversation or debate with the tireless stamina that could only maintain for so long in the young and impassioned, not to mention undead.

And busy herself though she might with the myriad of chores that Natty continued to assign, Mary simply couldn't seem to keep her attention from the horizon. Finally, as she was distractedly piling up scavenged kindling despite their lucrative supplies ("Stores are best saved for the times of utmost desperation" Natty had written when she ventured to object) the old skeleton tapped her on the shoulder and pointed two bony claws first at his own empty sockets, then to the pile of desiccated weeds and salvaged planks of wood Mary busied herself in collecting.

"I *am* focused!" she snapped back at him. "Do you mean to tell me you're not the least bit concerned about Jett? That girl seemed kind of psycho."

Natty folded his arms and sank back on his heels a moment, then put out one finger, dragged it across the exposed vertebra of his neck, and shrugged, to which Mary replied by hurling her armful of junk to the barren gravel.

"Yeah!" she snapped, "I get it! He's dead already, so why even give a shit, right? Well I'm sorry, but just in case you've failed to notice that doesn't exactly change the fact that he's still just a kid, and literally just met some crazy girl in the middle of this god-forsaken wasteland, and they've been out there for hours fighting about god-knows what!"

And at that point she was so overcome with emotion and ill-equipped to handle Natty's eyeless gaze that all she could think to do was kick the bumper of her car hard enough to send herself hopping about on stubbed toes.

"Damn it!" she cried, and then she let herself collapse to her knees beside the fire and simply cry. It was strange to realize that this was actually the first time after all of the terrible days that had followed the breakwater that she had actually been able to cry.

Eventually Natty held the dry-erase board out to her, and she slapped it away. He, in turn, tossed it down to the dust before her feet.

"We have not moved beyond the capacity to feel pain, ma'am," he had written somewhat hastily (for Natty anyway). "But ours is a different world than that in which you currently reside. Still, the boy is steadfast and strong, and I assure you he will be fine."

Mary nodded slowly, not quite able to make eye-contact with the dark pits in his skull.

"I know," she said. "I know he will. That doesn't make this any easier."

Natty took up the board and began again with his meticulous script. After a moment he handed it back to her.

"I do not mean to intrude, ma'am," Mary read as she wiped

away her snot and tears. "But may I inquire as to the nature of your loss? I dare to presume that it was a child."

And after she had driven for so many countless miles, picked up bodies, held it all in, she broke down completely. She let her head collapse down to her knees as the sobs overtook her. After a moment she felt a sharp but gentle pressure on her shoulder and she knew that it was his hand again. A dead man with no flesh and blood left to him trying to offer her a bit of compassion. Suddenly it seemed the most natural thing in the world to lurch over and throw her arms around him. And yes, she heard a crack or two, and it was like hugging a sack of old branches wrapped in autumn leaves, but the warmth she felt when he wrapped his arms around her was undeniable. In a fatherly way he stroked her hair while she sobbed uncontrollably until finally she got out enough to sit up again and wipe the tears away.

"H-h-how did you kn-n-now?"

Tossing his head slightly, Natty looked away almost embarrassed and tapped one bony claw to his own chest.

Mary looked down at her abnormally huge breasts beneath the pilfered truck stop dress and self-consciously put a hand up to cover the stain.

"Right," she said, then let a bitter laugh escape her. "Spilled milk."

The strangest thing that happened that night was that Mary eventually pulled herself together, finished the chores that Natty had assigned, and finally settled into her sleeping bag. Her eyes still fixated on the horizon as she put minimal effort into pretending she was asleep.

All the while Natty sat in a relaxed supine manner against a rock on the other side of the campfire. He ran a much-abused little tin harmonica, clickity-clacking, again and again over his broken teeth with an asymmetric sort of rhythm.

Turning on her back to look up at the stars, Mary asked him, "Can you hear the music the same way you see and talk to one-another? I'm only asking because ... well, it's been a few days now. I still don't hear anything."

After a second's silent contemplation, Natty extended that little strip of tarnished silver in one bony hand.

"I don't know how," Mary said.

The crunchy brown bones shrugged beneath the worn duster and pushed the harmonica an inch closer. He was tenacious enough that she finally accepted the tiny instrument. The skeleton pointed to the harmonica then pointed to his lipless grimace.

"I don't know how," she repeated.

Natty cocked his head and just kept tapping his bony finger against broken teeth until finally Mary gave up protesting and put the harmonica to her mouth.

What followed was a game of Dishwasher. He held his hands in pantomime and she did her best to move hers to reflect him. As she breathed into the harmonica a song finally began to form from it. And they continued softly humming in this strange collaboration until she finally began to drift off into restless slumber.

It had to be well past midnight when the cold thin desert wind carried with it the sick sweet smell of formaldehyde. Mary bolted up in her sleeping bag and squinted hard. She could just make out two figures very slowly approaching the camp. They stopped frequently to continue with what looked like pleading or arguing, turning back away, and back again.

She began the graceless process of stumbling out of her

sleeping bag when she heard a tapping and looked over to where Natty was comfortably slumped beside the dying embers of the fire. He held the board which had "Easy now," carefully scrawled across the entire surface.

"I just want to make sure he's okay!" Mary exclaimed, and with a forceful calm Natty motioned for her to maintain her position while he slowly penned out his next message.

"Of course he is okay, that is a girl not a dragon. You just sit tight. They will return in their own time."

Mary couldn't deny his logic, but neither could she dispel her anxiety to see Jett. So, much like a petulant child, she folded her arms and slumped over.

"Well they certainly are taking their own sweet time about it!" she finally huffed.

Instead of writing a response Natty just tossed over his harmonica again.

"It's no good," she told him, "I already forgot how to play the song you showed me."

Again he took up the board.

"Compose a new one, ma'am" he wrote and returned to prodding the life back into the dying fire.

"Damn it, Natty!" she cried, but in the end she found herself blowing an incoherent melody into the beat up instrument, which she had to admit was better than staring daggers as the two dead kids floundered again and again over whether or not to return to camp.

After what didn't quite seem like forever Natty rose to his feet and cupped one hand over the gaping black holes of his eye sockets as though scanning the distance. Mary stopped what we generously refer to as 'playing' the harmonica and very faintly she heard the wheezing rain-stick crunch sound she had come to recognize as Jett's voice. When she looked up the boy rapidly approached the camp while the girl steadfastly marched off in the opposite direction.

"What is it?" she asked.

Natty put up a finger for her to wait a second, which she did before speaking again.

"What's he saying?"

It was amusing to see how plainly Natty could convey his exasperation despite a complete lack of facial features. He crouched down again and with as much speed as he could muster he wrote a terse message for her.

"For once do as you are told and stand down."

He put on his hat with some swagger and started off, but before the ghoulish contours of his skull were outside the light of the flames, he flashed a friendly salute to let her know there were no hard feelings.

Jett seemed frantic as he ran up to Natty, whose long purposeful strides barely paused to dismiss the boy's agitation and pointed him back towards the camp. Jett seemed ruefully to comply as Natty carried on in the direction of the girl.

Quickly Mary laid back and pretended to be sleeping. It couldn't have been much long after when Jett slumped down to the desert earth beside her.

"I'm glad you're back," she tentatively whispered. "I was worried."

He shrugged and gave her a thumbs up.

"Where are the others?"

Jett grabbed the dry erase board and smeared Natty's last message away. When he finally handed the board over to her it read:

"Natty said they'd take a walk, and whatever she wanted to do afterwards that would be that. I don't know how I made her so mad. All I know is that I tried to let her know everything was okay and that made her mad, and I tried to talk about why, and then she got mad about something else, and it went on like that for a while. She didn't really want to talk to me, or anybody traveling with the living, but I bet he'll do a better job at explaining everything since he's a cool old-timey cowboy. And also I just started saying sentences backwards and my voice got all weird and screechy like it did when I was still in middle school. She won't say her name, but whatever it is I think I'm in love with her."

Mary considered telling him that that was a pretty weird conclusion to come to about a complete stranger he'd managed to argue with for hours and not even come out with a name, but instead she just smiled and said, "Good for you."

Jett wiped the board clean and started writing again.

"I've never been in love before. I had a girlfriend for a week and a half back in eighth grade and I guilt-tripped a hot nurse's assistant into kissing me after I got sick, but I never felt anything like this. It's like getting hit by lightning in the middle of a roller-coaster ride. I guess you don't believe in love at first sight?"

"I never used to," she said, "but I felt it when my son was born."

Jett's leathery fist punched playfully into her arm.

"Get out!" he wrote. "I didn't know you had a son! What's his name?"

"John," she said. "His middle name was Connor. We called him Johnny C."

"Cool! Like in Terminator?"

"Exactly," she said. "The man who could stand up to Armageddon."

Jett wrote, "How old?"

"Well," she said, "he was born a little more than two weeks ago. I'd gotten sick. I mean, not like you were, just ... a bad infection, but it complicated things. It was way too early." She couldn't look at Jett as she spoke so she looked down at her own hands as she cupped them together in her lap. "He could fit in my hands," she said. "They wouldn't let me hold him, but when I put my hand into the incubator he tried to hold onto me. He was so strong. He wanted to live so badly."

It was getting harder and harder to keep talking. And then, very suddenly, for the second time that evening she found herself embracing the dead. This time it was Jett who threw his arms around her, and despite his mummification she felt that embrace as strongly as she had felt that little fist close around her thumb.

And though she had thought she would have died from the shame and the sorrow, instead she found herself breathing easier now that her companions knew the truth, as though a great weight had been lifted from her chest.

"I'm alright," she finally stammered, "I think I'll finally be able to sleep again now."

And that was just what she did.

As the sun began to rise, Mary applied an ample coat of SPF 100. She gingerly peeled away the pink patches of sunburn when out of the corner of her eye she saw a flash of darkness. She let out a cry of alarm as she turned and saw the dead girl approach with a massive bowie knife in one hand.

"Christ, calm down, grandma!" the girl exclaimed.

"I'm thirty-one."

"Yeah, whatever. Lone Ranger over there says we need to try and get some water from a cactus and I should ask you for empty bottles."

Mary looked over to where Natty was knelt down calmly burying the remains of the campfire. Without looking up he shot them a bony salute.

"If you ask me, it was pretty stupid of you to drive into the middle of the desert without enough water. I mean, if you *do* intend to go on living and all."

She folded her gray-skinned arms and popped one hip out, the very soul of insolence.

"Sure," Mary said, "okay." And she went to the car to grab one of the liter plastic bottles she had drained the day before. The girl snatched it up and stomped off in the direction of a couple of barrel cacti, shimmering green in the hazy dawn.

"Um, Natty?" Mary said. "The trunk is practically brimming with bottled water."

He handed her the dry-erase board where a message was already pre-written.

"Finding water in inhospitable climbs is a skill that is not to be undervalued, ma'am. I advise you to accompany the young lady. Between yourselves you should be able to procure a bottle. She is not angry with you, she is angry to be dead."

"Where's Jett?"

Natty nodded off in the other direction where he apparently had set the boy to arbitrarily arrange stones in the sand. Jett saw her looking and waved merrily.

"Okay, what is the point of that?" she had to ask.

Natty tapped a finger to his skull as though to indicate that she should trust him as he knew what he was doing.

"Natty, even if there was any more to you than a skeleton, I do believe I could see right through you."

He flashed her a thumbs-up, very clearly a gesture he had picked up from Jett, and with a resigned sigh she started off to where the girl busily hacked away at the cactus in the distance.

"What do you want?" she demanded as Mary approached. The girl paused her repetitive hacking to shove her sunglasses up the top of her forehead and glare defiantly down at her with partially rotted eyes.

With an exasperated sigh Mary threw her arms out. "Nothing!" she exclaimed. "I thought I'd offer to help."

"Well, that'd make sense considering that you're the one who's going to be drinking this shit. However, we have just the one knife and I've already established my rhythm, so if there's nothing else?"

"Maybe you could tell me your name?"

The girl kept her one milky eye and one oozing socket turned down as she replaced the big retro sunglasses.

"For roller derby I was going to be Terran Tella," she said. "You know, like the mad Spanish dance that they used to think was the only way to survive the bite of a venomous spider. Nobody really got it, though."

"You got a real name?" Mary asked.

"Do you, Mary, full of grace?" the girl demanded with a bit of hostility, then took a breath she hardly needed and went back to chopping at the cactus with Natty's huge unwieldy bowie.

"Sure I do. My parents hooked up in a church basement in Cape Elizabeth when they were supposed to be at bible study. I just hope that Jett's parents weren't so literal."

"Ha ha ha," was the sarcastic reply. "How about Lupe?" she said, stab-stab-stabbing at the thick hide of the barrel cactus. "Like the great silent film star from the golden age, Lupe Valez. She used to say that she wasn't very beautiful, but she had beautiful eyes and she knew how to use them. You obviously can't tell from looking, but I did too."

"Didn't she drown in the toilette?"

The girl halted her rhythmic poking with a single violent stab that buried the blade halfway to the hilt in the succulent.

"That's an urban legend. Some racist fuck said she stumbled into the bathroom after her 'Mexi-spice' last meal didn't agree with the Seconal. Lupe was a fucking movie star, though, and she had access to the good stuff. She wouldn't have been able to move after that much Seconal.

"So what *really* happened," the girl continued, "is that Lupe Valez was pregnant and the man she thought had loved her supremely turned out to be full of shit. And this amazing and glamorous life as a beautiful movie star turned out to be a lot of shit as well. Edie Sedgwick played her in an Andy Warhol film, you know. Talk about Hollywood whitewashing!"

"Is that what happened to you?" Mary asked, feeling the emptiness churn inside her once again as she thought back to the small hand squeezing hers within

"Well, I wasn't pregnant," she pulled the bowie back out of the cactus and dutifully began to collect the trickle that spilled out with the empty bottle. "And I doubt any white factory girls are ever going to get cast in the biopic of my brief and inauspicious tenure among the living ... and I didn't exactly have a bunch of Seconal hanging around, just a whole lot of extra-strength Tylenol and some peppermint schnapps.

"I played a little game with myself, in fact. Arranged them all in a fun little spiral around the bottle. Wanted to see if I could get it all down without chugging. One sip per pill moving the spiral down gradually to the middle. In the end there was still a mouthful left.

"But sadly, I was not blessed with the paralysis and instant drift away of the movie stars. No, I got to live, however briefly, that urban legend. I did stagger towards the upstairs bathroom in my parents' house. I didn't quite make it before I couldn't hold back the vomit any longer, and it was messy, but not quite enough to delay the inevitable. The last thing I remember before waking up in a goddamn box was the bathroom tiles rushing up at me.

"They didn't bury me with a phone, thank God. You've heard about FOMO, right? 'Fear Of Missing Out.' The great scourge of our generation. Even when it was giving me panic attacks and night terrors I was pulling out that stupid thing several times an hour to see who was saying I was a slut, cunt, or bitch.

"If they buried me with my phone I probably would have started checking all the feeds again as soon as I woke up, see if maybe this was all it took for them to start saying nice things about me again. Check out the memorial page. Read the letters that they sent. They write you way more letters after you're dead. Some guy I met on the road told me that. He said I was much better off having sworn off the living like I did.

"I may be rotten, but you guys? You still get so thirsty, don't you?"

She held out the bottle of translucent gray fluid she had harvested from the succulent. Mary pushed it back at her.

"You know what the worst part is? I thought that no matter what happened it would be over after that night. Maybe there would be some kind of peace, some enlightened new plain of being. My family's pretty old-school Catholic, so yeah, a big part of me was afraid that there would be damnation, hellfire, eternal suffering. I guess I figured I could take it. But to be perfectly honest I was really counting on blinking out into nothing forever and ever. But none of that happened, did it?"

She took a moment to pause in her soliloquy and stare up at the endless blue sky that enveloped them, horizon to horizon. Then she turned to Mary.

"Do you have a phone?"

It had been off since she started driving, but still, Mary had somehow managed to transfer that dead weight from her dress pants to the pocket of her pilfered dress. She turned it on and immediately it began to buzz, vibrate, and chime.

"Lot of unseen messages, huh?"

"Did you want to check Facebook or something?"

"I want you to tell me today's date, plain and simple."

Mary did, and the girl put her hands into her hair and laughed with unnerving hysteria, turning around in a few circles before responding.

"You know Jett probably died when my dad was a little kid, right? And Natty? Jesus Christ! It has been less than a month for me. Nothing super profound or terrible happened, though. It's just that instead of waking up in the detox wing with everyone mad at me, I woke up in the ground. There's probably nothing left of me now but nostalgic pictures and bittersweet memories on a tribute page in the yearbook. At least Natty and even Jett got to wake up in the distant future. For me *nothing* has changed, and I'm just so goddamn mad I could scream."

Instead of screaming, though, she sank down against the base of the cactus. Leaning back the prickers made an audible *thunk* as they sank into her nicely embalmed flesh, but if she felt anything it didn't seem to bother her. After a moment's hesitation Mary walked over and, keeping a slightly wider berth, sank down to the gravel beside her.

"Nothing's changed," the girl said to the sky. "But now I have to go to the valley. That's all."

"We're all going that way," Mary told her. "And there's an extra seat in the Prius."

"So it's really true that you're not afraid of us?"

"My mom took me grave rubbing when I was a kid," Mary said, and even the slack face of the dead girl managed to register a look of unmistakable *ick*. "*Rubbing*," Mary carefully enunciated. "There are some pretty old graveyards where I'm from. A lot of the stones had death's head reliefs; skulls with angel wings. But me as a little kid made a wax rubbing of the entire stone not just the relief. I hung it above the head of my twin bed when I got home because I thought it was cool ... I mean, years later my mom said that it looked kind of creepy, but she always let me do me.

"The sun went down, bedtime came, and I started to put together the letters I was learning to read and it finally sunk in that it was a name over a dead body, just like grandma."

"What was it?"

"I hardly remember. Rebecca something. She may have been a Puritan.

"Anyway, I got scared, I ran into my mom's room because I was terrified that the ghost of this woman would be mad at me because I made a rubbing of her headstone and she was dead, just like Grandma. She told me 'Grandma wasn't mean.' She told me 'Most people aren't.' So maybe that did it. And maybe the past week I've had as much fear as I could handle and my reserves have run dry.

"My grandma will probably come along this way eventually, now that I think about it. She didn't have a Prius, and Jett's the only one I've actually come across who actually asked for a ride. Fuck, she's probably on her way, though."

"What about your mom?"

"Probably a dozen or so of those chimes you heard when I turned on my phone."

Sinking her head back into the thorns the girl sucked in her lower lip and chewed on it a second or so.

"I had a bad night," she finally said. "I mean, obviously there weren't a lot of good ones in the mix, but that was just a really *really* bad night. I can't take it back now." She breathed another long unnecessary sigh and finally looked directly at Mary. "I guess there's nothing else for it. Extra seat in the Prius? Let's go to the valley."

"Okay," Mary said, reaching out one hand. The one that

clasped it was dry, but it wouldn't be quite right to say that it was cold out beneath the burning sun.

"So. That Puritan chick, Rebecca. Her ghost ever come after you for making that rubbing?"

"I stopped believing in ghosts a long time ago."

"It's biblical, you know. 'Rebecca at the well.' She's the one who gave water to the stranger and all of his animals at the oasis."

Again she held out the bottle of liquid she had harvested. This time Mary took it with a whispered thanks and took a long swig. Her face screwed up immediately, but she managed to swallow.

"Christ," she said. "That's bitter."

"Let's just go with Becky," the girl said.

* * *

After that, quite in keeping with the immortal adage from, *Planet of the Apes* "Don't trust anyone over thirty," the kids took to keeping company with one another in the back seat. Becky, the only voice among the companions that Mary could actually hear and understand, kept to a conspiratorial whisper aside from moments every now and again when something Jett must have told her caused her to break out in a trill of high, clear, laughter only slightly gurgled by embalmed slow decay.

From time-to-time Jett still sat up front with Mary when Becky went to sleep. Perhaps being newer to death, the girl still carried on little habits like this, whether she needed to or not. Explaining that riding in the back seat had always been an easy way to soothe her into slumber, she slumped her forehead on the blazing glass of the back seat window, her eyelids softly closed over the mess beneath them, her chest rhythmically rose and fell with the breath she no longer needed.

Mary couldn't help wondering if Becky was pretending for a bit of respite from the increasingly exuberant Jett, but Mary was glad for any time she could get with her first passenger riding shotgun once again. He eagerly scribbled messages imploring her to explain the new slang and modern advancements that Becky spoke of. After securing his word that he would take the responsibility seriously and drive like he had at least one living person in the car, she even let him get behind the wheel a few more times.

They made one last stop before the desert completely enveloped them. It was a collection of small adobe buildings and tin shacks that was nearly a ghost town even before the living had fled *en masse* as the dead began to pass through on their way to the valley.

Becky, finding the Prius far less magical than Natty or even Jett, took the car to a deserted service station and, lacking any attendant, went about checking all of the fluid levels and prepared to change the oil.

"You *do* know what you're doing, right?" Mary had asked.

Becky flashed a gray-tinted smile. "Trust me."

Mary left money on the counter to cover any supplies and left with Jett to walk through the handful of streets that made up the town. Natty opted to stay behind, hat clenched against his chest as he watched Becky work. Somehow his fleshless façade still conveyed an air of trepidation as she casually explained the mechanics of the engine she worked on.

"My school had an auto-shop," she told him as she checked the dipstick. "It was always my favorite. Once you know what you're doing it's much simpler than it looks. And when something goes wrong it's just a matter of isolating what parts are not working and figuring out how to fix it."

As Mary and Jett wandered the streets, they found that the town was, for the most part, cracked, sun-bleached and, in places, practically submerged in the dust and gravel of the desert. There was, however, one notable exception that Jett was quick to spot. In one corner of that little outpost tucked behind the cracked adobe walls of the local school there was a small concrete courtyard sunken low among a cluster of massive wind-blasted rocks. A wide, shallow, stairway with an iron rail descended to a mosaic mandala made up of bits of colored rocks, glass, and semi-precious stone. Along all the edges there were strangely placed concrete ramps that seemed to lead to nowhere.

Jett's reaction to this little park seemed inordinately piqued, even considering his typically high-spirited demeanor. As he ran and veritably leapt down the stairs towards a pile of bikes that had been haphazardly abandoned, Mary began to understand. The local kids must have hung out there as the first waves of the dead began passing through. Parents, in a panic, had most-likely swooped in to gather them up and flee what-ever untold apocalypse this new legion surely heralded, demanding that they abandon bikes and skateboards, even leaving behind a backpack or two.

Jett searched through the abandoned property for a minute or so before he selected a skateboard and walked back to show it, with exaggerated reverence, to Mary. The wheels were acid green and the bottom of the deck was emblazoned with a garishly colored and slightly cartoonish pin-up girl with a tattered cloak and a reaper's scythe. He took the dry-erase board from Mary as she admired the graphics and penned a quick message.

"I think I may have found my edge."

This message turned out to be rather literal, Mary came to realize, cheering from the sidelines as Jett gained momentum then leapt up, grinding down the length of the stairway's iron rail, leaving a trail of sparks in his wake.

Becky had put her quads back on as well as a pair of large and badly scratched and taped up knee pads. She made a valiant attempt to mimic Jett's grind, but once again she fell almost immediately down to the concrete steps.

"I'm telling you!" she called with a laugh. If she felt any pain from the fall she didn't show it, but something told Mary she wouldn't have before dying either. "It can't be done with quads!"

Jett sank his weight low and leaned back so far that Mary feared he would topple over himself, but instead of falling he pulled the board into a wide arc back to Becky before jumping off and plopping down beside her. The clicking wheeze came out as he flipped his board over and moved the desiccated husks of his fingertips over the trucks of his own board then the ones on the bottoms of her feet. No doubt he was pointing out the similarities between the two.

"Maybe I could show you a few of my tricks?"

This time they chased one another in wide circles around the park. Becky leapt nimbly from skating forwards to backwards and reached out her hands. Jett grabbed her hand and she twisted her waist sharply, pulling him around and giving him a burst of crazy speed.

Becky let out a cry of exuberance and, judging by how Jett held out his arms, either emulating wings or a frantic attempt to keep his balance. He shouted in kind, and Mary felt a stab of jealousy that the dead girl could hear him while she herself could not.

"That's a whip!" Becky called. "You think you're brave enough to try hitting?"

. . .

In the end it proved close to impossible to pry the kids away from the park and, not having the heart to break into any of the local houses, Mary opted instead to scout out the schoolhouse to find a place to spend the night.

It made sense to pick a room on the first floor. There was less distance to carry the camping gear, and it was a smaller space, which was good considering that she was the only one with any body heat that needed conserving. It was a nice coincidence that this particular room happened to have a neat row of small folded white fleece blankets and rolled up sleeping mats against one wall. Garlands of construction paper chains hung draped along the walls, their vibrant colors paled in the light of the moon filtered through the dusty window panes, and self-portraits in heavy lines of wobbling crayon framed the blackboard.

Mary walked to the empty cluster of faded linoleum in the center of a semicircle of little desks that barely crested the top of her knees, and without really thinking about it she took one of the even smaller chairs and placed it in the center, then took another and set it facing the first. Still not thinking she sat down on one of them. After months of cravings and being too exhausted to move, her frame was still narrow, yet her hips spread out on either side regardless, and her knees rose up practically to her chest.

Would this be what it would have been like, even after four, maybe five years on this earth together? Would he still have been so small? Her little guy who fought so hard. Would she still have wanted to protect him so badly even when the years had gone by and the hormones had depleted. Perhaps that chair before her wasn't so small, really.

She had no doubt whatsoever that the scuff of a rotten leather boot on the tiles was made deliberately by a man who could move in a silence that was complete and absolute. But

Natty had seen enough tears from her already, so she tried to make it appear as though she had a convenient itch to scratch on the side of her eye as she turned to face him.

"Kids still playing?" she asked, and Natty nodded solemnly down at her.

"Thought this would be a decent place to spend the night," she said. "I mean, there's plenty of that shit pizza in the cafeteria. There's water. I can even shower in the gym. We *do* try to do that every day in the twenty-first century."

Natty walked past her miniature chair setup and plucked a piece of chalk from the blackboard ledge. Still in his elegant script, but huge and simple, he wrote on the board "A, B, C."

"Yes," she said. "I am aware of the fact that it's a classroom for little kids. But everything I said makes sense, and ... I'm just so damn tired, okay? And the park's right outside. Listen." The windows were all open, slanting inwards, and the sound of the skate wheels grinding against the pavement over and over again could be easily heard. "They're having so much fun."

That ceaseless grind carried on throughout the night while, keeping to himself in one dark corner, Natty's teeth clicked against his battered harmonica, comforting despite the lack of music it produced.

The night before was the first time she had been able to manage more than twenty minutes or so of straight slumber for days and days. That night, wrapped up in those white flannel blankets on a pile of yoga mats that still smelled like chalk and were slightly sticky with traces of apple juice and jam, finally she was able to dream once more.

* * *

They were on the road again in time to watch the dawn. The morning came to the desert differently than it did back north.

There was no silver mist to filter the sunrise, no softness of rolling hills and dark fragrant pines to shield her from its intensity. The world around them was a hard and vibrant sculpture of the wind. A world of naked and inescapably powerful beauty.

It was still just cool enough that the windows were down, and Mary relished the dry wind that made her hair dance in a sweat-christened halo even as her skin began to feel the burning kiss of the unchecked sun. Miraculously, she found herself smiling.

"It's beautiful," she said aloud, if mostly to herself, "here at the end of the world."

"Tell Susie's-got-a-pulse to get over it," a sleepy voice came from the back. "This is just the beginning as far as I'm concerned."

"Jett says—"

In an instant all of Mary's senses went numb. Next came the crash of overwhelming clarity.

"I heard him," she said, and when she looked up in the rear-view mirror in the unfiltered light of the dawn Becky's eyes were clear and brown. She was comfortably nestled in the arms of a skinny boy in a hoodie. He had dirty blonde hair that fell to his shoulders in messy waves, a pronounced nose, and huge eyes the color of honey with flecks of fungus green.

"Why's she looking at me like that?" he asked, and something in her face must have betrayed her. "Mary?"

"Watch the damn road, girl!"

A hand latched onto the wheel as the car began to veer off into the blistered sand. Mary looked over and didn't see a weathered skeleton sitting shotgun, but a man with graying five-day stubble and deep furrows between wild eyebrows that shaded vibrant hazel eyes.

"Oh my God, oh my God, oh my God!" Mary wailed. "I crashed the car, didn't I? I'm dead, I'm dead, I'm dead!"

"Hate to break it to you, grandma," Becky said, and made a show of waving her hand over her nose, "but counter to logic though it may seem, nobody dead smells that bad at the moment."

"You're not dead, Mary," Jett muttered in awe, and pointed to a sand-blasted sign on the side of the road. "Look. We made it."

"Madam," Natty said. "I believe it would be wise to bring this machine to a halt."

Mary's was the only car in the valley that morning. The rest of the myriad troupes of the dead slid into the valley like the sailing stones of the desert playa, and despite the weather-beaten signs by the side of the road, Mary knew they were entering a place without boundaries.

Somehow, in the shimmering sunlight, Mary finally found herself completely unable to distinguish the living from the dead. It was a bit like watching a festival crowd walk exhausted from an all-night jam only to learn that each and every one of their childhood heroes had just announced a surprise performance. Considering the crowd, eventually it just made sense to pull over.

Outside, among the glittering stone and rippling horizon, Mary stood out among the crowd. She was disheveled, sweating, stinking, and miserable ... physically speaking. Despite everything her journey had taken her through, there was a serenity in the scalding air.

Wiping again at the paste of sweat and grime that hung from her brow, Mary watched as Jett and Becky crouched by the side of the road and drew maps and plans and great ambitions with their fingers in the sand.

"Boys grow up."

If she had enough moisture reserves in her body, Mary knew that tears would be cutting through the grime.

"I wouldn't know," she said, and forced a smile.

"This is Nadua," Natty said with a terse nod to the woman who stood beside him. She was darker skinned, but had a similar leathery cast, with ink-black hair streaked white and cascading several inches below the waist of baggy overalls patched up with bits of fraying gingham. And slightly built though she was, perched up on her shoulders there was an immensely fat baby, perhaps a bit more than a year old, with shaggy blonde curls and big marble eyes.

"This one hasn't told me his name just yet," Nadua said. "We met on the journey." She looked up past her heavy black brows. "Say 'hello' to Miss Mary, little one."

The baby on her shoulders flapped both chubby arms and grinned to reveal two tiny sharp teeth. Mary, with a shrug, flapped her arms back at him, eliciting a shrill and delighted giggle and flapping so eager that he began to bop the head of his companion. Nadua raised an eyebrow but otherwise didn't seem to mind in the least.

"Care to tell her what you told me?" Natty prompted with gentle gruffness.

"I met the little one on my way here. He can walk a bit, but mostly crawling still. He was crossing Comanche lands all by himself. None of the living could see him at all. Scooped him up before a Jeep full of panicking white folk ran him down. Don't know what would have happened had they hit him. Seems he's got no body left to him at all. He's in good company. Biggest part that's left of me is my foot. Got it caught in a ravine a while back when times were hard. Meant to walk out to California, but the air had turned to dust when I was only a few days into my journey. Can't blame myself for losing my footing. Foot stayed trapped in the rocks. Tseena must have eaten the rest. Can't blame him either. Times were hard then, for men and men and wolves alike."

"Reckon all you'd see of the two of them a few miles back would be Nadua's foot, plodding on along the desert," Natty said, to which the woman rolled her eyes.

"Sacred vessel one day is meat for the wolf the next."

"Are there many children like him?" Mary asked. "Out there alone?"

"Not alone for long," Nadua said. "It's funny how our differences don't seem to matter now. When I was a child, I had family who remembered first-hand being driven from their homes and watching their kin slaughtered. And when I found work for the white families during the hard times their children played cowboys and Indians in the back yard, so very innocently reenacting that slaughter."

"Ain't none of us alone out here, ma'am," Natty said. Then very awkwardly he attempted to give her arm a comradely pat on the shoulder. "Not for long."

"We don't mean to say being dead is a better way to live," Nadua said. "But there may yet be some things you can learn from us."

A long silvery thread of drool slipped from the corner of the baby's mouth and fell down to land on the tip of Nadua's nose. She wiped it away and glared up with mock irritation.

"You may not have a body, little one," she said, "but you've been a weight for these weary shoulders to carry for some very long strides." She reached up and lifted him from her shoulders, held him against her hip for a moment to plant a rough kiss on his forehead, then held him out to Mary. "Give an old woman a moment's rest?" she said. "I have a feeling I'll be carrying him for a little while yet until it's time for his parents to make the journey down to the valley themselves."

The memory of the incubator still raw in her mind, her trembling fingers reaching through plastic, afraid to touch the little fist no bigger than a porcelain doll. JC didn't tremble while he fought to live. But he grabbed onto her finger ... her index finger on her left hand. Why could his fingers squeeze while his lungs couldn't breathe? Why couldn't his heart keep beating when hers just had to?

Mary took the robust toddler into her arms. She had to admit, he was as heavy as a bag of wet cement. Nadua was even tougher than she looked to carry him for so many miles. It was hard to notice the weight of him, though, when he looked up at her with shining blue eyes and smiled a wide two-tooth grin.

"Hi" she said, because it seemed as good a thing as any. He reached out one chubby arm and stroked her hair, then giggled hysterically at the moisture of her sweat that came off her nose and dripped down on his forehead.

Nadua stretched out her arms and twisted her torso. Despite her supposed lack of a body her joints audibly cracked. Squinting, she held one hand over her brow and scanned the undulating horizon.

"What say you, little one?" she asked, turning to the baby in Mary's arms. "If we keep to our feet, we may yet catch my father. He died a ways closer to the meeting place, so there's a bit of a head start."

Lurching in Mary's arms he laughed and clapped his hands. She handed him back to Nadua after planting a soft kiss on the top of his head (his curls smelled vaguely of Johnson and Johnson).

"The old man has many wonderful stories to tell," the older woman whispered to the child. "Most of them you should not believe in the slightest." She propped the squirming baby on one bony hip and turned to nod at Natty and Mary. "We were happy to meet you both," she said. "Safe travels until your journey's end." And then she turned her attention back to the child as she moved off towards the horizon. "Come on, young one. I think he's this way. I feel it in my bones."

"How does she know?" Mary whispered when they had moved far enough away.

Natty gave a cavalier shrug.

"She knows," he said. "Same as I know. Something about the valley, I guess. My wife and daughter are on their way.

"I've been gone from this world for a long time. And they departed long before that. Our daughter never drew her first breath as my wife was drowning in her last. When they were gone what else could I do? Rode out west. Lived out the rest of my days on the lonely trails."

"I'm so sorry, Natty."

"Ma'am, I always had faith that I would see them again. Back east she and I had a hill that we vowed we would always find a way to meet upon, no matter what. When the great war finally ended, I staggered back, more bloody than blue, and that was where she found me. Somehow, she managed to coax me back to life after I was certain that all the horrors I had seen had finally burned all the humanity away. She was the goodness in me, and that never did perish. Even when there was no longer anyone left to meet me on that hill. I suppose now we'll have a valley instead." He put a hand to his chest and closed his eyes as a smile of complete serenity spread over his worn and lined face. "I couldn't feel it on the road," he said, "but now ... it's like my own heart beating. I know they're on their way."

Mary smiled as well.

"What was ... is her name?"

Natty chuckled. "Marjorie," he said. "Means 'pearl.'"

"You give her my best when she gets here."

"That I certainly will, ma'am. As it happens, we had yet to decide on a name for the child. We buried her with Marjorie's name, but I feel certain my wife would have found this frightful vein. If it's all the same, I might see what she thinks about 'Mary.'"

"Awww, Natty!" she put her hands over her mouth and felt the sting from the saline residue of her own perspiration as her eyes began to well up once more.

"Aw, hell, not this again."

"Sorry," she said as she wiped at her tears.

"Ain't no need for it." He replaced his much-warn hat and settled down on a cluster of wind-scarred rock and gravel. "It has been a distinct honor, ma'am."

"Natty, I—"

"Go on, get. Don't go wasting your time here with me. Got a long while to wait right here for them before we go into the valley. But don't go fool yourself into thinking you got nothing but time once you're dead."

Before she could say another word, he'd pulled out his harmonica and begun to polish it on one of the faded linen lapels of his shirt. Nonchalant though he attempted to pretend, he couldn't stop his eyes darting off to the sandy pit in a tiny gorge a few feet below the level asphalt where two ridiculously blissful teenagers played carefree in the sand.

"Them two ain't looking to linger, ma'am," was all he said before putting the old harmonica to his lips and effortlessly exhaling a slow and melancholy sprinkle of notes.

* * *

The scalding desert wind made the light-weight fabric of her dress swirl and dance around her legs as she walked back towards where Jett and Becky had started rough-housing.

When Jett looked up and saw her coming, he smiled huge and, whispering a quick excuse to the wild young girl, he scrambled to his feet and trotted over to her.

"Looks like this is it for me, kid," she said. She nodded over her shoulder towards the rising sun. "Life is waiting for me."

Jett's face screwed up in what looked to be the attempt at a smile that for once wasn't coming easy. "I wouldn't have made it this far without you," he said, and she found the lie to be very touching.

"Sure you would," she said, then put her hands out in a shrug. "But you wouldn't have traveled in style."

"Aw hell," he stepped in and threw his arms around her and held her tight. Unlike the last time he was now composed of lean muscle with a heartbeat she could feel distinctly. He smelled like sweat and sunlight combined with that teenage boy propensity to wear just a bit too much cologne.

When he finally pulled away Jett looked down and made an attempt to wipe his eyes without making too big a deal of it.

"And tonight, on a very special episode of whatever!" Becky shouted from where she was doing hand-stands in the desert sand, her legs twisting this way and that in an attempt to keep balance. Jett rolled his eyes, but Mary didn't miss the depth of warmth in the gesture.

"It's happening kind of fast, don't you think?" she couldn't help saying.

"But I died slow," he said. "I mean, technically speaking, I am actually older than you. I've got a lot of time to make up for."

"Point taken."

"I wouldn't have met her if I didn't die when I did." His grin was fracture-the-earth kind of huge. "I was such a huge dork before I was stuck in that bed. I don't really get what she sees in me."

"I do," Mary said.

"Thank you, Mary," he said. "Really. Thank you for everything."

"You're going to get me tearing up again," she said, smiling despite her trembling lips. "Goodbye, Jett."

"Goodbye, Mary."

She touched his shoulder one last time and then turned and started back purposefully towards the Prius. She turned back after a few strides. Becky had run up to throw her arms around Jett's shoulders and plant a huge messy kiss on the side of his face.

"Maybe I should say, 'until we meet again.'"

"Damn straight, grandma!" Becky called. Mary rolled her eyes.

"I'm thirty-one!"

"Until we meet again," Jett said and leaned his head back against Becky's.

"Take care of each other," Mary said, and started back towards her car. She turned back one last time to call, "And stay out of trouble!"

Becky put her thumbs and forefingers into the shape of a halo above her head and intoned "Ding!" while Jett giggled mischievously. Mary shook her head and climbed into the driver's seat.

Her breath caught at the inferno that was the car's interior. She rolled down the windows as she waited for the AC to cool it down and turned on her phone.

It wouldn't be so ungodly early back on Eastern time, but she was dreading the call. Alec picked up almost before the first ring.

"Mary! Oh my God, where are you? Where have you been? I thought you were dead!"

"No," she said, a deep stab of remorse intertwining with her newfound hope. "I'm not dead. I'm coming home."

*Sun bleached bones were most wonderful against the blue –
that blue that will always be there as it is now after all man's
destruction is finished.*

— GEORGIA O'KEEFFE

BIOS

Brady Rose
A Canadian boy always looking for great stories to get lost in, trying to create a few of his own. Likes throwing his voice, smashing guitars, and studying faces in parking lots. Lives and writes in Calgary, Alberta.

C.H. Rosenberg
C. H. Rosenberg is a policy wonk, armchair economist, and real-life world traveler who has not actually visited any of the worlds mentioned in this novella—yet. Rosenberg's early career was spent fighting in the trenches of Southern California's local politics and they currently work at one of D.C.'s many alphabet soup think tanks, brainstorming all sorts of amazing ways to save the planet.

Anna K. Young
Anna K. Young is an emerging writer and an MFA candidate in creative writing at Western Washington University. She has been published in Crack the Spine's The Year anthology

(2019) and on Sheila-Na-Gig's Under 30 poetry feature. Originally from Montana, Young writes about rural life and explores
how upbringing affects young people and their perception of
the world. When not writing, reading, people-watching, or
eavesdropping, Young enjoys playing guitar, exploring the
Pacific Northwest, and taking long naps on her living room
futon.

Running Wild Press publishes stories that cross genres with great stories and writing. RIZE publishes great genre stories written by people of color and by authors who identify with other marginalized groups. Our team consists of:

Lisa Diane Kastner, Founder and Executive Editor
Andrea Johnson, Acquisitions Editor, RIZE
Rebecca Dimyan, Editor
Andrew DiPrinzio, Editor
Cecilia Kennedy, Editor
Barbara Lockwood, Editor
Cody Sisco, Editor
Chih Wang, Editor
Benjamin White, Editor
Peter A. Wright, Editor
Pulp Art Studios, Cover Design
Standout Books, Interior Design
Polgarus Studios, Interior Design
Nicole Tiskus, Production Manager
Alex Riklin, Production Manager
Alexis August, Production Manager

Learn more about us and our stories at www.runningwild-press.com

Loved these stories and want more? Follow us at www.runningwildpress.com, www.facebook.com/running-wildpress, on Twitter @lisadkastner @RunWildBooks @RwpRIZE